D1553716

WHAT
THIS MYSTERY IS ABOUT

Exploding pimps,

        drug-crazed cod,

                rats on PCP,

      hits with hornets,

truth serums,

        mind erasers,

            zombie potions,

      beatnik cops,

dirty detectives,

      a walking corpse,

an insanity-inducing virus
called the Willies,

      an adrenaline-boosting drug
            called Slaughter,
and a sick city
called Butchers Harbor.

WHO
THiS MYSTERY iS ABOUT

Leon Lynch,
alienated albino who sells strange drugs to strange people

Increase Lynch,
Leon's father & bohemian patriarch of a second-rate
crime syndicate

Wyatt Lynch,
Leon's rage-aholic half-brother and chief enforcement
officer of the Lynch mob

Macey Kick,
Lynch assassin with a killer body

Fuzzy Magee,
germaphobic Lynch gangster

Cracker Jack Farrell,
Lynch goon

Frankie Baloney Bologna,
Lynch goombah

Benny One Too Many Vega,
happy-go-lucky, drunken pothead

One-Eye Connivin' Ivan Wazowiecki,
horny little lawyer with a glass eye and a loose tongue

Billy Shakin' Blake,
unstable fullback hooked on Slaughter

Vladimir Borisova,
Russian mob boss pursuing an American dream based on
The Godfather Part II

Sergei Sickie Listyev,
Siberian hip-hop gangsta

KILL WHITEY

KEN HARVILL

UGLYTOWN
LOS ANGELES

First Edition

UGLYTOWN AND THE UGLYTOWN COIN LOGO SERVICEMARK REG. U.S. PAT. OFF.

Library of Congress Cataloging-in-Publication Data
Harvill, Ken, 1967–
Kill Whitey / Ken Harvill.
    p.   cm.
ISBN: 0-9724412-8-X
ISBN (Limited Ed.): 0-9758503-5-0
1. Albinos and albinism—Fiction. 2. Criminals—Crimes against—Fiction.
3. Inheritance and succession—Fiction. 4. Russian American criminals—Fiction.
5. Irish American criminals—Fiction. 6. Racially mixed people—Fiction.
7. Organized crime—Fiction. 8. Drug traffic—Fiction. 9. New England—Fiction.
I. Title.
PS3604.065 B87   2003
813'.6—dc21   2003012953
                      CIP

The author wishes to state that despite the cataloging efforts of the Library of Congress, this story
does not necessarily take place in New England.

Find out more of the mystery: UglyTown.com/KillWhitey

Printed in the United States of America

10 9 8 7 6 5 4 3 2 1

This book is dedicated to my family,
here and in the hereafter,
&
to my friends,
old, new, and undiscovered.

KILL WHITEY

1
BUZZED

Smutty McCafferty and Fuzzy Magee were eating burgers for breakfast at the Blue Loon Diner. Smutty hunched over his plate, gripping his burger with two meaty hands that were scabbed and bruised around the knuckles. As he chewed with an open mouth, crumbs gathered and settled in the grease at the corners of his lips.

Fuzzy reached across the table and pulled a paper napkin from a metal dispenser. He patted the napkin against his forehead, careful to avoid his stylishly trimmed hair. "Look at this," he said, holding up the wet napkin for Smutty's inspection. "You see this?"

Smutty stuffed a pickle spear into his mouth.

"I'm swimming in my own sweat," Fuzzy said. "I feel like a pig's ass in here." He tossed the napkin onto the floor. "There's no excuse for keeping an establishment this hot. Somebody ought to talk to the immigrant halfwits who own this shit-hole and tell them we aren't living in the fucking Bronze Age. These days, we got a little thing called air conditioning." He stirred a french fry in a blob of ketchup and shoved it in his mouth. He grunted and shook his head. "And look at this," he said, holding up a limp fry. "You see this rubbery piece of shit? French fries are supposed to be crisp. I like to bite into

13

a crispy fried potato shell surrounding a fluffy, moist center. That's the kind of fry I like. What I dislike is this lukewarm, floppy potato turd that's been sitting under a heat lamp since last week." Fuzzy tossed the droopy fry onto the floor next to the sweat-soaked napkin.

A construction worker in an adjacent booth saw the trash accumulating on the floor, and he cast an annoyed glare toward Smutty and Fuzzy. Smutty was a massive man with a potbelly, a barrel chest, and thick arms. He had a layer of fat on him, but under the fat was solid muscle cultivated by years of pumping iron in prison yards. Fuzzy was taller and leaner than his partner. The knotty muscles in his arms and neck twitched under his skin as he gestured with jerky, angry motions. Both men wore their shirts untucked: Smutty in a faded Hawaiian shirt over frayed jeans and Fuzzy in a crisp Italian jacquard sport shirt with tiny pistols woven into the fabric. Their shirttails bulged as they draped over pistols holstered on their belts. The construction worker decided the trash on the floor was none of his business, and he darted his eyes back to his own plate.

"This food blows," Fuzzy said. "I'd rather eat snot."

"You don't like, send it back," Smutty muttered though a mouthful of hamburger.

Fuzzy scoffed. "Send it back. Right. What are you, nuts? You know what happens when you return your food? You're lucky if they only spit on it. If you send back your meal, nine times out of ten, the cook wipes his balls on it. Never send back a meal, Smutty. Especially in this day and age, with all that viral shit out there waiting to fuck you up. You don't know what's being carried by the guy cooking your food. He could have loony plague or urban yellow fever or the fucking pigpox."

Smutty McCafferty belched through clenched teeth as he slid out of the booth. "I gotta take a shit," he said. He snatched the sports section of the *Butchers Harbor Register* from the table and lumbered to the back of the diner, still chewing his burger as he walked.

Smutty closed the bathroom door behind him and entered a stall. He unholstered his Colt Python .357 and set it on the back of the toilet. As he sat on the can, he inspected the graffiti on the chipped gray paint that surrounded him. It was the usual bathroom scrawl of swastikas, penises, and men's phone numbers. "Nazi fuckin' queers," Smutty muttered. He shook his head and opened the newspaper over his knees. The lead sports story was yet another article on Butchers Harbor's hometown hero, overnight NFL sensation Billy Blake.

Outside the bathroom, a middle-aged doofus with thick glasses and greasy, dandruff-caked hair slicked over his bald head was yammering on a pay phone. He glanced across the diner and saw that Fuzzy was distracted as he scraped a stain off the table with the handle of a spoon. The doofus abruptly hung up the phone and approached the bathroom. He stuck a key in the doorknob and locked it shut.

Smutty heard the door lock. He folded the newspaper, set it on the back of the toilet, and hoisted his .357. He heard a creak as someone opened the bathroom window from outside. With his left hand, Smutty drew a 9mm Beretta from his ankle holster. A gloved hand outside the window tossed a Mason jar filled with yellow jackets into the bathroom. The glass shattered on the tiled floor, and an angry swarm filled the room. Smutty burst out of his stall, tripping over the pants around his ankles as he swatted at the wasps with his guns.

KILL WHITEY

Back in the dining room, Fuzzy heard Smutty scream. Fuzzy drew his burner from his holster and raced to the back of the narrow diner. He slammed his shoulder against the bathroom door and kicked it near its lock, but the heavy door wouldn't give. Inside the restroom, Smutty hurled both his guns into the thickest part of the swarm. He turned and tugged at the door until the yellow jackets had covered his back. He then stumbled about the bathroom, cursing savagely as he pounded his fists on the walls and shattered a mirror with the fleshy side of his hand. He swung blindly, squinting his eyes against the wasps' stingers. The yellow jackets crawled up his nostrils and squirmed in his ears. They worked their way under his shirt and underwear, getting tangled in his armpit, chest, and pubic hair. Smutty slapped and clawed his body as he dropped to the filthy bathroom floor. As he howled, the wasps crawled over his tongue and stung the back of his throat.

When Fuzzy finally knocked the door down, he found his partner dead on the floor, swollen to the size of a Sumo. Smutty was allergic to wasps, but only his mother and a few of the boys on the Lynch crew knew it.

The scent of sunscreen lingered around Leon Lynch. The sunny smell of the beach was jarringly out of place in the dim basement bar. The thin woman dressed in a stylish beige pantsuit and seated in the booth opposite Leon did not belong in this dive either, and she knew it. She fidgeted, and her bug-eyes darted wildly around the dingy room. Her expensive suit hung loose on her bony body. Leon suspected she'd lost weight recently and rapidly. She tangled her fingers through her wiry black hair.

Leon studied her face. "You remind me a little of Marilyn Monroe," he said.

The woman cast a bleary glare at Leon. "Is that some kind of joke?"

Leon pointed at a ruby stud pierced through her cheek. The gem shimmered like a spot of fresh blood on a field of dirty snow. "It's that stone," Leon said. "You have it in the same spot as Monroe's beauty mark. Is that what you were going for?"

"Sure. Whatever," she said. "You look like George Hamilton. Alright?"

Leon glanced down at his pale hands and smiled.

The woman took a closer look at Leon. The first thing she had noticed about Leon, the first thing anyone noticed about Leon, was his whiteness. His eyebrows and his short dreadlocks were frost white. The only color in his face was the inky rings that circled his large, soulful eyes and a watery tint of violet pigment in his irises. At first glance, Leon looked sickly and grotesque, like some salamander pulled from under a rock. As the woman continued to study Leon, however, she saw that he actually had handsome features. He had a slim, solemn face, but an odd twist to his full lips made him look like he was always on the verge of smiling. The twists of his lips and a dimple in one cheek helped to soften his generally mopey disposition.

As the woman continued to study Leon, she cocked her head to one side. "What are you, anyhow?" she asked.

"What am I? I'm not sure what you mean," Leon said, knowing exactly what she meant.

"Well, I had heard you were an albino. It's just your face. It looks..." She circled her fingers around her own mouth and nose. "Your nose is kind of flat. And your lips." She leaned closer, staring at Leon until he squirmed. "Oh my God," she said with a little giggle. "Are you *black*? Are you a *black albino*?" She scrunched her face as she said the words. "I never knew there was such a thing."

Leon checked his watch. "Well, now you know."

"That's a little ironic, don't you think?" the woman asked. "You're a person of color without color." She chuckled smugly at her own joke.

"You have a shallow understanding of race."

"So you are black?" the woman asked.

"My mother was Haitian. My father's..." Leon shook his head. "Do you really care about my genealogy? When we spoke on the phone, I didn't get the feeling you wanted to discuss my family tree. As I recall, you wanted something from me. Are you ready to do business, or would you like to chat some more?"

The woman's smug smile faded, and her face fell into a haggard frown. She shook three packets of sugar, ripped them open, and dumped the contents into her Jack and Coke. Her hands were shaky, and she spilled half of the sugar onto the grimy table. The woman's ashen face and shaky hands bothered Leon. Everybody seemed to have the cold or flu these days, and nastier viruses were on the rise. HIV had mutated again. TB was rampant in the cities. Two cases of Ebola had been confirmed in New York City, and now there was this thing called the Willies that was killing people on the West Coast.

"You want to end the small talk, that's fine with me," the woman said. "I don't want sit in this toilet any longer than necessary." She looked up from her drink. "So how long will a dose keep me awake?" she asked.

Leon sipped his beer again and returned the pint glass to the table as far from the woman as possible. "A dose will keep you awake for four days. Sometimes five."

"Give me ten hits," the woman said.

Leon laughed. "Ten? Are you out of your mind? Listen, ma'am, Kava Mondo can't replace sleep. It only postpones it. What do want this stuff for, anyhow?"

The woman huffed. "I already told you on the phone. I'm on deadline, and I'm a little behind on my manuscript. I need to pull a few all-nighters to pull it all together."

"When's the deadline?"

"In a week."

"So why do you need ten doses?"

"A month. I meant to say a month." She gulped her drink. "Look, I have shit to do. Are we doing business or not?"

Leon shrugged. "I'm just trying to get a better idea of your situation."

"I was under the impression you were a dealer, not a therapist."

Leon smiled as he pushed two short white dreadlocks away from his eyes. "If you want ten hits of Kava Mondo, I'll sell you ten hits of Kava Mondo. I don't care. I'll sell you whatever you want. I just thought you might be interested in some of my other products, that's all. For instance, I have something that cures nightmares. Does that interest you?"

The woman glared angrily at Leon. "Listen, you sideshow freak," she began. She stopped as her voice started to crack. A tear slipped down her ashen face and collected on the ruby stud. She lifted her chin higher and maintained an icy stare on Leon. "I've been dealing with nightmares all my life. I know how to handle it." She reached for a cocktail napkin and dabbed her sunken cheeks. "I'm used to bad things happening to me in my dreams, just like I'm used to bad things happening to me when I'm awake. The comfort of bad dreams is that they're only dreams."

Her defiant pose started to crumble. She averted her eyes and slumped closer to the table. "But things have become complicated. My nightmares have started to change. I've become the one doing the bad things." She cleared her throat. "In my dreams, I'm hurting people. Not just people, but children. Infants. I'm hurting innocents. And I'm doing things I shouldn't even be able to imagine. They're only dreams, but they're *my* dreams."

Leon raised a hand. "Hey. Listen. Don't be so hard on yourself. It's not you. Not entirely. It's this sick city we live in." He tapped his temple with two fingers. "It infects our dreams. It's good you told me about it. I can help." He rummaged in the pouch of his light windbreaker and removed a white envelope. He checked the contents of the package then passed it under the table to the woman. "I'm giving you something that'll kill your dreams. Take some tonight and go to bed. You'll shut your eyes and open them again eight hours later. It'll feel like time travel. You'll have no dreams. Not even a memory of sleep."

The woman opened the envelope and examined its contents. "What is it?" she asked.

"It's tree bark," Leon said. "It comes from Australia, from a remote spot in the Outback. A small tribe of Aborigines has been using it for generations."

The woman closed the envelope and tucked it into her purse. "Thank you."

"Now, that dream-killer isn't much different than the Kava

Mondo," Leon warned. "It only postpones dreams. You can't live without dreams, you know. After you get a few good nights' sleep, you'll need to talk to someone. You need to cure whatever's ailing your mind. This disgusting city, it's bad for the soul, but your problems aren't entirely external. You need to look within. These children you hurt in your dreams, maybe they represent you—your true nature. Maybe there's some discord in your life that's destroying your inner child, your essential nature or something."

The woman finished wiping her sickly eyes with the cocktail napkin. She crumpled the paper and dropped it in an ashtray. "How much do I owe you?" she asked.

"That's two dimes," Leon said. He stuck his head out of the booth and scanned the dim bar.

The woman reached into her purse and discreetly folded two bills into her hand. She reached across the table, and Leon took the money as they shook hands. "Thanks."

The woman drained her bourbon and cola, slid out of the booth, and stood beside the table. "This shit better work," she said.

Leon smiled. "All of my products work. Remember what I said, though. This is only a short-term solution."

"Thanks for the advice. Want some in return?"

Leon shrugged.

"People come to you for drugs, not your opinion. Normal people aren't seeking guidance from lowlife mutants like you. People like me don't respect people like you. The last thing we want is your advice. Okay? So just sell us your drugs and keep your mouth shut." She turned and walked away, filling the low room with the click of her heels.

Leon smiled as he watched the woman leave the bar. "That's what makes it all worthwhile," he muttered.

KILL WHITEY

A week before the bee hit on Smutty, Wyatt Lynch had received a tip that some local fishermen were coming ashore with eleven kilos of heroin tucked under a load of flounder. The harbor was within the Lynches' district, and they hadn't authorized the import, so Wyatt sent a crew down to the piers to seize the cargo. They executed the six fishermen, packed their bodies with the fish, and tucked the skag into a rusty honey wagon. The crew was not on the road for more than five minutes before they were hijacked themselves. The incident raised considerable suspicion among the Lynches. As Increase had said, nobody robs a honey wagon unless someone got a tip it was hauling some good shit.

Around the same time, two enforcers had paid a visit on a pimp who wasn't paying his taxes to the Lynch family. They kicked in the pimp's door and searched his seedy townhouse. Eventually, they found him in the basement, huddled in a corner with an Uzi on his lap. The goons emptied their clips into the ass merchant, but he wouldn't die. He was already dead. The enforcers were shooting a mummified mack stuffed with C4 and embalmed with nitroglycerin. The ensuing blast leveled the pimp's townhouse and two adjacent homes.

"Our business is going down the shitter," Wyatt said. At five feet seven and one hundred forty pounds, Wyatt Lynch should not have been an intimidating figure, yet men twice his size were uneasy or plain scared when Wyatt was near. Of course, he was second-in-command of a crime family, and some intimidation came with the position, but even people who did not know Wyatt's background were wary around him. Wyatt had crazy eyes. His eyes sizzled with unstable rage, but for all the heat of his hate, his eyes were cold with cruel indifference. The ice in his stare revealed a soul unburdened with sympathy or regard for consequences.

Wyatt had the hard eyes of a young man who had been raised in deprivation and abuse, yet this was not his childhood. He had been pampered as a boy, raised by a wealthy and attentive father. His father, Increase, was tolerant and even-tempered, at least by crime boss standards. He had never raised his hand against the boy; he threw money at his son instead of punches. The most traumatic event in Wyatt's life was his parent's divorce, but a situation as common as divorce could not explain Wyatt's unbridled and unending anger.

Wyatt paced his second-story deck, expending energy to keep the fury within from boiling over. His dark black Irish hair, slicked back tight against his skull with too much gel, shimmered in the summer sun. He raised his arm and swirled two fingers through the humid air in a wide loop. "This is our business, Pop. A big fat dookie twirling in the crapper on its way down the pipes."

Times were indeed difficult for the Lynch organization. A new gang led by Russian immigrant Vladimir Borisova had moved into town a few years before. The Lynches' efforts to repel the Borisovas were failing. In fact, the Borisovas were forging alliances with institutions that had once belonged to Increase. The press had turned against the family. Unions wouldn't cooperate anymore. Dirty cops, crooked feds, and judges on the take had all turned their backs on the Lynches and were working with the Borisova syndicate. The Borisovas were not only usurping the Lynches' political connections and competing for market share, they were thinning the Lynches' ranks and outright stealing their product. The Borisovas were competing too efficiently. They seemed to have an unfair advantage.

Increase Lynch licked a patch of salt off the side of his cactus-shaped glass. He glanced down at his grandson, Wyatt Jr., who pushed a toy car under the railing, sending it tumbling onto the lawn below. Increase smiled lovingly at the boy, then turned his attention back to Wyatt Sr. "Son, nothing's over 'til it's over," he said. He cupped his hand to his ear. "I don't hear any fat chick singing, do you?" Increase lowered his hand from his ear and stroked his bushy salt-and-pepper goatee. He had grown the facial hair to compensate for his retreating hairline. He had always been proud of his hair, wearing it long even when it was no longer fashionable. He still kept his remaining hair in a ponytail that reached halfway down his back. He thought the ponytail and goatee made him look hip. Instead, he looked like what he was: an aging party animal.

"Let me lay a little history on you, boy," Increase said. He leaned back in his patio chair and rested his sandaled feet on the edge of a potted plant. "There was a time, not so long ago, when the world was gloating over the apparent demise of America. We had stumbled a bit, and a few other countries were beating us at our own games. So the world said the USA was a fallen empire. They said our time had passed. They wrote us off." Increase shrugged. "Well, God knows I'm no jingo. I know our nation has its problems. But there is one indisputable fact that no sensible resident of this planet will deny: the United States of America is the center of the world.

Every other nation is just a suburb of America." Increase fished a lime out of a pitcher of margaritas and squeezed its juice into his glass. "Right now, Butchers Harbor is writing off the Lynches. Let 'em. Take it as a good sign. We're just a few steps away from our most glorious moment."

"You think so?" Wyatt asked.

"Boy, I am dead-to-nuts certain. We just have to take the right steps to turn things around. What's the biggest threat to our organization at this moment?"

"The Borisovas," Wyatt said. He flopped into a chaise lounge beside his father.

Increase shook his head. "The Borisovas are just competition. Competition is an inevitable fact of life, son. We've built a beautiful thing here in Butchers Harbor. It's only natural that others will try to steal the fruits of our labor." Increase made a dismissive gesture with both hands. He was still holding his margarita in one hand, and some of the green drink sloshed out his glass and splattered on the deck. "The problem is we have a weakness that our competition is exploiting. When we conquer our weakness, we will conquer our competition. Now tell me, what is our weakness?"

Wyatt furrowed his brow. "We aren't angry enough? We aren't committed to total domination?"

Increase chuckled. "You're plenty angry, son. Besides, I'm not referring to our corporate culture. I'm talking about concrete problems. Our *specific* problem is that we have a traitor. Somebody set up our boys in that pimp explosion. Somebody knew Smutty was allergic to bees, and that somebody sold that information to the Borisovas. How does the fuzz always know where we're operating and where we're storing product? Someone's dropping a handful of dimes on us. How do the judges always manage to know which jurors are on our payroll? How does the press get so much dirt on our family? We've got ourselves a leak."

"Well no shit, Dad," Wyatt said. "Give me a little credit, will you? I know I'm not a genius, but I'm not a fucking retard either."

Wyatt Jr. looked up from his toys and laughed at his father's angry words.

Increase winced and leaned toward his son. "Hey, son. Easy with the language, alright?" He nodded toward Wyatt Jr. "I don't want a potty-mouth for a grandson."

"Oh. Right." Wyatt glared at this son with mild annoyance. He took a deep breath and exhaled. "Sorry, Pop. Sometimes my temper gets the best of me. But I'm working on it." He took another cleansing breath. "I am aware that my anger only stands in the way of my revenge."

"Fine," Increase said. "Let's get back to the task at hand. We've defined our problem. Now we need to establish the necessary steps to reach our objectives."

"It's pretty simple, Pop," Wyatt said. "All we gotta do is find the mothef—" He glanced at his son. "—the motherhumper who's been selling us out, and we clip him. Then we wage a full-on offensive against the Borisovas until we've chased those filthy immigrants back to the shit heap they came from. I mean, doo-doo heap. Sorry. After we've chased off the competition, we'll just settle up with all the rump-humpers that turned their backs on us and took sides with the Russkies. We whack the Borisova's pigs, their union bosses, their hacks, and any other cocksucker—sorry, dicksucker—that's been disloyal to our family."

"Well, that resembles a plan," Increase said. He rubbed the bridge of his nose with his forefinger and thumb. "More or less. But first you have to find your turncoat, don't you?"

"I'm already working on it," Wyatt said. He flicked his cigarette butt over the porch railing. "I've got my eyes open and my ear to the ground."

Increase snickered. "That's your strategy?"

"You have a better idea?"

"As a matter of fact, I do," Increase said. "I've got a nice, simple plan to find our traitor. It's so simple that even you could have thought of it if you weren't so preoccupied with the details of your revenge." Increase lifted the pitcher and refilled his glass. "One thing about a simple plan, though: it's easy to execute and even easier to botch. If this plan of mine is going to work, it'll require two things. First, we need absolute secrecy. I don't want you discussing this little endeavor with anyone. We'll do as much of the work as possible by ourselves—just you and me. We'll need some of the crew to carry out a few details, but you make sure your instructions are very limited. We can't trust anyone. Got it?"

Wyatt nodded. "What's the second thing we need?"

"We need your brother."

Wyatt groaned. "Whitey? Are you kidding me?"

Increase nodded patiently. "We need Leon."

Wyatt Jr. looked up from his toys and smiled. "Unca Peon?" he asked.

"Yeah, that's right, Junior!" Wyatt said with a sarcastic singsong tone. "That's Grandpa's great idea! We're gonna get help from your retarded uncle. Uncle Fucking Whitey, who turns everything he touches to shit, is gonna save our asses. Isn't that a neat idea? Isn't that just fucking super?

Wyatt Jr. giggled.

"Yeah, laugh it up," Wyatt snapped. "It's a fucking riot."

Leon drained his flat, foul lager and set the pint glass on the bar counter.

"Want another?" asked the bartender, a scrappy tattooed man in torn jeans and a faded Boy Scout shirt.

"Nah, I'm good," Leon said. He jerked his chin toward a television suspended from the ceiling behind the bar. A football game was playing on the set. "Is Blake playing today?"

"You bet your ass he is," the bartender said. He leaned against the bar and looked up at the set. "That Shakin' Blake came out of nowhere, didn't he?"

"He sure did," Leon said.

"You think he's on roids?"

"No, not steroids," Leon answered. He knew exactly what Billy Blake was on. Blake was one of his customers. He sold the running back a drug called Slaughter. Leon had developed the drug himself some years ago. Now, he regretted that he had ever made the poison. Slaughter, a.k.a. Rip, BMF, and Arnold, deadened nerves to pain, suppressed fear, and provided a powerful surge of strength and energy. It worked the way PCP worked in comic books, but without the delirium and amnesia. The user seemed to be in control of his actions. He was simply less preoccupied with self-preservation, and he could overturn a parked car.

When Leon had supplied BMF to Billy Blake, the formerly timid running back became an overnight sensation. He was a locomotive on the field, charging clear through the other team and shaking off any player who tried to tackle him. Unfortunately, the drug had some nasty side effects. For one thing, it lingered in the body for weeks, and habitual users of BMF tended to become sociopaths. When a teammate spilled a beer on Blake's leather jacket, Blake sent him to the hospital with a broken nose, two cracked ribs, and a fractured wrist. The teammate avoided further injury by claiming he'd fallen down a flight of stairs. Blake's wife had fled with their infant son and kept their whereabouts a secret. Even Blake's mother and father were afraid to meet with him. Recently, a reporter had implied during an interview that Blake was taking performance-enhancing drugs. The following night, a masked intruder stormed into the journalist's home and threw him out of his second-story window. The identity of the assailant was never determined, but reporters stopped asking nosey questions all the same.

As Blake grew crueler and crazier, Leon decided he would no longer supply him with BMF. Standing in the parking lot outside the Hegemonix Inc. Arena, Leon had explained to Blake, "Slaughter may help you on the field, but it's ruining your life off the field. I won't help you destroy yourself."

Blake nodded. "Yeah, I do have a problem," he said. He grabbed Leon's throat. "And now you have a problem." He squeezed Leon's windpipe until his pallid face was splotched with blue and purple. Finally, Blake released him, and Leon collapsed to the pavement, clutching his neck and gasping.

"Let me explain something to you, Whitey," Blake had said. "There is no life off the field. You understand?"

Leon nodded as he retched.

"Let's make a deal," Blake said. "You supply me with Rip, and I'll keep you supplied with air. You shut off my Rip, I'll shut off your oxygen. Permanently. Do we have an understanding?"

Leon nodded.

"Want to shake on it?" Blake asked.

"That won't be necessary," Leon croaked.

After their discussion, Leon continued to supply Blake with BMF, and he kept his opinions to himself.

Leon's attention had drifted away from the game as he contemplated his relationship with Billy Blake. When he heard a whistle, Leon returned his gaze to the TV. Blake had been flagged on a facemask call. Leon watched the running back coolly approach the referee. Blake raised his hand, his index finger locked behind his thumb, and flicked an eye out of the referee's face.

"Jesus!" Leon gasped.

"Dude! Did I just see what I think I saw?" the bartender asked.

Leon pressed his palms against his eyes. "Oh man! Aw shit! This can't be happening."

The bartender turned up the volume on the set. There was commotion in the stadium as the commentator stammered, "It appears that Blake has poked and possibly, uh, dislodged an eye from referee Dwight Newcastle." The commentator was silent for a moment. "We do have confirmation from observers on the field that the official has, in fact, lost his right eye. Dear God, ladies and gentlemen, I just don't know what to say."

The bartender slammed his hand on the bar and shouted, "Show the fucking replay!"

"Aw, man, this isn't good," Leon muttered. "This is bad." He reached into his windbreaker pouch and removed a pair of sunglasses and a few crumpled bills. He dropped the money on the bar, put on the shades, and pulled his hood over his head. "This is bad," he repeated as he stepped out of the bar.

Vials and hypodermics crunched under Leon's shoes as he walked along a short concrete pier. To reach the end of the dock, he had to step around a rusty abandoned shopping cart, several empty forty-ounce bottles of malt liquor, and the torso of a mannequin in a nurse's uniform. When he reached the edge of the pier, he paused to study the foul waters of Butchers Harbor. He took shallow breaths through his mouth in a failed attempt to avoid the stench. In his left hand, Leon clutched a plaid pillowcase that he had filled with his stash of Slaughter. Leon opened the pillowcase and looked at the thousands of purple capsules inside. He reached into the pillowcase, grabbed a handful of capsules, and stuffed the pills in the pocket of his windbreaker. Leon considered Billy Blake's earlier threat, and he grabbed another handful of BMF. Then he held the pillowcase over the edge of the pier and dumped the pills into the water. The capsules fizzed as they dissolved and sunk below the surface. "Good riddance," he muttered.

Leon turned away from the pier's edge and took a few uneasy steps toward the shore. He wondered how he would explain to Blake that Slaughter was no longer on the market. His thoughts were disrupted by loud splashes behind him. He turned back to face the harbor and saw the murky water around the dock starting to roil. A school of minnows burst through the oily skin of filthy water and leapt over the low waves like tiny dolphins. After a jellyfish floated to the surface with a sea bass thrashing in its tentacles, a cod shot out of the water and landed with a wet splat on the dock. It flopped its way toward Leon and slapped his shin with its tail. Leon took a step back, but the cod pursued him. He kicked the fish in the belly, sending it back into the ocean.

Two more cod leapt onto the pier and rolled in flips and convulsions toward Leon. They seemed to curse as their maws snapped in the lethal air. Leon stumbled in a backward retreat until he tripped over a tire. He cut his palm on a shard of green glass as he tried to break his fall, and his sunglasses fell off his face. Although the day was overcast, the dim glare off the water briefly blinded Leon. He fumbled on his hands and knees, looking for his shades, when a heavy wet fin slapped his cheek. "Son of a bitch!" Leon shouted just as the second fish body-slammed him. Leon pushed himself to his feet and sprinted for an oar five yards away. The cod were hot on his heels when he grabbed the oar and spun to face them. He brained one cod with a backhanded swing and cut the other in half with the tip of the oar's blade.

Clutching the oar in one hand, Leon used his bleeding free hand to shield his sensitive eyes from the sun. Squinting out at the harbor, he saw a dorsal fin slicing through the waves and heading in his direction. Having no desire to see what was connected to the fin, he abandoned the dock and retreated to the relative safety of the streets.

2
UNHOLY BAPTISM

Peter Volkov drove his sputtering old sedan into the narrow alley behind his apartment building. He parked in his space beside the Dumpster. The driver-side door was sticking, so Volkov had to slam his shoulder against the door to open it. He hated driving his wreck after a day of driving the boss's Cadillac, but he tried to be patient. Boss Vladimir Borisova trusted him, and Volkov hoped that, in time, he would be promoted to a more important position than chauffeur. Then he could finally pull down a decent salary and drive his own Cadillac. He tried to be optimistic, but things were looking bleak. At forty-five, Peter Volkov realized he had few years left as Borisova's bodyguard. There were rumors that Borisova was grooming Volkov for something big, but Volkov wasn't getting any younger, and his prospects for power seemed to be fading. He had to consider the possibility that he would never be anything more than the big man's driver. Even if this were the case, Volkov vowed to be always loyal to the Borisova family.

Volkov stepped out of his car and scanned the alley with his cold gray eyes. He was a short, broad-shouldered man who tended to walk with his fists clenched and his arms crooked, as if he was always ready to punch someone in the face. As he walked across the alley, he glared at a rat rummaging in a pile of trash. The rat stopped its rooting and returned a hostile glare. Volkov considered shooting the insolent little beast or at least throwing a brick its way, but the stench of rancid meat and soiled diapers festering in the summer heat was too overwhelming for Volkov to linger in the alley.

Covering his mouth with one hand, Volkov quickly unlocked the rear entrance to his building. When he stepped inside, he saw a longhaired young man with chronic acne waiting by the elevator. Volkov had seen this tenant before. The kid considered himself a musician or an actor or some damn thing, but he was nothing more than a junkie. The elevator door slid open, and the two men stepped inside. Peter pressed the button for the fifth floor, and the junkie pressed the button for the second. "Floor two!" Volkov shouted. "One goddamn floor of stairs you cannot walk?"

The punk leaned against the elevator wall. "I'm tired, dude."

Volkov grunted. "*Tva-ya mama sa-syot kor-rovie khuy-ee.*"

"Huh?"

"Your mother suck the dick of a cow." Volkov continued to mutter curses as the elevator rose one floor. When the door opened, he was greeted by three members of the Lynch mob. He saw Macey Kick, a lean, sinewy woman in her late twenties who was as attractive as she was dangerous. Beside her stood Cracker Jack Farrell, a pug-faced thug with a shaved head and bulging forearms. The third person standing outside the elevator was Swag Kilpatrick, a hulking old ghoul with long, greasy, gray hair that draped over his shoulders and hung down his back like some storybook wizard.

The three stepped inside the elevator and surrounded Volkov. Cracker Jack Farrell handed a balloon of heroin to the junkie and said, "We'll be at your place in a minute. Leave your door unlocked."

The junkie weighed the balloon in the palm of his hand. "It's a little light, dude."

Cracker grabbed the junkie by his hair, banged his head against the elevator wall, and threw him into the hallway. The kid held his head with one hand. "Hey, man, that's not cool. You're way out of line." Cracker took a step toward him, and the junkie turned and scurried down the hall.

Cracker Jack stepped back into the elevator, nodded hello to Volkov, then punched the Russian in the stomach. The blow knocked the wind out of Volkov's lungs so he could not shout. It was an unnecessary precaution; no one in this tenement would heed a call for help. Nevertheless, Swag Kilpatrick held the elevator door open and kept watch down the hall as Cracker and Macey pummeled Volkov to the floor and kicked him until he stopped squirming. Finally, they lifted the chauffeur by his arms and dragged him down the hall into the longhair's apartment. The junkie sat on his futon as he cooked his smack in a spoon. He jerked his pimpled chin toward a soiled Persian rug and said, "Hey, don't get any blood on the carpet, alright? That thing was imported."

The three enforcers dragged Volkov into the kitchen. Cracker and Swag pinned Volkov to the floor while Macey bound the Russian's wrists and ankles with duct tape. After she pulled a length of tape, she used her sharp canines to tear it free from the roll. Volkov was sick with humiliation as this woman tied him up like an animal. As he glared at her, his quivering eyes betrayed his disgrace and rage. Macey winked at him as she bit into the silver tape again. Volkov pulled his hands free from Macey's grasp and tried to strike her, but she quickly subdued him with a jab to the throat.

Although Volkov was no longer stirring, Swag Kilpatrick grabbed a heavy frying pan from the range and swung it down on the Russian's head. Swag raised the pan to pummel him further, but Cracker Jack reached out and grabbed the old goon's wrist. "Easy, Swag," Cracker warned. He looked down at the blood that welled on Volkov's scalp and stuck to the short gray spikes of his crew cut. "Wyatt wants him alive."

Swag jerked his arm free and tossed the frying pan back onto the range, filling the small kitchen with loud metallic clatter. "I just wanted to settle him down," Swag said. "What's the point of this kidnapping anyhow?"

Cracker shrugged. "Don't know. Increase and Wyatt want him. I ain't concerned with the reasons why."

Swag narrowed his hollow eyes. "Yeah? Well, I like to know why I'm doing a thing."

Macey rose slowly, stretching the muscles in her back and legs like a cat awaking from a nap. As she strolled out of the kitchen, she gave Volkov a playful kick in the ear. Volkov started to curse in Russian until Cracker covered his mouth with a strip of duct tape.

Macey returned to the kitchen dragging the worn Persian rug from the den. She dropped the carpet on the floor next to Volkov. Swag lifted Volkov by the shoulders, and Cracker grabbed his feet, and they tossed the Russian a few feet so he landed in the center of the rug. Then they rolled him up tightly in the carpet, forming an enormous cigar. Cracker and Swag hoisted the load onto their shoulders and carried the bound Russian out of the apartment. On their way out, they passed the junkie lying facedown on the floor. A syringe dangled from his arm, and blood streamed from his nose and mouth as he struggled to breathe. Macey stepped over the dying addict, careful to avoid the growing puddle of blood. "Looks like our friend sprung a leak," she said. "Good thing we moved his fancy imported carpet. Boy would've bled all over it."

Bea Carver sat on the front step of her duplex, sipping a cup of spicy tea and taking in the neighborhood as a cool evening breeze chased the day's heat off the asphalt. She savored the aroma of cinnamon and nutmeg wafting through her open kitchen window. In the house behind her, a girl was practicing her saxophone, playing "All of Me." The girl played the same song every night for the past three weeks. She never improved. Across the street, a couple argued about money. It was a common argument among couples, especially in this neighborhood. She'd had similar arguments with Lester when he was alive. Some things never change, Bea thought.

Other things do change. Like the language young people used these days. Bea enjoyed the bits of slang and jargon she overhead from people passing by. People spoke of technologies and fads that meant nothing to her, but she enjoyed the lingoes all the same. One thing she didn't care for was the way everyone used the f-word lately. She heard mothers using the word when they spoke to their children, for Pete's sake. It seemed as if everyone felt free to use the obscenity in every sentence until the word had as much meaning as a comma. When Bea was young, the word actually meant something. She shook her head and tried to enjoy a small patch of sunset in the valley of the surrounding buildings.

All her life, Bea Carver had enjoyed watching people and the world around her. It seemed cruel that her senses had dulled at a time when she could do little more than sit and observe. She had reached a point where she could barely recognize the blurry faces of those who leaned before her and shouted in her ear. She was happy when the pale young man moved into the abandoned florist shop next to her home. He grew exotic flowers, ferns, herbs, mushrooms, dwarf trees, and cacti in the greenhouse that occupied most of his back lot. He was an odd neighbor. He looked strange with his ghostly complexion and white hair. He behaved peculiarly as well, as if he was new to the planet. Still, he was friendly. Once a week, he would stop by Bea's home with a brown paper bag filled with dried herbs. She drank the herbs twice a day in a tea as the young man had instructed. Soon, her vision and hearing were restored almost to the condition of her youth. Her taste buds came alive, and she could smell as well as a hound. To show her gratitude, Bea used her restored powers of observation to keep watch over her neighbor's home. She worried that the greenhouse glass was too great a temptation for the neighborhood vandals.

Bea heard footsteps scuffling on the sidewalk. She turned and saw Leon rounding the corner of their block. He strolled slowly with his hands in his pockets. As usual, his eyes were shielded behind sunglasses, and his face was shaded under his oversized hood. A lot of younger kids dressed the same way, little fools wearing sunglasses at night and hoods in the sweltering heat, but Bea knew Leon wore the hood and sunglasses out of necessity rather than show. Leon smiled as he approached Bea's doorstep. "Mind if I join you?" he asked.

"Any time," she said, patting the stoop beside her. As Leon sat, he pulled his hands from his pockets, revealing a large bandage across one palm. "What happened to you?" Bea asked.

Leon looked with some embarrassment at the bandage. "I tripped the other day," he said. "I scuffed my hand on the sidewalk."

"That's a big bandage for a scrape."

"Well, I sort of fell on some glass too."

Bea nodded. She didn't believe Leon's explanation, but the young man obviously did not want to discuss the injury. The two sat for a few minutes, savoring the evening. Finally, Bea said, "I saw a boy loitering by the fence around your yard. I don't know what he was up to, but I got him to move along."

"I appreciate that, Mrs. Carver, but you really don't need to go to the trouble."

"You grow wonderful things back there, Leon. I don't want some dope fiend robbing you."

"I don't think many people in this neighborhood, besides you, have any idea what I'm growing," Leon said. "And if they did, I don't think many kids would go to the trouble of robbing me. I don't grow the kind of product they want. Anyhow, how are you feeling these days, Mrs. Carver?"

"Never better," she said.

"Good. Glad to hear it." Leon reached into his wind-breaker pouch and removed a paper bag. He set it on the stoop between him and the older woman.

"How much do I owe you?" Bea asked, as she did every week.

"Nothing," Leon said. "Neighbors have to look out for one another."

Bea smiled, creasing the dark, rough skin around her eyes. "And who else is looking out for you, Leon?"

Leon chuckled with embarrassment. "What do you mean?"

"Oh, I'm sure it's none of my business," Bea said. She ran the tip of her finger around the rim of the cup she was holding. "You just seem a little lonely to me, that's all. I never see you with many friends or family."

"Well, you know how it is. I guess I've lost touch with some old acquaintances."

"Well, you have family here in Butchers Harbor, don't you? Why don't you spend more time with them?"

Leon fidgeted on the stoop. "My family is complicated."

Bea laughed. "Every family is complicated, honey."

"Some families are more complicated than others." Leon said. He shrugged. "Then again, maybe it's very simple. My family doesn't respect me. And I guess the feeling is mutual. My brother and my dad … well, let's just say they aren't the best representatives of humanity. Especially my brother." Leon toyed with a drawstring on his windbreaker. "I could live without my brother in my life, but I do want to be closer to my dad. Other than DNA, my father and I don't have much in common. Still, the man's my dad, and if no one else in this world accepts me, at least my old man ought to."

Bea pursed her thin lips and wondered if she could offer any advice. Despite her inquiries, she was surprised by the sudden candidness from her normally private neighbor. As she considered Leon's situation, she detected a scent of burnt crust wafting out of her home. She felt an urgency to wrap this conversation up so she could get her pie out of the oven. "Well, it's probably none of my business," she said. "I'm just a nosey old lady who ought to mind her own affairs."

Leon forced a laugh. "Well, I ought to learn to keep my affairs to myself." He pushed himself off the stoop. "Anyhow, I guess I'd better tend to my plants. You take care, now, Mrs. Carver."

"You too, Leon," said Bea. She set down her tea and held up the paper bag. "Thanks again."

"Anytime. It's my pleasure." He turned his back on the old woman and took a few steps down the walk while Bea pulled herself to her feet and shuffled into her home. She had already shut the door behind her when Leon had turned to wave goodbye.

At the edge of Bea's yard, Leon turned and walked along the narrow stretch of grass between his house and his fence. His home was a cramped, single-story cottage with large front windows that once displayed floral arrangements and balloons. Leon hadn't bought the property for the house. He bought it for the deep backyard and the greenhouse that was more than twice the size of his home.

Leon unlocked his greenhouse, stepped inside, and inhaled the moist, fertile air. He took a moment to observe the spectacular display of colors and forms that surrounded him. A velvety black-and-red butterfly with eerie cat's eyes on its wings fluttered before Leon. Other butterflies and brilliant canaries flew near the glass ceiling or lit upon the branches of miniature trees. *My flying flowers*, Leon mused. He had to be careful to breathe only through his nose when he was in the greenhouse. Rare butterflies, no bigger than his smallest fingernail, also inhabited this space, and Leon could draw them into his lungs if he breathed through an open mouth.

Leon peeled off his windbreaker and set it on a hook. He started a fan set in the wall and hoisted a canvas bag filled with gardening supplies. He stepped over pots of cacti and ducked under vines as he walked through the greenhouse. He knelt on the concrete floor and used a small spade to loosen the dirt around a runty potted palm whose roots rose above the soil like stilts. Sap from the palm stabilized irregular heartbeats and

41

suppressed epileptic seizures. If people without heart conditions or epilepsy consumed the sap, they would feel pleasantly giddy. Leon moved on from the little palm to mix a bit of compost into the soil around a plant called Jade Rapture. Its firm, swollen leaves resembled shiny stones. They were full of a juice that tasted like limeade and helped people recall the smallest details of their vivid dreams. Some villagers in a mountain hamlet of the Bilauktang Range believed that the plant gave them the ability to perceive the shared soul of the universe. Leon never encountered this particular vision when he used the Jade. He tried to get the villagers to give him more instruction regarding the spiritual uses of this plant, but they were reticent people. One old woman gently suggested that the rapture of the plant could not be explained; it could only be experienced by the fortunate.

Leon put down the spade and worked the soil with his hands. He dug past the thin crust of gritty, dry dirt and burrowed his fingers into the cool, spongy soil below. He grabbed handfuls of black compost and kneaded it into the soil. As he was hunched over the pot, massaging the soil, he backed into one of the four-inch spikes protruding from the trunk of a Lemur tree. Leon yelped, startling a canary in a nearby shrub. He turned to face the spiked tree. "The next time that happens, you're mulch."

The tree had been sticking Leon ever since he'd uprooted it in Madagascar. He had spent hours working around the massive thorns, and when the small tree was finally unearthed, the sun had nearly set. Leon had to spend the night in the forest under a small plastic tarp. As he had slept, he dreamt of puppies nuzzling his ears and licking his nose. When one of the dream puppies scratched his lips, he awoke abruptly and found himself covered with cockroaches as big as his hand.

He had never returned to Madagascar since that trip. In fact, Leon hadn't returned to many places lately. He had traveled very little in the past eight months. He had been roaming the world since he was seventeen, and he had gathered a fine collection of plants. Now, he was able to cultivate his own crops. When he needed fresh supplies of a certain product, his contacts mailed him seeds or spores.

After it was no longer necessary for Leon to wander the globe, he had decided to return to Butchers Harbor. For all his traveling, he could not evade his habitual melancholy. He felt he should return to his roots, to his hometown and his family, to work through whatever it was that made him forever restless and depressed. Unfortunately, this plan was not working. He now shared a city with his family, but he felt as alienated here as he had felt on Earth's most remote territories. The family contacted Leon only when they had some demeaning chore for him. The rest of the time, the family liked to maintain some distance.

Leon stooped at the edge of a koi pond in the center of the greenhouse. As he tended to a few tiny, heart-shaped lily pads, carp with violet and crimson zebra stripes brushed against his knuckles. One of the koi tilted diagonally toward the surface and stared at Leon. Its fins fanned at its sides, and its mouth slowly opened and closed. Leon thought of the vicious fish in the harbor, and he was a little spooked by the carp's attention. He pulled his hand from the water and backed away from the pool. As Leon stepped backwards, he heard the door to the greenhouse creak open. The creaking startled the canaries, and the greenhouse became noisy with squawks and fluttering wings. Afraid that the intruder might be Shakin' Blake or some other BMF fiend, Leon snatched a pair of pruning shears and quietly ducked behind several pots of Buddha Grass. As he held his breath, he strained to hear the footsteps shuffling through his greenhouse and tried to catch a glimpse of the intruder through the concealing grass.

"White Boy!" a woman's voice called. "Where you at?"

Leon peered through the grass and saw Macey Kick stepping through his greenhouse. The few times the family had a job for Leon, they sent Macey to deliver the message. Leon suddenly felt weary. He continued to crouch behind the pot of Buddha Grass, waiting for Macey to leave.

Macey strolled between the plants, whistling back at the chirping canaries. As she passed Leon, she looked up at potted plants hanging from the glass ceiling. She took two steps past his hiding place and then turned to face him with a grin. "What're you doing behind those bushes, Whitey? Rubbing one out?"

Leon crawled out from behind the potted grass and waved at Macey with his shears. "Hey, what's up? I was just doing a little pruning. I didn't hear you come in."

Macey grinned, forming tiny dimples in her high cheeks. "Pruning, huh? I haven't heard it called that before."

Leon forced a chuckle. "That's a good one. No, really, I was pruning." For proof, he held up his shears and snipped at the air.

"I can come back in a few minutes. If you want to finish 'pruning.'" She watched small blotchy patches of red form on Leon's pallid face before she relented and laughed. "I'm just busting your balls, Whitey."

Leon continued to chuckle awkwardly. "Yeah, I know. That's funny." He knew he was blushing, and he knew if he looked directly into Macey's dark eyes, he would only blush harder, so he stared at his feet like a shy kid.

He didn't need to look at Macey to know she was gorgeous. Her image was engraved in his mind. Her face had traits of three continents. The inner corners of her eyelids had the epicanthic folds of Asians, yet the roundness of her eyes was more typical of Europeans. Her hair was long and black with a slight wave. Her lips were full and voluptuous, and her skin was the color of maple butter. She was lean and muscular with curves in the right places, but when the Lynch crew said she had a killer body, they were often speaking literally. Macey had put men in comas with nothing but her knuckles. She had used her thumbs to crush windpipes. Her knees and heels had punctured lungs with broken ribs. She was a walking weapon, which was useful when a hit went down on the other side of a metal detector.

Although Macey was a skilled assassin, she performed more than simple wet work for the Lynch family. She had quickly worked her way through the gang's hierarchy to attain a powerful position. She now worked with every division and rank in the organization. She met often with Increase, helping him develop long-term strategies and goals, and she worked with the soldiers, turning strategy into reality. Her combination of charm and intimidation helped her motivate the crew and mediate disputes. Some of the newer grunts made disparaging remarks about Macey, behind her back of course, calling her Increase's secretary. However, most of the crew accepted her. She was good at her job, and she knew how to play with the boys on their own terms. She traded insults and dirty jokes with ease, and she could drink any one of the crew under the table. Beauty, charisma, and deadliness had taken her far in her twenty-eight years.

Macey ran her fingers through vines dangling over her head. "So, White Boy, you're still growing plants?"

Leon glanced at the surrounding flora. "Sure looks that way."

"That's good." Macey nodded as she wandered around the greenhouse. "A green thumb can be a handy thing." She stopped by an eight-foot shrub with waxy yellow cones protruding from its leaves. "So what're you growing here?" she asked.

Leon held one of the waxy pods between two fingers. "This is an extremely rare and potent species of *galenggang* that I found in Suriname."

"What does it do?" Macey asked.

"It's the most powerful laxative-diuretic known on the planet."

Macey laughed. "Is there a much of a market for that sort of thing? "

"Well, not in this potency. I mean, if someone takes this to cure their constipation, they're in for a deeper colon cleansing than they might expect. I keep it on hand for overdoses or other poisonings. If something is too far along in the system for vomiting to help, this *galenggang* will flush it out of the body in a hurry. I've also run into a few models who wanted to use it for weight loss, but I don't sell it to promote bulimia."

"Why not? A sale's a sale, isn't it?"

"For some. In my line of work, I can't be too judgmental, and my ethics need to be a little flexible. But I still have to sleep at night, you know?"

"Come on, you don't have a plant that'll cure insomnia?"

Leon smiled. "Well, I have to be able to look at myself in the mirror too. I haven't found a plant that can cure a troubled conscience. Not for long, anyway. I wouldn't take it even if I found one."

Macey wagged a finger at Leon. "Now that, young man, is the kind of attitude that will hold you back in life." She dismissed any further discussion of ethics with a wave of her hand. "Anyhow, your laxative must be pretty good because it's boring the shit out of me just talking about it. Show me something else." She wandered through the rows of plants until she reached a low shrub with broad green and lavender leaves. "What's this?"

"It called a Dancing Lady," Leon said. He took a few awkward steps toward her but stopped at a respectable distance.

"What do you do, smoke it?"

"No," Leon said. "I just look at it." The Dancing Lady was an unusual plant in Leon's collection, as it had minimal medicinal or psychotropic properties. Leon simply liked the name. "When I was a kid, I used to call my mom 'Dancing Lady.' *La dame de la danse.*"

"You speak French?" Macey asked.

"*Un peu.* When you travel as much as I have, you learn a little of a lot of languages. Enough to find someone who speaks a bit of English, anyway. I also picked up a little Creole from my mother. Not much, though. She tried to speak only English when she was around me. I guess she figured that as a half-breed albino bastard, the other kids had enough material to use against me. I didn't need to be speaking a foreign language to boot."

"That was nice of her," Macey said. She tapped the base of the plant with her foot and set the colorful leaves slowly dancing. "It must have been a challenge for her, not speaking her native tongue even in her own home."

"She was a good mom," Leon said. His mother, Amabelle Voinché, was petite, beautiful, and young when Leon was a child. Leon remembered her soft, sad smile, and her loud belly laughs. Most of all, Leon remembered her dances. When she heard music, she threw her tiny body and enormous soul into the rhythm. Her dances were a wild mix of styles that she had learned as a child or had seen on television. She blended traditional Haitian meringue, itself a mix of African and French traditions, with Navaho war stomps, Irish step, Egyptian belly dance, jitterbug, salsa, samba, and swing. She would spin, hop, clap, slide, throw her arms into the air, and writhe her torso. No two dances were ever alike. Some days she danced for hours straight, until she collapsed on the floor, panting as she laughed or cried.

Amabelle combined drugs as wildly as she mixed dance styles. She took pills in the morning to help her roll out of bed, smoked pot with breakfast, and by afternoon, she was consuming a variety and quantity of narcotics that would have shocked Elvis. She had tried to hide her substance abuse from Leon, but it was hard to keep secrets in their cramped apartment. Leon's lifelong interest in drugs began by observing his mother. He found it fascinating that nature and mankind had devised so many means of getting high.

Thinking back, Leon realized his mother had a bipolar disorder. She tried to self-medicate her moods, but the endless intake of drugs only intensified her manic-depressive swings. Leon never resented his mother for her many problems. Even in her deepest depths of depression and addiction, she was always tender with her son. Forever doting. Her love for her boy always managed to shine through the haze caused by whatever chemicals were fighting for control of her brain. Leon thought she was brave and strong for enduring her struggles as long as she could manage.

Leon's father, Increase Lynch, had met Amabelle during one of his frequent business trips to Miami. Leon tried not to consider what his mother's profession in Miami had been, but Increase visited her on each trip after they had first met. Eventually, he brought her back to Butchers Harbor, set her up in an apartment, and gave her a job as a cocktail waitress at one of his clubs. Increase was already married to a pretty Irishwoman, and he had a boy he had named "Wyatt" over his wife's objections. This family did not stop Increase from pursuing a love affair with Amabelle, nor did the unexpected birth of her albino boy.

Growing up, Leon enjoyed the frequent visits from the friendly white man with the long hair. Each time Increase arrived at their small home, he brought expensive toys, stylish clothes, and other gifts, but Leon grew fond of Increase because he was a great playmate. When they played with action figures, Increase would lie down on the floor with Leon, and the two of them would simultaneously script and perform great action dramas with the little plastic men. When other adults played action figures with Leon, they made the characters say corny things, as if to remind Leon that they, the adults, were too old for this sort of play, that they were merely entertaining a kid who was too weird to have play-mates his own age. Increase never did that. When Increase spoke as Skelator or Aquaman or Darth Vader, his dialogue was perfectly suited for the character and the narratives that he and Leon crafted together. On the playground, Increase would make spaceship sounds as he pushed Leon on the swings, and he once poured vegetable oil down the length of the slide to make it a faster ride. When Leon's mother had complained that the oil had ruined Leon's clothes, Increase simply bought the boy a new wardrobe. As the years passed, Leon began to act with more maturity and responsibility than Increase, the perpetual child. However, Leon was always grateful for the man who was a friend to both him and his mom.

When Leon was twelve, he came home from school to find an Increase he had never seen before. This Increase was not laughing or singing goofy songs. This Increase had red, swollen eyes. He looked broken and old. He told Leon that his mother had taken a long trip that day. She was going to a nice place that was better than Butchers Harbor. Leon would not accept Increase's vague description of events, and eventually Increase told the boy that his mother had collapsed at the club where she waitressed. She was dead before the paramedics arrived.

In a rare act of responsibility, Increase legally recognized his illegitimate son and took him into his home. Leon was terribly unhappy in the Lynch house. Mrs. Lynch filed for divorce a month after Leon's arrival, and she was remarried within a year. Leon's half brother, Wyatt, hated the intruder who disrupted his family, and he honed his superb skills in psychological and physical torture with regular practice on Leon. Increase was no longer the happy playmate Leon had known while his mother was alive. While Increase was not overtly cruel like Wyatt, it was clear he resented the disorder Leon had created, and he treated the boy less like a son and more like an unwanted consequence.

After five years of dysfunctional family hell, Leon accepted a $25,000 gift from his dad to travel the world. As he toured far-flung rainforests, tundras, swamps, and deserts, he started collecting the powerful plants that formed the amazing pharmacopoeia that he still maintained. Leon had never abandoned his childhood fascination with drugs, but he always avoided the cheap, dangerous highs that killed his mother. Instead, he pursued the more exquisite and esoteric effects of nature's sundry bounty.

"How about these?" Macey asked, pulling Leon from his reverie. She was crouched by a long clay trough filled with rich, stinky soil and tiny coral-colored mushrooms. "Will these things get me high?"

"Oh yeah. And then some," Leon said. "I sell those mushrooms to die-hard heads who've been dropping acid since Nixon was in office. These old hippies have eaten a rainbow of LSD, from purple haze to orange sunshine. They've seen it all, and they're blown away by these little boomers. Owsley himself never mixed a thing that could touch these shrooms."

"So, you won't support bulimics, but you will support acidheads," Macey said.

"Well, these shrooms do give the mind a workout, but they have a fairly low impact on the brain. They're far more benign that the most of the garbage LSD that's out there today. Besides, they aren't the sort of thing that people consume habitually."

"Do you take them?" Macey asked.

"I ate a couple when I was gathering them down in Bolivia. They helped me work a few a kinks out of my psyche, but once was enough for me. My head's too fragile to repeat that experience."

"Well, if you won't eat them, they must be heavy duty," Macey said. She turned to take another slow survey of the greenhouse, stopping to study specific plants as if she was making a mental inventory. "Well, this is all very interesting," she said, "but I'll have to learn more about your collection some other day. I'm here on business. You feel like working tonight?"

Leon set his pruning shears on a bench beside a potted plant with long orange vines cascading to the floor. "What's the gig?"

"I wish I knew," Macey said. "All I know is your dad wants to see you, and he wants you to pack a full medicine bag. Be prepared for anything, he says."

"You don't have any more information than that?" Leon asked.

"Increase is providing information on a need-to-know basis. Apparently, I don't need to know."

"Give me a break. You're never out of the loop."

"I am this time."

Leon shook his head. "I have a tough time believing that. Come on, be straight with me. What kind of shit detail do they want me to do now?"

Macey threw up her hands. "I'm telling you, Leon, I have no idea. I doubt it's shit work, though. Your father and brother have some big, secret operation planned. They won't discuss it with anyone."

"And they want me?" Leon asked, his tone betraying pride and fear.

"Yeah, go figure. So you in?"

Leon hesitated. "Well, I can listen to what he has to say, I guess."

Macey smirked. "That's all they're asking."

Macey drove Leon through the streets of Butchers Harbor, past condemned slaughterhouses and abandoned factories, hollow fossils of an extinct economy. The only semi-thriving, semi-legal industries in Butchers Harbor were blocks upon blocks of dive bars, shot-and-a-beer liquor stores, strip clubs, pornographic superstores, pawn shops, and little offices with block-lettered signs advertising CASH FOR CAR TITLES, YOU KEEP CAR. Leon leaned his head against the passenger window and watched the citizens of Butchers Harbor drift by. The elderly tried to be invisible among packs of bored kids. Lunatics and addicts ranted to themselves or shouted at the darkening sky. Sidewalk geeks ate live roaches or hammered spikes into their nostrils for spare change. Even the people who weren't profoundly insane or deformed looked a little off, as if they had been drawn by an artist who had lost control of his pen and his mind.

Macey used her left knee and, occasionally, one hand to guide her '67 Mustang convertible through traffic. As she approached a red light, she pointed to the glove compartment before Leon's knees. "Open that up, will you?" she said. "I need something." Leon opened the hatch. Inside the compartment were a few maps, lip gloss, a Glock 20, and a pint bottle of Wild Turkey that was three-quarters empty. Leon was prepared to jump out of the car if she asked for the Glock. "Hand me that Turkey," she said. Leon handed her the whiskey and watched her with furtive, sidelong glances as she tilted the bottle back against her luscious lips.

While the car idled at the red light, Macey looked to her side and watched an obese woman sitting on the curb. Heavy, wet sobs shook the fat woman's shoulders and jiggled the loose flesh under her chin. Macey took another sip of whiskey and turned back to face Leon. "No place like home, huh?"

"Not like this home."

"You've been sticking around for a while this time, White

Boy." She passed the Wild Turkey back to Leon. "How long has it been now? Half a year?"

"Eight months," Leon said. He examined the label for a moment before taking a small sip. Leon was not a whiskey drinker, but he welcomed the intimacy of sharing a bottle with Macey. Most people were uneasy sharing a bottle or can with Leon. They seemed to worry that albinism might be contagious.

"So what brought you back to this city of freaks?" Macey asked.

Leon shrugged. "Just needed a break from traveling, I guess."

"I'd think you'd enjoy traveling," Macey said. "Seeing new places, meeting new people."

"When I began traveling, the first two countries I visited were Haiti and then Ireland. I had youthful notions about visiting my ancestral homelands." Leon was quiet for a moment. "You'd be surprised by the similarities between the two countries. Both have landscapes that are beautiful enough to move you to tears. Music is a big deal in both countries. Both the Haitians and the Irish like to visit and tell stories. Either group can talk for hours on end. And both islands have some tough locals who know how to give a stranger a hard time. Even the locals who didn't threaten to beat the shit out of me didn't exactly embrace me either." Leon shrugged. "Neither place felt like home. So, I kept traveling, hoping I'd find some place where I fit in. I never found it, though."

Macey smiled. "Then you've come back to the right place, Paleface. This is where you belong when you don't belong. We're all misfits in this city." The light changed and Macey punched the accelerator. The tires made a short burst of a squeal that startled the crying woman on the curb. "I traveled a bit myself before I wound up in this dung heap. I hate the place, but somehow, Butchers Harbor just feels like home. You know what I mean, Whitey?"

Leon took another sip of whiskey. "I don't mean to be a pain in the ass, Macey, but I'm not a big fan of the whole 'Whitey,' 'White Boy,' 'Paleface' thing. I'd like to think there's more to my identity than a pigment deficiency."

Macey reached for the bottle in Leon's hand. "I understand how you feel, but you have to consider the situation. Our industry embraces nicknames. It's part of our culture. Bugsy Siegel hated to be called 'Bugsy,' but who remembers his real name?" Macey tipped the bottle and drained the last of the bourbon. She tossed the empty pint toward a group of thuggy kids loitering outside a head shop. As the glass shattered, the kids scattered. The boys hurled threats and curses back at Macey as the Mustang drifted away. She smiled slightly as she watched them in her rearview mirror. "Anyhow," she said, "you have white hair and white skin. People are gonna call you 'Whitey.' You might as well accept it." She turned and winked. "Know what I mean, Leon?"

She gave the steering wheel a hard turn with the palm of one hand. Tires screeched and the engine growled as the car climbed a steep hill. They approached a high school, an ugly concrete and brick building mottled with graffiti.

"Where're we going?" Leon asked.

"For a walk down memory lane," Macey said, pulling into the high school parking lot. "You went to school here, didn't you?"

"Until I dropped out." As he scanned the parking lot and the nearby baseball and football fields, Leon recalled the endless adolescent ostracism and ridicule that had occurred here. Most of the abuse was orchestrated by his older brother.

Macey drove slowly through the empty parking lot, easing the Mustang to the right or left to crush empty beer cans and fast food litter beneath the tires as she circled to the back of the school. She parked the car on a patch of burnt lawn near a rear entrance. "Alright, follow me," she said. She shut off the car and twirled the key ring around her index finger as she eased out of the car.

Leon grabbed his medicine bag, followed Macey to rear entrance, and waited as she unlocked a deadbolt on a dented steel door. Inside the school, Macey locked the door again and led Leon down a narrow corridor into an unlit gymnasium. As they walked across the basketball court, the hollow thud of their feet against the floorboards echoed in the darkness. Finally, they entered a locker room lit with one flickering fluorescent bulb.

Macey sat on one of the benches and slumped against the tiled wall.

"Now what?" Leon asked.

She pointed toward a door at the far end of the room. "Your dad and brother are waiting for you in there. I'm supposed to wait here."

Leon walked across the locker room and stood before a metal door coated with layers of chipped paint. He turned and glanced back at Macey. She waved the fingers of one hand for Leon to move on.

As Leon opened the door, his nostrils tingled with fumes of chlorine and burning alcohol. Small blue flames formed a large, dotted rectangle around the perimeter of an enormous room. The flames cast shimmering reflections on a floor of water.

"We're down here, at the end of the pool," Increase called. Leon looked for his father in the darkness. He saw an ember rise slowly at the far end of the room. It hovered in one spot and grew brighter, illuminating his brother's angry eyes as he drew on his cigarette.

Leon walked around the edge of a pool lined with cans of burning Sterno. As his eyes adjusted to the blue light of the flames, he saw a middle-aged man tied to a chair set in the shallow end. Scattered around the bound man were floating candles that bobbed on the small waves. Dark spoors of blood swirled in the water, trailing from a gash on his jaw. The man raised his head to watch Leon, but he seemed disoriented by the choppy water reflecting the flickering light of a dozen flames. Torture by candlelight and canned heat. Typical Lynch modus operandi.

Leon averted his eyes from the man and walked on until he reached his family. Increase and Wyatt sat on a fiberglass bench by the pool. A bottle of wine sat on the floor between them. "Leon, my boy. Good to see you," Increase said. He stroked his goatee. "Damn good to see you." He grabbed the bottle of wine, rose from the bench, and strolled up to his son. He gave Leon a hearty clap on the shoulder. "How are you, kid? Been all right?"

Leon shrugged.

"Care for some wine?"

"No thanks," Leon said.

"You don't know what you're missing." He turned the bottle so Leon could see the label. "This here is a first-rate Müller-Thurgau. Top-notch grape." He took a swig from the bottle and swished the wine in his cheeks.

Leon walked past his father and sat wearily on the bench, careful to keep some distance between himself and his brother. "So," he said, setting his heavy medicine bag at his feet, "Macey says you've got a job for me."

Increase waved the bottle under his nose. "I've been told that a good Müller-Thurgau is supposed to smell like cat pee. Who's the piss-sniffing wino who came up with that comparison? Huh? Makes you wonder. I tell you something, though, Leon, if cat piss tastes like this wine here, I'm tempted to give genuine kitty wee-wee a little taste one of these days."

"That's a good idea, Dad," Leon said. "Let me know how that works out for you. In the meantime, maybe someone could tell me why there's a man tied up in the pool."

Increase glanced over his shoulder at the bloody man. "Oh, that's Peter Volkov. Heard of him?"

Leon shook his head.

Increase ambled back to the bench and sat between his sons. "Peter Volkov is Vladimir Borisova's chauffeur," he said. "You know who Vladimir Borisova is, don't you, Leon?"

Leon nodded. "He's your competition."

"That's right, son. He's our competition. Damn stiff competition at that. I'm not just losing market share to Borisova. I'm losing manpower. That Russian is killing some of my best employees. He's also disrupting longstanding business arrangements I've had with City Hall. He's causing all kinds of problems." Increase put his arm around Leon. "You know what wins a war, son?"

Leon shrugged.

"Information," Increase said. "Think about it. You've heard the expression, 'Loose lips sink ships'? You know why they say that, son? They say it 'cause it's the goddamn truth. The general with the right information wins the war. And this bastard Borisova's got the best kind of information. He's got inside information. That's information from the inside, Leon. One or more of our employees or associates are supplying our competition with trade secrets. If we want to win our war with the Borisovas, we need to plug our leaks."

Increase pointed the neck of the wine bottle toward the pool. "Peter Volkov is more than a mere driver or body-guard, Leon. He's also a trusted friend of Vladmir Borisova. Rumor has it that Volkov may be a captain some day. I suspect that Borisova shares a lot of family secrets with our man in the water. I also assume that Borisova conducts much of his business in the car while Volkov is driving. It's likely that Peter drives his boss to meetings with his informants. All of this makes Peter Volkov a very important man to us. We'd like to know what he knows. The long and short, I think he can name our traitor. Unfortunately, Pete's been a bit shy tonight. He's hardly said a word all evening." Increase took a quick swig off his bottle and patted Leon on the shoulder. "So what do you say, my boy? Do you think you can loosen the man's tongue?"

Wyatt took a drag on his cigarette then pointed the ember toward the medicine bag at Leon's feet. "You got any truth serum in your stash?"

"I could whip something up," Leon said.

Wyatt exhaled a thin plume of smoke from the side of his mouth. He squinted one eye against his smoke, form-ing deep crow's-feet on his otherwise boyish face. "Will it work?"

"All of my products work," Leon said. "But a truth serum is a tricky thing. It's a bit like Truth itself. You have to know how to work it. It requires some manipulation. You can't just pour the serum into your driver over there and expect him to spill the beans on whatever subject you choose. You need an experienced handler to manage his trip. You need some-one to guide him and coax the truth out of him. Otherwise, he'll just jabber like a mental patient. He'll make as much sense as Dad."

Increase chuckled.

"Are you an experienced handler?" Wyatt asked.

"Sure," Leon said.

"Fine. You're hired," Wyatt said. "Any other issues?"

The Russian in the pool groaned. His moans rumbled in the dark room. Leon shifted uncomfortably on the bench. "As a matter of fact, I do have a couple of other issues. There is a question of ethics."

Wyatt scoffed. "Ethics?"

Leon nodded. "Yeah, ethics. It's this business of you plugging your leaks. I'd rather not have my products or my services contributing to a killing spree. I've never been an accessory to murder, and I'd prefer to keep it that way."

Wyatt felt the throb of blood quicken in his neck. His cigarette bobbed on his lower lip as he muttered, "Fuckin' Whitey." Wyatt hated everyone, but Whitey filled him with new levels of loathing. It wasn't just Whitey's candyass reluctance to pitch in that made Wyatt angry. Everything about the whiny, wimpy shit pissed him off. He hated the way Whitey dressed, wearing tattered jeans and a ratty, decade-old windbreaker like some homeless bum. He was annoyed that Whitey wore a windbreaker even in the middle of the summer. The defective weakling had to cower under an oversized hood or the sun would turn him to toast. Fucking pussy couldn't even handle sunlight. Wyatt wanted to grab Leon by his nappy white dreadlocks and hammer his face into the concrete floor. He wanted to kick Leon in the head until he bled from his ears. He wanted to kill Whitey. He didn't want to merely snuff out Whitey's future; he wanted to wipe out his past as well. Wyatt wanted to kick the milky bastard so hard it would send him back into his junky mother's womb, and then he'd give the bitch an abortion. He wanted to kill Whitey before he was ever born, before he came into Wyatt's life and drove his mother away and turned everything to shit.

But that would have to wait for another day.

Wyatt struggled to keep his rage in check. He swallowed the bile at the back of his throat and reached into his ostrich-skin jacket. He removed a brick of bound bills and tossed it onto Leon's lap. "Alright, Mother Theresa, put your ethics on hold for a minute and count that pile."

Leon flipped through the bills with his thumb. When he was a quarter of the way through the stack, he stopped counting. "All this is for me?" he asked.

Wyatt nodded.

Leon set the stack of bills on the bench beside him. "That's a lot of cash. It would take me months to see this. More than half a year, I think. Maybe longer. Still, I don't think it's quite enough for me to facilitate a murder."

Increase cleared his throat. "You know, son, no one has actually used the word 'murder.' We just want to know who our turncoat is, that's all. This traitor has helped our enemies kill people in our organization. Good people have died." He pursed his lips and shook his head to demonstrate his sorrow. "Murdered in cold blood, son. Now, if you help us find our traitor, you can *save* lives. Saving lives is never a bad thing, is it, Leon? You believe that life is precious, don't you?"

"Of course I do," Leon said.

"Yeah, life is precious," Wyatt said. He flicked his cigarette into the pool. It hissed as it hit the water. "So we'll pay for your products, your services, and your scruples. Now, can we get down to business?"

"Well, there is one final matter," Leon said. "There is my pride."

Wyatt smirked. "That shouldn't cost much."

"You'd be surprised," Leon said. "The price is based on a few factors. The first factor is, you two are in deep shit. The family business is headed down the toilet, and it looks like I'm the only one who can turn things around. The second factor is, I don't care if the family business goes down the shitter. It's not like I've ever been included in it. Refresh my memory, Wyatt. How did you describe my profession? I believe you've called me a 'two-bit dealer selling boutique drugs with no market value.' Well, I think it's a little ironic that you now depend on me and my useless drugs to save your ass. Maybe I'd like to see you grovel a little. In fact, maybe I'd like you to lose everything. Then you might know how I feel."

"Jesus Christ, you whine like a fucking bitch," Wyatt said. "You know who you sound like? You sound like Fredo. You remember that dickhead in *The Godfather*? 'I'm smot! Not stupid! Not like everybody says! I'm smot!'" Wyatt laughed. "Listen, Peon, don't overestimate your importance. I have my own truth serum. I'll just give that old fart a little baptism. Once his head's been submerged for a minute or two, he'll develop a new appreciation for oxygen, and he'll be glad to name all of our informants. Or maybe I'll interview the man with a blowtorch. After I burn his pecker off, he'll rat out his own mother. So we don't need your fucking truth serum, Whitey. In fact, get your punk ass out of here before I throw you in the pool too. I'll give you and the Russki your baptisms and your last rites."

"Wyatt, that's no way to talk to your brother," Increase said.

"Half brother," Wyatt corrected. "And fuck him, Dad. He disrespected our family."

"Come on, now. Leon's only venting," Increase said. "He's blowing off a little steam, is all. And that's fine, Leon, but try to save the drama for your therapist, okay? Your brother needs your help, and I need your help. If we've done wrong by you in the past, we can make it up to you in the future."

"Oh, you need my help," Leon said. "Well, after all you've done for me, how can I turn you down?"

"Leon, this is an opportunity to show me your mettle. Don't blow it by acting like a sarcastic little snot," Increase said. "Prove your worth tonight. If I've underestimated you, I won't repeat that mistake. Now it's up to you. You have the power to change your role in the family right now."

"Really?" Leon asked. "You're offering me something meaningful instead of the occasional shit work?"

"Of course. You're involved tonight, aren't you? We've turned to you at this critical moment." Increase slapped his hands together. "So let's get to work."

Leon turned his gaze to Volkov. The driver lifted his chin from the water and squinted at Leon. "Maybe I have one other issue," Leon said.

"You feel bad for Volkov? Is that it?" Increase asked. "I'm only trying to defend our family, Leon. To do that, we need to make the man talk. Wyatt is right; we don't need your truth serum to make Volkov sing. Obviously, I won't have Wyatt climbing in that pool to drown the man, but we do have other employees who are skilled at that sort of thing. Unfortunately, I may call in the wrong employee, someone who's working for the other team. This traitorous employee may 'accidentally' kill Volkov before he confesses.

"Also, Leon, I want to move quickly on this thing. I want a

confession from the man before anybody misses him. Volkov is a tough old Russian. He won't die as coward or a traitor. Not soon enough for us, at any rate. It may take days to get a word out of him. If you want to know the truth, I admire Volkov's strength and loyalty. I wish I had more people of his ilk working on my team. That's why I don't want him to suffer. If you can make him talk quickly, then I can afford to be compassionate."

Increase put a hand on Leon's shoulder. "Using your truth serum is the humane way, son. Don't you see that? If you don't want to lend a hand, well then, I will to turn to more barbaric means. I'll make Volkov talk one way or another. Trust me, we can make him sing like a choirboy. But that won't be pleasant for anyone. So, do the right thing, Leon. Give Volkov your truth serum and consider it an act of kindness."

Leon averted his eyes from the driver and watched the reflection of the glowing exit sign squirming on the choppy water. He knew what he should do. The right thing was to leave the high school and call the police before Volkov was beaten too severely. Then again, many of the cops were crooked, and some of them still worked for the Lynches. Also, Increase and Wyatt might move the driver to a new location. And there was always the Wyatt factor. Wyatt was unpredictable, but if Leon had noticed any trend over the years, it was that he always underestimated his older brother's capacity for cruelty. Boredom alone made Wyatt nasty. If he felt slighted, he turned vicious. If he felt threatened, Wyatt could be as deadly as a dirty nuke. If Wyatt suspected that Leon could put him in jail, Wyatt would just take his half brother out of the equation. No hesitation. No doubt. Leon wanted to do the right thing, but he also wanted to live. As shitty as his life was, he still wanted to keep it, the way a starving man might cling to a hunk of moldy bread.

Self-preservation is a powerful drive in the animal kingdom, but this instinct alone did not explain why Leon found himself contemplating his family's offer. If Leon was so hell-bent on avoiding danger, he would have never returned to a city as perilous as Butchers Harbor, and he certainly would have steered clear of his brother. It wasn't just a desire to return to his roots that brought Leon back to the Harbor. He was loath to admit it, even to himself, but Leon wanted to be a gangster. He had shuffled across the globe buying and selling product and hoping to find closeness or camaraderie along the way. All he found were customers, suppliers, and alienation. Some years back, he had seen a coming-of-age gangster flick in which a kid asked a local street hood, "Would you rather be loved or feared?" Well, nobody loved Leon, so maybe folks should fear him just a bit. If becoming affiliated with his mobster family brought Leon a measure of respect, he was ready for it. He was weary of his days of wandering, moping, and being treated like a loser.

"So what's it gonna be, Fredo?" Wyatt asked. "Are you with us or against us? Shit or get off the pot."

"If no one's going to get hurt," Leon muttered. "I guess I don't have much choice."

Wyatt and Increase smiled.

Leon unzipped his medicine bag and lifted the brick of bills. He avoided looking at the cash as he stuffed it into his bag. "Just so you know, I'm not doing this for the money."

Wyatt scoffed.

Leon gave his brother a brief, angry glare. "I'm not," he said forcefully. He turned his gaze back to his father. "I'm doing this for you, Dad. You're my father. You need my help, so I'm helping the family. But I want something in return. I want involvement. I want respect."

"Son, the issue has already been addressed," Increase said.

Leon nodded. "Alright, then." He waited for something more, some words from his father, a small gesture, or even a feeling within himself to mark this transition, but the moment was filled nothing but silence and fidgeting. "Alright, then," he repeated.

Leon reached into his medicine bag and rummaged among the baggies and corked vials until he removed a tiny cauldron slightly larger than his fist. He filled the pot with two drams of spring water and placed it over one of the cans of burning fuel. Then he milked the stamens of a rare iris that grows in the Truong Son Mountains of Vietnam. The juice formed swirls of creamy emerald in the cauldron's water. Next, Leon crushed five crimson berries from the tiny Alaskan Unaija tree. He added the juice, pulp, and skin of the berries to the pot, along with the caps of three mushrooms that he had grown from spores imported from a lonely bog in County Mayo. Finally, he ground the bark of a Mwerugani in a wooden mortar and poured the powder into the brew.

After the mix had simmered for several minutes, Leon looked up and said, "It's ready." He dipped a large eyedropper into the cauldron and drew the solution into the tube. Holding the eyedropper above the water, he descended the steps into the pool and trudged through the water toward Volkov. The driver lifted his chin from the water and glared at Leon. "I'm sorry, sir," Leon said. "This will help you. Lean your head back and open your eyes."

Volkov squeezed his eyes shut and put his face in the water. As Leon stepped closer, Volkov turned his face in the other direction so that his right ear faced the ceiling. Leon steadied the dropper and shot the solution into Volkov's ear canal. He then grabbed Volkov's head and struggled to keep it still for a minute so the driver would not shake the solution into the water. Each time the Russian pushed his skull against the cut on Leon's palm, Leon grimaced with pain. Volkov's thrashing and Leon's grunts echoed in the concrete room. Several of the floating candles tipped into the water, but others managed to stay afloat on the growing waves. Their flames cast serpentine shadows on the walls. Gradually, Volkov began to settle down, and Leon released his head. As the Russian coughed and gasped, Leon waded to the edge of the pool and leaned against the side.

Volkov's breathing began to settle. He felt vaguely protected in the water, and his fear began to ebb. His deep contempt for the Lynches and his sad acceptance of death dissolved in the warm water around him. He watched the burning Sterno's blue hue turn slowly into a neon violet. Furry beads of water worked their way into his pores. Charmed hydrogen and oxygen atoms rolled between his cells, through organs and bones, up his spine and into his brain, where they effervesced and tickled his cerebellum. The chlorine that drenched the air smelled like thick slices of ginger. Volkov lost any sense of past or future. Sitting in the pool was the first moment in his life. The water that lapped against his chin was singing hymns.

Leon pushed himself off the side of the pool and sloshed back to Volkov. He put a comforting hand on the Russian's shoulder. "You okay?" he asked. This simple question touched Volkov. These were the kindest words anyone had ever spoken to him. He struggled to keep from weeping.

"When I was child, I swam in river that was cold," Volkov

said. "It made my fingers blue. I shiver then, but I stay in water. When a cat purrs, you know, it prove that God exist. Yes?"

Leon nodded thoughtfully. "Yes. Right. Why else would a cat purr? It's the Voice of God, isn't it?" Leon took his hand off Volkov's shoulder and walked in a circle around the bound man. "You're a wise man, Mr. Volkov. Or may I call you Peter? I'm hungry for knowledge, Peter. I could learn much from a man as wise as you. Tell me more." Leon's voice was the music of clouds passing before a winter moon. His words were psalms. Leon spoke a little more, but the words were lost on Volkov. Although he could not understand him, Volkov believed what Leon said. As Leon walked around the Russian, he left a luminescent wake. His white hair glowed, forming a halo around his head. Volkov saw that Leon was a benevolent spirit. This young shadow of light was a baptist sent from Heaven to cleanse Volkov's soul.

The driver talked. He began by describing his childhood, and he saw the world through the eyes of an innocent. When these pure eyes saw himself as he was today, he knew he was evil. He saw his reflection in the choppy water before him. He looked into the rotting face of a demon. His wickedness caused him insufferable pain. The strong man wept and choked on his sobs.

"I can free you from your pain," Leon said. "It's so much easier than you believe. All you have to do is purge yourself of deceit. The dark secrets that you clutch are toxins in your soul. They blister your heart and warp your mind. Why do you keep secrets that hurt you so deeply and harm so many more?"

It was a good question, one the driver could not answer. He saw the Borisovas through his pure vision and saw that they were more evil than he. It was senseless and wicked to hold secrets that promoted so much harm. This young man before him was good. Leon was the only righteous man he had ever known, and he alone deserved loyalty. He alone deserved the truth.

With Leon's gentle coaxing, the driver named all of the enemies of Increase and Wyatt Lynch. They had two-timers and double-crossers on the force, in the unions, in the press, and in the courts. As Increase had suspected, they also had traitors within their organization. Ivan Wazowiecki, a one-eyed, occasional attorney for the family, had tattled every tidbit he had ever been privy to, though he had never been trusted with much. Benny One Too Many Vega, a drunken pothead thief who performed frequent freelance work with the Lynches and often socialized with the crew, was also a good listener and a key informant for the Borisovas. The greatest traitor, however, was Swag Kilpatrick, boss of the Mud Hollow crew and Increase's oldest friend.

When the Russian had finished his confession, Increase groaned and held his forehead in his hands. "Damn," he said. "Why'd it have to be Swag?"

"It doesn't surprise me," Wyatt said. "I never trusted that gooney motherfucker for a second. He's got this way of look-ing at me, like he thinks he's smarter than me. Fucking dick-head. I've been waiting for an excuse to take that geezer out."

Volvov struggled against his ropes as he mumbled a Russian poem.

Increase lifted his head and fortified himself with a swig of Müller-Thurgau. "You did put a tail on Swag, didn't you?" he asked.

"Yeah. I put a tail on Swag, Macey, and Cracker Jack. And I tapped their phones, just like you said."

"Good. I'm glad we took the precautions. I never would have thought any of those three would have been a rat. Least of all Swag. But I'm glad we took the precaution. You don't think he could have contacted the Borisovas, do you?"

Wyatt shrugged. "He hasn't called anyone."

"Well, we'd better move quickly with him."

Leon turned his back on the Russian and trudged toward the steps leading out of the water. He followed the conversation between his father and brother with mounting concern.

"The dead speak to me when I dream," Volkov said loudly. "Hungry ghosts are honest with sleepers."

Wyatt paced along the pool and rubbed hands together. "Okay, then. Swag dies tomorrow night. Then we'll whack out Benny and that weasel shit lawyer Wazowiecki. And we'd better hit the Russkies' five-O and their feds before they get any heads up. After that, we'll take out our unfriendly judges, hacks, and the union ass wipes." Wyatt laughed. "God damn almighty, I'm looking forward to this little bloodbath!"

As he listened to his brother, Leon's lungs tightened and his knees felt rubbery. He sat down on the blue pool steps, the water up to his chest. He gripped the stainless steel railing to keep from slipping underwater.

"Let's not get carried away," Increase said. "I don't think we'll get the police and unions back on our team if you starting killing them. That's the sort of hotheaded overreaction of yours that has alienated our family from these institutions in the first place."

"Dad! They turned their backs on us! They hung us out to dry! Now you want to kiss and make up?"

"Pray for the dead," Volkov murmured. "Their souls are near."

"Will somebody shut that fucker up?" Wyatt shouted.

"It's a phase of the truth serum," Leon explained. "He'll go on like this for a little while. There isn't much I can do."

"Once in while, every body pick their nose. No shame in this," Volkov explained.

Wyatt pulled a revolver from his jacket. "Fuck it. I'll quiet him down."

"Hey, whoa! Wait a minute!" Leon said as he stumbled to his feet.

"Put that gun away!" Increase demanded.

"Do what? Has everybody lost their minds?" Wyatt asked. "This is a Borisova here! This is the enemy, remember? So now we're letting our enemies go too?"

"Volkov is more use to us if he's alive," Increase said. "If he's missing, Borisova will assume we killed him, and he'll also assume that we interrogated him before he died. We'll lose any element of surprise." Increase turned to Leon. "Do you have anything in your bag of tricks that would make Volkov forget about this night?"

"Sure," Leon said eagerly. He pulled himself out of the pool and scrambled over to his medicine bag. "I have just the thing," he said as he rummaged through his powders and potions. "When I was in Taipei, I bought a hundred vials of venom from a guy in Snake Alley. Here it is." He held up a glass vial of a viscous red liquid. Fat drops of water dripped off Leon's clothes and slapped the concrete. "This stuff is a mind eraser. It's liquid amnesia. I can make somebody forget hours, days, or weeks. You know, I'm lucky to have any left. It's been a great seller. Everybody has something they want to forget."

"Excellent," Increase said. "Can you substitute another memory as well?"

"Sure, no problem."

"Very good, Leon. Well done. Make Volkov forget about his kidnapping and interview. Make him believe he was mugged as he stepped out of his car tonight. We'll have Cracker Jack and Macey take his wallet and dump him in the alley behind his home."

"Good idea, Dad," Leon said. He climbed back down the steps into the pool and splashed toward Volkov. "I'll medicate him right now. Everything'll be cool. No one needs to get hurt, right?"

"Naw, no one needs to get hurt," Wyatt said. "In fact, let's all drive over to Swag's and give him a big hug for being such a wonderful traitor! We'll make him the man of honor at our Enemy Appreciation Day picnic."

Increase chuckled. "Don't worry, Wyatt. If you want revenge so badly, I'll put you in charge of plugging our leaks. Will that make you happy?"

"A little," Wyatt said, "but don't expect me to exercise any of your restraint. I want to make an example of our traitors."

"By all means," Increase said. "I wouldn't have it any other way."

Leon felt ill again. He gripped the back of Volkov's chair for balance.

Volkov nodded solemnly, his bloody chin dunking in and out of the water. "However bad is the dying, the dead are suffering more. Excuse me now. I pee in pool."

3
WHACKED

The shades in Swag Kilpatrick's small Mud Hollow house were drawn day and night to deter sniper attacks. He had installed security bars over the windows, and he had added steel door braces and several more deadbolts to his front and back doors. As for weapons, he had a Calico M-960A mini submachine gun hanging on a coat rack by the front door, a Mossberg automatic shotgun propped against the wall by the back door, a Colt Commando in the hall closet, and a Steyr tactical machine pistol in the oven. Grenades were tucked away in cupboards, drawers, and under furniture throughout the house like chocolate eggs on Easter morning. He had a Ruger service revolver stuffed in the pocket of his ratty bathrobe, and an AMT Hardballer was holstered to his ankle. He wore the Hardballer at all times, even when he was sleeping. Not that he slept much. He had been running on amphetamines and alcohol for two days, ever since he had kidnapped that driver, Peter Volkov.

Swag Kilpatrick wanted to call Vladimir Borisova and warn him that the Lynches were onto him, but he suspected his phone was tapped. Wyatt Lynch was a halfwit lunatic, Swag thought, but he did get one thing right. When he had told Swag to kidnap Borisovas' driver, he had given the instructions to Macey and Cracker Jack at the same time, and he had ordered them to kidnap the man that same day. That left Swag no opportunity to murder the driver before the grab. He had no choice but to help kidnap the man who would finger him as a traitor.

Swag had known Increase Lynch for most of his life. They had grown up in the same neighborhood, and Swag had developed an early friendship with Increase and his brother, Timmy. The boys were the sons of Paddy Lynch, a brutal mobster who maintained his monopoly of Butchers Harbor's loan sharking, prostitution, protection, and gambling through the sheer intimation of no more than a few gun-crazy Irish goons.

Swag and the Lynch boys spent their days and nights roaming the rough streets of Mud Hollow, the bad end of a bad town. They were just pups when they first began boosting cars for joy rides. The kids were so small, one had to steer while another worked the pedals. As Timmy and Increase became teenagers, Paddy Lynch introduced his sons and their friend to the family trade, and the boys pursued crime as a vocation rather than a pastime. Increase developed talents as a schemer, charmer, and con artist as he negotiated with various elements of the Butchers Harbor underground, while Timmy and Swag grew up to be a pair of hulking, nasty thugs. The combination of charisma and intimidation made the boys a powerful trio in the Lynch operations.

The Lynches' monopoly on crime in Butchers Harbor did not go unchallenged. Competing gangs and crooked cops tried several times to take out Paddy Lynch, but luck, grit, and paranoia kept him alive. Paddy had survived so many assassination attempts that he began to believe he was charmed. One night, after playing cards and swilling

Tullamore Dew into the wee hours, Paddy stood and made an announcement to the bleary-eyed players slumped around the table. "Did you boys ever wonder why I'm still livin' and breathin'? Why do you t'ink it is them coppers and wops in this city can't manage to rub me out? It ain't for a lack of trying, I'll assure you. I got a notion Ol' Nick is looking out for me. I reckon he wants me to learn as much up here so I can help him run t'ings down below after I wind up in Hell. So if you feckers ever get the notion that you want to rub out Ol' Paddy Lynch, just remember one t'ing. I'm feckin' bulletproof. The bullets just waltz around me." To prove his claim, he hoisted a pistol off the card table, pressed the muzzle against his temple, and squeezed the trigger.

Increase and Timmy Lynch inherited their father's business that morning at the youthful ages of twenty and twenty-one. They soon made Swag Kilpatrick their number-three guy. The older gangsters in the Lynch mob did not immediately embrace the leadership of these young men. To counter this resistance, Timmy and Swag abruptly terminated most of the old guard while Increase recruited fresh blood. The few old-timers who had survived the cut were more than willing to follow the instructions of their new, younger bosses.

In the early years, Swag was grateful that the Lynch boys had stood by him, and he had put his life in jeopardy many times to defend their asses and their honor. Swag did more than his share to elevate the new, young outfit from a gang of thugs to a first-class operation. The growth of the gang was not without a few hiccups. Timmy was murdered only three years after he had inherited his father's business. A boy whose father had been gunned down by Timmy had returned the favor. With Timmy dead, Swag assumed the role of the family's enforcer. The position made him a target, both for enemies of the family and for jealous elements within the organization. Nevertheless, Swag relished his job. As Wyatt grew up, however, it became clear that Swag was only holding the position until Wyatt was old enough to take over.

Back in the day, Increase Lynch used to prattle on with lofty hippie notions about the empire he hoped to build. He told Swag that he wanted to be a benevolent titan of underground industry. Like the counter-cultural products and services he provided, the organizational structure of the Lynch enterprises would also defy the conventional business model. Increase spoke of an egalitarian syndicate, one that rewarded loyalty and hard work with a generous slice of the pie.

Swag knew it was all bullshit. Players in their operations were as expendable as employees in any other business, mere raw material, gears in the machine no more cherished than cubicle partitions or rolls of cheap toilet paper. Nevertheless, Swag was dismayed that Increase planned to hand over his entire operations to his idiot son. It wasn't merely the nepotism that infuriated Swag, but the idiocy of it. Wyatt was an imbecile. The average street-level banger, some shithead clocker too stupid to sell dope on his own, had more business acumen than Wyatt. A lifer fucked out of his skull on prison dust demonstrated better judgment and self-restraint than Wyatt. Yet, Increase was willing to step over his old friend Swag and disregard everything he had done for the family, just to let his retarded son drive the business into the ground.

Swag took a good look around at the shithole that was his home, and what he saw pissed him off. He was living like a goddamn bum. Swag had to admit he was never good with money. He lost a fortune to his degenerate gambling. Still, if

Increase had given Swag a little more scratch, he wouldn't have had to try to improve his position through gaming and other unwise investments. Fuck Increase. That shanty Irish piece of shit had fucked Swag over. He had been as loyal as a brother to Increase, but he was treated with less respect than the family dog. Well, this dog was turning. He was biting the hand that barely fed him. Increase had no one to blame but himself.

Angry as Swag was, it wasn't spite alone that drove him to the Borisovas. Swag was also thinking of the future. The Lynch family was putting itself out of business. Soon, the Borisovas would run the city, and Swag wanted to develop a relationship with the new owners.

"Man's got a right to look out for himself," Swag muttered. He stood over his stove, eating a fried egg out of the pan and drinking cold sake from the bottle. As he hunched over his meal, his long gray hair dipped into the grease of the frying pan. The only light in the cramped house came from the television. The canned laughter on some old sitcom pissed Swag off. This was no time for laughing.

As Swag gulped his sake, he heard something scuffle. He put down the bottle and drew his Ruger from his bathrobe pocket. He walked across the den and peeked though the corner of a tattered shade, but he saw no one outside. All he saw was the stillness of his slummy neighborhood awash under the cool glow of a gibbous moon. He heard the rustle again. It was above him. The muffled scratches grew louder and seemed to cover his entire ceiling. Swag holstered his revolver, walked to the back door, and grabbed the Mossberg. He stepped back into his living room and fired four rounds through the ceiling into his attic. Chunks of plaster and bits of pink fiberglass fell to the floor. The scuffling stopped.

KILL WHITEY

Swag walked to the trap door leading to the attic and pulled on the rope to open the hatch. Ten rats, each the size of a bulldog, dropped through the opening and landed on Swag. He yelped as jagged teeth bore into his legs, back, and neck. He slammed his body against the wall, crushing two of the animals. He grabbed another that was chewing his ear and gouged its eyes with his thumbs. A dozen more rats dropped through the hatch and pounced on Swag. He howled as he dropped his empty jungle gun and drew the Hardballer from his ankle. He fired five shots wildly about him. Two rats writhed at his feet, but more were pouring through the attic hatch and squirming through the shotgun holes in the ceiling.

Swag ran to his front door with three rats still gnawing at his back. He unlocked his several deadbolts, kicked the security bar out of the way, and tugged on the doorknob, but the door would not open. As he struggled with the door, a rat climbed up his bare leg and bit his gonad. "Mother-goddamn-fucker!" Swag shouted. He pulled the rat off his nuts and held the squirming beast by the scruff of its neck. The rat snarled and spit as Swag jammed the muzzle of the Hardballer against its ear. The room reverberated with a wet explosion, and brain rained down on the other invading rats.

Swag hurled the carcass and his empty gun at the surrounding rats and checked the locks again. He tried to open the door a second time. When it would not budge, he ran to the back door, tripping and stumbling over the biting throng that filled his home. He had no luck opening his back door either. Someone had bolted the doors from the outside. He threw an end table at a picture window. The glass shattered, but the table bounced back into the house when it hit the security bars. The cages Swag had installed to thwart an invasion now prevented his escape.

Exhausted, Swag waded through the mob of rats for his Calico. Smaller rats dangled from his robe and his hair. He grabbed the submachine gun and fired it into the teaming swarm, shouting, "Filthy, ball-bitin', shit-eatin' motherfuckers! Get the fuck outta my motherfuckin' home!" Rats exploded and fell, but few retreated. They continued to leap onto Swag and tear off ragged strips of his skin. As the stink of Swag's blood saturated the air, the pack intensified their attack.

Sitting atop Swag's roof, Günther and Gerhard Schlüter continued to stuff rats through an attic vent until their cages were empty. Günther and Gerhard, identical twin sons of a Nazi fugitive, had raised and bred the animals themselves. Continuing their father's avid interest in genetic engineering, the two rat handlers had developed a line of Master Race rodents designed to crave human flesh with refined ferocity. On Wyatt's orders, they had also fed the rats links of bratwurst spiked with PCP and boar adrenaline. Wyatt would have doped the little monsters with Slaughter, but the idiot Whitey had dumped his supply of the drug into the harbor. All the same, the rats did their job, and before the sun rose, Swag was little more than a pile of bones with the odd bit of cartilage remaining in a few hard-to-reach joints.

Fat, flashing, multi-colored bulbs lined the arched windows, neon poles, and raised dance floor of the Aphrodite Lounge. Fuzzy Magee and the lawyer One-Eye Connivin' Ivan Wazowiecki were seated at a table a short distance from the strippers, who gyrated and rubbed themselves to heavy metal and a strobe light. Fuzzy was a silent partner in the club, and he had invited Ivan over to discuss a few legal issues concerning the business.

"Oh, baby, where do you find these girls?" Ivan asked. He swung his legs with horny glee, his feet not quite touching the floor.

Fuzzy shrugged as he cut a short rib loose from its rack. "I don't get too involved in recruiting. I think they find us for the most part."

"Oh, baby, I love this place," Ivan said. He loosened his wide tie and shrugged out of his cheap suit jacket. "Any one of these girls could be a model. A celebrity model, any one of them. This is Heaven, Fuzzy. Mmmm, mmmm, mmmm! Heaven, I tell you."

Fuzzy sipped his warm vodka tonic and glanced around the club. "Yeah, well, it makes me a few bucks anyway."

"Oh my God, look at that one," Ivan said, pointing at a leggy dancer. "Oh, baby, I think she likes me. She's making eye contact. See that? She wants me, Fuzzy. She definitely wants me."

Fuzzy laughed. Ivan was barely four feet tall, yet his ears and nose would have been oversized even on a giant of a man. Ivan had tried to toughen up his appearance by wearing his hair a little long and by growing scraggly sideburns, but this didn't help much. He still got smirks and giggles from people who saw him.

Ivan leaned forward. "So tell me something. How are these ladies?"

Fuzzy was distracted by the runty lawyer's glass eye, which was pointed somewhere over Fuzzy's shoulder. He turned to see if Ivan was speaking to someone behind him. Seeing no one, he turned back to Ivan. "What did you ask me?"

"I'm just asking how these ladies are, that's all. You know what I mean, Fuzz Man. How are they in the old sack-a-roo?"

Fuzzy gave Ivan a disgusted look. "How would I know? I don't fuck these whores."

One-Eye winked unnaturally. "Come on, Fuzzster. You're telling me you've never sampled the merchandise? It's okay for the butcher to taste the meat. I mean, just look at these hotties. How could you resist that kind of grade-A tail?"

"The same way I resist drinking out of a toilet," Fuzzy said. "I look at these strippers, and I see walking sacks of viruses. I wouldn't stick anything in any one of these skanks unless she had a certificate of cleanliness from two gynos and a tamper-proof seal on her twat. Even then, I'd be double-bagging my knob. Christ, just sitting in this clap-hole gives me the heebie-fucking-jeebies."

Ivan surveyed the room, looking each stripper up and down. "I don't know, Fuzzy. These honeys could have the plague, and I wouldn't kick them out of bed." He ended the subject with the wave of one hand. "Anyhow, let's talk shop. How's business been? You guys still having a hard time with the competition?"

"Well, we've taken our hits," Fuzzy said. "Literally. But things are turning around. Things are about to get a whole lot better."

"Oh yeah? You guys have something planned?"

"We have a number of things planned," Fuzzy said. "In fact, we're correcting some internal and external problems even as we speak."

"Oh yeah? What does that mean?" Ivan asked. "You gonna whack out some of the Borisovas? You gonna kick some ass and take names? Huh? How you gonna do it, Fuzzy?"

Fuzzy glanced about to see if any patrons might be listening. "I'm no lawyer like you, Eye," he said, "but isn't murder illegal?"

"Yeah," Ivan said. He laughed in a high-pitched titter. "What was I thinking? Seriously though, how are you gonna hit those Russian sons of bitches? How you gonna set them up? Gimme some details."

"Really, Eye, this is no place to discuss this sort of thing. What if this place is bugged?"

"Oh, I wouldn't worry about that," Ivan said. "There's too much noise in this club. I think the cops would have a tough time recording anything in here."

"It's not the pigs I'm worried about," Fuzzy said. "It's the Borisovas. I don't know how they do it, but they always seem to be one step ahead of us. They either have some kind of kick-ass surveillance, or they're working with a spy within our own organization."

Ivan erupted in a convulsion of nervous titters.

Fuzzy stopped sawing at his ribs and pointed his knife at Ivan. "Did I tell a joke, Eye? Is a traitor among us comedy to you?"

"No, no," Ivan said. "It's just sort of funny to think that anyone would mess with the Lynch mob like that. I mean, who's that stupid?"

"Money has a way of making most people a little stupid."

"Well, not me," said Ivan. "I mean, you guys have always been great to me. I love you guys. I mean it. I love you guys. And I'll tell you something else, I know better than to cross the Lynches, believe you me. Your boss Wyatt is a friggin' lunatic. I don't mean that in a bad way, Fuzzy. I mean, I have great respect for the man, but I wouldn't tick him off either. I mean, I can't even imagine anyone in your organization—this, this family of ours—selling dirt to the Borisovas. I mean, that's like science fiction or something. Science freakin' fiction, Fuzzy. I mean, I know one thing for sure. I wouldn't ever cross the Lynches, and that's a fact."

"Well, of course you wouldn't, Eye." Fuzzy said. "You're as loyal as a dog. But maybe a few of our greedier associates have turned on us. It's a possibility." Fuzzy shrugged. "Then again, maybe I'm wrong. Maybe it's all my imagination. What do I know?"

"Yeah, Fuzzy, it's all in your head," Ivan said. He hoisted his martini and downed it in two gulps. He set the glass clumsily on the table and said, "Wowie, man. I'm hammered! I'm annihilated. Annihilated, I tell you." He sprung out of his chair and boogied up to the stage to dance with a stripper. He swung his midgety hips and twirled his hands like a drunken boxer working a speed bag. The stripper looked down at Ivan and laughed. Ivan giggled with her and continued to dance. When the stripper moved along to a tipper, One-Eye Connivin' Ivan staggered back to the table.

"Man, oh man, I love this place," he said to Fuzzy. He was panting from his dance with the stripper. "Man, oh man, I love this fun house. That's what it is, Fuzzy. That's what it is, you know. It's a great big fun house for grownups. And I friggin' love it, Fuzzy." Ivan slapped the table repeatedly with both hands, as if he was playing the bongos. "I love this pace!"

Fuzzy glanced about the club and shrugged. "It's alright, I guess. Of course, it doesn't hold a candle to the scene downstairs."

Ivan focused his good eye on Fuzzy. "Downstairs?" he asked. "This place has a downstairs?"

"You're a member, aren't you?" Fuzzy asked.

"Member of what?" Ivan asked.

"Damn, I must be drunk," Fuzzy said. He shook his head. "I thought you had already been initiated. Listen, forget I said anything. You're right, Eye, there's no downstairs to this place."

One-Eye grabbed Fuzzy's forearm. "Fuzzy, my man. Don't hold out on me. If this club has some secret operation downstairs, you gotta let me in on it. I mean, hey, Fuzzy, this is me! This is Ivan you're talking to."

Fuzzy stared fiercely at Ivan's hand gripping his arm. "I only make this warning once," he said. "Get your fucking hand off me." Ivan jerked his hand away as if Fuzzy's arm had caught fire. "I don't like being touched," Fuzzy said, "and I don't like my Armani getting wrinkled."

"Sorry, Fuzzy," Ivan said. His eyes were wide, and one of his pupils quivered. "I got carried away."

Fuzzy forced a smile. "No problem."

Ivan relaxed. "But seriously, though. I gotta know about this downstairs situation."

"The downstairs club is invitation only." Fuzzy looked over his shoulder. "It's a real scene down there, but it's hardcore taboo shit. I'm talking Bangkok hardcore. Hell, I shouldn't even be talking about this."

Ivan leaned forward again, putting his hand dangerously close to Fuzzy's wrist. "You gotta let me in, Fuzzy. The cat's already out of the bag. Why not let me check it out? I can keep a secret."

"I don't know, Eye. It's the sort of experience you might feel compelled to talk about."

"If there's one thing in this world I know how to do, it's keep a secret," Ivan said. "Now, Fuzzy, baby, there is no way you can tell me about this private club and then refuse to bring me downstairs. I mean, that's just cruel, Fuzzy!"

"Well, like you said, the cat is already out of the bag. I'm warning you though, Eye, this place will blow your mind."

"Fuzzy, believe me," Ivan said with a giggle, "I'm ready to be blown. Bring it on." The little man shook with anticipation.

Fuzzy finished his vodka tonic. "You promise you'll never tell another soul about what you're about to see?"

Ivan tittered. "Mum's the word."

Fuzzy leaned back in his chair so he could examine himself in a nearby mirrored column. He straightened his narrow silk tie, perfecting the crease under the knot. Then he smoothed each of his trimmed eyebrows with the tip of his little finger. As he tilted his head, he examined several angles of his hundred-dollar haircut. Everything seemed in order. "Alright, Eye. Follow me. But don't say I didn't warn you." He stood from the table and led Connivin' Ivan away from the dance floor, past rows of pool tables, and beyond the Champagne Room. Ivan tried to walk nonchalantly, his hands crossed before his waist. Finally, they reached a skinny steel door at the end of a narrow hallway. As Fuzzy searched his pocket for the key to the door, Ivan heard footsteps quickly approaching behind him. He turned to see Cracker Jack Farrell bearing down on him with a handkerchief in his right hand. "Hey, Cracker," Ivan said uncertainly.

Cracker pushed Ivan against the wall and pressed the wet cloth over the lawyer's face. Ivan struggled briefly, gagging on the fumes from the handkerchief until he slipped into darkness.

KILL WHITEY

Ivan awoke abruptly and found himself in a dark, dank base-ment. Fuzzy stood before him waving smelling salts under his nose. "Wake up, Ivan," Fuzzy said. He slapped the lawyer's face. "Wake up, you one-eyed piece of shit."

Ivan jerked his head away from the smelling salts and tried to back away from Fuzzy. He was alarmed by his inability to move and soon realized he was bound to a wooden chair. He tried to shout for help, but he was also gagged with a red rubber ball attached to a black leather strap. The sounds of the strip club above hammered through the basement ceiling.

A lamp swung above Ivan's head, casting a swaying cone of light in the darkness. Fuzzy and Cracker stood before Ivan, the swinging light casting odd pendulum shadows down the length of their faces. Fuzzy had changed out of his suit. He was now dressed in pressed jeans and an ironed white T-shirt. Cracker wore an outfit befitting a garbage collector. As the two men stepped closer to Ivan, their feet crunched a sheet of clear plastic that covered the floor. Cracker Jack had an axe resting on his shoulder, and Fuzzy held a bone saw.

"You've made some bad decisions, One-Eye," Fuzzy said. "We have word from a reliable source that you've been disclosing confidential information to our competition. The Lynch organization demands loyalty and integrity from its employees and associates. I know I'm proud to give the family my utmost loyalty. You, unfortunately, have demonstrated a profound lack of loyalty. So, as Increase is fond of saying, your services will no longer be tolerated. The Lynches are letting you go, One-Eye." He smiled slightly. "We're giving you the axe."

Ivan tried to protest through his S&M gag.

"I'm not gonna lie to you, One-Eye," Fuzzy said. "Wyatt has ordered up a long and horrific night for you. I can only imagine the kind of pain you're about to endure. However, you should keep in mind that Smutty McCafferty died a fairly gruesome death of his own thanks to your betrayal. We know you told the Borisovas that Smutty was allergic to bees. So when you're suffering tonight, just chalk it up to karma."

Ivan shook his head, and his eye began to water.

"If it were up to me, I'd just pop a pill in your ear and be done with you," Fuzzy said. "But you know Wyatt. He wants to make an example of you. He wants people to think about One-Eye Connivin' Ivan the next time they consider double-crossing our gang. I have to say, Wyatt does make a good point." Fuzzy put down his saw, reached into a large paper bag at his feet, and removed a yellow rain suit. He stepped into the pants and buttoned up the slicker jacket. Cracker watched with mild amusement, and Ivan watched with profound terror, as Fuzzy continued to dress, slipping his hands into latex gloves, tying a surgical mask over his face, and securing oversized goggles over his eyes.

"The hell you doin'?" Cracker asked.

"I'm suiting up," Fuzzy said. "What does it look like?"

"Like you lost your mind."

"Hey, if you want to expose yourself to AIDS or the Willies, you go right ahead," Fuzzy said. He picked up the bone saw and tapped the handle against his rain suit. "As for me, I wear protection."

Cracker set his axe blade on the plastic-covered floor and leaned on the handle. "I tell you something," he said. "I ain't so sure I got the stomach for this shit."

"You've got to be kidding me," Fuzzy said. "You're a god-damn sadist, Cracker. Next to Wyatt, you're the sickest fuck

I've ever met. You can't be getting queasy over a bit of dwarf chopping."

"Tell you what. Let's just crack his head first and do the rest after he's dead."

Tears and snot streamed down Ivan's face, and a wet spot formed on his lap.

"I don't know," Fuzzy said. "Wyatt gave us explicit instructions."

"When we're finished, ain't Wyatt or nobody else gonna know the difference."

"Yeah, but this midget as good as murdered Smutty. Smutty was my friend. This shyster runt needs to suffer."

"Think about it," said Cracker. "If we do it Wyatt's way, he'll be squirming the whole time. He'll be spraying blood, piss, and shit all over us."

Fuzzy examined his rain suit and studied the gaps between the buttons. He looked doubtfully at his thin latex gloves. "You've got a point," he said. "Alright. We'll do it your way."

"Good," Cracker said. He raised the axe over Ivan's head and said, "Don't say I never did nothing for you, One-Eye."

Benny One Too Many Vega sat at his usual stool at the Sit & Drink. A garish, oversized design of flames, skulls, and naked women adorned the front and back of his untucked sports shirt. The stink of a hangover and morning bong hits mixed unpleasantly with his cheap cologne. He nursed a Bloody Mary with extra horseradish as he played along with a morning game show on the bar television. "What's a supernova?" Benny called to the television.

The contestant answered: "*What is a black hole?*" His

response received a harsh buzz followed by a condescending tone from the host. "*No, that is incorrect. The correct response is 'supernova.' That will cost you $200.*"

"You should a listen to me," Benny said. "Survey says, 'Go back to school, homes.'"

The bartender, a craggy-faced man with thick hair dyed jet black, shifted his gaze from the TV. "How do you know this all shit, Benny?"

"Education, my man. Education. I ain't some nine-to-five chump wasting my life behind a punch press or a computer. I make my money fast—minimum time, minimum effort, maximum profit. So I got time to tutor my ass watching the Discovery Channel."

The door to the club swung open, and Fuzzy Magee stepped inside. He walked slowly and stiffly to a stool near Benny.

"Damn, look what the cat drag in," Benny said. "What brings you in so early, Fuzz?"

Fuzzy sat heavily on the stool and leaned his forearms on the bar. The bartender was already pouring him a glass of Ketel One. "It's not early. It's late," Fuzzy said. He rubbed his shoulder, which was sore from sawing One-Eye Connivin' Ivan. The bartender set the vodka before Fuzzy, who nodded his thanks. "So what about you, Benny? What brings you in at this hour?"

Benny raised his Bloody Mary. "Hair of the dog, man."

"What the hell does that mean?"

"Hair of the dog that bit you," Benny said. "It's an expression. It means you cure your hangover by drinking a little of whatever fucked you up the night before. Last night, I was drinking kamikazes, so today, I'm drinking a Bloody Mary. Vodka for a vodka hangover. The remedy don't fail."

"I've heard the expression before," Fuzzy said. "I hear you say it every morning I see you. What I don't understand is what dog hair has to do with some wethead swilling booze for his hangover. It makes no sense."

"Ah, but it would if you know your own history," Benny said. He assumed a smug, learned tone. "See, you Irish used to believe that if a dog bit you, you gotta stick some of its hair in the bite so you don't get rabies."

Fuzzy cringed. "That's disgusting. Who'd want to stick some greasy, flea-infested mutt hair in an open wound?"

"You expectin' sound medical practice from an island of drunks?" Benny asked. "There ain't no Louis Pasteur coming out of Ireland, homes. When you *borrachos* learned the art of fermentation, y'all had all the science you wanted. Y'all were like, 'Class dismissed, man. Let's party.'"

"You'd better not let Wyatt hear you talking like that," Fuzzy said. "He'd clip you. Besides, you're one to talk about drunks."

Benny shrugged. "Shit, I drink just to fit in with you Irish dudes. It's like, peer pressure, homes." He drained his Bloody Mary and held his glass out to the bartender for a refill. "And as far as Wyatt goes, what he don't know won't hurt him."

"That reminds me," Fuzzy said. He unclipped his cell phone from his belt and punched a number onto the keypad. "Wyatt, it's me," he said into the phone. "I finished that job for you."

"Yeah? How'd it go?" Wyatt asked on the other end.

"It got messy."

"What happened? Something get fucked up?"

"No, everything went down per your instructions. To the letter. That's why it got messy."

Wyatt chuckled. "*Good. Glad to hear it. Wish I could've been there. So that's two down and one to go.*"

"One to go?"

"*Yeah. Benny is number three.*"

Fuzzy was silent.

"*You still there?*"

"Yeah, absolutely," Fuzzy said. He pressed the phone against his ear so only he could hear Wyatt. "Yeah, I'm just hanging out here at the Sit & Drink."

"*Oh … Is our boy there?*"

"Right. Okay."

"*Just say fucking 'yes' or 'no.'*"

"Yes."

"*Well that's perfect. Take our friend out. You know … for golf or something.*"

"Right now?"

"*You got something else on your agenda?*"

"I'm just a little tired, that's all. It's been a long night. Can someone else play golf?"

"*Naw, I want you on the links, Fuzz. Wrap this up now while we have the opportunity.*"

"Okay. So do you have any instructions? I mean, is there a certain … course you want me to play?"

"*Yeah, I did have something planned, but it's hard to discuss on the phone, if you know what I mean. Use your own discretion. Play a game that will set an example. Understand?*"

"Understood."

"*Alright, Fuzz. Go make a mess.*" Wyatt clicked off.

Fuzzy re-holstered his phone. He turned to face Benny, who was staring with glazed eyes at the bar television. "What is the Taj Mahal?" Benny said to the set.

Fuzzy waited to hear the correct answer. The answer was

Taj Mahal. Fuzzy nodded. "So, that was Wyatt on the phone," he said.

Benny continued to watch the TV. "Oh yeah?"

"Yeah. He wants me to visit a delinquent account. Want to come with me?"

Benny looked down at the fresh Bloody Mary that the bartender had set before him. He lifted the glass and drained it with four chugs. "Yeah, I'll go with you," Benny said, clapping the empty glass on the counter. He wiped his lips with the back of his hand. "I'm ready to stretch my legs."

"Good," Fuzzy said. "You packing?"

"Ah, nah, man. I left my piece at home."

"Don't worry about it," Fuzzy said. He patted his suit jacket. "One is all we need."

Benny slid off his barstool. "Let me take a piss before we go."

Fuzzy nodded. He watched Benny closely as the chubby man ambled toward the restrooms at back of the club.

As he stood before the urinal, Benny One Too Many considered the previous few minutes. He had been listening to Fuzzy's side of the phone call, and Fuzzy had been discussing messy jobs and golf, not deadbeats. Benny had watched Fuzzy in the bar mirror as he abruptly announced that he was at the Sit & Drink, and he had seen that Fuzzy went slightly tense after that point. And why had Fuzzy asked Benny if he was packing, only to tell him he didn't need a gun? Benny had a bad feeling the Lynches had discovered he was working with the Borisovas. Benny was pretty sure he was about to get whacked. He looked around the bathroom. There was one window, but it was far too small for Benny's potbelly and fat ass. He pictured the layout of the bar. There were two exits, but neither was near the restrooms. Benny flushed the urinal and stepped back out into the bar.

Fuzzy was already waiting by the door as Benny approached. Benny willed himself to walk in a slow, pothead sort of shuffle. He focused on taking measured, steady breaths. "Can we stop for, like, a snack on the way to the gig?" Benny asked. "Get some drive-thru or something? I got some fierce munchies."

"Sure. If something's on the way," Fuzzy said. He turned and stepped through the door with Benny close behind him.

As Benny approached the exit, he swung the door shut and twisted the lock. He then stepped quickly but casually behind the bar. The bartender, who was unpacking a case of beer, looked over his shoulder. "What do you need, Benny?"

Benny slid a sawed-off shotgun out from beneath the register. "This," he said. The bartender nodded, his hands raised at his sides. Benny walked toward the unlocked side exit. As he stepped outside, Fuzzy was rounding the corner of the alley. Benny leveled the shotgun and fired just as Fuzzy dove for cover. Shot tore through a metal trashcan and ricocheted off brick and concrete. "You stay put, Fuzz," Benny called. "You my boy. Don't make me lead you up." He took backward steps until he reached the far end of the alley. When he emerged from the alley, Benny sprinted down the block as fast as his tubby legs would carry him. He heard gunshots behind him as he leaped over a low chain-link fence. He ran diagonally through a block of yards, dropping the shotgun in a sandbox along the way. He continued to run, sprinting down alleys and cutting through the projects until he collapsed, gasping and retching in unfamiliar territory.

Benny spent the rest of the day hiding in an alcove beneath a highway overpass. As he sat on the concrete, among empty plastic vodka jugs and the stench of piss, he considered how he would slip out of Butchers Harbor. His car was back at the Sit & Drink, so that option was out. He didn't have so much as a screwdriver to help him boost another ride. He suspected the Lynches would post someone at Riverside Station, so he couldn't take a bus or train out of the city. He was even reluctant to call a cab on the chance that Wyatt had a dispatcher on the payroll. To complicate matters, Benny had only a few dollars in his pocket. He was stoned when he drove to the Sit & Drink that morning, and he had forgotten to take his wallet. Everything he needed to survive—his cash, his credit cards, his gun, and his weed—were back at his apartment. He simply could not leave the city until he first made a stop at his crib.

When the sun had set, Benny used the cover of night to creep through the city back to his neighborhood. He realized that one of the Lynch mob would likely be posted outside or inside his apartment, so he needed a spot to monitor his building for activity. He chose a bar that was two blocks away from his home yet still offered him a line of sight.

The dive he entered was having Karaoke Night, but no music or videos were playing. They had simply passed a half-dozen cordless microphones around the crowd. The amplified voices of several people reverberated in the low room. A couple of drunks competed to see who could sing a cappella Elvis the loudest. One sang "Are You Lonesome Tonight?" while the other screeched "Viva Las Vegas." A woman too intoxicated to speak slurred sentences that sounded like a record played in reverse, and a plump, pasty businessman whispered, "I am Beelzebub, the Prince of Eternal Darkness. Submit to my will, freaky sheep. Let's go to Hell for kicks."

Benny One Too Many sat at a beer-soaked table by a large window and strained to see his apartment building in the dim illumination of the streetlights. As he scanned for familiar cars, he heard a young woman making raunchy comments into her microphone. He shifted his gaze from the window and saw the thin twenty-something staggering through the bar, one hand holding a cosmopolitan while the other held the cordless mike to her lips. She approached a group of underage frat boys and taunted them by asking, "Which one of you faggots has the balls to fuck me?"

Benny leered at the young woman as he muttered to himself, "Damn. *¡Yo tengo los cojones para clavarte como un cerdo cabróna!* On a better night, I'd fuck you to pieces." The woman wore a white half shirt with spaghetti straps, cheap cotton sweatpants, and a pair of muddy hiking boots. She was all skin and bones, but there was something about a young woman demanding sex from strangers that Benny found appealing. He shook his head, sorry that circumstances would keep him from spending the night with this dirty girl. He looked out the window again and tried to ignore any distractions from within the bar. His concentration was shattered, however, when the skinny woman sat beside him in the booth, set her cosmo on the table, and ran one finger around the gaudy designs on his shirt. "Well, hello Fancy Pants," she announced into the mike.

Benny wrenched the microphone from her hand and tossed it across the bar. As the mike hit the floor, a rumble of heavy thuds was broadcast over the club's speakers. The dirty girl smiled coyly at Benny as she drained the last of her cosmopolitan. Then she tried to smash the empty glass against his face. Benny managed to catch her wrist before she struck him. They struggled with each other in the booth as Benny said, "Whoa! Hey! Settle down, firecracker! Take it easy!"

"You took my microphone, asshole!" She tried to scratch his eyes.

Benny laughed as he swatted her hands away. "Hey, you wanna play with your microphone, go ahead. Just play away from me, okay? I'm trying to stay low key, you know?"

The woman lowered her hands, and she slumped back in the booth as she examined Benny. Her mood shifted into curiosity as abruptly as she had turned violent seconds before. "Why so shy?" she asked. "Are you married?"

"I don't know," Benny said, covering his left hand with his right. "You into married dudes?"

She leaned forward and dropped her right hand between Benny's legs. "I'm into this right here," she said, giving his package a gentle squeeze. "I don't care what it's attached to."

Benny chuckled uncomfortably. "Nice! That's a good attitude."

"You want to come back to my place and get laid?"

Benny turned serious. "Okay. Sure."

The skinny woman grabbed his wrist and pulled him through the bar, bouncing him off drunks with microphones until they reached the exit. She continued to pull him across the street and into a three-story apartment building. "I'm Priscilla," she said as they hustled up a flight of muddy stairs. "You've never met anyone like me."

As Benny One Too Many climbed the steps, he thought that things were working out just fine. He had a place to

96

lie low for the night, and he was going to have wild, kinky sex with a woman ten years younger. Priscilla led him into a small studio at the top floor. She lifted a battery-powered lantern from the floor and turned it on. "Bastards turned off my electricity," she explained. "If they wanted the bills paid, they should have sent them to my father. He's the one with the money." She struck a long fireplace match and walked about the studio, lighting candles until the room glowed like a shrine. In the center of the room was a complex, multi-leveled maze made out of pasta and cereal boxes, paper plates, and empty soup and coffee cans with the tops and bottoms removed. The maze had five levels, and it covered most of the studio.

"Isn't this cool?" Priscilla asked.

Benny studied the maze with genuine awe. "This is amazing," he said. He stooped for a closer look and saw tiny cardboard gargoyles on the walls. Sections of the maze were supported with squat Doric columns made from empty toilet paper rolls. "Just amazing," he said. Realizing he'd made a pun, Benny repeated the word, "A-*maze*-ing." He grinned, feeling very witty. Priscilla didn't seem to notice. "So ... did you, like, make this yourself?" he asked.

Priscilla nodded proudly. "You want to run through it? We can sleep in one of the towers." She pointed to a beer can, the top of which had been cut and bent to form a battlement.

Benny chuckled. "Yeah, that'd be cool. Too bad we ain't mice, huh?"

Priscilla looked confused. "What's that supposed to mean?"

"Well, we're too big to run through the maze," Benny said. He chuckled again, trying to understand Priscilla's weird sense of humor. Her perplexed stare indicated she wasn't joking. "I mean, the paths are only three inches wide, you know? We wouldn't fit. It's, you know ... impossible."

Priscilla stared at Benny for a moment. The candlelight flickered over the sheen of her dingy hazel hair. She smiled and said, "Anything's possible if you want it bad enough."

Benny nodded uneasily. "Yeah. That's a good attitude. Power of positive thinking. So ... do you, like, have any pot?"

"You don't get it, do you?" Priscilla asked. She began a slow walk around the perimeter of the maze. "It's all in here, man. It's all in here."

"Oh yeah, I get it. It's all in there. That's cool. That's the shit," Benny said. "So, if you got any weed or anything, I could go for a little bong hit right now. It's been a long day, you know?"

Priscilla continued to walk steadily around the maze. She was muttering softly and incoherently.

"Or a drink or something," Benny said. "I never got a chance to order nothing at the bar. So if you got beer or something, that'd be real cool." He waited patiently for a response, but Priscilla was lost in her own internal maze. Benny decided to conduct his own search for booze, weed, or any other variety of sedative. He stepped into the kitchenette and opened the refrigerator, which wasn't running. All he found in the fridge were a few rotten pieces of fruit and a nasty stink. He shut the refrigerator and began opening cupboards and drawers. Eventually, he found a half-full bottle of tequila under the sink.

Benny took a swig from the bottle and sat on a mattress lying on the kitchen floor. The mattress had no sheets, blankets, or box spring. "So, I'm gonna turn in. Call it a night, you know?" Benny said. He waited a moment for Priscilla to respond. "You want to join me?" he asked. He patted the mattress as if he were calling a pet. "It's nice and comfy here. It's nap time, okay?" The skinny girl continued to mumble to people only she could see. "Yo, I don't mean to be rude, but I have a recollection you said something about me getting laid? You know, back at the bar?" Benny said. "I hope you didn't lure me up here under, like, false pretenses."

Priscilla stopped her mumbling and wandering when she reached a Popsicle-stick drawbridge at the entrance to the maze. She lowered herself to her hands and knees and searched the paper-mâché moat until she found a can of black spray paint. She shook the can vigorously, clacking the metal ball inside.

"Oh shit," Benny said. He gripped the tequila bottle by its neck.

Priscilla approached a mirror and sprayed it with black paint. Then she moved on to the studio's windows and blacked out each pane. "I'm tired of seeing myself," she explained. "You ever get that way? Tonight is a no-reflection evening."

Benny guzzled the tequila, set the bottle on the floor, and flopped back onto the mattress. After a few minutes of listening to the hiss of the spray paint and the patter of Priscilla's frantic pacing, he rolled onto his side, pulled his knees to his belly, and tried to coax himself to sleep. After a few more pulls on the bottle at his side, Benny managed to sink into an uneasy slumber. He dreamt that the Lynches had all turned to sand figures that crumbled in the hot wind of some alien desert. The pleasant dream was cruelly shattered when Priscilla grabbed his arm and shook him until he was awake.

"What?" Benny mumbled, glaring at Priscilla through one bleary, half-shut eye.

"*Yellow Submarine* is on TV!" she said. She was smiling with sweet excitement. "Quick, you have to see it!"

"I seen it before," Benny groaned.

"Watch it again. Let's set a record." She pulled Benny off the mattress and dragged him to a small television set on the floor. The screen had been covered with stickers of Blue Meanies, Glove, Sergeant Pepper, Jeremy the Nowhere Man, and John, Paul, George, and Ringo, all decked out in their cartoon bell bottoms.

"Pepperland kicks ass," Priscilla said.

"I'm going back to bed," Benny said.

"No!" Priscilla said sternly. "You have to watch!"

"I can't watch. I can't stay awake."

"You'll stay awake if you focus. Now, concentrate!" She turned to face the TV as she grabbed Benny's hand.

Benny yanked his hand away from Priscilla. "It's not even a movie, you fucking *puta loca*!" he shouted. "They're stickers! You took stickers and stuck them on your TV. This is paper and glue you're watching. You're out of your mind!"

Benny tried to crawl back to the mattress, but Priscilla pounced on him and twisted his head until he was watching the set again. "Focus! Concentrate!"

Benny was surprised to feel warm tears running down his cheeks. He began to sob. "I just wanna sleep. I'll watch the cartoon stickers in the morning. I swear to God I will. But right now, I need to sleep. If I don't get some sleep, I'll lose my mind." He wiped his tears with the heel of his hand. "Listen to me, Priscilla. I'm in deep shit. For real trouble. People are trying to kill me. And I ain't talking about imaginary people, neither. I'm talking about real people with real guns or worse. These are scary fuckers who want to cause me a lot of pain. I just need a place to hide, and I need a little sleep to get my head together. Have some sympathy, Priscilla. Okay?"

Priscilla dug her nails into Benny's cheeks. "I said concentrate! Now quit your whining and watch the fucking movie!"

Priscilla and Benny watched the *Yellow Submarine* stickers until dawn. Priscilla recited the movie's entire dialogue from memory. Benny sat cross-legged at her side, staring at the immobile pieces of paper and wondering what Priscilla saw. Unfortunately, her vision of the world was not so warped that should could not keenly monitor Benny. Whenever he started to shut his eyes or his head began to roll to the side, she would shake his shoulders and repeat whichever line of the movie he had missed.

At around 10:00 A.M., Priscilla abruptly lost her interest in the cartoon Beatles and shouted, "Hey, I know! Let's play 'Inside-Outside.' Check it out." She pulled a scuffed hiking boot off her foot and ran toward one of her blacked-out window. She pulled open the window and held the boot up for Benny's attention. "Inside," she said, then lobbed the shoe out the window. "Outside." She pulled off her other boot. "Indoors." The boot tumbled out the window. "Outdoors." She lifted a wine bottle from the floor. Stuck in the mouth of the bottle was the stump of a candle that had burned all night. Wax had drizzled down the side of the glass, but a flame still flickered. "Inside. Indoors. My world," Priscilla chanted. She tossed the lit candle out the window and shouted to the neighborhood, "Outside! Outdoors! Your world!" The glass shattered as it hit the sidewalk.

She ran to the sticker-covered television and hoisted it off the floor. "Inside," she grunted as she hefted the set toward the window. Seeing that her back was turned, Benny retreated into the bathroom and locked the door behind him. Even with the door closed, he could hear the television explode on the street outside. Benny sighed wearily and folded a thin towel on the linoleum floor to serve as a pillow. He had just stretched out and laid his head on the meager cloth when Priscilla began pounding and kicking the door.

"Get out here!" she screamed. "I'm still playing Inside-Outside!"

"Play with yourself!" Benny shouted. He hoped she would follow the instruction literally and throw herself out the window.

"I'm playing with you, candyass!" A plate, a wineglass, and a fluorescent light bulb shattered against the door in rapid succession.

Benny heard a neighbor pound on the wall and threaten to call the police. "Time to go," he muttered. He stood, took a deep breath, unlocked the door, and bolted out of the bathroom and out of the apartment. As he fled down the stairs, plates and bowls shattered about him, and a coffee mug struck him in the back of the neck. As Benny reached the door to the street, he heard Priscilla shout, "Call me!" The hallway echoed with her hostile laughter.

Benny ran across the street, back into the dive where he had met the insane Priscilla. The bar was nearly empty now, although there were still a few microphones left on some of the tables. A pale man in a baseball cap sat in a corner booth with his back to the door. Benny ordered a beer and took his seat by the window. He divided his attention by monitoring both his and Priscilla's apartment buildings. The street was quiet.

As Benny drained the beer, the alcohol went straight to his exhausted brain. He ordered a second beer, set the glass on his table, and headed for the men's room. Inside the single-toilet bathroom, Benny stood before a small sink. The porcelain was marred with dozens of brown burn-tracks left by neglected cigarettes. He turned on the faucet and cupped his hands under the water. He poured water down his dry throat, splashed water on his face, and ran his wet hands through his thinning hair. He desperately wanted to return to his apartment. He needed the comfort of a wallet in his jeans pocket, a pistol in his hand, and a bong hit in his lungs. Returning to his crib was lunacy, but Benny felt he had no choice. He barely had enough money in his pocket to pay for the two beers he had just ordered. Besides, he had laid low for nearly twenty-four hours. Maybe the Lynches would think he had already slipped out of town.

Benny returned to his booth and continued to watch the street as he considered his next move. As he thought, he worked on his second beer. This beer made him more relaxed but less exhausted, and he settled into a numb state of static thought. The pale guy in a baseball cap stepped out of his distant booth and walked toward Benny. He set a large leather bag on the table as he took a seat across from Benny. He removed his baseball cap, revealing short white dreadlocks. He smelled of sunscreen.

"I don't think we've met," the pale guy said. He extended his hand. "My name's Leon Lynch."

As Benny shook Leon's hand, his own arm felt thick and heavy, as if he were wearing a glove made of lead. "Whitey," he said.

"Call me Leon."

"Leon. Yeah, I know you. You're Wyatt's brother."

Leon nodded.

Benny put his elbows on the table and slumped forward. He stared for a while at a brownish-red stain on the table. When he looked up again, he was surprised that Leon was still sitting across from him. "So," he said, "how'd you find me, homes?"

"You practically walked right into me," Leon said. "I came into this bar to keep an eye on your apartment. I was sitting right where you are now until I saw you bolt out from that building across the street. I thought I might see you lurking around outside your apartment. I didn't expecting to find you running around in the street then hanging out in your local bar. You might want to keep a lower profile."

Benny bobbed his head slowly up and down. "Yeah, live and learn. Not for long, though, huh?"

"You may live a little longer," Leon said. "I have a plan that might save you."

"Save me?" Benny was having trouble following the conversation. He felt like he was watching a television program and he had missed the start of the scene. He rubbed his forehead briskly. "You're Lynch. You'll kill me, right?"

"Drink some more beer," Leon said.

Benny gulped his beer, and he felt more compliant.

"You know who Peter Volkov is?" asked Leon.

"Yeah, I know Volkov," Benny said. He felt like he was giving an answer on a game show. "He's that driver for Vladimir Borisova. I seen that dude a few times when I was talking to Borisova."

"When you were selling Lynch secrets to our competition," Leon said.

"Yeah," Benny said. "Right. You know something? That Volkov is an angry *cabrón*. He got issues."

"Yeah, well, Volkov talked to my father and brother," Leon said. "Actually, I'm the one who got Volkov to talk. I gave him a truth serum. He identified several of the family's enemies, include you, Swag Kilpatrick, and Ivan Wazowiecki."

"Oh."

"I don't know what happened to Swag and Ivan, but I'm guessing they're dead. I haven't been able to reach either one of them," Leon said. "My truth serum probably got them both killed. Swag wasn't a very good man, and Ivan knew what he was getting into, I suppose. Maybe they both got what they deserved. I don't know. What I do know is their fates weigh on my conscience. I'll be damned if I'm going to feel guilty about your sorry ass as well."

Benny sipped his beer again, carefully raising the glass with both hands.

"That's good," Leon said. "Keep drinking that beer."

Benny took another gulp, then set the glass before him. He stared at the suds in his beer. "Is this a dream?" he asked.

"No," Leon said. "When you left to use the bathroom, I spiked your beer with *burundanga*."

"Oh yeah, I heard of that shit," Benny said. "That's like roofies or something, right?"

"Sort of. *Burundanga* puts you in a kind of voodoo trance and makes you open to suggestion. Thieves use it to get their victims to clean out their own bank accounts. But I don't want your money, Benny. I just wanted to keep you from running away from me."

"No problem, man," Benny said. "My ass is staying right here."

"Well, we will need to take a short walk out to the alley," Leon said. "Here's my plan. We're gonna step out back, and I'm gonna give you another drug. It's a zombie potion that

will slow your breathing and heart rate down to impercep-
tible levels. I'll leave you in the alley, and I'll come back in
here to call an ambulance. When the paramedics arrive, they
won't be able to find a pulse. So they'll just bring you to the
hospital, where you'll most likely be brought straight to the
morgue."

"How come your eyes are funny colors?" Benny asked.
"They're, like, light purple or something."

"Pay attention," Leon said. "I know a guy in the morgue
who owes me a favor." He checked his watch. "He should be
on duty as we speak."

"Why's somebody in the morgue owe you a favor?"

Leon sighed. "He's a doctor with a drug problem. He has
a habit of dipping into the narcotics cabinet. I sell him a drug
that helps him flush the gunk out of his system when he's
due for a drug test or when he's trying to clean himself up.
He always relapses, though, so he's sort of a repeat customer.
But none of that should concern you. All you need to know
is that my man in the morgue is going to write up a false
autopsy that says you died of an overdose. He'll write up a
death certificate and file some paperwork that says you've
been shipped to a funeral parlor outside the state. Where do
your parents live?"

"My dad died when I was a kid."

"I'm sorry to hear that. Where does your mom live?"

"She lives on Sodville Street."

"What town, Benny?"

"Oh. Sinton, Texas."

"Okay, so the paperwork will say you died and your body
was shipped to Texas. Meanwhile, I'll show up at the morgue,
and I'll give you another drug that'll gently ease you out of

the zombie coma. Then you get your ass out of Butchers Harbor, and you never come back. You start over."

Benny sensed that there were potential flaws in Leon's plan, but he couldn't think clearly to pinpoint his exact concerns. Finally he shrugged and said, "Yeah, okay. That's a good plan, I guess."

"Good. Follow me," Leon said. He put on his sunglasses, hoisted his medicine bag, dropped a few bills on the table, and then led Benny through the bar and out a back exit. Benny squinted against the sunlight as he continued to follow Leon into a narrow alley between the bar and a corner market. They walked a few feet into the cramped space. Leon set his medicine bag on the dirt and rummaged through it until he found a long, slender bottle wrapped in strips of tanned hide. He uncorked the bottle and handed it to Benny. "Bottoms up."

Benny stared at the thick, brown fluid inside the bottle. Traces of thought lingered in his sedated mind. "How do I know this won't kill me?" he asked.

"I'm not so sure it won't," Leon said. "That's some strong mojo you're about to drink. I'm no witch doctor, either, so I may have the dosage wrong. But I do know one thing. Whatever that stuff does to you, it'll be a lot easier than any-thing Wyatt has planned."

Benny nodded and lifted the bottle.

Leon held Benny's wrist before he could drink the potion. "One more thing, Benny. Don't get any bright ideas about talking to the police or the feds. My family still has a few cops and G-men on the payroll, so you just might be talking to one of my brother's friends. That would be bad—for both of us. If I hear you're planning to squeal, I'll send you to the morgue again, but the next time, it'll be a one-way trip. I can slip a little something into your food that'll turn your intestines to pulp. You'll be finding your internal organs in a toilet bowl. So keep your mouth shut for a change. Alright?"

Benny nodded.

"Alright," Leon said, helping Benny lift the bottle to his lips. "Bon voyage."

Benny tilted his head back and drained the slender bottle.

"You'd better lie down," Leon said.

Benny leaned against the brick wall as he lowered himself to the ground. He sat with his back against the wall. Soon his eyes closed, and his head slumped forward so that his chin touched his chest. His body swayed, and he slid down the brick until he was lying in the dirt. Leon stood over him, watching his chest raise and fall in slower and slower rhythms.

Leon returned the empty bottle to his medicine bag and zipped it up. He stepped out of the alley and walked back to the bar. He stopped abruptly just as he was stepping over the threshold. Cracker Jack Farrell was sitting in the same booth where Leon and Benny had been moments before. Cracker had his back to Leon as he looked out the window.

Leon quietly stepped backwards through the door. He leaned against the exterior of the bar and buried his face in one hand as he tried to quell the frenzy within him. There's no reason to panic, he told himself. Cracker hadn't seen him. All he had to do now was find another telephone. Easy peasy. He lowered his hand and let out a long, shaky breath. As he scanned the small parking lot behind the bar, he saw an elderly homeless woman walking behind the nearby corner market and approaching the narrow alley. "No, no, no," Leon whispered. He watched her turn and step into the alley. "No, no, no, no."

The woman screamed as she ran out of the alley. She dropped the two heavy bags she had been lugging and ran toward Leon as fast as her frail legs would carry her. "Call 911!" she shouted. "There's a body in the alley!"

Leon held one finger to his lips. "Shh. Shh." The woman continued to scream and stumble toward Leon. He turned and ran in the other direction.

Cracker sipped his Guinness as he glowered through the window. He had spent the night wandering around Benny's apartment building on the slim chance that the pothead might return to his crib. It was a bullshit assignment. He couldn't understand why Wyatt had him wasting his time with this sort of shit detail. Fuzzy was the idiot who lost Benny One Too Many. Fuzzy should have been the one to spend the night loitering in alleys and sitting on fire escapes. Cracker eventually decided that he could just easily keep an eye on Benny's building from the comfort of a bar.

An old lady dressed in layers of filthy clothes staggered into the bar through the backdoor. "There's a body in the alley!" she shouted, pointing behind her. "There's a body in the alley."

The bartender, a skinny, hunchbacked old man, looked up from the newspaper he had been reading. "Aw, for chrissake! Getchya homeless piece a shit ass outta my bah."

She continued walking up to the bar counter. "There's a body in the alley! Call 911!"

"Ya seein' shit, ya ol' hoowah. It's the DTs for chrissake. Go sleep it off."

"I seen a body in the alley, and he ain't breathing," the woman said. She pointed a bony finger at the hunchbacked bartender. "I'll call the cops myself, and I'll tell them you didn't lift a finger to help a dying man!"

"Aw, for chrissake!" the man said. He crumpled the paper and threw it on the floor. He called to Cracker. "Hey, buddy, you wanna help me out?"

Cracker looked to see if there was anyone else in the bar. "You talkin' to me?"

"Yeah, buddy. Help me out heeya."

"What do you want me to do?"

"Jez take a walk out back and see if this crazy bitch is seein' shit."

Cracker sipped his Guinness and looked out the window again. "I'm busy."

"Aw, for chrissake, buddy. Len' me a fuckin' hand, will ya? I can't leave the till unattendit. I'll give ya a drink on the house for yafuckin' trouble. Whatdaya say?"

Cracker shrugged. He was bored and needed something to do. Looking at a corpse would be better than looking at a building. As he stood, the woman clasped her hands before her. "Thank you, sir. Thank you." She turned and scampered out of the bar with Cracker ambling behind her.

The woman approached the entrance to the alley, but she would not step inside. "He's in there," she said, pointing. Cracker took his time reaching her. He glanced into the alley and was surprise to find an actual body crumpled on the ground. He had carried his glass outside, and he took a sip of stout as he stepped into the alley. He smiled as he looked down at Benny's face.

"See? See?" the woman called from behind. "Now can we call 911?"

Cracker finished his beer and dropped the empty pint glass on the ground next to Benny. As he stepped out of the alley, he removed a roll of bills from his front pants pocket. "I don't see nothin'," he said. He peeled off a pair of Benjamins and held them toward the old woman. "Do you?"

The old woman stared at the money then looked up at Cracker.

"One way or another, I'm gonna keep you quiet," Cracker said. "Take the money. Or end up like the guy that ain't in the alley." He took the woman's hand, pressed the bills against her palm, and closed her fingers over the money. "Now screw," he said.

The woman's lips quivered as she glanced at the alley then back at the scary man with the big arms and the shaved head. She backed away from Cracker, forgetting to take the bags she had dropped. When she felt she had reached a safe distance, she turned and continued walking.

Cracker removed his cell phone from his belt and made a call. "Wyatt," he said. "I found our friend."

9
HEAD

Wyatt drove a stolen floral delivery van down a narrow, wooded country road. There were no streetlights, but a full moon illuminated the pavement and trees in a blue sheen. Wyatt's loudmouth goombah pal, Frankie Baloney Bologna, was riding shotgun, while Cracker sat on an uncomfortable seat that folded out of the side of the van. Cracker had to ride in back with the cargo, among heavy-duty garbage bags filled with Swag Kilpatrick and One-Eye Connivin' Ivan. Thrown on top of the bags was the stiff body of Benny One Too Many Vega. Each time the van hit a deep pothole, the bags of Swag rattled and the bags of Ivan sloshed. Although the bags were tied tightly, the stink of blood and decomposition mixed foully with the lingering scent of roses, lilies, and heather.

The boys were on their way to an incinerator shop, where they planned to destroy the remains of Swag, Ivan, and Benny. Wyatt had been a little depressed for the past few days, ever since his father had refused to allow him to participate in the actual hands-on killing of the rats. Considering that the organization was having a problem with loose lips, Increase wanted Wyatt to cut down on the number of times he committed a felony in the company of potential state's

112

witnesses. Wyatt obeyed his father up to a point. He let his soldiers commit the actual murders, but Wyatt wanted to see his enemies burn. He wanted to be present when the traitors turned to ash. Wyatt was also angry that Benny had managed to die of an overdose instead of torture. At least Wyatt would get a little satisfaction by chopping the pothead up and watching his body parts ignite.

Frankie Baloney sipped from a pint of butterscotch schnapps. He dribbled some of the liqueur down his bushy goatee. "Want a swig?" he asked, offering the bottle to Wyatt.

"Get that sissy shit out of my face," Wyatt snapped. He began to drive a little faster. Cracker Jack watched the road through the rear window, looking for signs of a tail. They seemed to be alone until they saw a Jeep approaching at one of the few intersections ahead. The Jeep coasted past a stop sign and pulled in front of the delivery van. Instead of applying the brakes, Wyatt mashed down on the accelerator, bringing their van within a few feet of the Jeep. Both vehicles traveled down the road for about a half-minute, maintaining a dangerously small gap between them until the driver of the Jeep stomped on his brakes. Wyatt braked hard, and the van fishtailed. The garbage bags sloshed and rattled to one side, and Benny was sent sliding off the bags. Benny landed with a heavy thud on the metal floor of the van. His eyes began to flutter.

"Douche bag!" Wyatt shouted after he regained control of the van. The Jeep accelerated after its sudden braking and shot away from the gangsters. Wyatt punched the gas to close the gap.

Benny could hear voices. He heard Frankie Baloney laughing as he said, "Yeah, Wyatt! Run that fuck off the road!"

Benny could not move his limbs, but he could open and move his eyes. He watched Cracker Jack Farrell ease out of his foldout chair and crouch between Wyatt and Frankie's seats. "Your advice ain't exactly prudent, Frankie," Cracker said. "Seein' how we got a stiff Benny and a dozen bags of Swag and One-Eye stuffed in the back of a hot van, maybe the reckless drivin' ain't such a great idea."

Wyatt ignored Cracker's warning and continued to race behind the Jeep. He clenched his teeth so tightly that a muscle on his jaw quivered in spasms. Meanwhile, Benny tried to move his fingers. He discovered that he could clench and unclench his fists. He could turn his head slightly, and he tried to make sense of his surroundings. Garbage bags surrounded him, and the air he breathed was foul.

As Wyatt chased the Jeep at speeds over eighty miles per hour, he began to consider how he would explain his cargo to a police officer. He knew Cracker was right. This was no time to be playing fucky-fuck with some asswipe in a Jeep, but he didn't want the brake-testing dicksucker to think he had won. With an enormous amount of effort, Wyatt eased off the gas and allowed the Jeep to pull away. As the gap between the vehicles increased, Wyatt couldn't help bidding farewell by flashing his high beams.

The Jeep came to a screeching halt and turned diagonally to block the narrow road. Wyatt groaned as he brought the floral delivery van to a slow stop before the blocking vehicle. Cracker muttered, "This ain't good." Wyatt reached to open his door, but Cracker put a hand on his shoulder. "Let's all be cool now," Cracker warned. "Don't nobody do nothing stupid. I'll memorize his plate so we can kill him later."

Wyatt snorted. "Whatever."

Wyatt and Frankie Baloney opened their doors and

stepped out of the van at the same time. Cracker stepped over the disrupted garbage bags and opened the rear door. He hopped out of the van and headed to the front to join Wyatt and Frankie.

Benny slowly raised his head and saw the open gate. He dropped his head back to the metal floor with a clunk. He released a long, raspy gasp and pushed himself onto his side. He felt his face get slick with clammy sweat, but he pushed on. He reached for the back of the seat before him, and gasping and grunting like a tubby boy doing a chin-up, he pulled himself to his knees.

As Wyatt, Cracker, and Frankie stood before the van, the driver stepped out of his Jeep. He wore a leather baseball cap, a long leather jacket over his bare chest, leather pants, and leather cowboy boots with silver buckles. He slapped a wooden souvenir baseball bat against the palm of his hand. The Leather Man was surprised to see that three men had emerged from the van with pink roses painted on its side. He had expected to confront some skinny teenager or maybe even a chick. He hadn't anticipated a tangle with three dudes, particularly these three, who didn't resemble florists. He wasn't scared, though. He was a big boy who pumped iron for two to three hours a day, seven days a week. He also knew karate, judo, and tae kwon do. Then there was his ace in the hole, a Smith & Wesson .357 Magnum tucked in his boot. He wasn't about to back down from these three chumps. They had no idea who they were messing with.

"Any chance we can get you to move your vehicle?" Cracker Jack asked.

"No problem," said Leather Man. "I'll move it right after the three of you finish sucking my crank."

Cracker took a step closer. Leather Man was a little

worried about this one. The pug-faced man looked a little tougher than the other two. He had scar tissue about his eyes, and it seemed as if his nose had been broken more than once. Still, that didn't mean the guy could fight. It just meant he'd had his ass kicked a few times. Leather Man remained confident.

"Here's the thing," Cracker said calmly. "You're blockin' the road, and we're in a hurry."

Leather Man shrugged. "I'm not."

A muscle twitched on Wyatt's jaw. "Listen, pal," he said, "I think I might have overreacted when you cut me off back there. Maybe I shouldn't have tailgated you, and maybe I shouldn't have flashed my high beams at you. I'm, uh…" Wyatt grimaced as he finished his short sentence. "I apologize."

"That's real sweet of you, Nancy," said Leather Man. "I'll let you blow me first."

Wyatt chuckled. He opened his jacket to reveal a Heckler & Koch P7 holstered at his side. "I'll bet you wish you hadn't said that."

"Mine's bigger," Leather Man said. He tossed the souvenir bat aside and stooped to draw his Smith & Wesson from his boot. He had barely bent over before Wyatt shot him in the shoulder. Leather Man stumbled backward and fell onto his ass. He sat on the pavement for a moment, staring with disbelief at the jagged hole in his leather jacket.

"Good thinking, quickdraw," Wyatt said.

Leather Man put his hand under his jacket. His chest was wet.

"Now say you're sorry," Wyatt said.

Leather Man looked up at Wyatt with confusion. "I don't want any trouble," he said.

"Come on, Wyatt. Let's wrap this up," Cracker said. "We got shit to do."

"You're lucky I'm in a hurry," Wyatt said. He fired another round between Leather Man's eyes.

Benny had been watching the entire episode through the windshield. He let go of the seat he had been gripping and dropped to the floor. The effort of moving had drained him. He lay on the metal floor, struck with paralysis again.

Wyatt holstered his piece. He and Cracker Jack strolled toward the torn man sprawled on the pavement. Wyatt grabbed the man's feet, and Cracker hoisted him by the shoulders. They grunted as they hefted the heavy body to the back of the van. Cracker opened the back doors with an elbow, and he and Wyatt gave Leather Man a few swings before hurling the corpse into the van. They threw the body to avoid the garbage bags. If the heavy musclehead had landed on the bags, he would have burst the plastic, so Leather Man was tossed onto the unbreakable piece of real estate. He landed heavily on Benny.

Although Benny was immobile with paralysis, he was all too cognizant. He felt the crushing weight of Leather Man upon him, and he felt the hot blood that leaked from the fresh corpse and soaked his clothes. Even as Cracker climbed back into the van and returned to his foldout seat, Benny would have screamed and shoved the body away from him. It was only the drug-induced paralysis that kept One Too Many still, silent, and alive.

Frankie Baloney lingered outside of the van, struggling to suppress a bout of nervous giggles. He had never seen a man get shot before, never mind shot to death. He was a little freaked out, but he was also excited. He was new to the crew, and so far his assignments had been kind of boring.

Seeing some guy get whacked was cool. Even though he hadn't done the actual shooting, he felt his presence alone was enough to promote him a few ranks in the organization. He'd probably get tapped to do some enforcement work pretty soon. In no time, he could be a captain. But first, he had to pull his shit together. After a few deep breaths, he managed to suppress his giddy snickers. He then strutted up to the van, opened the passenger side door, and took his seat, awaiting a new level of respect.

Wyatt opened the driver side door and sat behind the wheel. He turned toward Frankie B. "What're you doing, dickface?"

Frankie's hopeful expression dissolved into a wide-eyed, wounded gape. "Uh ... Just sitting here?"

"Yeah, I see that," Wyatt said. "So you think it's a good idea to leave that Jeep parked in the middle of the fucking road?"

"You want me to move it?"

"No, I want the cocksucker we just clipped to move his ride."

Frankie pouted as he opened his door. "Alright. I'll move it. All you had to do was ask."

Cracker gave addition instructions from the back of the van. "Take it to Mud Hollow. Ditch it in the ghetto."

"Why can't I just leave it on the side of the road?" Frankie asked.

"'Cause we don't want some cop seein' an abandoned Jeep next to a blood trail," Cracker said. "People ain't likely to notice a smear on the road unless there's an empty ride nearby."

"What do I do after I ditch the ride in the ghetto?" Frankie asked. "How do I get out of Mud Hollow?"

"Call a cab. Walk. You figure it out," Cracker said.

"This is bullshit!" Frankie appealed to Wyatt. "How come I gotta take a ride to Mud Hollow? Why can't Cracker do it?"

"Do as you're fucking told," Wyatt said.

Frankie snatched his bottle of butterscotch schnapps from the front seat and slammed the door. "Fucking bullshit!" he shouted as he stomped toward the Jeep.

Wyatt drummed his fingers on the dashboard as Frankie turned the Jeep with a series of K-turns. Tired of waiting, Wyatt gunned the van toward the Jeep. Frankie had to accelerate quickly, taking the Jeep off the road, in order to avoid a collision.

Wyatt drove the van along the wooded road until they reached a small industrial park at the top of a hill. He turned the van into the driveway and parked it behind the last unit of a low building. Wyatt stepped outside and unlocked the door to an incinerator shop. The shop was run by one man with no staff. Inside the unit were two incinerators used to burn biological waste. The owner burned road kill, medical waste, veterinary amputations, carcasses from animal control shelters, and offal from a few small butcheries that still operated in Butchers Harbor. After-hours and off the books, the owner allowed the Lynches to use the incinerators to burn whatever it was they needed to burn. He didn't want to know the details.

Cracker and Wyatt made several trips from the van into the shop, hefting Benny One Too Many, Leather Man, and the bags of Ivan and Swag. They piled the garbage bags before one of the incinerators. Benny and Leather Man were dumped beside a metal butcher's table equipped with a circular saw. Through the slits of his eyelids, Benny watched Cracker fire up the first chamber of the incinerator. He tried to clench his hands again, as he had in the van, but he could only twitch his fingers.

Wyatt stepped out of the shop to retrieve the last bag from the van. He was tired, and his grip on the bag was weak. The bag slipped through his fingers, hit the pavement, and burst open. He was about to launch into a string of obscenities, but he quickly gagged on the putrid fumes that were released. He stepped away from the bag for fresher air. One Eye Connivin' Ivan's undersized head and one of his stubby arms had spilled out of the bag, and a bloody gunk oozed across the blacktop. "This is just fucking beautiful," Wyatt muttered. "This is just a kick in the dick." He held his hand over his mouth and approached the mess. He looked down at Ivan, who stared back at him with one cloudy eye and one clear eye. "What are you looking at!" Wyatt shouted. He kicked the head, sending it skittering off the pavement and tumbling across the short lawn. Then, to Wyatt's horror, the head rolled down the hill and disappeared in some woods. Wyatt bit his knuckle to stifle a scream.

Inside the incinerator shop, Cracker grabbed Benny by one leg of his jeans and by the collar of his shirt. He hoisted Benny off the floor and dropped him on the metal surface of the butcher's table. The stainless steel beneath Benny sloped inward from the sides into a drain. Cracker pulled on a pair of heavy rubber gloves, then turned on the circular saw. He slid Benny on the table so that the spinning blade was centered over the joint where Benny's arm met his shoulder

Wyatt rushed into the shop, shouting, "Cracker! Cracker!"

Cracker Jack turned off the saw so he could hear Wyatt.

"The bag ripped," Wyatt said. "I need another bag."

"The bag what?"

"It was defective," Wyatt said. "The fucking bag ripped

open while I was taking it out of the van. We need another one." He scrambled about the shop looking for a new bag.

Cracker Jack stood motionless for a moment, resisting the urge to shoot Wyatt in the back of the head. He exhaled slowly, careful to avoid an audible sigh that might offend Wyatt. He opened a cabinet door beneath the butcher's table and removed a second pair of plastic gloves. As Wyatt frantically opened drawers and closet doors, Cracker stood in one spot and scanned the room. He quickly spotted a trash barrel on wheels tucked in a corner of the shop. On a nearby wall was a rack with miscellaneous tools, including a snow shovel. Cracker walked to the corner and examined the barrel. It was already lined with a large plastic bag, and several more bags were loosely tied to its handle. As he took down the shovel, he said, "We got all the shit we need over here." Cracker rolled the barrel outside, and Wyatt followed.

As he stood over the pile of One-Eye, Cracker handed the second pair of gloves to Wyatt. "Here. You may need these." Wyatt tucked the gloves in his back pocket and crossed his arms. He supervised as Cracker shoveled the mess into the barrel. When had had finished, Cracker nodded toward the wet pavement and said, "We gotta scrub that spot down. Park the van over the puddle 'til we get a chance to clean it up. I'm gonna take the barrel inside."

"I got something else I have to do first," Wyatt said. "Ivan's head rolled down that hill into the woods."

"Christ," Cracker muttered. "How'd that happen?"

"It just rolled." A muscle on Wyatt's jaw twitched. "It's a goddamn head. They tend to roll when they aren't attached to a body. Okay? Now you gonna ask questions all night, or do you want me to find the little fucker?"

Cracker Jack cleared his throat, turned his back to Wyatt, and rolled the trash barrel into the shop. Wyatt glared at Cracker and muttered quietly, "Yeah, you better walk away." He gave the finger to Cracker's back, and then he turned and scrambled into the woods.

The light of the full moon was not much help under the trees. Wyatt opened his Zippo lighter and held the flame before him as he stepped carefully down the hill. The grade was steep, and he slipped on a patch of damp leaves. He slid a few yards down the embankment until the hill leveled out before a stream. He cursed as he stood and brushed leaves and dirt off his pants. He lit his lighter again and stumbled around in the gloom.

After a few minutes, Cracker called from the top of the hill. "Did you find 'im?"

"Yeah, I did!" Wyatt called back. "That's why I'm still down here! 'Cause I like walking around in the woods with a one-eyed midget's head!"

Cracker walked down the hill, carrying a flashlight from the van. When he reached Wyatt, he studied the nearby stream. "You didn't hear a splash or nothin', did you?"

Wyatt ignored the question. "Here, gimme that," he said, taking Cracker's flashlight and handing him the lighter instead. Cracker looked at the Zippo as if he had been handed a turd. "Alright, let's do a grid search or something," Wyatt instructed without really knowing what he meant. He turned and walked up the hill, waving the light before him and walking haphazardly among the trees.

Cracker sat on a fallen tree. He flipped back the Zippo top, ignited the lighter, and then closed the top on the flame. He repeated this sequence several times as he watched the moon's shattered reflection on the surface of the stream.

Fucking Wyatt, he thought. The psycho couldn't control his temper if his life depended on it. Only a maniac would pick a fight with another driver when he was carrying the load they were carrying that night. Only Wyatt. Thanks to Wyatt, they had to chop and burn a fourth body, they had left a trail of DNA from at least two stiffs, and they were searching for a lost head in the woods in the middle of the night. The night was a disaster, just like the state of the Lynch operations. The entire war with the Borisovas was all about Wyatt's ego and insane temper. The war had nothing to do with sensible business. But what could Cracker do? He was just a grunt. He could only bite his tongue and put up with the bullshit. To do otherwise was to end up like Swag Kilpatrick.

Wyatt thrashed through the woods, using the flashlight to knock away branches and brush as he plodded forward. He spotted a fuzzy mound by a tree and hustled toward it with high hopes, but it turned out to be a moss-covered rock. Wyatt began to wonder if it would be okay to leave the head in the woods. As he stood in one spot, his flashlight attracted a small swarm of moths and mosquitoes. He began to slap at the exposed skin on his forearms and neck. "God-damnit!" He staggered backwards, swatting at the air with the flashlight, until he tripped over One Eye's head.

Wyatt scrambled back onto his feet. When he saw what had tripped him, he nearly kicked the head again, but he managed to restrain himself. He examined the head under the beam of the flashlight. The roll down the hill had mashed Ivan's face into a mournful expression. He had also lost his glass eye in the tumble, but Wyatt had no intention to look for that. He pulled on the rubber gloves that he had stuffed in his back pocket and grabbed One Eye by the hair. "Okay fuckface, playtime's over. You can roll, but you can't hide."

Wyatt shone his flashlight down the hill. "Cracker, get up here!" he called. "Shake a leg!"

Wyatt heard Cracker crushing leaves beneath his boots as he trudged up the hill. Cracker had to tear through a thicket to join Wyatt in the small clearing. "Hey, check it out," Wyatt said. He held the flashlight under One Eye's chin, casting long shadows up his face. "Ooooo! Oogity boogity," Wyatt said. "Pretty creepy, huh? Yah–ha–ha–ha!"

Cracker checked his watch.

"Nothing like getting a little head, right, Cracker? It makes your night, don't it?" Wyatt cackled again.

"Yeah," Cracker said. "So you wanna take that thing inside now? We still gotta cut up Benny and the guy you clipped on the way down here. Then we gotta clean the parking lot. So we better get started."

Wyatt lowered the flashlight and the head. "Jesus, Cracker, what crawled up your ass? We can't take a minute to share a few jokes? I'm just trying to take the edge off the night with a little humor."

"Yeah, well maybe you should just take that thing indoors."

"Yeah? Well maybe you should mellow the fuck out," Wyatt retorted. "You'd better watch your fucking tone with me, Cracker. Don't forget who I am. The way you're talk- ing, I think you're getting a little unglued." He pointed a finger at Cracker, using the same hand that gripped Leather Man's hair. "You take a deep breath and settle the fuck down, Cracker. This is no time to be losing your head!"

Cracker Jack turned and continued his trudge up the hill. Wyatt felt a throbbing in his left temple. Sometimes, he wished Cracker wasn't such an asset to the family. He sighed and followed Cracker out of the woods.

The two men plodded across the parking lot and into the incinerator shop. Wyatt plunked Ivan's head down on the empty butcher's table. "Alright. You want me to do anything?" he asked. He turned to face Cracker and was surprised to see that the large man's eyes were wide with apparent shock. Wyatt had never seen much of any expression on Cracker before. He followed Cracker's alarmed gaze to the butcher's table, but all Wyatt saw was a severed head. No cause for alarm there. "What's the matter?" Wyatt asked.

"Where the fuck's Benny?"

Wyatt gave a cursory glance around the shop. "You didn't cut him up yet?"

With uncharacteristic haste, Cracker scrambled around the shop, looking under counters and opening doors. "Where the fuck's Benny!"

"You must have cut him up already," Wyatt said.

Cracker ran back to the butcher's table and examined the stainless steel top and the saw blade. "There's no blood. Where the fuck did he go?"

Wyatt looked down at Leather Man. He grabbed one of the musclehead's boots and lifted his leg. He glanced at the floor under the corpse, then dropped the leg. "Well, he's gotta be here somewhere," Wyatt said. "It's not like Benny could just up and walk away."

5
BASH

Leon cut the price tags off his new jacket and tie. He sprayed heavy starch on his shirt and slacks and tried to iron creases that would look like a professional pressing. When he was dressed, he carefully lifted a present that had been set on his couch. The present was wrapped in paper that Leon had painted himself. Dozens of different cartoon animals all proclaimed the same message in voice balloons: "Happy 3rd Birthday, Wyatt Jr.!" The present inside was a collection of musical instruments that Leon had gathered during his trips around the world. He had painted a map of the Earth on the bottom of a shallow 3x5-foot wooden box and had fixed slots over various nations so the instruments could be set over their country of origin. Over Haiti, he had a pair of traditional maracas made of hollow gourds filled with dried seeds. South Africa had an mbira, an instrument made of bamboo tongues fastened with rattan braids over a wooden board. Alaska featured a cedar flute carved by a Tlingit fisherman. Hanging from a peg on Ireland was a penny whistle, and small brass sajat finger-cymbals rested on Egypt. The slots on China held three glossy red mu yüs, wooden temple blocks of different sizes and tone.

As Leon carried the large box out of his house to his car, the various instruments inside clinked, jingled, and rattled. He carefully loaded the present onto the folded-down seats of his hatchback. His neighbor, Bea Carver, opened her screen door and leaned outside, squinting in Leon's direction. "Leon? Is that you?"

Leon formed a visor with his hand as he turned to face Bea. "Yes. Hello, Mrs. Carver."

She stepped uneasily down the short stoop to the sidewalk. "I wasn't sure if it was you. My vision is getting a little unclear again."

Leon paused for a moment before he understood Bea's point. "Ah, shoot," he said. "I forgot to deliver your tea this week. I'm sorry Mrs. Carver. I've just been so busy that I forgot."

"I insist that I pay for the tea this week, Leon," Bea said, tottering closer.

"No, I insist that you don't. I'll never charge you for the tea, not after all you've done for me. I just have to mix some up." Leon looked at the gift in his car. "I have to go to my nephew's birthday party, but I promise I'll be back in a few hours to mix your tea."

"I don't want to be a pest, Leon. I just like to be able to see and hear."

"Of course you do, Mrs. Carver. There's no excuse for my absentmindedness. I've just been so preoccupied." Leon looked at his watch. "I'll just deliver this gift to my nephew, and I'll be right back to mix your tea." Leon opened the door to his Escort and put one foot in the car.

"Someone was snooping around your house," Bea said. "A big fellow."

"A big guy, you say?"

"Yes, a big fellow, and not very nice. I came over right away to see what he wanted."

"What did he want?"

"He wanted you."

"What did he look like?" Leon asked, still standing with one foot in the car and one foot on his driveway.

"It was hard to tell, with my vision going and all," said Bea, "but I think he looked like somebody famous. Some actor, I think."

Leon nodded. "Or an athlete, maybe?"

"Yes, that's it," Bea said, raising a crooked finger. "He looked like that football player that was on the news. The one that knocked the eye out of that poor referee. Do you know a man that looks like that football player?"

"Yeah, I do," Leon said. He looked down the street in both directions.

"Is he a friend of yours?" Bea asked.

"No, he's not a friend," Leon said. "Could you do me a favor, Mrs. Carver? If this man comes by again, could you tell him I'm never around? Could you tell him you haven't seen me for weeks?"

"Does he want to hurt you, Leon?"

"No, of course not. He's just an annoying guy. I'm trying to brush him off."

Bea laughed. "Oh, don't I know the type. Don't worry, Leon. I'll help you lose the deadweight."

"Thanks, Mrs. Carver," Leon said. He climbed behind the wheel and started the engine. He hesitated, leaving the car door open. "Come to think of it, Mrs. C, this annoying friend of mine does have a bit of a temper. So, don't go out of your way to talk to him. In fact, just avoid him altogether, okay?"

Bea gave Leon a concerned look.

"It's not a big deal. He's kind of a ...Well, don't talk to him if you don't have to," Leon said. "So anyhow, I have to go. I'll drop by with your tea later today."

East Wilt is a working-class suburb of Butcher's Harbor. Behind the town's factories are rows of duplexes and boxy single-story homes. East Wilt was also the home of Wyatt Lynch. His oversized house hulked over the other modest homes like a class bully repeating the second grade for a third year. The three-story home was vaguely Victorian in design, with a great porch, several balconies, and little towers with sloped turrets. The small mansion, crammed onto a half-acre lot, had black vinyl siding, silver shutters, and gold trim. The shallow front lawn was littered with post-modern sculptures, gaudy steel mobiles, and a life-size resin reproduction of *The Thinker*. The backyard was consumed by a swimming pool in the shape of a chubby "W."

As Leon drove into the neighborhood, the streets were clogged with the parked cars of gangsters attending Wyatt's party. Cadillacs, Town Cars, Acuras, and Irocs were parked too far from the curb on both sides of the road. Traffic had to trickle past Wyatt's home straddling the center line on what amounted to a single lane of useable road.

Leon parked his Escort a few blocks away from Wyatt's house. He checked his reflection in the rearview mirror. He wore a white straw Gambler he had picked up in Panama, and a pair of small wire-rimmed sunglasses. Leon liked the shades, which he saved for special occasions, but he thought the headgear looked silly. The straw hat looked fine on a

Panamanian, but it seemed like a goofy affectation on Leon. However, he needed some protection from the sun, and he couldn't show up at Wyatt's party wearing a shirt, tie, and baseball cap. He stepped out of his car and lugged his gift to the party.

When Leon stepped inside the house, he saw Wyatt's wife, Tina, seated in the living room sipping a Long Island iced tea. Tina was a half-foot taller than her husband or Leon. She had a muscular physique and a stunning boob job. She was surrounded by other gangster wives, all smoking and swilling strong drinks with tiny umbrellas. Tina spotted Leon and whispered something to the women around her. They all laughed as Leon approached.

"Hi, Leon," Tina said flatly. "Glad you could make it."

Leon smiled. "I brought a little something for Wyatt Jr.," he said. He raised the large box before him and hit the elbow of a nearby thug. "Oh, sorry," Leon said to the annoyed goon.

Tina and her friends were laughing again. "The present looks great," Tina said. She pointed her cigarette toward a side room. "People are piling their gifts in there."

Leon hovered for a moment, clutching the gift before him. He was about to ask Tina how she had been, but she quickly resumed a conversation with the other wives.

"Alright then," Leon said, nodding. "I'll just put this present in with the others." He stumbled through the living room, careful to avoid knocking over lamps or guests with the gift, and entered a dining room brimming with presents. Huge boxes, some larger than Leon, had been piled as high as the ceiling. Leon figured the boxes contained television sets, stereo systems, kitchen appliances, and other electronic goods that had disappeared from trucks or warehouses on their way to retailers. Leon tried to imagine how Wyatt and the other hoods would react when Wyatt Jr. opened Leon's gift, a box of mostly handmade musical instruments. He thought of removing his card from the present so nobody would know it was from him. He just hoped the boy might be able to play with the instruments for a few hours before Wyatt threw them all into the trash along with the hand-painted wrapping paper. Leon hid his gift on a low pile of gifts between two refrigerator-sized boxes.

He milled through several rooms without recognizing anyone and eventually stepped into the kitchen, hoping to find a plate of appetizers or a drink to keep him occupied. All he found was a cluster of somber, gray-skinned men gathered around the kitchen table. Leon stood in a corner, as far from the group as possible. The men stopped their hushed conversation and glared over their shoulders at Leon until he left the room.

He stepped onto the porch and worked his way down the steps to the backyard. He wandered around the pool, which was bordered by a patio made of interlocking W-shaped bricks. A clown on stilts entertained several children by juggling a bowling ball, a flaming torch, and a miniature chainsaw. The clown teetered on his stilts as the children stepped closer. At the opposite end of the yard, a burly old Seminole wrestled an alligator. Children as young as three gathered around and laughed as the big man sat on the alligator's head.

Leon was relieved to find a small bar set up at the corner of the pool. He gave the heavyset bartender a cheerful hello and ordered a beer. There were no stools at the bar, but Leon lingered there, leaning an elbow on the counter. "Good beer," he said to the bartender.

"What?"

"Good beer," Leon said, raising the bottle. "Hits the spot."

The bartender eyed Leon with suspicion. "Glad you like it."

Leon glanced up at the clear sky. "Not a bad day."

"What?"

"Not a bad day," Leon repeated.

The bartender looked up at the sky and back at Leon. He seemed annoyed. Leon sipped his beer and tried to think of a new topic. He wished he knew more about sports; maybe the bartender would want to talk about a game or something. As Leon drank, the heavy man took advantage of the silence to turn his wide back on Leon. He busied himself with packing fresh ice around bottles of beer.

Fuzzy Magee approached the bar and waited briefly for the fat man's attention. When the bartended failed to turn around, Fuzzy rapped his knuckles on the bar and said, "Hey Slim, I'm a little parched over here. You think you could summon up the energy to pour me a drink?"

The bartender continued to pack ice into the cooler. When he had finished, he turned slowly to face Fuzzy. "What do you want?"

"Manhattan. No ice."

The bartender nodded and poured Fuzzy's drink. When he reached for a maraschino cherry, Fuzzy barked, "Hey! Doughboy! What do you think you're doing? I don't want that nasty chunk of crap in my drink."

The man was confused. "It's a cherry. You don't want a cherry in your Manhattan?"

"What I'd just say?" Fuzzy asked. He picked up a cocktail napkin, wrapped it around the glass, and carefully examined the rim. He turned and saw Leon standing beside him. "Hey. You're Wyatt's kid brother, aren't you?" Fuzzy pointed at a white dreadlock poking out from Leon's hat. "Whitey, right?"

Leon nodded and smiled. "I prefer to be called Leon," he said, extending his hand.

Fuzzy recoiled. "I don't shake hands."

"Oh. Sorry." Leon dropped his hand awkwardly to his side. "I didn't know."

"Handshaking is a filthy ritual," Fuzzy said. He loosened the silver tie around his knotty neck. "It's why we're all sick. Smearing germs all over each other."

"Yeah, I guess so," Leon said.

"You guess so? There's nothing to guess about. Just think of all the disgusting shit that people do with their hands. They pick their noses. Wipe their asses. Jack off. And God knows what else. Who wants to touch something that's been doing that?"

"I should have know better. I'm sorry."

"I mean, why don't you just wipe a booger in my eye?" Fuzzy asked. "Or maybe you could take a leak in my beverage here. That'd be a nice custom. Why don't we all start doing that now?"

"I see your point. I apologize," Leon said.

"Whatever," Fuzzy said. "Well, I'll see you around, Whitey." He took a sip of his cocktail and strode across the lawn toward Wyatt's house.

Leon turned back to the bartender, who was smirking broadly. "Well, I guess I'll be running along too," Leon said. "Nice talking to you." He shuffled away from the bar and tried to find a spot where he could blend into the scenery. He found a cluster of unoccupied lounge chairs not far from the shirtless alligator wrestler. Leon slumped into one of the chairs, crossed his legs at the ankles, and rested his beer on an armrest. He watched as the wrestler put the alligator into a headlock and poked the writhing animal in the nostrils with two of his fingers. The crowd of children pressing around him squealed with laughter.

The shrinking space between the children and the alligator concerned Leon, and he looked around to see if any adults were supervising this situation. A pair of floozies and three overweight thugs were splashing about in the pool nearby, but they clearly were not interested in the alligator or the children. Another wise guy was seated in a plastic chair near the ring of kids, but his head had fallen forward so his chin touched his chest, and drool had spilled from his lower lip onto his black polyester shirt. The Seminole who was handling the alligator had ragged scars on his arms and belly. He did not seem too concerned with his own safety, never mind the safety of the children about him. In fact, the cross-eyed old man seemed to be in a bit of a trance as he lethargically abused the alligator. Leon wondered if the wrestler and the gator were both stoned.

With a sinking feeling, Leon realized he was the only responsible adult in sight. He rose from his chair and stepped before the kids, saying, "Okay, guys, let's give the wrestler a little room now. Let's all take a few steps back and give the man and his alligator a little breathing space, okay?"

The children ignored Leon, so he clapped his hands to get their attention. He succeeded only in gaining the attention of the alligator, which lurched out of the wrestler's arms and snapped at Leon's backside. "Shit!" Leon gasped, hopping away from the beast. The dirty word made the children laugh. Leon laughed along with them and said, "See? Now you don't want to become an alligator snack, do you? Huh?" Leon glanced nervously over his shoulder at the animal. "Now everybody listen to the grownup and take five big steps backward."

"Hey Unca Whitey! You in da way!" a boy called.

Leon scanned the group and found his nephew standing by the alligator's tail. Even at three, the boy was cocky. He stood with his head tilted back and his hands tucked in his front jeans pockets. Cracker Jack Farrell's two boys stood on either side of Wyatt Jr. The Farrells were older than little Wyatt. Mick Farrell was six, and Rocky Farrell was eight. Both boys tried to look as hard as their old man. They wore crew cuts, black denim jeans, black T-shirts, and black combat boots.

"Hey, guys. What's up?" Leon said, crouching before Wyatt Jr. The Farrell boys put their hands on their hips and took a step closer to Leon. Feeling a little intimidated by the six- and eight-year-olds, Leon directed his attention to Wyatt Jr. "How you doing, little man?"

"Arright," Wyatt Jr. said.

"Yeah? You having a good time being the birthday boy today?"

"Yeah. Forgit abitit."

Leon chuckled. "Yeah, forget about it," he repeated. "Hey, want to take a walk with your Uncle Leon?"

Wyatt Jr. shook his head. "Naw."

"No? Well how about you just step back from the alligator a little bit, okay?"

"Naw," the boy said, shaking his head again.

"Come on, little buddy, make your Uncle Leon happy."

Wyatt Jr. took a defiant step closer to the alligator. When Leon put a hand on the boy's shoulder, Mick and Rocky Farrell crossed their arms and stepped between Leon and Wyatt Jr. Leon chuckled, "Are you fellas security?"

Mick and Rocky kept silent.

Leon nodded seriously. "Alright, guys. You're doing a good job. But what do you say we get our little kingpin away from the gator? Okay? That's what grown-up bodyguards would do."

As the Farrell boys considered this, Wyatt Jr. punched his uncle in the cheek. "Hey!" Leon scolded, holding his face. "Watch it!" Wyatt Jr. swung again with both hands, boxing Leon's ears.

"Okay, that's enough," Leon said, rising to his feet. The moment he stood, he realized he had made a poor decision. His groin was at prime punching height for little Wyatt, and Leon had to fend off a flurry of jabs directed below his belt. "Hey! Hey! Come on! Enough already!" Leon pleaded, swatting away the little fists. Wyatt Jr. was laughing loudly, as were several of the surrounding children. The Farrell boys, however, maintained an icy silence as they stood by the three-year-old's side.

"That's enough, little killer," said a stern but seductive voice behind Leon. Wyatt Jr. immediately dropped his fists, and even the Farrell boys backed off and looked bashfully at their feet. Leon turned to see Macey Kick standing behind him. She glared down at the group of kids and said, "All of you do what Mr. Lynch says. Back away from the gator. Now!" The kids obeyed without hesitation, particularly the boys, who all had crushes on the lean woman with pretty eyes.

Macey gave Leon a lopsided smile, forming one tiny dimple near the corner of her mouth. Leon jerked his thumb toward the kids who were still stepping away from the alligator. "Thanks with that," he said. He met her dark eyes for just a moment. Then he lowered his gaze to study one of the W tiles on the patio.

"Hanging with the hoods today?" Macey asked.

"I guess so," Leon answered. He ventured a half-glance toward Macey. "So how've you been since the other night?"

"Busy."

"Yeah. So I've heard."

"Your father finally filled me in on what you were doing for the family back at the pool," Macey said. "I hear you did a good job."

Leon returned his gaze to his feet, and he began pulling distractedly at one of the short dreadlocks spilling from under his straw hat. "Yeah, well. I like to do my part. When I'm allowed to anyway."

"What does that mean?"

"It means I'm tired of being taken for granted by my family. I agreed to lend a hand the other night on the condition that I would have more involvement in the business. It's been over two weeks now since I did that bit of work with the driver, and I haven't had any further assignments, a phone call, or even a simple attaboy from my dad. The first contact of any sort I've had from my family was my invitation to this party."

Macey smirked.

"What's so funny?" Leon asked.

"You. And your notion that you want to be a gangster."

"Why not?" Leon threw his shoulders back and tried to assume the swagger of the hoods milling around the pool. "I've been in some tough situations before. I've run into some bad elements as I've been plying my trade. I know how to handle myself."

Macey's smirk broke into a wide grin. "You know how to handle yourself. That's cute."

"Forget it," Leon said. "Enjoy the party." He turned and

took a step away, but when Macey touched his elbow, he stopped mid-stride.

"You say you want more assignments. Do you even know what kind of work we do? Most of us don't spend our days mixing truth serums, you know."

Leon kept his back to Macey and did not respond.

"Not that you don't already have a little blood on your hands," she said. "I'm sure you've considered the consequences of your last assignment. Haven't you?"

Leon had. For the previous two weeks, he had spent several hours a day considering the fates of Swag, One Eye, and Benny. He didn't want to think of them. He didn't want to imagine the details of their disappearance, wondering what kind of sick tortures Wyatt had ordered and how much they surely suffered. Leon wished he could feel something other than responsibility for the fates of these three men, but he'd never had much luck controlling the course of his thoughts. Yet despite the bouts of nausea, insomnia, and shame, Leon still wanted more involvement in the family trade. He wondered if the combination of repulsion and attraction to the family was a form of impending insanity.

"Say you do get more assignments. What then?" Macey asked. "What do you hope to get out of it?"

"Respect."

"You think a lot of people respect us?" She smiled. "Whose respect do you want, anyhow?"

Yours, Leon thought. He turned to face Macey and saw that she was still smirking. He shook his head and tried to storm off, but Macey kept her hand on his forearm. She was barely touching him, but it was enough to keep him still.

"One other thing," Macey said. "What do you plan to bring to the table? Increase may be your dad, but if you want a bigger role in the family business, you need to appeal to him as a businessman. What can you bring to the business?"

"Products," Leon said. "My product line is unsurpassed. No one comes close to offering the variety and quality of my stash."

"That may be an in. Maybe. Which reminds me, are you still selling BMF?"

"BMF?" Leon repeated. "Don't tell me you want Slaughter."

"Of course not. I have no need for it," she said. "I just don't like you selling it to anyone else. People get a mistaken notion they're invincible when they're on BMF. Sometimes it takes me a while to convince them otherwise."

"Oh. Well, you'll be happy to hear that I've discontinued that line."

"You sure?" Macey asked. She looked him hard in the eye and gripped his arm a little tighter.

Leon squirmed under her grip and stare. "It's gone. I swear. I dumped my stash into the harbor after Blake messed up that ref. Slaughter was a serious liability. I'm glad to be rid of it."

"Whatever other products you want to sell, you go right ahead. As long as your livelihood doesn't interfere with mine, we won't have a problem."

"OK. I get it. No more BMF."

Macey release his arm. "Alright. Let me take you to your dad. Let's see what he thinks of the rest of your product line." She led Leon across the yard to a bulkhead leading down into a basement, where Wyatt had built a game room filled with antique torture and execution devices. In the center of the room hung a chandelier made from a Middle Ages break-ing wheel. Dangling from the wheel were thumbscrews and rectal pears. A pool table had been set into a stretching rack, and an open iron maiden set by the door functioned as a coat stand. The counter of a small bar was a Medieval pressing stone. The pores in the thick slab of granite still contained specks of dried blood that once flowed through the veins of heretics and witches. Behind the bar, a highly polished guillotine blade served as a mirror.

Cracker Jack Farrell and Fuzzy Magee were starting a game of pool on the stretching rack. Wyatt and Frankie Baloney were playing a game of cards at a table made of two abutting pillory stocks; the holes for the victim's wrists were handy for holding drinks or poker chips. Increase was in the corner of the basement, slouched in one of two electric chairs set before an entertainment center. He sat with one hand clutching a can of beer while the other hand fired a plastic revolver at the oversized HDTV flat screen. The sounds of his video game muffled the sparse conversation.

The terse chatter stopped altogether as Macey stepped into the basement and strode across the room. She stepped behind the bar and began to fix herself a drink. As Leon descended the steps, he removed his sunglasses and tucked them in his shirt so he could see in the dim, hazy room. He coughed on the smoke of Wyatt and Frankie's cigarettes. Wyatt looked up from his cards and said, "Well, look who's here."

Increase did not turn from his video game, but he called out, "Who is it?"

"It's Whitey," Wyatt answered. "How ya doin', bro?"

Leon nodded to his brother and looked uneasily around the room.

"Leon!" Increase called. He jerked an elbow toward the

empty electric chair beside him. "Get over here, son. I need your help."

Leon hustled across the room. With a twinge of anxiety, he sat in the hot seat beside his father. "What do you need, Dad?"

"Pick up a gun and give me a hand here."

"Oh." He stared at the screen. "How do I play?"

"It's called *Cattle's Revenge*. We're cowboys, and a toxic dumpsite near our ranch has turned all our cattle into heavily-armed mutants." Increase fired several rounds into a deformed cow that was racing forward with a flame-thrower. Chunks of flesh were torn off the cow until it collapsed, spurting blood from its wounds and udder. When the cow finally died, it shrank and morphed into a hamburger. "The game is fairly simple," Increase continued. "If something moves, kill it. Wyatt entered one of those—what do you call its?—cheat codes. We have unlimited ammo, we don't loose points for hitting innocent bystanders, and we don't have to worry about freeing the hostages that pop up now and then. So it's just kill, kill, kill."

Leon picked up a pistol and fired at a bull lurking behind a saloon.

"So what's up?" Increase asked.

"Oh not much, I guess," Leon said. "How have you been? Everything going okay since the other night?"

"Everything's been fine," Increase said. His glazed eyes never left the video screen. "We're all grateful for that bit of work you did. You were a big help to the family."

"So everything is going well then?"

"Sure. For the most part anyway. There was one snafu. Benny One Too Many disappeared before he disappeared."

Leon waited a beat. "What does that mean?"

"He gave Fuzzy the slip, and no one's seen him since. Wyatt and Cracker think he had help slipping out of town."

As Leon pondered this, a cow with a shotgun fired on him twice, and his character lost half of his life points.

"We'll find him, though. We have some boys flying down to his hometown in Texas. He may turn up there. A guy like Benny is bound to screw up eventually, and when he does, we'll find him. In the meantime, Swag Kilpatrick and One-Eye Connivin' Ivan have been taken care of. Those two won't be talking to anyone this side of Hell."

Leon lowered his plastic gun at the mention of Swag and Ivan. On the video game, a cow burst out of a brothel window and lobbed an axe at Leon's side of the screen. A splash of digital blood appeared before Leon. Increase reached over with his revolver and tapped the gun in his son's hand. "You supposed to shoot the cattle, Leon, not gawk at 'em. These cows are kicking our asses."

Leon shot back and hit a bull between the horns. The bull's head exploded with a wet splat.

"Atta boy," Increase said. "You get extra points for a head shot. Tagging them in the nuts is another bonus zone."

"So, you were happy with my work with the driver?" Leon asked.

"What'd I just say? We're all perfectly happy."

"Good," Leon said. "That's good to hear." Leon glanced over his shoulder. Wyatt and the other boys seemed preoccupied with their various games. Leon mumbled to his father, "I remember you said that I could be more involved with the family if everything went well."

"You are involved," Increase said. "We're killing cows together, aren't we?"

"Yeah, we sure are," Leon said quietly. "And this is fun and all, but I thought you meant I would be more involved in the family business."

Increase grimaced and set his gun down. "Do we really need to talk about it now? I mean, is it worth losing the farm to lunatic cows?" Increase chuckled when he saw Leon scowl. "I'm just busting your stones, son. We'll kill cows later." He pointed a remote control at the set and turned it off. "Come on," he said. He rose from the electric chair and drained the last of his beer. "Let's fix us a couple of drinks."

Macey was sitting on a stool behind the bar. Increase and Leon sat on stools on the other side of the pressing stone. "What are you drinking, Macey?" Increase asked. She held up an old fashioned glass filled with ice and a light amber whiskey. "Ah! Girl after me own heart," Increase said. "Pour us a couple, will you, Macey?" She obliged, dropping a handful of ice into two glasses and filling them with generous levels of Tullamore Dew. Increase held the whiskey under his nose and savored the earthy aroma. "This was your grandfather's drink," he said to Leon. "Did you know that?"

Leon nodded. "I've heard."

"There was nothing I enjoyed more than sitting next to my old man, knocking back one whiskey after another." He raised his drink. Leon did the same. "Here's to fathers and sons," Increase said. Leon smiled as he clinked glass with his father. The men drank then set their glasses on the stone counter. Increase patted his son's shoulder. "Now, what's on your mind?"

Leon watched his brother's reflection in the polished guillotine blade. Wyatt did not seem to be paying any attention to their conversation. "Well," Leon said, "I just want to know if I can do more for the family." He removed his Gambler and set it on the bar.

Increase took another sip of his drink. "What did you have in mind, exactly?"

"Well, nothing too specific. I just have a general notion that I could do something a little more substantial."

Macey joined the conversation. "Leon had just mentioned to me that we might to consider selling some of his products."

"Right," Leon said. "I could offer my products and, you know, manage that part of the business."

Increase raised his eyebrow. "Tell me again, what kind of products do you have?"

"He has a diarrhea plant," Macey said.

Leon laughed. "Well, I have other products, too."

"Such as?" Increase asked.

"Well, for example, I have dream-amplifiers. It's a plant called Jade Rapture. You eat a few leaves before you go to bed, and all night you have the most beautiful dreams. And when you wake up, you remember every detail."

Increase tried to maintain a neutral expression. "Hm. Interesting. So what else could you do for the family?"

"Okay, well, as you know, I've traveled all over the world, and I've made a lot of contacts. I've set up business arrangements with people on every continent except Antarctica. That demonstrates that I have people skills. That shows I have business, uh…"—Leon grasped at the air with his hand—"…business acumen. I mean, I could function as a project coordinator or something."

Increase and Macey laughed. "A project what?" Increase asked.

"You know what I mean," Leon said.

Increase tried to stop smiling. "Okay, Leon. You have people skills." He looked over his shoulder at the crew behind him, then turned back to face his son. "Are these your kind of people?" he asked, keeping his voice low.

Leon turned to watch Fuzzy racking another set of billiards as Cracker chalked his cue. Wyatt drummed his fingers impatiently on the pillory card table as he waited for Frankie Baloney to finish picking his nose and make his wager. Leon turned back to his father and shrugged. "They seem okay."

"Yeah? You like these guys?" Increase asked. "You can see yourself working with them one day after another? Hanging out with them?"

Leon nodded.

"Then go over strike up a conversation with Wyatt's idiot pal Frankie," Increase said. "You probably have a lot of similar interests. Maybe the two of you could start a book club or something."

Macey snickered. "First, you'd have to teach Frankie how to read."

"Maybe Frankie Baloney is a bad choice," Increase said. "Maybe you should make friends with Fuzzy Magee. He's a nice guy, isn't he, Macey?"

"Yeah. He's the salt of the earth," she answered. "We met at a restaurant the other day, and a waiter accidentally let his thumb touch Fuzzy's food as he was setting down a plate. Fuzzy dragged the kid outside and pistol-whipped him."

"Yeah, Fuzzy has some issues," Increase said. "Maybe you don't want to hang around with him either, Leon. But there is Cracker. He's an interesting guy. I'm sure he'd love to tell you about his days as a police officer. From what I've heard, every nickel-bag dealer, small-time booster, and flat-back whore would soil their pants just seeing Cracker. He didn't make many arrests, but he did issue a lot of fines."

"He wanted his cut," Macey said. "And he didn't care if business was sluggish."

"Back in the days when Officer Farrell was on the beat, the papers used to pin all sorts of grisly 'gangland slayings' on our family," Increase said. "The truth is, we had nothing to do with 'em. Most of the killings were Cracker's work. He was just taking care of business on the street. A one-man protection racket." Increase took a hearty swig of whiskey. "I wasn't so sure about Cracker when I first took him on. I'd send that boy out to talk to someone, and he'd practically draw and quarter the poor bastard. I tell you, I've had a deuce of a time trying to pull the reigns in on that one."

"Alright. I get the picture," Leon said. "These guys aren't very nice."

"No, they're not," Increase said. He gave his son a soft punch to the upper arm. "You *are* a nice person, though, Leon. You have a conscience. You're sympathetic, considerate, and compassionate. Those are all good qualities, but being a good person doesn't make you a good goodfella."

Leon started to protest, but Increase put up his hand. "Your mother, rest her soul, never wanted you in the business. She told me, 'Don't ever bring Leon into your world.' She saw that you were a creative, sensitive kid. She wanted you to grow up to be a musician or an artist. One of those nice careers."

"What about Wyatt's mother?" Leon asked. "His mother didn't care if he worked in the family trade?"

"Well, Wyatt's mom seemed to lose all interest in her son the same time she lost interest in his father. After you ... I mean, after I ..." Increase paused to consider his words. "After Kathleen discovered my indiscretion, she just took off and never really wanted to have anything to do with me or my son—my sons—ever again. And by 'indiscretion,' I don't mean 'regret.' I have no regrets about the time I spent with your mother. No regrets at all. Amabelle was special, and without my, uh … time with her, I would have never had you in my life, Leon. And you mean the world to me."

Leon chuckled bitterly and took a good swig from his whiskey. "Well, this is just a Hallmark moment."

After an embarrassing moment of silence, Macey said, "Maybe I should excuse myself."

"Don't bother," Leon said. "I'm leaving." He stood and took his Gambler hat from the bar. Before he could storm away, Wyatt approached the bar and put his arm around his brother.

"Hey, bro! You aren't leaving so soon are you?" Wyatt slapped his brother's chest. "Sit down. Have another fucking drink." He pressed his brother back onto the stool and sat beside him. "So, what's up, Whitey? What's everyone talking about over here?"

Leon shrugged. "Nothing."

"Nothing? Whole lot of talk going on for nothing." Wyatt scanned the rest of the group at the bar. "Anything here concern me?"

"We're just having a little chat," Increase said.

"Fine, keep your secrets," Wyatt said. "See if I give a shit." He took the Gambler from Leon's hands and placed it at a crooked angle on his brother's head. "Love your hat!"

Leon calmly removed the Gambler and set it on the bar.

Wyatt snickered. "So, anyhow, Whitey. You got any weed?"

Leon scoffed. "Any what?"

"Ganja. Reefer," Wyatt said. "Let's fire some up. I feel like getting retarded."

"You know, that's not a bad idea," Increase said. "That

could do us all a world of good right now. It's hard to stay angry when you're stoned."

Wyatt leaned closer toward his brother. "So, you holding or not?"

"No, I'm not holding," Leon said sharply. "I don't sell pot."

"Yeah, that's right," Wyatt said. He turned to face the rest of the crew in the game room. "My little half blood doesn't sell drugs with market value. He's a not-for-profit dealer."

Frankie Baloney snickered.

"I guess that's true," Leon said. He felt his cheeks burning. "But I've been thinking. I think I might change my line of work."

"Oh yeah?" Wyatt turned back to face his brother. "You plan to start pushing smack now?"

Leon shook his head. "Actually, I'm asking Dad for a bigger role in the family. I think I could do a lot to help out."

Increase slumped slightly and briefly covered his face with one hand.

"You want to help? That's super! Hey, guys, Whitey wants to help! Whitey's on the team!" Wyatt applauded. "I've got just the assignment for you, Peon. You can stay the fuck out of our way. Think you can handle that? That would be a big help."

Frankie Baloney chortled loudly.

"Alright, Wyatt, there's no need for that," Increase said. He lifted the bottle from the bar and added some booze to his glass. He leaned closer to Leon and spoke softly. "Wyatt does have a point, though. Maybe you should just stay out of our way. The truth is, you don't belong in our business, son. You can't do us much good, and we can't do you much good."

Leon looked at his reflection in the guillotine mirror

behind the bar. He could see splotchy red patches forming under his translucent cheeks. He stepped away from the bar. "Alright. I'll get out of your hair." He put on his hat and fumbled in his shirt pocket for his sunglasses.

"You don't have to leave," Increase said. He reached for his son's arm, but Leon yanked it away.

"No, I have to go," Leon muttered. "I promised my neighbor I would help her out with something."

"You mean that old lady that lives next door to you?" Macey asked.

"Yeah. Mrs. Carver."

"See, that's what I'm talking about," Increase said. "It's great that you're rushing home to help the elderly and all, but I don't see the rest of the crew doing that sort of thing very often. Don't get me wrong. I'm glad you're the nice kid you are, but that's why you shouldn't get too involved in this messy business of ours."

"Just looking out for me," Leon said flatly.

"I am," Increase said.

"Well, I appreciate that," Leon said. "So I guess I'll see you the next time you need me to do some shit detail. I guess that sort of involvement is okay." He turned and walked for the door.

"Hey, don't leave angry," Increase called.

"Yeah, just leave," Wyatt said.

Frankie Baloney laughed loudly as Leon stomped up the basement stairs.

The party continued for several more hours, until the sun had set and the children had all grown tired and cranky. Mothers tried to comfort their kids while the gangsters continued drinking. Wyatt sat on the porch with the goombah Frankie Baloney. Cans of beer, shots glasses, and two bottles of liquor were set before them on a glass table. Wyatt looked over the porch railing and watched his father playing with Wyatt Jr. and a few other kids. The old man was pretending to be a demented robot as he chased the laughing children around the small patches of yard lit with colored Tiki lights.

Wyatt poured himself a shot of tequila. "What do you think of my dad?" he asked Frankie Baloney.

"Your old man? Forget about it. He's the fuckin' bomb." Frankie poured himself a shot of watermelon schnapps.

"Yeah, he's the bomb and all that shit," Wyatt said. "But are you afraid of him?"

"Nah, I ain't afraid of him."

"Exactly. Nobody fears my father, and that's why he's not a great leader." Wyatt tossed back his tequila, set the shot glass on the table, and punched Frankie in the ear.

Frankie stumbled out of his chair, holding his hand to the side of his head. "Shit, Wyatt! What the fuck?"

"You're afraid of me, aren't you Frankie?"

"Yeah, you're a fuckin' psycho!"

"Right," Wyatt said. He poured himself another shot. "Now sit down."

Frankie remained standing and rubbing his ear.

"Come on, sit down," Wyatt said.

"You hit me in the ear, Wyatt. It fuckin' smarts."

"I was just making a point," Wyatt said.

"Yeah, but how do I know you won't make another point? I mean, what do you want to discuss next?"

Fuzzy Magee ran around the side of the house and up the

KEN HARVILL

stairs leading to the porch. "Hey, Wyatt!" he shouted. "We got a situation!"

Before Fuzzy could explain, a man and a woman rounded the corner of the house. They were both in their early thirties, and they both wore business attire that was cheap and dated. The pair climbed the wooden stairs leading to the porch. When they reached the top, the man approached Wyatt and showed him a detective's shield. "Good evening, Mr. Lynch. We'd like to have a word with you, if you don't mind."

"Who's we?" Wyatt asked.

"Detective Kerns," he said. He was a slim, pallid man with thick brown hair and glassy eyes.

The woman detective fumbled with her shield and awkwardly displayed it to Wyatt and the surrounding gangsters. "I'm Detective Janes," she said. Like her partner, she was thin and had the gaunt, wasted appearance of an OxyContin addict. The look was oddly attractive on her. "We're from Homicide."

"Are you now?" Wyatt said. "Well, I sure am proud of you. What do you want?"

"We'd like to talk to you about Walter Kamerowski," said Detective Kerns, returning his badge to a pocket inside his jacket. He chomped on a wad of gum.

"Never heard of him," Wyatt said. He turned to Frankie Baloney. "You ever hear of a guy named Kamerowski?"

Frankie shrugged. "Name don't ring any bells."

Wyatt turned back to Kerns and shrugged. "Wish we could help, Detective, but we never heard of the Polack." He pulled a fresh can of beer from the cooler.

"Are you sure don't know him?" Kerns asked. "He was a big guy. A bodybuilder type. Wore a lot of leather."

KILL WHITEY

Frankie busied himself with pouring a shot of watermelon schnapps. Wyatt pursed his lips and tapped his chin with one finger. "Hmm. Bodybuilder in leather, huh? No, I can't think of anybody who matches that description. Doesn't sound like the kind of crowd I run around with. Maybe you could ask around at the gay bar after you get off of work."

"No, I don't think I'll be going to the gay bar tonight," Kerns said. He turned toward Janes and smirked. Janes returned a tired smile.

Increase climbed the stairs to the porch. He was holding his grandson's hand. "What seems to be the problem here?"

Detective Janes pushed a lock of reddish-brown hair away from her eyes and tucked the hair behind her ear. "Good evening, Mr. Lynch," she said. "We're from Homicide. We'd like to discuss a few matters with your son."

"You pigs are something else," Wyatt said. "You've got nothing better to do than fuck up my son's birthday?"

"I do apologize for the disruption," Kerns said with a creepy grin. "Unfortunately, we can't plan our murder investigations around your social calendar." He spit his gum over the porch railing.

"We understand," Increase said. He let go of his grandson's hand and took a step closer to the detectives. "If there has been any sort of crime, my family will do all we can to assist your investigation." He clasped his hands before him. "Now, what can we do for you, exactly?"

"Well, as we were trying to explain to your son, we'd like him to accompany us to the station so we could ask him a few questions," said Detective Janes.

"We can't talk here?" Increase asked.

The male detective nodded toward little Wyatt. "The matter we'd like to discuss is the murder of a certain Walter

152

Kamerowski. The man's death was pretty gruesome, and some of the questions we need to ask might frighten the little ones."

Increase glanced at his grandson. "No, we don't want to frighten the youngsters." He turned back toward Kerns. "May I have a moment to speak with my son in private?"

"By all means."

"Thank you," Increase said. "Fuzzy, put some burgers on the grill for the detectives."

"No, thank you, sir," Kerns said. "I don't think we'll be sticking around long enough to dine."

"Well, at least help yourself to a beer," Increase said.

"Oh, no. We can't do that either," Kerns answered. He reached into the cooler and grabbed two cans of beer. As he handed a cold one to his partner, he said, "We can't drink while we're on duty."

Increase stooped before his grandson and patted the boy on the head. "Okay, little Wyatt, you stay out here with the detective while I talk to your dad." Increase motioned for Wyatt Sr. to join him inside the house.

Wyatt glared at the police as he walked across the porch. He followed his father into the house, shutting the glass slider behind him. When the two Lynches were alone, Increase quietly asked, "So who's Walter Kamerowski?"

Wyatt shrugged. "I never heard of him."

"Tell the truth, son."

Wyatt laughed. "I am, Dad. This is the first I've heard of the guy."

"Listen to me very carefully, Wyatt," Increase said. "I need you to tell me the truth so I know how to respond to the fuzz."

"Dad! Listen to *me*," Wyatt said. "I … never … heard … of … the … fucking … Polack."

"You haven't been killing anyone without my permission, have you?" Increase whispered.

"No way," Wyatt lied.

Increase looked back at the police. Detective Janes leaned against the porch railing as she held the cold can beside one of her weary eyes. Kerns chugged his beer like a marathon runner tossing back a plastic cup of water. "So they're just busting our balls, then," Increase said.

"Yeah, fucking pigs."

"I'll call our lawyers," Increase said. "We'll all go down to the station together."

"What do you mean?" Wyatt asked. "You want me to talk to these assholes?"

"Sure. I mean, if you didn't kill this dude, then why not?"

"I don't know, Dad."

"Listen, this can be useful. This incident helps to establish a pattern of police harassment and our cooperation. That can be helpful when we get pinched for something legit." Increase chuckled. "You know how many times I've been interrogated for something I *have* done? Man, I've lost count. In all those interrogations, they never got anything to stick. Zip. Nada. This time, you haven't even done the crime. Hell, this'll be a cinch."

"Still, Dad, what if they're up to something?"

"What can they do? If you haven't killed the man, you've got nothing to worry about. Come on, let's call our lawyers and get this thing over with."

6
HOOKED

eon sat at the edge of his tiny front yard, hovering four inches above a wooden bench. A tropical storm raged around him, bending trees and rattling street signs. Leon wore a plastic poncho that fluttered and flapped with the powerful gusts. He kept a thermos tucked under one arm, and when the rain was not too heavy, he unscrewed the canister and poured a little tea into a heavy Korean rice bowl at his side. As he sipped the salty brew, the steam warmed his face.

A nearby shop window exploded under the force of a hard gust, and Leon thought, *This is a night I won't forget.* He really had no choice. He would always remember just how the telephone wires keened in the wind. He would remember each movement of a plastic shopping bag, full with air, soaring overhead and passing fast as freeway traffic until a heavy sheet of rain hammered it to the pavement. Even the smallest details, like the thin trail of water snaking down his neck and chest, were seared into his mind, indelible as a brand on flesh.

The tea Leon drank was made from seaweed that grows off the coast of Molokai. Leon grew his own supply in pressurized saltwater tanks in his basement. This tea gave its user photographic memory for several hours. A pleasant side effect was a feeling of weightlessness, as if the drinker was floating four inches above the earth. Leon sold the seaweed to graduate students who needed help passing their comprehensive exams. The tea was also popular with corporate spies who were reluctant to be caught with miniature cameras or handheld copiers.

Leon drank *ho' omana'o 'ana* just to help him savor life, to keep an album in his mind filled with sights, motion, sounds, and smells. A day like this, when the black sky nearly touched the ground and the air was soaked with water, this was a good time to sip a little *ho' omana'o 'ana*. He didn't care for those who drank "Hoom" for base, utilitarian reasons, but these were his customers. They subsidized his craft. They were the patrons of his art, and they kept Leon and his plants alive.

He gazed down and saw a gray tree frog leaping along the sidewalk. It hopped onto the lawn and stopped when it reached Leon's feet. The tiny frog looked up at Leon, and the two studied each other for over a minute. Leon stared back into the animal's bulging, dark eyes, and he watched its rough skin change from gray to green to match the lawn. The frog resumed its travel, hopping under the bench and beyond. *That was a nice image for the Hoom memory scrapbook*, Leon thought.

Next, Leon listened to the sound of tires splashing along the road as a silver sport utility vehicle approached. When he heard the familiar music of Carl Orff's *Carmina Burana* blaring from the SUV, Leon worried that the next few minutes would soon become unwanted memories. He did not listen regularly to classical music, but he knew *Carmina Burana* all too well. It was the favorite composition of one of his customers, the NFL's notorious Billy Shakin' Blake.

The SUV splashed to a stop across the street from Leon. Blake sat in the driver's seat, emotionally swaying his head to the unsettling vocals of "O Fortuna" until the piece concluded in an orchestral crescendo. When the music stopped, Blake continued to sit for a few moments longer with his eyes closed. He opened his eyes, and then he opened the car door. He stepped out of the vehicle and walked with quick, long strides toward Leon.

"I've been looking for you, Whitey," Blake said. He stood before Leon, his powerful arms crooked at his side and his fists clenched. His jersey and his slick nylon sweat pants flapped in the wind as they were soaked with rain.

"Well, I'm right here, Billy," Leon said. He tried to maintain a calm and steady tone. "What do you need?"

"You know what I need. Hand it over."

"If you're talking about Slaughter, I don't have it anymore," Leon said. "I dumped everything I had into the harbor."

"Well I guess you'd better make some more."

"I can't do that. I burned the recipe."

"I'll trust your memory."

Leon studied his hands protruding from the plastic poncho. "That won't work either. I took a mind eraser. I burned the recipe out of my memory."

"That sounds improbable," Blake said.

"But true. Slaughter is like clove cigarettes and old-school communism, Billy. It's extinct." Leon regretted his last word as soon as he spoke it.

"Then you have a problem," Blake said. He took a step closer.

Down the street, a heavy limb snapped off a tree. The crack sounded like a shotgun blast, and Leon nearly hopped off the bench. Blake also flinched, but he continued to glare down at Leon. "You got air in your lungs, Whitey?"

Leon nodded with some reluctance.

"You got air in your lungs, but I got no Rip in my blood," Blake said. "That's a violation of our agreement. You do remember our agreement, don't you, Whitey? So long as you keep me supplied with Rip, I'll keep you supplied with oxygen?"

"I remember the arrangement," Leon said.

"Well, I always keep my end of the bargain," Blake said. He thrust his right hand out toward Leon, stopping a half-inch from his neck. "You sure you don't have a few doses of Rip tucked away somewhere?"

Leon noticed two things about Blake that gave him a grain of comfort. First, Blake had flinched. Then, Blake had hesitated. The old Blake had not hesitated to strangle Leon outside of the Hegemonix Arena. The man who stood before Leon at this moment was the Blake that Leon had met months earlier. This was the Blake who had traces of timidity and uncertainty. This was the Blake who was skittish on the field, the one who needed a drug to give him courage and strength to play the game. Leon spoke cautiously as he watched the hand by his neck. "Billy. Why don't you sit down for a minute."

"I'm serious, Whitey. I'll break your neck right here and now if you don't cough up some Rip."

"I know you will. But have a seat first. Let's talk for a minute." He carefully pushed the thermos and the rice bowl off the bench and onto the lawn to make room for Blake.

Blake lowered his hand. "Damn it, Whitey!" He paced

on the sidewalk for a moment before dropping heavily onto the bench beside Leon. He sat with his elbows on his knees. As he hunched forward, rain dripped off his forehead, nose, and chin.

"How long ago did you run out of Rip?" Leon asked.

"About two weeks."

"So it's out of your system. Why do you want to put more of that poison back in yourself? I mean, you've been kicked out of the league. You don't need it for the sport anymore."

"I need Rip now more than ever," Blake said. "I'm headed to the joint for de-eyeing that ref. When I'm inside, I don't plan to be anyone's bitch."

"Come on, Billy, you don't have to worry about that," Leon said. "You're a big guy."

"The madhouse is full of big men, and all of them will be trying to build a reputation by tearing into my ass. But that won't happen so long as I have Rip in my blood."

Leon was quiet. If he were going to prison, he would want a supply of BMF too.

"So you understand my situation?" Blake asked.

Leon nodded.

"Will you help me out?"

"I told you, Billy. I can't help you. The Slaughter's gone."

Blake sat up straight and draped his right arm over Leon's shoulders. Leon chuckled uncomfortably. His discomfort increased as Blake pulled him into a headlock.

"What's going on, Billy?" Leon asked. Billy reached into one of the deep side pockets of his nylon pants with his free hand and removed an ice pick. He stuck the tip in Leon's ear.

"You and I, Whitey, we're in a world of shit, aren't we? You sure you don't have a dose or two of Rip tucked away for a rainy day?" Blake glanced at the black clouds and the deluge that pelted his face. He returned his gaze to Leon. "It doesn't rain much harder than this, Whitey."

"Let's talk a little more, Billy."

"I'm done talking. Give me all the Rip you got. Then make some more." He spun the tip of the pick in Leon's ear. "I think you'll remember the recipe before push comes to shove."

"Let him go!"

Blake looked up from Leon and saw an elderly woman dressed in a bathrobe and slippers shuffling down the sidewalk toward the bench. She used one hand to clutch her terrycloth robe against the wind and rain. With her other hand, she gripped a cleaver.

Leon strained to see the old woman without moving his head. "Mrs. Carver!" he shouted. "Go back inside!"

Bea Carver stood before Blake and waved the cleaver. "Let him go! Now!" A heavy gust of wind made her sway in the rain.

"This is a friend of mine," Leon said. "We're just fooling around. Now please go back inside."

"Leon's right," Blake said. He pulled the ice pick out of Leon's ear and stuck it in the wooden bench. "We're just fooling around."

"Now let him go!" Bea said.

Blake released Leon from the headlock. Leon straightened up on the bench and rubbed his neck. "See? We're just horsing around, Mrs. C. Get inside before you catch cold."

"That's right ma'am," Blake said as he rose to his feet. "Go on back inside where it's dry." He grabbed the old woman's wrist and pried the cleaver out of her hand. She tried to run, but Blake pulled her into his chest with his massive arm crossed over her frail body. He held the cleaver blade near her neck. "Let's all go inside and have a talk."

"Jesus, Billy! Let her go!" Leon pleaded.

"I'm finished playing around, Whitey!" Blake shouted. "Take a look at me! Look what you've done to me! Look what I've become!" Mrs. Carver trembled as Blake waved the cleaver wildly before her. "This is your doing, Whitey. You did this to me. You turned me into this monster."

"You're not a monster," Leon said. He held his hands up with his palms facing Blake, as if he were trying to cast a spell of sanity. "The Rip's out of your system. You don't need to act this way anymore."

Blake shook with bitter laughter. "How do you live with yourself, Whitey? How do you look in the mirror? You gave me a drug that turned me into a sociopath. And now that I'm going to a place where I need to be a sociopath to survive, you shut me off!" He laughed again. "How can you live with yourself?"

"I tried to warn you," Leon muttered. He looked into Blake's frightened, wild eyes. He watched Mrs. Carver quaking with terror and struggling to breathe, and he worried that she would have a heart attack at any minute. These were images he did not want to carry with him for the rest of his life. This was a bad night for drinking Hoom. "Alright," Leon said. "You're right. I have a stash. Just let Mrs. C go, and I'll give you whatever you need."

"I'll let her go when I have my Rip," Blake said. He shook his head and spoke wearily, "Why'd it have to come to this, Whitey?"

"I don't know," Leon said. "I just mess things up." He rose

slowly to his feet, careful to keep his distance from Blake so he would not be alarmed. "Let's all go inside. I'll try to fix everything."

Blake heard a car sloshing down the street. He lowered the cleaver so it could not be seen from the road, but he continued to hold Mrs. Carver by the back of her drenched bathrobe. A candy-apple red Mustang slowly approached from the left and parked at the curb before Leon's house. "Now what?" Blake muttered.

Macey Kick emerged from the Mustang and took a moment to study the group. As she stood, the rain flattened her wavy hair, and droplets collected on her lips. "How's it going, Leon? Everything okay here?"

"Get back in your car, lady," Blake said. "This doesn't concern you."

Macey walked around her Mustang and stepped onto the sidewalk. She glanced down at the cleaver Blake held at his side. "What do you got there?" she asked.

Speaking through clenched teeth, Blake warned, "Get in your car, and drive away. You have no idea what you're walking into."

"I have a pretty good idea," Macey said. "Anyone who's read a sports page in this town in the last month knows who you are, Blake. And anyone who sees you with a cleaver in one hand and an old woman in the other knows something must be wrong. As an upright citizen of this community, I can't simply turn and walk away."

"Fine," Blake said. He released Mrs. Carver.

The old woman took a few steps before she began to stumble. Leon quickly grabbed her. "I've got you, Mrs. C," he said. "We'll get you inside now." He began to help her toward her home.

"No, no, no!" Blake shouted. "Nobody goes anywhere until we've finished business."

Macey took a step toward Blake, but he quickly turned on her, swinging the cleaver before him. As she ducked under the cleaver, she spun on one heel and extended her other leg. She was trying to sweep Blake's legs out from under himself, but the running back was denser than she had anticipated. Her foot bounced off his ankle, and he remained standing. Now she was in the uncomfortable position of crouching on the sidewalk while he hovered over her.

Blake swung the cleaver at Macey's neck. She flipped onto her back and grabbed Blake's wrist as he swung the cleaver down. Using the momentum of his attack, Macey pulled him headlong into the sidewalk. Still holding his cleaver-wielding wrist, Macey writhed out from under his 240 pounds then drove her knee into his forearm three times. Each time her knee connected, she heard his radius and ulna crack. On the third blow, Blake released his grip on the cleaver, and it clattered on the concrete. She kicked the weapon away and released Blake's wrist.

Blake used his good arm to push himself up to his knees. He panted hard as he looked up at Macey. Blood, thinned by the rainwater, ran from a gash on his forehead and covered his face. "Had enough?" Macey asked.

Blake charged her, driving his shoulder into her stomach and wrapping his left arm fully around her thin waist. He hoisted her off the ground and slammed her into the bench. Two of the wooden slats cracked behind Macey's back. As she struggled to pull in air, Blake swung his fist at her jaw. She managed to deflect the blow with her forearm.

Leon released Mrs. Carver and darted for the cleaver. He lifted it off the ground and swung it onto Blake's back. The cleaver bounced off Blake without even tearing his jersey. Leon swung the cleaver down a second again, this time aiming for his head. Blake turned to see the cleaver coming at his face, and he instinctively blocked the blow with his hand. He howled and the blade sliced his palm.

Macey looked to her side and saw the ice pick stuck into the wood beside her. She plucked the pick from the bench and jammed the tip into the center of Blake's forehead, driving it a good quarter-inch into his skull. Blake howled again as he backed away from his two attackers. Macey rose from the bench, and Leon stepped forward, holding the cleaver waist level at his side. Blake continued to step backward until he bumped into Macey's Mustang. Macey held the palm of her hand over the ice pick, prepared to drive it through his skull and into his brain.

"Wait," Leon said. "See if he's had enough now."

Macey continued to keep her hand raised and her arm cocked, ready to deliver the deathblow. "Well?" she asked Blake.

Blake looked down at his sliced left hand. He turned his head to look at his broken right arm hanging limply at his side. The ice pick followed his gaze like a unicorn's horn.

"Had enough now?" Macey asked.

As Blake nodded, the handle of the ice pick bounced.

"Will you bother Leon again?"

He shook his head, and the handle quivered.

"Good. Right answers," Macey said. "Now stay still. I'm gonna take this out for you." She put one hand on Blake's head and used the other to grip the handle of the ice pick. She pushed against his forehead and yanked back on the ice pick. After a few tugs, she managed to pluck it out of his skull. Her hand still on his head, she gripped his hair and swung his face downward into her thrusting knee. She released Blake's hair, and he crumpled to the ground.

Leon looked behind him and saw Mrs. Carver sitting on the muddy lawn. She was shaking badly. "Oh my god," Leon gasped. He dropped the cleaver, raced toward Bea, and helped her to her feet. "My god, Mrs. Carver. I'm so sorry. Let me get you inside."

Mrs. Carver struggled out of Leon's grasp. When he tried to take her arm again, she slapped his hand away. "Don't touch me." Her lips quivered as she spoke. "Don't come near me again. I've misjudged you, Leon. You're a dangerous man." Leon watched with sadness as the woman doddered back toward her home. Her hair, robe, and body drooped in the downpour.

Macey rubbed her back, feeling lumps forming where Blake had thrown her into the bench. "Don't worry about the old lady," she advised Leon. "She'll get over it."

Leon shook his head. "I don't know. I don't what's going on anymore." He looked down at the clump of Blake by the edge of the road. "So what are we gonna do with him?"

"I'll make a call," Macey said. "Someone'll pick him up."

"They aren't going to . . . "

"No. They'll just dump him in a park or something. Unless you want us to . . . "

"No, no," he said. "No, he's due to be locked up soon, so I don't think I have to worry about him for a while."

"Alright then," Macey said. She tugged at Leon's poncho. "Let's get out of this goddamn rain."

Leon laughed with a sudden, wild sense of relief. "Holy shit! I hit Billy Blake with a cleaver! Did you see me?"

"Yeah, you did good, Leon. But next time, go for the face or the jugular."

"Next time!" Leon continued laughing. "Jesus, Macey, your timing was perfect. If you hadn't showed up when you did ... How did you know I was in trouble, anyhow?"

"I didn't. Did you think I drove all the way over here just to save your ass?" She smiled. "I'm here to pick you up. Your father has urgent business to discuss with you."

Macey drove Leon across Butchers Harbor to Skirmish Bluffs, where Increase lived in a renovated lighthouse on a rocky peak overlooking the city and the harbor. The wind coming off the ocean was fierce. Leon and Macey ran from the Mustang to the small porch before the lighthouse, rang the doorbell, and waited for Increase to let them inside.

"Hey kids, come on in," Increase said. He wore a striped bathrobe over a tie-dyed shirt and plaid pajama bottoms. His hair was untied and hung loose down his shoulders. "Come on in."

Leon and Macey stepped out of the rain and followed Increase into the den. Three logs and a pile of orange coals burned in a fireplace made of fat, century-old bricks. The fire and two kerosene lanterns hanging from rough oak beams filled the room with stark, writhing shadows. The walls of the den were covered with hundreds of tiny, framed photographs of faces. Some of the photos were mug shots of petty criminals. Some were glamour shots of models and actors. Leon recognized a few authors, their photos cut from the back of book jackets. Some of the faces on the wall appeared to be nothing but random photos collected from magazines and newspapers.

Leon peeled off his plastic poncho and hung it on a

wooden peg. Macey ran her fingers though her wet hair and shook rainwater onto the hardwood floor. Increase grimaced at the water collecting on the floor. "Macey, why don't you get yourself a towel?" he suggested. "The bathroom is just around the corner, past the kitchen. Dry off. Fix yourself a drink. Make yourself at home. I need a moment alone with Leon."

Macey nodded and left the den, leaving a trail of droplets.

Increase lifted a coarse Mexican blanket from a couch and handed it to Leon. "Here. Wrap yourself in this and have a seat by the fire."

A leather recliner and a simple wooden chair were set before the hearth. Leon approached the wooden chair, but Increase steered him toward the more comfortable recliner.

Increase tossed a log onto the blaze, sending embers spiraling up the chimney. He pushed his chair closer to the fireplace and sat. He was silent for a moment as he watched the flames.

"Is something wrong, Dad?"

Increase nodded. He lifted a poker and jabbed a log until it crumbled. "Your brother is in trouble," he said.

Leon struggled to suppress a grin. "What happened?"

"He's in jail. He's been charged with murder."

"Oh. Who'd they pinch him for? Swag Kilpatrick? Ivan Wazowiecki?"

"No. They say he murdered some Polish bodybuilder. Some guy named Walter Kamerowski."

"Who's he?"

"He's nobody," Increase said. "He's got no connection with our family. As far as we can tell, he's never placed a bet with a bookie. Never been to a whore. The only controlled substance he's ever bought is steroids, something we don't distribute. Wyatt had no reason to even know him the guy, never mind kill him." Increase turned away from the fire. "You want a drink or something?"

"No. No thanks," Leon said. He fidgeted in his chair. "So, *did* Wyatt kill the guy?"

"Of course not. It's a bullshit charge. The cops don't even have a body. This Kamerowski is missing, that's all." Increase sighed. "They also have a supposed witness. According to my source in the B.H.P.D., Benny Vega says he saw Wyatt shoot a man matching Kamerowski's description. Benny has some wild story that we was in the back of a van playing possum or something while Wyatt and few boys were hauling body parts to an incinerator."

"Benny was playing possum?" Leon said carefully. His pulse was quickening. "What does that mean?"

"He says he was playing dead. The boys thought they were hauling a corpse or something. I don't know. It doesn't make any sense to me either. I mean, Cracker knows what a stiff looks like. He would have taken a pulse or something. And Wyatt wouldn't even be involved in that kind of grunt work. I gave him explicit orders to avoid all incriminating activities."

"Did you talk to Cracker?"

"He says they never found Benny. He says Benny must have had help slipping out of Butchers Harbor. Which doesn't make any sense either. Why would Benny put his neck on the line coming back to the Harbor just to rat out Wyatt?"

Leon exhaled and inhaled quietly, fearful that his breathing might somehow reveal his complicity. "What does your source in the department say?"

"About what?"

"Why is Benny offering testimony?"

"He says Benny's afraid. He says Benny claimed he had some sort of traumatic experience, and he's scared out of his wits, so he's offering testimony in exchange for police protection."

Leon shook his head and muttered, "That stupid son of a bitch."

"Exactly," Increase said. "That drunken pothead mustn't have more than two brain cells left in his skull if he thinks for a minute that the B.H.P.D. can protect him from us. And I'll tell you something else, if I find out that someone helped Benny slip out of town, Wyatt's gonna have a new name for his shit list."

The pop and hiss of a burning log filled the silence. Increase sprung up from his chair and crossed the room. "I need a drink."

"Me too," Leon said.

Increase opened a liquor cabinet and removed two glasses. "Have you ever heard of anyone being arrested on such absurd testimony?" he asked. He unscrewed a bottle of Tullamore Dew and filled both glasses nearly to the top. "If the Borisovas didn't own the courts and the police these days, there wouldn't even be an arrest. Yet Wyatt is locked up without bail." Increase carried the two glasses of whiskey back to the fireplace. He handed one glass to Leon. "The whole thing is a setup and a charade orchestrated by the Borisovas to put my boy in the gas chamber."

Increase sat heavily in his chair, took a gulp of whiskey, and set his glass on the floor. "With the pull Vladimir Borisova has in the courts these days, he'll be able to stack the jury and have the judge in his pocket. Wyatt is as good as convicted and executed. That goddamn Borisova is going to kill my boy." Increase reached over and grabbed Leon's shoulder. "You have to help me, Leon. You have to help me save your brother."

Leon ran a hand through his wet hair. "Yeah, Dad, of course. I'll do whatever you want. What do you want me to do?"

Increase tightened his grip on Leon's shoulder. "Get rid of the witness."

"Get rid of the witness?" Leon repeated. "I don't understand."

"The witness is all they've got against Wyatt. No witness, no case."

Leon laughed nervously. "So what do you want me to do? Rub Benny out?"

Increase nodded.

Leon laughed again. "This is a joke, right? I mean, you have a small army of killers working for you. Why would you want me to carry out a hit?"

"We can't just put a bullet in Benny's head. The fuzz and the feds would be all over us. We'd be in worse shape than before. A traditional hit just won't do. This witness has to die of natural causes." Increase patted Leon's shoulder. "You must have some poison you can whip up. Give the witness a heart attack."

Leon gulped his whiskey. He lowered the glass and wiped his mouth with the back of his hand. The room was starting to feel a little wobbly to Leon. The tension did not agree with his Hoom buzz. "You can't ask me to do this, Dad," he said, nearly whispering. "I can't kill another human being."

"Benny no longer is a human as far as I'm concerned," Increase said. "He was a rat, and now he's a liar. He's a paid liar working for the Borisovas. Don't you get it? It was the

Borisovas that killed this Kamerowski. Think about it, Leon. Russkis and Polacks, they're practically the same thing. The Borisovas must have had some beef with the bodybuilder, so they whacked him, and now they want to pin the murder on Wyatt. To back their story up, they contacted Benny, someone who had already been supplying them with Lynch family secrets. Benny is the best witness they can get because he's supposedly working for us. It all makes sense, Leon."

"I don't know, Dad. You're making a lot of assumptions and speculations. What if Wyatt really did kill this guy? What if Benny is telling the truth? Then I'd be killing an innocent man."

Increase narrowed his eyes. "Innocent man? You're the one who got Volkov to identify Benny as one of our family's traitors. You heard it with your own ears. How can you call him an innocent man?" Increase slapped the leather armrest of Leon's chair. "For Christ's sake, Leon! How many times have you come to me, whimpering and whining that you wanted more involvement in the family business? What did you think I was going to have you do? Did you think I'd make you our purchasing manager? You know what our business is, Leon. You know what we do. Now you make a decision, right here and right now." He jabbed his index finger into Leon's arm. "Do you want to be a part of this family or not? Are you going to side with your brother, or will you side with a liar who wants to harm your family?"

Leon released a shaky sigh. "I want to belong to our family. I do. I want to be part of the business too, Dad. I want to belong to something, you know? And I want respect, starting with respect from you."

Increase leaned closer to Leon. "You want my respect? Then start acting like a man. Start acting like a Lynch. If you turn your back on us now, Wyatt will be the only son I have. If you refuse to help your family, you won't have a family. You'll be dead to me."

"Come on, Dad, don't say that," Leon said. "You have no idea how much that hurts." Leon finished the rest of his whiskey and set the glass on the armrest. The glass slid off the slick leather and shattered on the floor.

Leon stared at the broken glass at his feet. He watched the light of the flames flicker over the edges of the shards. "Sorry," he muttered. "I'll clean that up." He slumped in the chair and held his forehead with one hand. "And I'll help with Wyatt. He's my brother. You're my father. Family comes first." As the words passed his lips, Leon felt hollow. It wasn't a pleasant feeling, and he knew he would always remember it, even if he wasn't on the memory tea.

Increase patted his son's forearm. "That's my boy," he said softy. "You're doing the right thing. This was a tough decision for you, I know. But you've made the right decision. You've made a commitment to the family. Now the family will make a commitment to you. Everything changes now. No more shit detail. Now, you'll be calling the shots, Leon. I'm moving you to a position of power, starting with this assignment. I'm giving you a crew to help you take out the witness. You pick anyone you want. I suggest you take on Cracker Jack and Macey. They're the best I've got."

Leon nodded slowly.

Increase leaned closer toward Leon to study his son's sickly face. "You okay?" he asked. "You look pale. Even for you."

Leon pulled the coarse blanket up to his chin. "I'm okay."

Increase picked up the poker and turned the half-burnt log to give the fire some air. A half-burned log crumbled, and orange coals fell to the hearth. "Alright. Let's get down to some details on this operation. With the judge denying Wyatt bail, our lawyers are demanding a speedy trial. His case should be brought to court soon. So you have to get moving on this witness, okay? I want you to take the witness out the night before he's scheduled to testify. Let's catch the prosecution with their pants down. We won't give them time to react. So get your crew together, and do what you have to do."

Leon felt dizzy. He felt as if he, the leather recliner, and the entire lighthouse were plummeting down a great abyss. "Dad, let's discuss this some other time," he said hoarsely. "I need to absorb ... " He waved his hand in a weary circle.

Increase chuckled uneasily. "You can handle this, can't you, son?"

Leon nodded slowly. "I'll do what I have to do."

"Alright," Increase said. "We can wait a night to discuss the details. You've made a commitment. That's the important part." Increase returned the poker to its stand. "So, you want another drink? Huh? Why not?"

"I think I should be alone," Leon said.

"Yeah? Okay, fine," Increase said. "Yeah, you don't look so good, now that I look at you. You want Macey to drive you home?"

Leon shook his head. "I don't want to move."

"No? Alright, crash here, then," Increase said. "I'll send Macey home, and I'll turn in early tonight. I'll leave you alone to contemplate things. Is that what you want?"

Leon nodded.

"Alright," Increase said. He rose from his chair and held out his hand. Leon gave his father a weak handshake. "Welcome to the family," Increase said. "I'm proud of you."

He smiled at his son, then turned and walked out of the room.

Leon leaned closer to the fire to dry the cold sweat that had formed on his brow. He stared at the flames and tried to will a change in himself. He had to pull himself together. He belonged to a family now. He had obligations. He had a commitment to honor. He could not be a weakling any longer. He would have to transform himself to suit his new position.

7
HIT

Leon and Macey Kick sat in a corner booth in a Greek diner. The rest of the diner was filled with churchgoers stopping for lunch after Sunday services. Leon took a bite of his tuna salad on wheat and washed it down with a gulp of Bloody Mary. He checked his watch. "Where the hell's Cracker?" he asked.

Macey jerked her chin toward the entrance. Cracker Jack Farrell had just stepped through the front door, and he was making his way toward Leon and Macey. He grabbed a chair from a nearby table and set it at the end of the booth. He sat in the chair and hunched over the table. "Alright," he said. "I talked to our guy at B.H.P.D. They got Benny holed up at the Queen of Hearts motel."

"Where's that?" Leon asked.

"It's the stop'n'fuck on Mingus Ave., just before you hit the airfield. It's got a strip of ten or twelve rooms. Big card for a sign."

"Oh, yeah. I've seen the place," Leon said.

"You know which room he's in?" Macey asked.

"The last unit. End of the strip."

"Points of entry?" she asked.

"One front door. No doors between rooms. Little window in the bathroom at the back of the unit."

"Security?"

"Two cops. One each in unmarked cars. One car parked in front. The other parked in a back lot by the bathroom window."

As Leon listened to the exchange, he stirred his Bloody Mary with a celery stalk to work up bits of horseradish that had settled to the bottom. He lifted his glass and drained it in two hard swallows. Leon had never been a heavy drinker, yet here he was swilling his second drink only a few minutes into the afternoon.

A slim, well-groomed waiter with bleached hair approached Cracker. "Excuse me sir. Your seat is blocking the rear exit." Cracker glanced up at the waiter and awaited further information. The waiter chuckled apologetically. "We have to maintain clear passages to all exits in the establishment. Fire codes, you see. So if you don't mind, maybe you could just go ahead and sit in the booth with your friends, and we'll just move the chair back to the table. Okay?"

"I'll have a cheeseburger platter," Cracker said. "With a glass of milk."

"Okay, I'll get that order in for you right away, sir," the waiter said. "And about the chair..." He glanced briefly into Cracker's hard eyes. "You know what? Just go ahead and sit where you are. If there's a fire, I'm sure you'll move the chair. It's really not a big deal." He turned and walked directly to the kitchen to place Cracker's order.

"So does Benny get out of the room at all?" Leon asked.

Cracker shook his head. "Not much. From what I was told, he's afraid to look out the window. Spends all day inside with the curtains shut. Heard he's as white as you."

Leon nodded.

"What does he eat?" Macey asked.

"They bring 'im fast food, but he don't eat much."

"Does he order a regular meal?" Leon asked.

"Nah. And he's real careful to mix up which joint he's orderin' from. He must be figerin' we might poison his food. And like I said, he ain't eatin' much anyhow, so doping his food might be a dicey way to go."

"Is he still drinking?" Macey asked. She popped a stuffed grape leaf into her mouth.

Cracker snorted. "Yeah. Like a fish. But it's the same deal. He insists the cops get the booze from a different store each time they make a run, and he's erratic with his beverage choice. On any night, it could be gin, vodka, tequila, or rum. Some nights, he's even drinking sherry like he's some old broad. He ain't doin' nothing with no consistency."

"Except getting high?" Macey asked.

"Yeah, he's doin' that. Every morning it's wake and bake. Then bong hits all day long."

"The cops let him get high?" Leon asked.

Cracker shrugged.

"So where does he get his weed?" Leon asked. He looked at his empty glass. He wanted to order a third Bloody Mary, but he worried this would send a bad message to the crew. "Does he have a dealer coming to his room?"

"Nah. He must have bought a pound or two before he contacted the cops." He reached into the inside pocket of his denim jacket and removed a pack of cigarettes. He slapped the bottom of the pack against the palm of one hand.

"I guess he would stock up on the essentials," Leon said.

"He's always bought his pot a pound at a time. All for

personal consumption." Cracker shook a cigarette out of the pack and stuck it in the corner of his mouth.

Leon turned to Macey. "It sounds like we go with the weed, then."

"Sounds that way," Macey said. "You have something that'll work with pot?"

"I guess so." Leon looked out the window at the dingy sky. "I don't have a lot of experience with products that … do what we want this product to do. If we're working with reefer instead of food … I guess I could work with something in a leaf form instead of a liquid." He drummed his fingers on the table for a moment. "Yeah. I got something. I know what'll work."

"Good," Macey said. She turned back to Cracker. "Do you have names of the cops guarding the room?"

"Night watch?" Cracker asked. He lit his cigarette with a disposable plastic lighter.

Macey nodded.

"Zeldin and Brisbane."

"You know them?"

Cracker shook his head. "They both joined the force after I was canned."

"How about their watch over Benny?" Leon asked. "Do they ever leave their cars?"

"They ain't supposed to. Most cops might take a break and walk over to his buddy to shoot the shit. It's gettin' cold at night, though, so there's more incentive to sit in the car and use the two-way." Cracker flicked ash onto the floor. "My guess, the night before Wyatt's trial, neither guy'll leave his car."

Leon slid an ashtray toward Cracker. "What's their routine before their shift? Where do they get their coffee and donuts?"

"It ain't coffee and donuts for these two," Cracker said. "It's espresso and scones. These guys hang out at a coffeehouse for an hour or two before work. On their way out, they both pick up an extra-large latte to go."

"Lattes, huh?" Leon said. "Okay, I think we have something to work with. Did you get a map of the area?"

Cracker set his cigarette directly on the table a few inches from the ashtray. He reached into his jeans jacket and fished out two folded sheets of paper. One was a map of the ten blocks surrounding the motel, and the second was a satellite image of the same area. He had retrieved both images from the Internet. Cracker returned his cigarette to his mouth as he unfolded the sheets and set them on the table before Leon.

Leon quietly studied the map. "Alright, let's form a plan," he said.

Officer Zeldin sat on a tall stool set on a small stage before an audience in the Own Zone Coffeehouse. He wore a sweater with thick blue and black horizontal stripes, a black leather vest, black khakis, and sandals. His hair was just long enough to be tied in a short ponytail, and he had a neatly trimmed goatee the size of a guitar pick under his lower lip. He was dressed for plainclothes duty, but he wore his badge on a long strap around his neck. The badge and his sidearm glinted in the dim spotlight suspended over the stage.

A cigarette dangled from Zeldin's lower lip as he looked lazily over the crowd. "The name of my next poem is 'Junkie Girl.'" He glanced at a scrap of paper in his hand and began to read:

KILL WHITEY

Junkie Girl, Junkie Girl,
  wasted from your last Score,
    lying on a Basement floor,
      you are not Breathing anymore.

Needle Dangling from your arm,
  still holds the Poison that did you Harm.
    You are not breathing, Junkie Girl.

I Put a Plastic airway tube over your Mouth,
  between your lips as cold as Ice,
    and I breathe through the Resuscitation device.

One Breath, Two Breaths, Five Breaths, Ten,
  I blow through the Mouth-to-Mask
  over and over again.
    Still You Do Not Breathe.

Twenty, Forty, Fifty Breaths.
  Damn you! I have seen too many Deaths!
    Junkie Girl, I must Breathe for you!

My lungs ache. My Shirt is Soaked with perspiration.
  Yet on I Struggle to Renew your Respiration.

Yes! Now I See your chest Rise and fall,
  as your Spirit Stirs to heed Life's call.

Junkie Girl, you Breathe! My job is done.
Junkie Girl, now we Breathe as one.

KEN HARVILL

The poet's partner, Officer Brisbane, leapt to his feet and clapped loudly. Brisbane had wild, electric-blue eyes and spiky bleached-bond hair with black roots. He wore a Harrington jacket over a T-shirt with the blue, white, and red Mod target. The rest of the Own Zone offered only a tepid smattering of applause. From the corner of the coffeehouse, someone shouted through a concealing hand, "Fuck you, pig!" A few of the younger people in the audience snickered.

Officer Zeldin scoffed forgivingly and shook his head. "Man, some of you cats just don't get it," he said. "You just don't get it." He folded the paper he had been reading and tucked it into his breast pocket. The next poem he recited from memory:

> when trouble knocks on your door,
>   thump thump thump,
> and the knights in blue arrive to rescue you,
>   will you call me pig?
> when I save your petit-bourgeois ass,
>   will you call me pig?
>
> others have said this before me,
>   yet I will say it again:
> for me, P.I.G. stands for
>   Pride
>   Integrity
>   Guts.

Officer Brisbane slapped his hands together in booming claps. "Right on, Zeldin! Right on, brother! Set 'em straight, man!"

KILL WHITEY

Officer Zeldin stepped off the stage. He glared coolly at the crowd as he sauntered to his booth. When he sat at the table, Officer Brisbane smiled and said, "Nice work, man. You're making them think." Brisbane tapped the side of his head with two fingers. "You're making them think, man."

Leon Lynch and Macey Kick sat at a table near the cash register. Macey had pulled her hair in a ponytail through a baseball cap, making her look several years younger. Her features were disguised under heavy makeup. Leon wore baggy pants and an open flannel shirt over a Jimmy Cliff T-shirt. Like Macey, he wore makeup; his face and other exposed skin were the color of a light coffee. His short white dreadlocks were tucked under a wig of slightly longer, black dreads. Blue-tinted sunglasses disguised his light violet eyes. Leon felt good with the artificial pigmentation. He toyed with the idea of wearing this getup on other occasions.

Leon sipped a cappuccino as he watched the officers.

"Stop looking at them," Macey said.

"Sorry," Leon said. He shifted his attention from the officers to Macey. Their eyes met for a brief moment before Leon glanced away.

"You nervous?" Macey asked. She nibbled at a slice of banana nut bread.

Leon shrugged. "I don't know."

"Everything should go fine," Macey said. She pulled a compact mirror from her purse and applied a little more lipstick. As she did, she watched the policemen in the booth behind her. "Those boys better shake a leg, or they'll be late for their shift."

Leon nodded, careful not to look in the officers' direction. He reached into his pants pocket and pulled out a small bottle of pills. Holding the plastic canister with one hand, he deftly popped off the childproof cap with his fingertips. He shook a pair of pills onto his tongue and swallowed them without water.

Macey folded her compact and returned it to her purse. "What are you taking?" she asked.

"A couple of Vicodens," Leon said.

Macey arched an eyebrow. "We want to keep our wits tonight," she said.

"Yeah. That's why I'm taking a couple of Vicodens. If they sold beer in this dump, I'd have a couple of those too."

"I thought the only drugs you took were the ones you grew yourself."

"Well, that used to be the case, but lately I'm doing all kinds of things I never used to do."

Macey rolled her eyes. "Are you sure you're up for this, Leon?"

"I have to be. My father's depending on me."

"Your father could manage without you. If you want my opinion, he shouldn't be asking you to do this."

"I'm glad he came to me. I'm glad my father needs me." Leon picked a piece of nut bread off Macey's plate. "You'd have to have a family to understand."

Macey smiled. She had been spending more time with Leon as the two were planning the operation to silence Benny One Too Many. They met often at Leon's home. When they we weren't discussing the operation, Macey questioned Leon about his past travels and his collection of plants. In return, Macey revealed small pieces of information regarding her secretive past. Her biggest disclosure, something she hoped Leon would keep between them, was that she was an orphan. She had been raised in a series of difficult foster homes and bleak institutions. "You'd have to have a family to understand," she said, mocking Leon's arrogant tone. "You're charming when you're on prescription painkillers."

"I didn't mean it like that," Leon said. "Families are over-rated. 'Family' is just a corporate concept designed to sell greeting cards." The Vicoden was already kicking in. He fidgeted and looked around the coffee shop. "Macey, do you ever get tired of this life?" he asked. "Do you ever wish you were doing something else?"

"Like what?"

Lone shrugged. "Well, for one thing, do you think you'll ever leave Butchers Harbor? I mean, what if you could just travel the world, like on a permanent vacation?"

"Like you used to do?" Macey asked.

"Yeah."

"Are you asking me to travel the world with you?"

Leon shrugged. He was feeling cocky and loose thanks to his costume and a steady intake of painkillers throughout the day. He knew Macey was trying to embarrass him, but he played along. "Sure, why not? I had good times travelling. I saw some cool places. Met some interesting people."

"I already have traveled the world," Macey said. "Like you, I've seen some 'cool' places. And I've met some interesting people. Some of those people had a shorter life after we were introduced, but it was still nice to meet them."

"Yeah? So let's take it up again. You and me, a couple of world travelers. Screw this job. Screw my family. What did they ever do for me?"

"I guess I'd have to have a family to understand," Macey said flatly. "Now stop acting weird. We have a job to do, so pull your shit together. After we hit Benny, we can make travel plans." Macey checked her compact again and saw that the officers were rising from their table. "Alright. It looks like Ginsberg and Kerouac are on the road. Let's get started."

Brisbane and Zeldin sauntered past Leon and Macey. The two officers were engaged in a mild argument comparing the merits of Sartre and Derrida. The cashier saw the officers approaching, and she began to prepare their latte grandes to go. Leon and Macey rose lazily from their table and ambled toward the two cops. When the cashier had placed the officers' cups on the counter, Macey triggered a remote control hidden in her purse. Three loud, popping explosions sounded from the women's room. Officers Zeldin and Brisbane spun from the counter and drew their weapons. "Police officers! Everyone hit the floor!" Zeldin shouted. The cool crowd in the Own Zone erupted in panic as customers dove under their tables. The cashier scrambled for cover under a glass display case, flattening biscotti and lemon-ginseng muffins under her body.

The two officers slowly approached the women's room. "This is the police!" Zeldin shouted when they had reached the door. "Drop your weapon and come out with your hands up!"

When no one answered, Zeldin kicked the door open, and the two men entered the bathroom. Their chins touched their biceps as they aimed their weapons before them. The patrons were either cowering with their faces to the floor or watching the bathroom, waiting for more gunfire. No one noticed Leon and Macey as they lifted the lids off the officers' to-go cups and spiked their coffees with a viscous, milky fluid that slowly seeped into the latte foam.

Officer Zeldin stepped out of the women's room, holstering his pistol. "All right, everybody. False alarm." There was a general murmur of relief among the crowd as they climbed out from under their tables.

Officer Brisbane stepped alongside his partner. "Somebody had the bright idea to set off some firecrackers." A few of the kids snickered. Brisbane narrowed his wild eyes. "Yeah, real funny stuff. Now I'm sure all of you are aware that class C fireworks are illegal in this state. I guess that doesn't bother you, whoever you are. What you may not know is that these fireworks were probably made by some poverty-stricken twelve-year-old girl in China who risks blowing up her fingers every day so you can have some juvenile entertainment. I hope you're proud of yourself."

Officer Zeldin shook his head. "Funny stuff, man. Big laughs."

The two officers scowled at the crowd as they made their way back to the register to pay for their lattes. The cashier climbed out of the display case. Cheesecake covered her clothes. Leon and Macey had already slipped out the front door.

Officer Zeldin sat in his patrol car, staring blankly before him at the door to Benny Vega's room at the Queen of Hearts Motel. Occasionally, he glanced around the parking lot for any newcomers or suspicious behavior. On the neon sign for the motel, a trampy queen of hearts opened and closed one eye in an endless series of winks. Neighbor kids had smashed out several of the neon letters, so the sign advertised the motel as the "Queen of _ea_t_ M_ _e_."

Zeldin was unusually tired. He took a gulp from his cup of latte. The caffeine wasn't helping much tonight. If anything, he seemed to be getting sleepier. He closed one eye and watched the motel with the other. *I'll just let half of my body sleep*, he thought. *Then when I'm half-rested, I'll switch and let the other half sleep.* As Zeldin tried to allow his left side to fall asleep, he sipped some more coffee to keep the other half awake. He lowered the coffee to his lap, and the cup slipped out of his hand, spilling lukewarm latte in his crotch. Zeldin watched the coffee cup fall to the floor, and he wondered how he would stay awake without the caffeine. As he slumped forward, a thin line of drool seeped over his lip and collected in his tiny goatee.

Across the street from the motel, Cracker Jack Farrell sat in a pickup parked in the far corner of an adult bookstore parking lot. He was watching Officer Zeldin through night-vision binoculars. He lowered the binoculars and sent a pre-programmed text message over a stolen cell phone: "Candle 1 out."

Leon sat in a fast food restaurant a half-block down the street from the motel. He replied to the text message he had received from Cracker. "Thank you." He then sent a message to Macey's phone: "Candle 2?"

Macey was crouched behind an embankment for train tracks running behind the motel. Her cell phone vibrated at her side. She replied to Leon with her own text message: "Still flickering." She felt foolish using the code Leon had developed for this operation. However, Increase had made it clear that Leon's orders were to be followed to the letter. She raised her night-vision binocs and watched Brisbane crack his window for some fresh air. He took a series of deep breaths, shook his head, and drank some more coffee. He took a deep, desperate gulp. He lowered the coffee, and his head rolled to the side, flattening his blond spikes against the window. His irises glazed as his eyelids slowly drooped shut. Macey sent her text message: "Candle 2 out."

KILL WHITEY

Leon was chatty in his response to Cracker and Macey: "Watch candles 1 minute. Then we cut cake. Minute starts now." He piled his empty paper cup and burger wrapper onto his plastic tray and dumped them in a trashcan on his way out of the restaurant. As he walked down the poorly lit street toward the motel, he nervously checked inside his black backpack and saw the night-vision goggles and a plastic bag of the product. He approached the motel from the end farthest from the office and headed for the lot on the backside of the rooms. As he approached Benny's unit, he pulled the hood of a black sweatshirt over his head. He had abandoned his costume from the coffeehouse, but he had kept the dark makeup on his skin for better night cover.

Macey and Cracker Jack were already waiting by the back bathroom window. Leon was about to examine Brisbane to verify that he was out, but Macey held Leon's chin to keep him facing the motel. "Don't show your face to the car," she whispered. "It may have a camera."

Cracker removed a glasscutter from his duffel bag and cut a circle of glass out of the pane. He reached through the hole and unlocked the window. Then he slowly lifted the sash, careful to avoid any noise. Macey crawled through the window first, and Leon followed. Macey already had her night-vision goggles on as Leon squirmed through the window. She first took his backpack, then helped Leon lower himself to the bathroom floor without making a racket. She waited as Leon put on his own goggles.

Cracker was too big to fit through the window, so he stayed outside. He returned the glasscutter to his duffel bag and removed a putty knife, which he used to carefully pry away the old, cracked putty that surrounded the window-pane with the cut-hole.

Macey crept to the edge of the bathroom and listened. All she could hear were Benny's snoring and the grating buzz of the small refrigerator. She gestured for Leon to follow her into the room. Seeing the room in the murky green of the night-vision, Leon navigated his way between the bed and a dresser covered with scratches and cigarette burns. Empty beer cans littered the floor. A half-filled glass of rum sat on the nightstand, and Benny was sprawled on the mattress facedown in the pillow.

Leon and Macey began a quiet search of the room, silently opening drawers and rummaging among clothes. Macey found a gallon-size freezer bag of marijuana in an underwear drawer and carried it over to Leon. He removed a large baggie of his own from his backpack and set it on the dresser. After scooping half of Benny's stash into his backpack, Leon combined the crushed leaves from his own bag into Benny's shake. He mixed the bag well so One Too Many would be sure to smoke some of the new leaves.

Macey found a bong tucked behind the nightstand. She checked the bowl to make sure Benny did not have a hit already packed for the morning. He didn't. They carefully tucked the bag of weed back under Benny's underwear and stepped back into the bathroom, where Cracker had already removed the windowpane. Leon and Macey squirmed through the window, back onto the parking lot outside. They removed their goggles, tucked them in the backpack, and strolled away from the motel toward the fast food restaurant where Leon had parked a rented car. Cracker stayed behind. He removed a pane of glass loosely wrapped in newspaper from the duffel bag and began to putty it in place in the bathroom window.

Leon and Macey climbed into the rented sedan. Leon

took the wheel and Macey sat beside him. Leon drove slowly down the road, and neither he nor Macey spoke until they were on the highway. Finally, Macey said, "Well, that was easy enough. As long as Benny fires up his bong tomorrow morning, we should be all set."

"Right," Leon said.

Macey turned on the radio and tuned it to an oldies station. Louis Jordan sang, "Let the Good Times Roll."

"You did a good job, Leon," Macey said. "Not bad at all for your first hit."

"Thanks." Leon was seized with the same dizzy, plummeting feeling he had experienced in his father's lighthouse. He struggled to keep the car from hitting a guardrail. He tried to shake his nausea and regain his composure. *I'm fighting for my family,* he told himself. *This is what we do. I can handle this. This is who I am.*

8
ACID TEST

Wyatt spent most of his trial slumped in his chair as he doodled on a yellow legal pad. Occasionally, he would take a break from his scribbles to yawn, stretch, or check his watch. During a detailed forensic presentation, he entertained the jury by pulling off his thin tie, undoing two buttons of his burgundy shirt, and laying his head on the table for a nap. His lumpy attorney spent most of the proceedings blowing his nose and hacking great blobs of phlegm into a handkerchief. Neither man seemed particularly concerned with the trial, which was remarkable since things did not seem to be going Wyatt's way.

The prosecution had presented the testimony of Helen Kamerowski, the wife of the allegedly murdered man. She had testified that her husband, Walter, had not been seen by her or any of their friends or relatives for three and a half months. She offered further testimony extolling the virtues of Walter Kamerowski, including his dedication to her and their children. During cross-examination, Wyatt's lawyer, Lester Funk, tried to establish a history of discord between Walter and Helen. He referred to police records documenting three occasions when the police were called to the Kamerowski residence to settle domestic disputes. Funk badgered the woman until she admitted that her husband did have a tendency to provoke fights, was often violent, and had abused both alcohol and steroids. Funk suggested that Walter Kamerowski was the sort of unstable man who might very well abandon his wife and children. Furthermore, he implied, if anyone had a motive to murder Kamerowski, it just might be someone who was forced to live with this abusive man.

Forensic scientists testified for the prosecution that traces of human blood had been detected on the parking lot outside of an incinerator shop where Benny One Too Many claimed Wyatt had taken several bodies, including Kamerowski's, for destruction. State police offered evidence that tentatively linked the owner of the incinerator shop to the Lynch organized crime family. However, scientists hired by the defense testified that, although the blood sample in the parking lot was in an advanced stage of decomposition, the DNA almost certainly was not a match for Walter Kamerowski. Moreover, the defense argued, the incinerator shop was frequently used to destroy amputations and other medical waste from several hospitals; therefore, the suggestion that human blood was proof of foul play was simply an absurd charge.

Increase sat in the gallery just behind his son. He wore a sleek aloe-green suit over an aqua shirt with no tie. His hair was oiled and pulled back in a ponytail. Wyatt's wife, Tina, sat at the end of the row dressed in a style of business attire that women wore in pornos or television shows about lawyers: a tight jacket, a low-cut blouse, and a skirt with a hemline just below her crotch. Leon was the frumpiest member of the defendant's family. His suit was rumpled and out-of-fashion. His complexion was a few shades paler than normal, and the rings under his eyes were a few tints inkier. A large stress-zit had formed on the side of his nose. Leon imagined the pimple was a beacon drawing the attention of anyone who looked his way. In fact, many people were looking in his direction. A pack of journalists was seated to the right of the family. At critical moments in the trial, the reporters would turn and watch the family to gauge their reactions.

Leon leaned toward his father and muttered, "This Judge Rivera seems awfully biased against Wyatt. I think it's clear she's on the take with the Borisovas."

Increase nodded toward the journalists in the courtroom. "Don't worry. We still have a few hacks working for our family. They'll get that point across for us." Increase leaned closer to his son and whispered, "Besides, I think the prosecution is about ready to realize they no longer have their star witness. Get ready to act surprised."

As if he was following Increase's cue, the prosecutor, Dennis Calloway, approached the bench and said, "The prosecution would like to call Mr. Benicio Vega."

There was a silent pause as the court waited for Benny to approach the witness stand. Wyatt looked up from the scribbles on his legal pad, turned to his lawyer, and snickered. Returning his attention to his artwork, he picked up a red pen and drew little drips of blood along the blade of a guillotine.

The door at the rear of the court opened, and Benny One Too Many walked down the aisle toward the bench. He was dressed in a shiny blue suit with unbuttoned French cuffs and oversized lapels spilling out of the jacket. He was paler and thinner than he had been three months earlier, but otherwise, he seemed to be in fine health. He tried to avoid eye contact with the Lynches as he approached the witness stand. Benny was particularly unnerved by Wyatt's hostile glare; he was relieved when Wyatt shifted his angry gaze toward his half brother.

Increase cleared his throat and glanced sidelong at Leon. Leon stared directly ahead, focusing his attention on Judge Rivera's mound of thickly moussed hair. He tried to dry the sweat off his hands by rubbing his palms on the knees of his pants. Increase pressed his shoulder against Leon's and whispered, "Why is Vega alive?" He glanced at the journalists and smiled sweetly.

"I don't know," Leon whispered. He continued to stare toward the front of the courtroom. "Maybe he skipped his bong hit this morning."

"This wasn't supposed to happen," Increase said. "We were counting on you, Leon."

Benny sat beside the judge and placed his hand on a Bible that a bailiff presented before him. When the bailiff asked him if he swore to tell the truth, Benny answered, "Ring Dings."

The bailiff looked up at Judge Rivera, who shrugged and nodded her assent.

Dennis Calloway approached the witness. He ran his fingers through his neatly trimmed hair and positioned himself so the jury would see the best profile of his handsome face. "Sir, would you please state your name?"

"Blister Twister," said Benny.

"I beg your pardon?" the prosecutor asked.

"Mister Blister Twister to you, Moody Doodie."

Calloway cleared his throat. "I, um…Your name is Benicio Vega."

"We know his name," Judge Rivera snapped. "Move on."

"Right," Calloway said. "So, Mr. Vega, please describe to the court your association with the defendant, Mr. Wyatt Lynch."

Benny nodded solemnly and said, "*Bebo cerveza porque me cago en la leche.*"

Calloway smiled patiently. "Could you repeat that in English for those of us who aren't bilingual?"

"Fetch the bone, homegrown. Me and Mary Jane did the boogy woogy 'til the kazoo turned blue. You dig? Conjunction Junction all night long, motherfucker." Benny licked his fingertips and smoothed one of his bushy eyebrows. "Lock, stock, post hoc ergo pop rock."

Calloway stared blankly at the witness. "Come again?"

Benny laughed. "Yeah, I'm flying all over the world!"

Calloway leaned toward the judge and whispered, "Your honor, I think we have a problem."

Judge Rivera pretended to cough. As she held her hand over her thin lips, she muttered, "Stop talking to me and get his goddamn testimony."

Benny winked at the judge and asked, "Is he fizzy, Miss Lizzy?"

Calloway glanced with some embarrassment toward the jury before he stepped back toward Benny. Clasping his hands before him, Calloway said, "Mr. Vega. Please tell us—in English, in the clearest possible terms, without any slang or jargon that might be unfamiliar to some us here in the courtroom—please describe to us the events you witnessed on July 13th, the night of Mr. Kamerowski's disappearance."

"I am ready, and I am willing, and I am able to wammy the jammy. All I need is a mammary." Benny clapped his hands twice, snapped his fingers once, and pointed two fingers back at Calloway.

Dennis Calloway wiped a film of sweat from his forehead. "Your honor, I'm having a little trouble understanding the witness."

"Get his testimony in writing," Judge Rivera said.

"What?"

"I believe the witness is nervous," Rivera said. "I believe he is intimidated by the notoriety of the person against whom he is testifying. And I believe this is making him tongue-tied. Perhaps he can express himself more clearly in writing."

Lester Funk stood from his seat. He snorted loudly, swallowed a gob of snot, and objected, "Your honor, this is highly irregular."

"So are you," the judge said, "but you don't see me delaying this court's proceedings. Now zip it, or I'll hold you in contempt."

The bailiff and a few of the reporters snickered.

Rivera turned back to the prosecutor. "Come on, get his testimony so we can wrap this up."

"Right," Calloway said. He presented a legal pad and a pen to Benny. He looked pleadingly into the witness's glassy eyes and said, "Mr. Vega. Please tell us, in writing, how you know Wyatt Lynch. Also, tell us where you were late in the evening on July 13th, and describe anything unusual that you witnessed." Calloway glanced up to the judge, and she nodded her approval.

Benny hunched over the pad and wrote furiously for five minutes. He tapped the pen against his mouth as he proofread his work, made three corrections, and handed the pad back to Calloway. The prosecutor looked at the pad and muttered, "Oh shit."

Funk rose from his chair, waddled up to Calloway, and looked over the prosecutor's shoulder so he could see Vega's testimony. Funk laughed loudly as he snatched the legal pad from Calloway's hands. Despite the prosecutor's efforts to restrain him, Funk managed to display the legal pad to both the jury and the bank of reporters.

Judge Rivera sounded two sharp raps with her gavel. "Back in your seat, counselor! You are clearly out of order!"

Lester Funk ignored the judge, and said, between coughs, "Ladies and gentlemen, I present the witness's testimony." Vega had drawn a border of arrows and saw-toothed waves around the edge of the legal pad. Inside this frame were five columns of crudely drawn male and female genitalia.

Rivera rapped her gavel again and barked at Wyatt's lawyer, "Get back in your seat, Mr. Funk, or I will hold in contempt of court!"

Funk smirked as he handed the pad back to Calloway. "Good work, counselor," he said. He swaggered back to his chair and patted Wyatt's shoulder. "This is in the bag," he whispered.

Dennis Calloway threw the legal pad to the floor. He turned to the witness and said, "Mr. Vega, why don't you just point to the person who shot and killed Kamerowski?"

"Objection!" Funk shouted as he lumbered out of his seat. "The prosecution is testifying for the witness."

"Settle down, Mr. Funk," Judge Rivera warned.

"I will not!" Funk said. "I demand that the court consider the actual testimony of this witness. I demand that the jury consider the incoherent ranting of this unbalanced man." Funk snatched the legal pad from the floor and held it before the jury. "This is the witness's testimony!" Funk pointed at one of the penis scribbles. "This is what the witness saw the night Walter Kamerowski disappeared!" Funk coughed as he walked away from the jury and displayed the scribbles to the reporters. "I appeal not only to the jury, but also to the vigilant press and the very citizens of Butchers Harbor to witness this, the testimony against my client. I was prepared to call to the stand a veritable parade of witnesses who would testify that Mr. Bencicio Vega is a thief, and an alcoholic, and a habitual drug user. However, no testimony can be more damning to this supposed witness than his own demented gibberish uttered in this very court!"

Judge Rivera banged her gavel, but Funk ignored her. He wheezed as he pulled in more air to conclude his argument. "Clearly, Mr. Vega is a deeply disturbed man. Clearly! Whatever he believes he saw or heard existed only within his delusional mind. Yet, the entire case against my client is based on the testimony of this deranged man." Funk pointed a shaky finger at Benny.

The confused witness scratched his ear. He looked sadly at the lawyer and tried to explain. "I got ballistic mistletoe in my pocket."

Funk shook his head. "What *legitimate* court could possibly consider the delusions and hallucinations of a raving lunatic as evidence against a defendant?" Funk breathed heavily. "I demand in the name of justice that this witness be dismissed, and I demand that the case against my client be dropped at once!"

Judge Rivera banged her gavel and pointed it at Funk. "Sit down and shut your mouth!" She heard the scribble of the reporters taking notes and the rustle of court artists sketching her angry face. A blood vessel burst in the corner of her eye. "I call a recess," she said. "Counselors, in my chambers! Now!"

Increase Lynch stood outside on the metal walkway that

ringed the tower of his lighthouse. He puffed a cigar and listened to the tobacco crackle. He exhaled the Cuban smoke and inhaled it again through his nose. The rhythm of weak waves rolling ashore competed with the noise of a party inside the house below. Wyatt had been acquitted, and the family was celebrating with a spontaneous post-trial party. Increase was happy for Wyatt, but he was not in a celebratory mood. He was preoccupied with his other son. Leon was a good boy, he thought. Increase still did not know what Leon had done exactly to sabotage Benny's testimony, but he was pleased with the results. Leon did have something to offer the family after all, and Increase regretted the years he had neglected and underestimated the boy. He felt like a bad father.

As Increase considered the matter, he decided he wasn't a bad father; he was a horrible father. What kind of scum would order his own child to murder another human being? Increase was filled with self-loathing. He was grateful that Leon had defied him and allowed Benny to live. Leon's peaceful solution reminded Increase of his own idealism he had held when he was young.

Increase had inherited his father's business in 1967, the Summer of Love. America was in the midst of social revolution. Kids were marching for civil rights and putting flowers in riffle barrels. The youth were discovering personal liberation through drugs and free love. It was a beautiful time. Increase had tried to carry the spirit of the sixties into his newly acquired enterprises. It made sense. He represented the underground economy, the businesses that served the people and defied the oppressive laws of the government. If people wanted reefer, acid, or smack, they should have the freedom to get it, and Increase would ensure their rights to elevated states of consciousness. He supported the feminist movement by granting women the opportunity to earn a living sharing their sexuality. He would not tolerate the government's attempts to control how a woman could use her body. Moreover, he supported sexual equality by ensuring that any individual—regardless of physical appearance, social skills, or personal hygiene—could enjoy the natural gift of sex at a reasonable price. He also fostered ties with the proletariat. Working with transportation and construction unions, he helped the working men of Butchers Harbor bring the fat cats to their knees.

Increase had never wanted violence to be a part of his enterprises. His brother and his father had been violent men, and they had died violent deaths. Timmy Lynch died in the tit-for-tat cycle of revenge that was all too common among his breed of businessmen. Paddy Lynch had been so steeped in blood that he had been driven to destroy himself when no one else could get the job done. Increase wanted to learn from the mistakes of his family. He wanted to believe that there were alternatives to murder and mayhem.

Unfortunately, competing gangs were entrenched in the status quo, and they would not let go of violence as a tool of trade. So, Increase reluctantly relied on the savage skills of his buddy Swag Kilpatrick to deal with those in Butchers Harbor who refused to give peace a chance. It was an uneasy alliance, however. Increase worried that his aversion to brutality put him in a weak position; he worried that Swag might take advantage of his soft heart to usurp power. Increase was privately relieved to see antisocial tendencies in his son Wyatt. When Wyatt was old enough to participate in the family trade, Increase was willing to delegate some of the messier matters of industry to the boy.

Regrettably, Wyatt grew up to be an extremist. His unrestrained belligerence seemed to be destroying the family. The war with the Borisovas was supposed to protect the family from unwanted competition. Instead, the bloodshed was putting the family out of business. Their ranks were thinning, and they were losing their best contacts. All the police, judges, and the rest that Increase had worked so hard to buy were turning their backs on the family. After a few more years of this, Increase would have nothing left.

Leon's recent actions reminded Increase that there was another way. He had ordered Leon to kill Benny. Instead, Leon had allowed the witness to live, and things could not have worked out better for the family. Leon chose a more peaceful path, and that path lead to positive resolution. Increase believed he had more to learn from his forgotten son.

Increase stepped off the gallery and into the beacon room of the lighthouse. When he had bought the lighthouse, Increase had removed the beacon and installed a Jacuzzi and small bar at the top of the tower. He stepped behind the bar and fixed a fresh shaker of martinis. There was a knock at the door. "Come on in," Increase said.

The arched wooden door swung open, and Leon and Wyatt stepped inside. Each brother gravitated toward points in the circular room that were farthest from the other.

"Macey said you wanted to see us," Wyatt said.

Increase studied his sons standing on opposite ends of the room. "Look at you two," he said. "You're like a pair a magnets. Only you're both turned the wrong way so that you repel each other." He held up his hands with the palms facing each other and separated. "I need to turn one of you around so that the right ends are lined up. That way, the two of you will be drawn together." He twisted one hand so the knuckles of the right faced the palm of the left, and he slapped the back of his right hand into his left palm.

As the brothers contemplated the implications of this metaphor, Increase stepped around the bar and gave Wyatt a bear hug. "Congratulations, my boy! Thank God you dodged that bullet!" He slapped Wyatt on the back and moved on to Leon. As he embraced his younger son, he said, "And Leon! Job well done! Excellent work, my boy! I'm so goddamn proud of you." He waved toward three stools by the bar. "Have a seat, kids. Let's have a drink."

They took their places at the bar, Increase seated between his sons. He lifted the shaker and filled the three martini glasses before him. Slivers of ice circled in the vodka as Increase dropped a thin red chili pepper into each glass. "To Wyatt's acquittal," he said, raising his glass.

"Here, here," Leon said, clinking the surrounding glasses.

Wyatt sullenly participated in the toast, as if raising his glass was hard labor. He tossed back the martini with a bit more vigor.

Increase patted Leon on the back and squeezed his shoulder. "Leon, my boy. I can't get over Benny's testimony. It was beautiful. Absolutely beautiful. I was waiting for Benny to start singing scat." Increase laughed as he recalled the moment. "So tell me, Leon, what did you do to him?"

"I mixed some aphasia leaves in with his pot," Leon said. "I had meant to turn him into a mute. I didn't expect him to be able to say anything, but the leaves must have had some kind of funny interaction with the weed he was smoking. He was able to speak, but he could only speak gibberish. Weird, huh?"

"Weird but perfect," Increase said. "I'd say an insane witness has less credibility than a mute one."

Wyatt snorted.

"Do you have something you'd like to add?" Increase asked.

Wyatt sulked for a moment before he spoke. "Whitey was supposed to kill that piece of shit. He took a gamble on my life with his antics. This is not an appropriate time to be sucking his dick."

"Wyatt, if that man had been killed by a stray meteor, we would have been blamed. Leon's plan was better." Increase leaned toward Leon and gave him a stern look. "However, son, I am not happy that you changed our plans without my permission."

"I'm sorry, Dad."

"You should be. The chain of command is important in any well-run organization. You need to obey orders." Increase's stern countenance softened. "To be fair, though, if you had asked to keep the man alive, I would have said no. What you did turned out for the best, so it's all water under the bridge as far as I'm concerned. I've learned something from the incident. I hope you have too."

"I have," Leon said.

"Good," Increase said. "This family has been having problems lately, and I blame myself. I've been a lax leader. I've delegated too many responsibilities, and I haven't ruled with a firm hand. However, that will change tonight. I want there to be no mistake: I am a benevolent but absolute dictator of this family."

Leon nodded. "Understood."

Increase turned toward his oldest son. "Wyatt?"

"What?"

"Do you understand that I run this family?"

"Sure, Dad. You're in charge." He gave his father a sarcastic salute.

"Good. I'm glad that's clear in everyone's mind," Increase said. He stepped away from the bar and walked to the edge of the room. He clasped his hands behind his back as he looked out the window, out to the dark ocean horizon that blended with the smoggy sky. "Every successful ruler has relied on competent advisors to help him reach and implement his decisions. An effective leader needs skilled officers to help him manage his empire. I'm no different." He turned to face his eldest. "Wyatt, you are my chief advisor in matters of war, discipline, enforcement, and defense. That hasn't changed. However, I am making a few changes to the organizational chart."

The muscle on Wyatt's jaw began to twitch.

"I have a new advisor," Increase continued. "I will call on a second advisor who will counsel me in matters of public relations, diplomacy, and joint ventures. My advisor in these areas will be Leon. He demonstrated a genuine gift handling Benny One Too Many. I'll need more of Leon's help as we pursue a cease-fire with the Borisovas."

Leon grinned broadly. "Thanks, Dad."

"A cease-what!" Wyatt stood abruptly, and his barstool clattered to the floor. "What the fuck are you talking about?"

Increase held up his hand to silence Wyatt. "We've tried war, and it isn't working. We're only making our family weaker. We're going to have to learn to live with the Borisovas if we want to survive. We've enjoyed a monopoly for years, but there is plenty of vice in Butchers Harbor to support two families. If we work with the Borisovas, we can form a partnership to keep out any additional competition."

Wyatt grabbed his hair with two hands as he paced the length of the room.

Increase sighed and directed his attention to younger son. "Leon, I want you to work with Macey to arrange a sit-down with the Borisovas. You listen closely to Macey. She can teach you a lot."

Leon nodded. "Yeah, I know. She's . . . She's something else."

"I want you involved too, Wyatt," Increase said. "We'll need your input on our terms for a cease-fire."

Wyatt lowered his hands from his head. His heavily gelled hair stood up in wild shocks. "Great. I'm glad you still need my fucking 'input.'"

Increase held his chin in his hand as he studied his boys. "Well, I suppose we can discuss all this in more detail at another time. There is one last matter we need to discuss, though. How do you want you want to handle the Benny situation?"

Wyatt uprighted the fallen stool and sat at the bar. "I'm already taking care of it." He snatched the shaker and refilled his glass.

"How?" Increase asked.

"I called our guy at B.H.P.D. They're booting One Too Many out of witness protection. His testimony was garbage, so they figure he didn't live up to his end of the bargain. I got Cracker waiting outside of the Queen of Hearts to pick him up as soon as the pigs end their watch."

Leon waited apprehensively for his father's response.

"Okay," Increase said. "Pick him up and bring him to a secure location for questioning. We ought to find out who helped him slip out of town. And we need to be sure he plans to keep him mouth shut."

"Oh, he'll keep his mouth shut," Wyatt said. "Or let's just say he won't be talking to anyone. Technically, I don't think he'll actually have a mouth when I'm done with him."

"There you go again, Wyatt," Increase scolded. "Thinking like your old, angry self. Haven't you learned anything from your arrest? Let me state this clearly so there is no misunderstanding. Do not kill Benny. Not unless I say so. If you kill Benny without my say-so, you're out of this business. Am I clear?"

Wyatt stared at his father with disbelief. "Dad. What are you thinking? We let a rat live? What kind of message are we sending? That we're a bunch of pussies?"

"What kind of message do we send if we kill Benny?" Increase asked. "That he was telling the truth when he spoke to the fuzz. That you really did kill this Kamerowski shithead. That's the message we would send. Listen, Wyatt. Benny is thoroughly discredited, and so is the B.H.P.D. The next time one of us goes to trial, all we have to do is point back to Benny's past gibberish on the stand. It's proof that the fuzz have always been out to get us with trumped-up bullshit charges. We can milk this day for years, Wyatt. Why would you want to screw that up by killing Benny?"

"That's not how things are done, Dad!" Wyatt shouted.

Increase held a finger to his lips. "Shhh. Settle down, son. You need to abandon your old, violent ways. We all do. That's the lesson I've taken away from this experience. If we don't learn from history, we're bound to repeat its mistakes. Start thinking outside of the box, son. Try acting a little more like your brother for a change."

Wyatt glared at Leon, who stared uncomfortably into his martini. Wyatt raised his own glass with a shaky hand and drained the vodka. His chin puckered, as if he were on the verge of crying. He closed his eyes, released a long sigh, and began breathing slowly. Gradually, he began to smile. When he opened his eyes, he seemed to be almost at peace. He held out a hand toward Leon.

Leon stared at his brother with some confusion. He gingerly shook his brother's hand. To his surprise, Wyatt gave his hand a firm, warm clasp, and he patted Leon on the side of the shoulder. "Dad's right," Wyatt said. "I've been an asshole. You saved my life, and I should be grateful."

Increase applauded. "Now that's what I'm talking about! That's what I'm goddamn talking about!" He threw his arms over both of his sons' shoulders. "This is a great day for the Lynches, boys! Together, the three of us are going to do great things!" Leon smiled awkwardly as his father patted his back.

Wyatt lit a cigarette. "So," he said. "Getting back to Benny. Cracker should probably be picking him up tonight. I'll start interviewing him tomorrow."

Increase's broad grin became a little strained. "Oh. Okay. Take Leon with you."

Wyatt smiled. "Leon? Why's that, Dad?"

"So both of you can question Benny," he answered. His grin was fixed. "Maybe you could learn more if you have two interviewers. Plus, Leon can bring along some of his truth serum. It seemed to work well the last time around."

"Sounds good," Wyatt said. He nodded to Leon. "We'll be working together, then."

"Great," Leon said. He didn't bother to smile.

"Okay, then," Increase said. "You can play good cop, bad cop. I'll let you two decide which roles you want to play."

In the silence that followed, Increase and Leon finished their martinis.

Wyatt raised his empty martini glass. "To the future," he said.

Leon and Increase raised their own empty glasses and repeated, "To the future."

Stubby purple pods, twisted and shaped like Gila monster tails, sat in a pile before Leon on his kitchen table. He gathered the pods three at time, crossed their stems to form an asterisk, and tied them with a short length of white string. He then tied each cluster to a wire coat hanger, and when the hanger was full, he hung it on a curtain rod before his sunniest window. Four hangers with dangling pods hung before the window to dry.

Leon felt both weary and restless as he trudged back to his kitchen table. His fingers, elbows, shoulders, and back all ached, and he was overwhelmed with a combination of anxiety and boredom. He opened one of his kitchen drawers and found his bottle of painkillers. He popped off the cap, shook two pills onto his hand, and ambled back toward the table to continue tying pods. He stopped for a moment, stood in the center of his kitchen, and rattled the pills in his cupped hand. He thought about his mother.

Leon had been taking drugs for all of his adult life, but he had never considered himself an addict. He understood the chemistry of the plants he consumed, and he knew what effects they would have on his body. He enjoyed a variety of nature's abundant treasures, both rare and common. In Leon's mind, savoring the weightlessness and photographic memory of a Hoom high was no different than relishing the thick sweetness of fresh pineapple, the soothing scent of Spanish saffron, or the exhilaration of a woman's touch.

While Leon thought there was nothing wrong with an

occasional Hoom buzz, he had also seen enough of the world to have encountered thousands of different addictions. He had known whole families of opium addicts in Iran and Pakistan, and some of his Thai contacts were dangerously unstable yaa baa fiends. He hadn't visited one country that was untouched by alcoholism. Of course, he didn't need to travel any farther than his front doorstep to see dozens of different brands of addiction in a single day. Now, he worried that he needn't travel any farther than his bathroom mirror to see a budding addict.

Leon walked to his kitchen sink and dropped the pain-killers down the drain. He opened a cupboard, gathering two other medicine bottles that he had tucked away, and added their contents to the drain. As he ran hot water down the drain to dissolve the pills, he raised his chin to look out the window over his sink. "Wah!" he shouted, and stumbled backward in three jerky steps. When he had looked through the window, he had met the eyes of his brother staring back at him.

Wyatt cackled as he stood outside Leon's window.

Leon held his hand to his chest and felt his heart slam against his sternum. "What the hell is wrong with you!" he shouted at his brother.

Wyatt continued laughing as he walked from the kitchen window to Leon's front door. He rattled the doorknob as his way of knocking. Leon crossed his kitchen to his small den and let Wyatt into his home. "What's wrong with you?" he asked again.

"I just saw you in the window, so I thought I'd fuck with you," Wyatt gave his brother a hard punch to arm. "So what were you doing back there?"

Leon rubbed his arm. "Where?"

"Back in the kitchen. By the sink."

"Oh, nothing," Leon said. "Why are you here, anyhow?"

"We have an assignment, bro. Remember? Dad's wants us to talk to Benny?" Wyatt strolled into the kitchen. "Mind if I have a glass of water?"

"I'll get it for you." Leon stepped ahead of his brother and tried to block the empty pill bottles with his body as he reached for a glass in the cupboard. He turned on the faucet and let the water run.

"You don't have any bottled water?" Wyatt asked. "I can't drink Butchers Harbor tap."

"I don't have any bottled water," Leon said.

"Well at least put some ice in the glass. I mean, I don't want to put you out or anything."

"No problem," Leon said. He reluctantly stepped away from the sink to carry the glass to the freezer.

Wyatt stepped up to the sink and examined the empty pill bottles on the countertop. "Hmm. What do we have here?" Leon ignored his brother as he filled the glass with ice. "What's the matter?" Wyatt asked. "Got a toothache?"

"Something like that." Leon handed the glass to his brother.

"Yeah? I got a wicked kink in my neck. Fucking killing me. Wanna help me out with a couple of Vikes?"

"I took my last one," Leon said. "Finished the prescription."

Wyatt dumped the ice into the sink and turned off the faucet. "That's what I figured. One Way Whitey. So does Dad know about your toothache?"

Leon gave his brother a cold stare. "I thought we were going to talk to Benny."

"We are. But we can socialize first, can't we?" Wyatt held one of the empty pill bottles. "You really ought to be careful with these things, Whitey. Junkies do run in *your* family." He smirked.

Leon nodded. "Thanks for looking out for me."

"That's what big brothers are for." Wyatt returned the bottle to the countertop. "Now let's hit the road."

Leon squirmed and gripped the door handle at his side as Wyatt ran red lights, tailgated other motorists, waved his middle finger, and blared his horn across Butchers Harbor until they reached the landfill on the East End. Wyatt nodded to the dump hag tending the booth at the gate, then drove his Porsche Turbo past tottering stacks of doorless refrigerators, dented and rusting appliances, worn furniture, and heaps of bald tires. Filthy seagulls, perched atop hills of trash, pecked at scraps of rotten food as they glared down at the Porsche rolling through the foul valley. Leon looked up at the slope of multicolored garbage bags and imagined their contents: disposable razors and pens, toilet paper rolls, forgotten toys, junk food wrappers, chicken bones, fish guts, cat shit, snotty tissues, used tampons, spent condoms, drained liquor nips, empty pill bottles, broken syringes, family photos torn in anger, unread love letters, practice suicide notes, and discarded sympathy cards. Leon pictured the city of Butchers Harbor as one hellish factory churning out a high-yield production of refuse and misery.

Butchers Harbor Animal Control maintained its facilities at the far end of the dump. Wyatt rolled the car to a stop before a low, long cinderblock building surrounded by cages of barking dogs. He lit a fresh cigarette as he stepped out of his Porsche. As Leon emerged from the car, he looked uneasily at the building before him. "This is where you have Benny?"

Wyatt returned his silver Zippo to his pants pocket. "Yep. Picked up him late last night. I've been softening him up. Getting him ready for our interview."

"What do you mean 'softening him up'?" Leon asked.

"Take a wild fucking guess."

Leon felt queasy. He regretted dumping his painkillers down the drain. "Dad said you weren't supposed to hurt Benny." A Doberman with chunks of missing fur lunged at the chain-link fence and snarled at the brothers.

"Dad said I wasn't supposed to *kill* Benny," Wyatt corrected.

"What have you done to him?" Leon asked.

"Just letting him play with the dogs."

Leon stepped back to the car and opened the passenger door. "I want to go home."

"Fuck you, Whitey. This is how we do business. You wanted in, and now you're in. Grow a dick."

Leon closed the door but continued to linger by the car. "What has he said so far?"

"Thanks to you and the shit you put in his reefer, he hasn't said anything that makes any sense," Wyatt said. "Anyhow, I don't ask a lot of questions right off the bat. When I'm conducting an interview, I might work the fucker over for a full day before I ask a single question. Sometimes, I tape their mouths shut to keep them from confessing. That way, when I finally do ask a question, they're more than willing to answer."

"Does Dad know you're doing this?"

"I don't tell Dad everything. Do you? Maybe he'd like to know about your little toothache problem."

Leon scoffed. "Go ahead and tell him. You think Dad hasn't popped a few pills in his day? You need something better than that to hold over my head."

Wyatt took another drag off his cigarette and flicked the butt onto a pile of empty dog food cans. "Well, maybe I will. Let's see if Benny has anything to say about his walking corpse act." Wyatt swaggered up to the entrance of the cinderblock building and stepped through the metal door.

Leon lingered by the Porsche. He was terrified of what he might see inside the pound, but he needed to hear what Benny had to say. He took a few deep breaths to steady himself, but the stink of the nearby sewage treatment plant made him gag. He stepped forward, past dogs that slobbered through jagged yellow teeth and slammed their bodies against their wire pens.

He stepped into a dingy room with stacks of wire cages holding old and disfigured cats. A stoop-shouldered middle-aged man with dandruff caked in his greasy hair looked up from his metal desk and squinted at Leon. "Who're you?" he asked.

Wyatt was crouched before the metal desk examining a strange grayish-brown mammal in a small cage. "That's my brother Whitey. Whitey, meet Fritz."

Fritz continued to squint at Leon. "Pleasure to make your acquaintance," he said, his tongue clacking against his toothless gums.

"What is this thing?" Wyatt asked. He wrapped his knuckles on the cage. The animal whipped its thin tail as it hissed and spat at Wyatt.

"Dunno," Fritz said. "Cops found it in the projects. Bit some little colored kid." He chuckled at that.

Leon looked into the cage. The animal had a long white snout and small, frightened eyes. Although naturally long and slender, it was malnourished and bony. "It's a coati," Leon said. He noticed blood around its mouth and on its long front claws.

"Learn something new every day," Fritz said. "Anyhow, the thing don't like your friend much. They had a little scuffle."

Wyatt straightened up and glared down at Fritz. "Have you been playing with the detainee? I told you to leave him alone."

"I was bored. I needed something to do. You try sitting around here all day with nothing to do but scoop shit." Fritz glanced at his watch. "At least I get to start putting down cats in one hour and forty-two minutes." He pointed at a mangy, one-eyed cat in the corner and wagged his finger. "Tick-tock, tick-tock, Mrs. Whiskers."

"Get the keys," Wyatt said. "I want to see Benny."

Fritz removed a large ring of keys from his top desk drawer and pushed himself away from his desk. He shuffled out of the main office toward a side door. Wyatt pushed Leon to follow Fritz. They walked down a narrow hallway lined with cages on both sides. Cats and small dogs quaked as the warden passed. Fritz inserted a key into a heavy door at the end of the hall. With Wyatt shoving him from behind, Leon followed Fritz into a dark, windowless room. He gagged on the stench of urine, excrement, and blood.

Fritz pulled a chain for an overhead light that illuminated the room in a green fluorescent hue. Wire dog crates, stacked two high, lined the room. Leon looked down and saw a coal-black spider, almost two inches long, crawling by his foot. He stepped back and bumped into Wyatt.

"Watch it, stupid," Wyatt said.

Leon looked around the room and saw more of the spiders creeping across the floor, walls, and ceiling. They had hard, bulbous bodies and long legs that looked like human finger bones dipped in tar. "This place is filled with spiders."

Wyatt scanned the room. "What the hell's going on in here Fritz?"

Fritz crunched a few arachnids under his sneakers. "We got a box of spiders the other day. So I showed them to your friend."

"Alright, Fritz. Unlock Benny's cage."

Fritz crouched by a kennel in the corner and unlocked the wire door. He winced as he looked inside, then looked up sheepishly at Wyatt. Wyatt grabbed Leon by his shirtsleeve and dragged him to the corner of the room, and the two brothers looked into the kennel. Benny was crammed into the wire crate. Two dozen funnel-web spiders crawled over his body or clung to the cage. Wisps of webs stretched from Benny's legs to the corner of the pen. His clothes, torn and soaked with blood, rippled as more funnel-webs squirmed under the fabric. The flesh that was not punctured or torn by various animal teeth was grossly swollen with spider bites. Curled beside Benny was a dead porcupine. Several of its quills dangled from Benny's face and body.

"Take his pulse," Wyatt said.

Fritz reached into the cage, flicked a few spiders away from Benny's neck, and pressed his fingers against his carotid. He continued to press his fingers against Benny's cold flesh until he finally gave up with a shrug. "I don't feel nothing."

Leon tore his arm free from Wyatt's grip and staggered out of the room. He made his way to the front office, where he stopped to puke into a wastebasket. Wyatt followed him into the office with his Heckler & Koch drawn. "What's the matter, Princess? Tummy upset?"

Leon dropped to the floor and sat with his back to a file

cabinet. He breathed heavily, keeping the wastebasket at his side. "This is fucking insane," he muttered.

Wyatt shrugged. "Welcome aboard."

Leon shook his head. "It doesn't have to be this way. Dad said he wanted things to change."

Fritz stepped into the office and loitered uncomfortably in the corner. Wyatt leaned against the desk. The coati reached through its cage at clawed at his leather jacket. Wyatt shoved the cage, and it landed with a loud clatter on the tiled floor. The animal whined, hissed, and tumbled frantically in its cage. Wyatt waited for the coati to settle down. "You want to talk about Dad? Fine. First of all, the old man is out of his mind. He always has been. He named me after a fucking cowboy, for Christ's sake." He tapped the butt of his pistol against two fingers. "Secondly, he's full of shit. Even *he* doesn't believe half of what he says. Today, he wants us to act like hippies. Tomorrow, who knows? Third of all, he's soft. He's always depended on me to do the dirty work to keep business running, and I intend to continue doing that, no matter what the changes to the organizational chart." As Wyatt crossed his arms, he pressed the barrel of the Heckler & Koch against one of his biceps. "So I don't give a goddamn shit what Dad wants. I'll do whatever the fuck I want whenever the fuck I feel like it. And the last thing I'll do is allow you or Dad to pussy up this organization."

"I could wait outside if you boys want some privacy," Fritz said.

"Stay where you are," Wyatt said. "I need to talk to you."

"This wasn't supposed to happen," Leon said. He put his elbows on his knees and held his forehead in his hands. "Benny wasn't supposed to die."

"Well I didn't kill him! It was this asshole here!" Wyatt

pointed his 9mm at Fritz and fired a round into his chest. Fritz staggered backward into a bank of cages. His feet slipped out before him, and he dropped to the floor with his back slamming against the tiles. Wyatt turned the pistol on his brother.

"Oh my god!" Leon shouted. He held his hands before his face, as if he could somehow block a bullet with his palms.

"Settle down," Wyatt sneered. Behind him, Fritz breathed raggedly as he held a trembling hand over his wound. "I'm not gonna shoot you, Whitey. Not right now, anyway. You and I both know that Dad would freak out if I killed you. I'd have to clip him too, and I'm not so sure I want to do that." Wyatt seemed to consider this option as he kept the Heckler & Koch aimed at his brother. "I don't know what kind of charm you cast over our father, but he's pretty smitten with you these days. Maybe you just remind him of the junkie whore he used to fuck." Wyatt lowered the gun. "Anyhow, Dad won't live forever. You'd better mix up some magic brew that will let the old man outlive me. 'Cause when Dad takes a dirt nap, there won't be a goddamn thing to keep me from capping you."

Leon slumped against the file cabinet.

"Who knows. Maybe I won't even have to wait for Dad to kick," Wyatt said. "You got this big assignment coming up with the Borisova sit-down. You think you got any chance of survival with those deranged motherfuckers? They'll cut you into chum. They'll be carrying you out of that sit-down in buckets. And when you're dead, Dad will be so pissed that I'll have free reign to kill anything with a pulse. So go play with the Russians and go get your fucking head blown off. It'll be business as usual in no time."

Wyatt pushed off the desk, sauntered up to Fritz, and fired

two more bullets into the man's chest. He holstered the piece under his jacket as he approached Leon. "Alright. Let's work out a few details. All we have to do is tell Dad the truth. When we got here, Benny was dead. The psycho dog warden feed him to the pit bulls, spiders, and whatever the fuck this thing is here." He kicked the coati's cage, which set the animal snapping and crying. "Then I capped Fritz for screwing up our interview with the rat. This works out best for both of us, Whitey. With Benny dead, Dad'll never know that I let a stiff walk away, and he won't know that you turned Benny into a mobile corpse."

"What are you talking about?" Leon stammered. "Mobile corpse. What's that supposed to mean?"

"Give it a rest, Peon. It doesn't take Sherlock Fucking Holmes to figure out that you've got the drugs to make an alkie wetback look like a stiff. So get on board with my story, and we'll keep both our secrets safe. Sound like a plan?"

Leon stared dully at the floor. Eventually, he nodded.

Wyatt unholstered his cell phone and dialed a number. "Cracker. I'm at the place where our friend was staying. You're on cleanup detail. Bring supplies for two."

Wyatt holstered the phone and gave his brother a light kick to the ribs. "Come on. Let's go."

Leon grabbed a handle of one of the upper drawers of the file cabinet and pulled himself to his feet. He looked to the corner of the office, toward the warden lying on his back with patches of red spreading across the chest of his gray uniform.

"Look on the bright side," Wyatt said. "Mrs. Whiskers gets a reprieve." He gave his brother a shove toward the door. As they stepped outside, Wyatt said, "So tell me. How much time, effort, and thought did you put into saving Benny's life? It wasn't just once, but twice you tried to save that drunken pothead lowlife. Didn't do him much good, though, did it? You don't have a knack for doing things right. Do you, Whitey?" Wyatt paused to light a cigarette as he studied the rolling landscape of trash. "Well, maybe things will work out better with the Russians."

9
RUSSIAN ROULETTE

Peter Volkov sat at the counter of the Restaurant Georgia, hunched over a plate of khachapuri and the business section of the *Butchers Harbor Register*. Volkov had been feeling out of sorts for months, ever since he had been mugged outside of his apartment building. He was left with a scar over his upper lip that ran through the stubble of his perpetual five-o'clock shadow. His front tooth was chipped, which gave an eerily boyish appearance to his haggard face. Volkov wished he could summon a clearer memory of his attackers. All he could recall were vague silhouettes rushing him as he stepped out of his car. These shadows punched and kicked him to the ground, took his wallet, and ran into the hazy night. If Volkov could only remember his assailants' faces, he would hunt them down and kill them. The Borisovas had made inquiries on the street, all to no avail. Some had suspected the Lynches were behind the attack, but the idea didn't make much sense because Volkov was still alive.

Volkov sprinkled salt on a wedge of khachapuri and washed it down with a gulp of lukewarm coffee. There was no one else in the diner except a young waitress with slime-green hair. She filed her purple nails over a stack of plates as she listened to a virus report on the radio.

The smallpox outbreak in Seattle is reportedly under control, thanks largely to a quarantine of the entire Puget Sound area. Residents have requested a lifting of the quarantine, but authorities are standing firm by their decision to let the epidemic run its course. Elsewhere in the United States, the Sin Nombre virus appears to be spreading beyond the Four Corners as reports of high fevers, lung failures, and other hantavirus symptoms have been reported in Santa Fe, Denver, Flagstaff, and Cedar City, Utah. Locally, we have seen a decline in outbreaks of Hong Kong flu, but hepatitis and tuberculosis appear to be gaining momentum in urban areas. STDs, including HIV-3, are maintaining steady rates of infection, so be sure to wear a condom. Finally, we have a report of a possible case of Gupta-Comstock in suburban Butchers Harbor.

At the mention of Gupta-Comstock, Peter Volkov looked up from his paper and the green-haired waitress stopped filing her nails.

A female voice was heard on the radio: *Gupta-Comstock is a new disease on this coast, isn't it Dan?*

Yes it is, Diane. Our listeners may know it better as pigpox or the Willies. Gupta-Comstock is a suppressed porcine virus that apparently jumped species after a pig-to-human liver transplant. The symptoms of pigpox are muscle fatigue and headaches, followed by intense shivering, dementia, and, finally, hemorrhagic fever. Fortunately, the virus usually kills its host within 48 hours of infection, which helps to contain its spread.

Volkov dropped his fork in his plate and called to the waitress. "This is not good listening when I am eating."

The waitress slid off the counter and changed the radio to a country music station.

Volkov looked around the diner. A layer of grease had settled everywhere, over countertops, floor tiles, walls, and booths. Dust and grime had clung to the grease until the entire diner had a yellow-brown hue. "How much are you washing the dishes here?" He asked, eyeing his food uneasily.

"We're very sanitary," she said, retreating to the kitchen to avoid further discussion.

Volkov pushed his food aside and pulled a pack of unfiltered cigarettes from his green plaid jacket. The door to the restaurant opened, jingling a small bell set over the entrance. A scruffy young man in faded jeans and a hooded sweatshirt stepped inside and sat at the counter two stools away from Volkov. The kid took off his sunglasses, revealing pale violet eyes. Volkov glared at the white-haired stranger, annoyed that he was taking a seat so close to him in an otherwise empty diner. He grunted and returned his attention to the *Butchers Harbor Register*.

The new customer plucked a menu from its stand and glanced at the entrees. "What's good here?" he asked Volkov.

"Nothing. Everything bad. Go eat someplace else." Volkov gave him another disgusted glare. The kid looked familiar to Volkov, and he searched his memory for a connection. It seemed he should have had no trouble remembering such an odd-looking person. Then Volkov recalled that Increase Lynch had a second son, some kind of freak. The kid was supposed to be a social dropout with little involvement in the family business.

Leon smiled. "You recognize me, don't you."

"What is your name, please?" Peter demanded.

"Leon Lynch." He extended his hand.

Peter Volkov regarded Leon's hand with disgust. "What are you wanting?"

"I was in the mood for a veggie wrap, but they don't seem to have that here," Leon said. "As long as I'm here, though, maybe you and I could talk about peace."

"Peace?" Volkov said.

"Peace between our organizations."

Volkov scoffed. "We are not interesting in peace. Our side is winning war."

"You *were* winning," Leon corrected. "Things have changed a bit, haven't they? You don't have your tipsters inside our business anymore, do you? Your family has taken a few beatings lately, too. The tide is turning, my friend. Now we have the edge. We could bury you, but there are members in my organization who value the bottom line over revenge. Recent history has demonstrated that retaliation is not profitable. Maybe both of our families would benefit from a cease-fire." Leon set the menu on the table and leaned closer to Volkov. "You don't seem so stupid to me. I think you want to make money like the rest of us. I think you're as tired of the bloodshed as I am. I'll tell you what I want, Peter. I want you and me to work together to negotiate a peace between the Lynches and Borisovas."

The waitress emerged from the kitchen and approached Leon. She tapped a pencil on a green and white pad. "What are we having today?" she asked.

"Hi," Leon said with a smile. "How's the borscht here?"

The waitress shrugged.

"Well, borscht it is, then. And a cup of coffee too, please."

"Anything else?"

"A few minutes of privacy," Leon said. "No offense."

"No problem," the waitress said, walking back to the kitchen. "Call me when you want your coffee."

Leon turned back to Volkov. "So what do you say? Can the two of us work together?"

Volkov tapped an unfiltered cigarette against the side of his pack. He stuck the cigarette in his craggy lips and struck a match. He couldn't shake the feeling that he had met Leon before. He had a weird notion that the two had been on a long journey together. "Why do you come to me, please?" he asked.

"From what I hear, Vladimir Borisova has a high opinion of you. He trusts you and your judgment. Your suggestions regarding a cease-fire would carry a lot of weight with him. This would also be good for your career, Peter. Negotiating a peace accord between two families would be a nice feather in your cap. This could move you along in the family hierarchy."

Volkov nodded and lit his cigarette. He shook out the match and tossed it over the counter. "And why do *you* come to me? You are not big cheese in your family, no?"

"No and yes," Leon said. "I wasn't much of a player in the past, that's true. Times change, though, and I am now one of my father's closest advisors. The fact that my father seeks my counsel reflects a major change in our business strategy. You see, I'm not a violent man. I'm no peacenik either, but all things being equal, I prefer to minimize the number of killed and maimed in most business transactions."

Volkov eyed Leon through a haze of smoke. "And why should I trust you?"

Leon shrugged. "Do you?"

Volkov did. He trusted Leon for no sensible reason, and this made him distrust Leon, the way he would be suspicious of a con man's charm.

The bell over the door jingled again, and a muscle-bound, pale man in his early twenties swaggered into the diner. He wore ridiculously baggy pants, a baseball cap turned sideways, and a tank top with an image of Al Pacino as Scarface. On his shirt, beneath Pacino wielding a machine gun, were the words ORIGINAL GANGSTER. SERIAL KILLER. Gold medallions hanging from thick gold chains jangled together as the young man pimp-rolled toward Peter Volkov.

"Yo, yo, yo! What is word, Peter V?" said the young man. He spoke slowly, with a thick Slavic accent, pronouncing the "V" as "We." "How is my G original home dog?" He extended his hand. Oversized gold rings representing chess pieces separated his fingers.

Volkov ignored the young man, but Leon eyed him warily. This clown matched Macey's description of Sergei Sickie Listyev, one of the nastiest Siberian thugs in the Borisova syndicate. Sickie noticed Leon glancing at him. "Yo! What are you looking at, bitch?"

"This is Leon Lynch," Volkov said. He smiled and blew a thin plume of smoke into Leon's face. "This is son of Increase Lynch."

Sickie leaned on the counter and held his face close to Leon's. "You kidnap Lynch? This is big score, my dog." The Siberian smiled broadly as he spoke, an affectation that allowed him to show off the gold incisor in his upper jaw. "Tell me dilly. How you kidnap this Lynch fuckermother? Give me the four hundred and eleven."

Volkov chuckled. "He walk in here, Sickie. He says he want to talk."

Sickie patted Leon on the shoulder. "This is wery phat and hype. This is bomb, da? We take him now to Vladimir, yo?"

The waitress approached Leon with his coffee and borscht. Leon removed his wallet and dropped several bills on the counter. "Well, I've said everything I have to say. I guess I'll be moving on then." He nodded as coolly as he could toward Volkov and Sickie, rose from his stool, and stepped toward the front exit.

Sickie Listyev put an arm around Leon's shoulder and turned him in the other direction. "We go out back way, yo?" He steered Leon to the rear exit and pushed him into a back alley that reeked of fish and rotting vegetables. Peter Volkov followed them outside and closed the back door to the restaurant.

Leon backed up until he tripped over a garbage bag and stumbled into a concrete wall. Sickie grabbed him by the shirt and pushed him into a corner. Leon raised his hands in weak protest. "Gentlemen, I'm here for peaceful reasons. I don't want to cause any trouble."

"You will be no trouble," Volkov said. "You will be great help. When your father knows you are in custody of Vladimir Borisova, he will be very agreeable to all of our many demands, yes?"

"This won't help the peace process," Leon said.

Sickie found a piece of pipe among the trash and tapped it against Leon's chin. "Fuck peace process."

Leon appealed to Volkov. "Peter, come on, man. We're tired of the bloodshed, remember? Peace is good for business, right?"

Volkov nodded. "Maybe so. But we want peace on our terms, yes?" Volvov gave Leon a playful slap on the face. "This is how you help us, my friend."

Macey had been sitting in a car parked across the street, monitoring the diner through a pair of binoculars. When she saw the Russians push Leon out the back door, she walked around the Restaurant Georgia and stepped into the back alley. When Sickie Listyev saw her approaching, he lowered the pipe he had been brandishing and hid it behind his baggy pants. "Yo, shorty," he called. "This is priwate conwersation. Step off."

Macey continued walking slowly with her hands in her loose khaki pockets until she reached Sickie. "What's up?" she asked.

"Nothing is up," Sickie said. "I am just talking to my peeps. Now step off, boo. Do not get in my grill. Yo? You are knowing what I am saying?"

Macey turned to Leon. "You finished talking to these assholes?" she asked.

Leon nodded. "More or less."

"Good. Let's go." She grabbed Leon's arm and started to pull him away.

Sickie lifted the pipe he had been hiding and pointed it at Macey. "Are you smoking on crack? You are rock star, skank bitch? I told you step off!"

Macey looked at the pipe in Sickie's hand. "Are you threatening me?" she asked.

"Shit yes, this is threat!" Sickie shouted. "What are you going do about it, chicken head?"

Macey let go of Leon and dropped Sickie with a roundhouse kick. He landed in a cardboard box filled with wilted cabbage and eggshells. Macey spun toward Volkov and knocked him to the pavement with three punches to his face and a knee to his groin. Then she turned her attention back to Sickie, kicking him twice in the head with her heavy boots. Finally, she lifted a garbage can and smashed it onto Volkov's chest and stomach. She threw the barrel aside and searched Volkov's jacket for his gun. She pulled the piece from its holster and pressed the barrel against the bridge of Volkov's nose. Volkov struggled to remain conscious as he stared cross-eyed at the gun.

Macey turned back to Leon and said, "Finish what you have to say."

"Right," Leon said. He crouched on one knee beside Volkov. "Um. So basically, Peter, my offer still stands. I'd like the two of us to work together to forge a peace between our families." Leon looked behind him to see if Sickie was moving. He wasn't. Leon turned back to Volkov. "My family is willing to change. I think you're seeing some evidence of this change today. You and your friend here just tried to kidnap me. Under the old rules, we would've killed you, right here and now in this alley. But that's not going to happen today. We're willing to let bygones be bygones, and I hope your side is willing to do the same. People can change, Peter, the same as everything else in the universe. Like water that falls from the sky, fills the reservoir, and winds up as an ice cube in your soda, nothing stays the same forever."

Macey glanced over her shoulder at Leon. She raised an eyebrow to express impatience.

"My point is that things change," Leon continued, "and we can change too. Enemies can become partners. So, will you talk to Vladimir for me and tell him we want a sit-down?"

Macey slid the gun up to Volkov's forehead. "Answer the question."

Volkov nodded his head carefully. "I will do what you are asking."

"Good, then," Leon said. "So we're cool?"

Volkov tried to nod with his eyes.

Leon smiled. "Great. Okay, then. So I guess we'll be talking again pretty soon." Leon stooped to shake Volkov's hand. Volkov winced in pain as Leon jerked his arm. "I think we're doing a good thing, Peter. I'm sure you won't regret this."

"Are you done?" Macey asked.

Leon nodded.

"Good," Macey said and smashed the butt of the gun against Volkov's head, knocking him unconscious.

In the 1970s, Vladimir Borisova was just another thug running his little niche of the black market in Volgograd. He sold just about anything, as long as it was stolen or forbidden. One of his suppliers, a chemist who manufactured speed and LSD, was also one of his favorite customers. This chemist, Aleksey Hollywood Shvidkovsky, was an avid fan of American movies, and Vladimir supplied him with bootleg prints. Sometimes, Vladimir watched the films with Aleksey. Vladimir spoke a bit of English, and Aleksey translated the parts that he did not understand.

It was in Hollywood Aleksey's apartment, on a frigid winter night in 1979, that Vladimir saw the film that would change his life. In that apartment, Vladimir saw the American dream projected on a cracked plaster wall. He saw a movie about an immigrant boy who had arrived in the United States without parents or property yet lived to build an empire. At first, Vladimir tried to dismiss the movie as blatant American propaganda, but he could not deny the film's poetry and beauty. He asked to see the movie again, and Hollywood was pleased to oblige. On the second viewing, Vladimir was convinced that the film was as true and honest as anything he had ever known. He embraced *The Godfather Part II* as his gospel.

The story of Don Vito Corleone haunted Vladimir Borisova for weeks. It spoke to him, and it said, *You belong in America, Vladimir.* The United States was a land for men who were willing to work hard for a better life. It was a land for men of honor and integrity. In America, any man could succeed if he was ambitious and willing to defy written laws. It truly was the land of opportunity, and it was the land for Vladimir Borisova.

Within a month, Vladimir had sold all of his possessions and contraband, and he had bribed a captain to smuggle him and his family aboard a freighter bound for Cuba. From Cuba he hired a boat to Mexico, where he stalked a family of American tourists and robbed them of their car and luggage. He doctored their passports with photographs of himself, his wife, Lyudmila, and his son, Josef. As it turned out, the phony passports were unnecessary because he simply drove into America without any interference from the border guards.

Vladimir drove north along the East Coast until he found a city where the buildings were boxy and drab, the overcast skies were smeared with smog, and poverty, decay, and alcoholism were rampant. He drove until he found Butchers Harbor, a place that reminded him of home. Butchers Harbor was a city where Vladimir could live for the dream of *The Godfather II*.

Now, Vladimir Borisova sat behind a great oak desk in his library. American, Russian, and Italian flags hung on the wall behind his desk. Portraits of great Italian-Americans, from Christopher Columbus to Lucky Luciano, adorned the walls. Vladimir removed a cigar from a humidor and trimmed the tip. Before him sat Peter Volkov and Sickie Sergei Listyev. Peter's left cheek was swollen and bruised, and seven stitches on his left temple held a gash closed. Beside him, Sickie Listyev wore a plastic neck brace. White adhesive tape and a splint covered his broken nose.

"Tell me what happened," Vladimir said.

"Ay you treep and check this out," said Sickie Listyev, rasping through a wired jaw. "This chump Leon Lynch approach me and Peter at Restaurant Georgia, yo? He act as distraction while some thumb popper whore sneak up behind us."

"Macey Kick?" asked Borisova.

"Da, that is chicken head pigeon bitch. This chicken head hit me with sucker punch. She use baseball bat or some crazy ill shit. I never see her coming. These goddamn Lynch fuckermothers set us up," Sickie said. He leaned toward Borisova and pounded his fist on the oak table. "I want retribution, Vladimir. I got homies back in Omsk got mad stash of military hardware. I say we smuggle grenade launcher into Butchers Harbor. We fire rocket into crib of Increase Lynch. Yo?" Sickie wiped away some spit that was collecting on his lower lip. "Next we go after psycho chump Wyatt. We put him in bathtub with piranhas. I can score piranhas. I have connection. This is dope, no? This is mad revenge."

Sickie glanced toward Peter Volkov for support. He continued, sputtering through most of his consonants. "Then we grab other brother, this Whitey fuckermother who distract me and Peter. I am saying we cover head of this albino shit with honey. Also, we pour chocolate syrup in his ears, yo? Then we stick his head in box filled with red ants. Ants eat out his eyes and crawl through ears into brain. Fuck him up wery good. Last but not for least, we go after bitch Macey Kick and clip the pigeon's wings. But this shorty, I am saying we do not kill her right away." Sickie smiled and grabbed his groin. "I have many nut to bust. I make her pay for disrespecting Sickie."

Vladimir lit a wooden match and held the flame to his cigar. He puffed several times as he drew the fire into the tobacco. When the cigar was burning nicely, he flicked the lit match onto Sickie's lap. Sickie struggled to find the flame, but his brace prevented him from bending his neck for a better view. Borisova and Volkov chuckled.

Vladimir spoke around the cigar clenched in his teeth. "Sergie, you sound like a mental patient." He had a deep, Russian voice, but his accent was less severe than Sickie or Volkov's. "Enough with your ridiculous yo-yo rap bullshit. You do not need to sound any dumber than you already are." Vladimir dismissed Sickie with a lethargic backhanded wave. "You disturb me, Sergie. Now leave me and Peter alone. Fuck off, please."

"Yo! Vladimir! Hear me for what I say!" Sickie protested.

Borisova rose from his chair and walked around the desk. He stood for a moment, towering over Sickie. Then he grabbed Sickie by the lapel of his leather jacket and hoisted the Siberian to his feet. "Yo! Vladimir!" Sickie snapped. He tried to pry Borisova's hands from his jacket. "You are creasing my Wersache!"

Vladimir let go of Sickie's jacket and grabbed him by the neck brace. He began to push Sickie backward across the room. "Vladimir!" Sickie shouted as he struggled to stay on his feet. "You are being bugging!" Borisova slammed the back of Sickie's head into a heavy oak door. He then opened the door and shoved Sickie outside. As Borisova tried to slam the door, Sickie struggled to get back inside the office. "What is dilly?" he asked. "I warn you, Vladimir. You should not dog me in this manner!"

"Get out!" Borisova shouted, kicking Sickie's shin. Sickie hopped backward, and Borisova closed the door.

Borisova returned to his seat and raised his hands in exasperation. "Fucking Sergei. What a fucking crackpot, yes?"

Volkov chuckled. "Yes, he has shit for his brains."

"Yes. Forget about it," Borisova said. "Now, Peter, what really happened to you and Sergei?"

Volkov rubbed his bruised face. "I was eating in Restaurant Georgia, and this white hair boy, this Leon Lynch, he approach me with offer. Before we much talk, Sergei walk into restaurant, and he propose we kidnap Leon Lynch for ransom. We think we can use him as bargaining coin with Increase Lynch. This seem like good plan at time, no?"

Borisova nodded.

Volkov continued, "Before we could kidnap this Leon Lynch, the Macey woman approach us. Then she does the karate on me and Sergei."

Vladimir Borisova laughed. "Poor Peter! Did she pull your hair too? Did she try to scratch your eyes out?"

"I tell you, she has black belt or something. She move like Bruce Fucking Lee."

"Yes, I am sure she was a very scary girl," Borisova said. He puffed his cigar. "So tell me, Peter, what was this Leon Lynch's offer?"

"He says his family wants sit-down."

"To arrange a cease-fire?" Borisova asked.

Volkov nodded.

"I have not heard much of Leon Lynch. What type of man is he?"

Volkov shrugged. "I did not speak to him long. He appears honest. But this is only impression."

"Do you believe he speaks for his father?"

"He tells me that he is new advisor to his father."

Borisova tapped an ash off his cigar. "I do not trust changes of heart, Peter. Maybe Increase Lynch uses his naïve son as a decoy or as bait."

"So you think it is trap?" Volkov asked.

Borisova shrugged. "Maybe. Or perhaps we have beaten some sense into the Lynches. Peace, I think, sounds good to the Lynches these days, yes?" Borisova puffed on his cigar thoughtfully. "We will have this sit-down. We will listen to Increase's offers. We negotiate, then I agree to most of Increase's terms. We put them at ease, yes? We all shake hands and talk of the future of peace. Then the sit-down is over. Everybody goes home. But we put Sergei down the road with his fucking grenade launcher. When the Lynch car stops at an intersection, Sergei detonates the Lynch family. Then we have our peace."

Volkov nodded uneasily. "This is good plan, Vladimir. But maybe this grenade launcher is … how is it said? … extreme? This is not Moscow, you know."

"Ah, if we miss our target and hit a school bus or some fucking shit, then maybe we have bad press. But I will tell Sergei to take careful aim. Everybody in this city will be glad to be rid of the fucking Lynches. I will talk to Police Chief McLean and make proper arrangements. He will say the explosion was from a car bomb, and he will call it an inside job." Borisova waved his hand to dismiss any further concern. "Get back in touch with this peacemaker Leon Lynch. Tell him we want the sit-down and make arrangements for finding a safe and neutral location. Let's wipe out this fucking Lynch menace once and for all."

10
TWISTED

Macey Kick drove a rented Town Car through crowds of drunks partying in the wind and rain. Although it was early in the afternoon, the sky was as dark as dusk. A low-grade hurricane was moving up the coast, bearing down on Butchers Harbor. Heavy winds rattled street signs, tore limbs from trees, and blasted sheets of rain across the streets. Increase sat in the passenger's seat beside Macey. Leon sat in the backseat. The Town Car tailed closely behind a black Jeep driven by Fuzzy Magee with Frankie Baloney Bologna riding shotgun.

Macey and the three Lynches were on their way to the sit-down with the Borisovas. The two families were meeting in a seafood restaurant located on a pier. The restaurant, named Something Fishy on the Harbor, had no affiliation with either family. The Lynches and Borisovas had agreed to limit the number of members from either side that would be allowed into Something Fishy. Leon would accompany his father, and Macey would be their bodyguard. Wyatt refused to attend the sit-down, and none of the other Lynches had tried to change his mind. As for the Borisovas, Vladimir would be accompanied by his only son, Josef, and Peter Volkov would serve as their bodyguard and advisor.

KILL WHITEY

The preliminary negotiations with the Borisovas had been surprisingly easy. The Borisovas seemed as eager for peace as Leon. This willingness to arrange a sit-down made Macey suspicious. She drove cautiously, expecting an ambush around every corner. To deter such an attack, Macey had insisted on arriving in a rented car, which would be unfamiliar to their enemies. Still, the drunks partying in the rain made Macey uneasy. When they stopped at one light, a teenage boy dressed in a toga climbed onto the hood of the Town Car and began to dance and sing. Macey punched the accelerator, ran the red light, and dumped the boy onto an oncoming Volvo.

The only structures near Something Fishy on the Harbor were a small bar across the street and a four-story warehouse a block down the road. Cracker Jack Farrell climbed a fire escape up the side of the warehouse with a Stoner SR-25 automatic sniping rifle slung over his shoulder. When he approached the top of the warehouse, he peered carefully over the side of the building onto the roof. He saw a lean Ukrainian dressed in black khakis and a navy blue pea jacket. The pale man was perched at the edge of the warehouse, surveying the piers through a pair of high-powered binoculars as he hunkered against the wind and rain. Beside him was a Beretta Sniper mounted on a bipod and pointed toward Something Fishy.

Cracker climbed onto the roof. The rush of wind and rain masked the sound of his footsteps as he crept up to the Ukrainian. He pressed the muzzle of his rifle against the back of the man's head. "Move away from the Beretta," he said. The startled gunman dropped his binoculars and slowly looked over his shoulder. Cracker waved his rifle, and the Ukrainian inched away from his own weapon as he had been instructed. "You offense or defense?" Cracker asked.

The Ukrainian shook his head. "I do not understand."

"Who you plannin' to kill today?" Cracker asked.

The Ukrainian raised his hands. "I am protection only. The Borisovas have no plans to kill anyone. Not unless your side fires first."

Cracker studied the Ukrainian for a nearly minute and finally said, "Alright. I'm protection too. You can live for now." Cracker Jack patted down the gunman, then he unloaded the Beretta. He instructed the Ukrainian to sit away from the edge of the roof, within Cracker's sight but out of the view of anyone on the ground. "Stay put and keep quiet." Cracker lifted the binoculars and surveyed the piers around the restaurant. The Borisovas approached first, pulling alongside the restaurant in a pair of red sport utility vehicles. Two men emerged from the first SUV and cautiously eyed their surroundings. Cracker kept his rifle low and eased away from the edge of the roof. Soon, the Lynches arrived. Fuzzy and Frankie stepped out of the Jeep, surveyed the area and nodded to Borisova's men. Finally, the heads of both families stepped out of their vehicles, cautiously approached one another, and shook hands.

Cracker Jack Farrell was not the only one watching the activity outside the restaurant. Sickie Listyev, dressed in a Phat Farm jeans jacket and a red doo rag, sat by a window in the bar across the street. He used a straw to sip beer through his wired jaw. When he saw Macey and the Lynches emerge from their Town Car, he jotted down the license plate number, paid for his drink, and slipped out an exit at the back of the bar. He stepped into a van and drove to an apartment building a mile down the road. Sickie opened the back of the van and dragged out a rolled carpet that concealed his newly purchased RPG-7V grenade launcher and a Kalashnikov AK-74. He lugged the weapons up the stairs to an empty third-floor apartment.

Back at the restaurant, Fuzzy Magee, dressed in his sharpest pinstripe suit and a Joseph & Feiss double-breasted raincoat, ran a handheld metal detector over Vladimir Borisova, his son Josef, and Peter Volkov. The Lynches submitted to the same search by one of the Borisova bodyguards. Finally, the two parties stepped inside the restaurant while the guards waited outside.

The windows of Something Fishy were all boarded in preparation for the approaching storm. Only the owner, a waitress, and two chefs were on hand to serve the families. No other diners were present. When news of the hurricane was first reported, the families had considered postponing the sit-down, but Vladimir suggested the storm would help keep the meeting private.

The owner of Something Fishy nervously collected the gangster's overcoats, and the two families were seated at a round table in the center of the dining room, beneath fishnets and lobster traps suspended from the ceiling. Macey Kick and Peter Volkov left the table and inspected the bathrooms to make sure no one would pull a Michael Corleone. Their search of the rest rooms was slow, as each one tried to keep an eye on the other. When Volkov stooped to check behind a toilet, the side of his head began to throb and burn. He held his hand over his stitches. "Nasty cut you've got there," Macey said. "Hope it doesn't scar." Volkov ignored her and continued his search for hidden weapons. Finding nothing, the two bodyguards returned to the dining room and the negotiations began in earnest.

Vladimir Borisova crossed his arms as he studied his competition on the other side of the table. "Increase, it is good we finally meet," he said.

Increase nodded. "I agree."

"It is a shame your son Wyatt could not attend," Vladimir said. He was sincere. He had wanted to take out all of the Lynches in one clean sweep. Still, two dead Lynches were better than none, and Wyatt clearly was not the brains in the organization. The Borisovas could bump off the psycho later.

Increase put his arm around Leon and nodded toward Macey. "I've got my diplomacy advisor and my operations manager with me. They're all we need today."

"I suppose so," Vladimir said. He unfolded a napkin and tucked it over the collar of his black silk shirt. "I want you to know, Increase, that I have washed my hands quite recently."

Increase ran a hand over the bald portion of his head. "What does that mean?" he asked. "You wash your hands of the killings?"

"No, I wash my hands of germs and dirt. Before we come here, I put my hands under the faucet and I rub them with soap. I work up a good lather and clean under the fingernails." Vladimir held up his hands for Increase's inspection. "Very clean hands."

Increase nodded patiently. "That's good."

"Yes, for both of us. I also brush my teeth just before we leave for this dinner. I brush, then floss, then use the mouthwash." Vladimir tapped his square jaw. "Clean mouth."

"Marvelous," Increase said. He smirked broadly. "I can see you're a man who's proud of his personal hygiene. Good for you, Vlady."

"You know why I tell you this?" Vladimir asked.

Increase shrugged. "Because you're a little kooky?"

"I tell you this because today we share our meals," said Vladimir.

"Yeah, in a manner of speaking, I guess."

"Not in a manner of speaking only. In literal speaking, we share our meals. I drink half of my glass of wine, and you drink half of your wine. Then we exchange glasses. We both eat half of our dinner plates, then we trade. Everything I eat, you eat also."

"What the hell for?" Increase asked.

"Because your younger son here is an excellent pharmacist," Vladimir said. "This is what I hear. I think maybe your son could make me ill, yes?"

"Ah, Leon wouldn't do that," Increase said. He reached over and tousled his son's short white dreads. "He's not that sort of boy."

"Good. Then you do not mind sharing meals with me, no?"

Increase glanced at Leon. Leon gave his father a subtle, reassuring nod. "No, I don't mind sharing meals," Increase said. "And I have a clean mouth too, by the way. I'm a brushing and flossing machine. And the mouthwash too. I love that shit. I use it all the time."

"This is reassuring," Vladimir said.

"Do we all have to share our meals?" Leon asked.

"I think it is enough that the fathers share meals," Vladimir said. "However, you are welcome to share a meal with my son, if you feel safer."

"I think we'll pass on that, Dad," said Josef Borisova. Josef was much thinner than his father, and his spiky brown hair and long sideburns made him look younger than his twenty-eight years. He wore a suit, but the top button of his shirt was unbuttoned, and his narrow tie was loose and crooked. A faint odor of marijuana lingered about him. He looked at Leon and said, "I think my fear of the Willies or some other virus exceeds my fear of being poisoned." His accent had no trace of Russian, but he didn't sound exactly American either. He sounded vaguely English. "No offense," he said to Leon.

"None taken," Leon said.

The owner of the restaurant lingered uneasily by the table. He had received a call the night before warning him to stay open for this meeting despite the weather. "Folks, would you care to begin with some appetizers?" he asked from a safe distance.

The table ordered a round of Bombay Sapphire martinis, shrimp cocktails, and smoked salmon. Increase dipped a shrimp in cocktail sauce and bit it. He pointed the shrimp stump at Borisova and said, "So, Vladimir, I hope you're as committed to the idea of peace as I am. I think enough blood has been shed between our families. We've both lost some good players. If we continued to whack out our best guys like this, neither of our organizations will have a chance of standing up to the greaseballs if they decide to move into Butchers Harbor."

Vladimir glared at Increase. "Grease balls?" he said, pronouncing 'balls' as 'bowls.'

"Yeah," Increase said, sipping his gin. He smirked at Vladimir, who seemed perplexed. "The Wops, man," Increase explained. "The Degos. Those Mafioso Guinea bastards." Increase fished an olive out of his drink and popped it in his mouth. "I mean, those greasy goombahs are some stupid sons of bitches, but they do have strength in numbers. Am I right?"

"I admire Cosa Nostra," Vladimir said sternly. "They are great Americans." He considered pushing his chair from the table and storming out of the restaurant, but he managed to calm himself with the knowledge that Increase would be dead within a few hours.

Increase snickered. "I didn't mean any offense, Vladimir. I mean, I'm sure the Cosa Nostra are a great bunch of guys, but right now, that's really neither here nor there. Let's talk about us." Increase used both hands to tap his chest, and then he gestured to indicate the entire group at the table. "Let's talk about our situation. Can we arrange a cease-fire? Are we going to put an end to these killings?"

"You did start this war first, yes?" Vladimir asked.

"Yeah," Increase agreed, "and we were here first, too. You can't blame us for defending our interests, can you?"

Josef Borisova slathered horseradish dressing over a slice of pink salmon. "Mr. Lynch, I doubt McDonald's was delighted when Burger King started selling Whoppers, but that's the nature of a free market, isn't it?"

"I suppose it is, Sport," Increase said, "and I suppose there's enough appetite in Butchers Harbor to support two burger joints, but as they say, two's company and three's a crowd. Can we at least work together to makes sure we won't have to contend with Wendy's moving onto the block?"

"That's what we're here to discuss," said Josef.

Vladimir Borisova cleared his throat. "Before we take this discussion further, let us get one fact straight. Cosa Nostra are not Wendy's. Cosa Nostra are the Big Mac of our industry. We are not even Burger King compared to the Mafia. We are just family businesses flipping burgers. Let us show proper respect."

Increase tossed a shrimp tail into an ashtray. "Okay, Vladimir, we're a couple of local burger joints. I'm glad we straightened that out." He looked over his shoulder toward the kitchen. "I'll tell you one thing," he said. "All these metaphors are making my tummy growl. I'm about ready for my supper."

Down the road, Sickie Listyev sat on the floor of a dingy corner apartment as he loaded an anti-tank grenade into his RPG. He stood and looked out the windows. He had a clear view down the road leading from the piers. He also had a view of the drawbridge across the street. The heavyset drawbridge operator saw Sickie in the window and waved. Sickie turned his back without responding. When Sickie sighted the Lynches approaching the bridge, he was to wave a red handkerchief before the window. This was the signal for the drawbridge operator to raise the bridge and lower the gate, which would keep the Lynches' car idling just below Sickie Listyev. He would have plenty of time to take aim and fire a grenade into the Town Car. If any Lynches survived the grenade attack, he would mow them down with the AK-74.

Sickie checked his watch. The sit-down would probably last another hour or so. He picked up the RPG and practiced taking aim on a few of the lonely cars that passed on the wet streets below. The neck brace made it difficult for Sickie to center his eye over the sight. However, Sickie wouldn't need to be a perfect marksman when he was firing anti-tank grenades.

KILL WHITEY

Increase stirred his spoon in a bowl of gumbo, searching for a calamari ring among the okra, crawfish, andouille sausage, and rattlesnake. "Obviously, you love America. That's good to see. You have an immigrant's fresh perspective of this nation, and I admire you for that," Increase said to Vladimir. "But you have to admit, my Russian friend, America is full of shit most of the time. Take this whole notion of 'freedom' as an example. This is the land of the free, right? When America was having its little cold war with the Soviet Union, we were told that there was no freedom in your country. Yet what kind of freedom do we have in the good old USA? If you took an unbiased poll, the overwhelming majority of Americans would favor legalization of our industry's products and services. They vote for our products every day with their wallets, right? Their demand for our goods keeps us in business. Still, the tiny percentage of our population that writes the laws has decided to deny the masses the simple pleasures they crave. I mean, a guy can go to jail just for smoking Mother Nature. Is that freedom? No, I don't think it is, comrade."

Vladimir Borisova chuckled. "Let us be honest, Increase. We do not want that kind of freedom. If Mr. Joe Six Pack could walk into his local supermarket and buy a pack of Easy Smokes Light Marijuana or a trial-size balloon of heroin, we would not be successful men, no? This is a good country. It is prudent to regulate the drugs and the prostitution and so on. It prevents the huge corporations from dominating our markets. As we know, there already are some powerful syndicates that control many of the largest cities, but in the little niches like Butchers Harbor, there is still the opportunity for the average man to thrive." Vladimir switched bowls of gumbo with Increase. "Face it, my friend," he said, "you and I, we were not born with spoons of silver in our mouths. In other countries, we could not have pulled our boots by the straps to become the wealthy men that we are today. This is a good country. It is the land of opportunity." Vladimir extended his arm and placed his hand on his son's shoulder. "Now the question is how can we share the bounty and protect our wealth for our children?"

Increase raised his glass and said, "Vladimir, my friend, I think we can work something out." The two men sipped their wine and exchange glasses. Despite the tension both had felt when they first sat down to dinner, the two men were warming up to one another. In fact, everyone at the table was enjoying the company. As he had felt in the Restaurant Georgia, Peter Volkov had a hazy notion that he had met Leon before. He felt a strange urge to confess his sins and grief to the pale young man. Macey Kick and Josef Borisova were engaged in a conversation about administrative strategies. They joked about the egos and personal quirks of the families they managed. Leon, for his part, was drawn to Macey. He had always thought she was beautiful, and he had felt they shared a common loneliness in this world, but tonight he was desperately in love with her. He had to remind himself that chemicals were at work in his brain, and his emotions might not be genuine. He had a difficult time controlling his lust, however, when Macey reached under the table and brushed the inside of his thigh with her fingernails. This was not typical behavior for Macey.

The apparent success of the sit-down had less to do with the chemistry between the Lynches and Borisovas than it had to do with the chemistry of the various berries and leaves that Leon had boiled in his kitchen three weeks earlier. As Vladimir had feared, Leon had doped the meals they ate, but only Leon was aware of this. He had learned which company supplied Something Fishy with its produce and herbs, and he had bribed the man who delivered these goods to the restaurant to allow him onto the truck before it stopped at the harbor-side restaurant. As the truck bounced over potholes, Leon sprayed a harmony potion over crates of plum tomatoes, green onions, habañero peppers, and okra. He dipped cloves of garlic and bundles of parsley, mint, and cilantro into the drug.

Unsure of how soon the restaurant might use a certain supply of vegetables, Leon had been doping the produce for over two weeks. During this time, couples had entered the restaurant with one spouse planning to ask the other for a divorce; instead, the couples returned home and made love like newlyweds. Children who had revealed to their parents that they were gay or dropping out of college were embraced and accepted by their mothers and fathers. Every business deal that was discussed in those two weeks at Something Fishy was the beginning a solid partnership.

"Excuse me, please, for one moment," Vladimir said. He rose from his chair and walked toward the front door of the restaurant. Macey gave Increase a concerned look, but he dismissed her suspicions with a slight wave of the hand. Vladimir stepped outside the restaurant, took the arm of one of his burly guards, and led him some distance from the shelter of the awning. The two men stood in the driving rain, and Vladimir said sternly in Russian, "Get to Sergei Listyev and tell him the plan is off."

"The assassination?" the guard asked. Rain collected in fat beads on his gold hoop earring.

"Yes. If any harm comes to the Lynches, I will personally execute every individual that contributed to their deaths. That includes you if you do not deliver my message. Go now. Tell Sergei the hit is off."

Sickie Listyev stuck a coat hanger down his brace and tried to scratch the back of his neck. He grunted with relief as he worked his itch. He peered out the window, watching an elderly woman fill a bucket from a rainspout. "Crazy old pigeon," he muttered to himself. A red SUV sped through a puddle and splashed the old woman before it came to a stop by the curb. Sickie watched as one of the Borisovas guards stepped out of the SUV. Sickie stepped away from the window and listened to the footsteps climbing the stairs. There was a knock at the door. Sickie opened the door and allowed the guard from Something Fishy to step inside.

"The hit is off," the guard said. He bit a piece of dead skin off the side of his thumb.

"You are shitting me, no?" Sickie asked.

The guard shook his head. "If Lynches die, you die."

"Who says this?" Sickie asked.

"Vladimir. He wants to make friends now."

"No! Fuck this shit noise!" Sickie shouted. He ripped his doo rag off his head and threw it across the room. "The Lynch fuckermothers disrespected me. I kill them all and their whore chicken head bodyguard too. I will make streets flow red with their blood."

The guard shook his head. "No. Vladimir says if Lynches die, he kills both you and me." He stuck the tip of his thumb in mouth again and gnawed at his thumbnail.

"Then I kill Vladimir," Sickie said. "That bunk cracker dogged me too. Nobody fuck with Sickie anymore." He picked up the AK-74 and fired it into the guard's stomach. The guard dropped to the floor and gurgled as he fumbled for his revolver. Sickie fired another round into the guard's head. "Nobody fuck with Sickie!" he shouted, pointing his finger at the dead man. "Nobody fuck with Sickie!" He slung the machine gun over his shoulder, picked up the grenade launcher, and marched down the stairs to the street. He threw the weapons onto the passenger's seat of the van, climbed behind the wheel, and sped toward Something Fishy on the Harbor.

By the time the Lynches and Borisovas had finished dessert, everyone was pretty drunk, which only improved the effects of Leon's harmony potion. Impulsively, Vladimir Borisova stood on a chair and sang a Russian folk song in booming, off-key notes. The rest of the table laughed heartily at his wretched singing. Josef Borisova held his hands over his ears and said, "Father! Spare us!"

When Vladimir finished his song, he thumped his chest and shouted, "I love you fucking people! All of you are good fucking people! Here's to the best two damn fucking families to ever run a city!"

"Here, here, comrade!" Increase shouted. He leapt onto an adjacent chair and threw his arm over Vladimir's shoulder. "Here is to the Lynches and Borisovas! The best partnership since Luciano and Lansky!"

Leon, Macey, Peter Volkov, and Josef Borisova all stood,

raising their glasses and voices in boisterous assent. Even the raging storm outside seemed to cheer and applaud as the wind howled and the windows rattled.

Up on the warehouse across from the restaurant, the wind was picking up. Cracker Jack Farrell and the Ukrainian clung to a vent hood. "I think we should go down!" the Ukrainian shouted over the wind.

"I ain't leaving," Cracker said, "and you ain't leaving my sight."

On the other side of the piers, Sickie Listyev mashed the accelerator and sped through a red light. He formed a plan of attack as he drove. First, he would run over the guards with the van. Then he would fire a few grenades into the restaurant. Then he would move in and clean up with the automatic rifle. He hoped that Vladimir and the chicken head Macey would survive the grenades so he could kill them with the machine gun. Let them beg for mercy. Let them know who was killing them.

Sickie heard a freight train rumbling beside him. He turned but only saw warehouses on either side. By the sound of it, Sickie figured the train must be very close, probably on the other side of the buildings. The rumble of the train grew louder until Sickie heard an explosion behind him. When he looked into his rearview mirror, he saw a storehouse crumbling as its bricks and concrete swirled into a black funnel cloud. The funnel twisted onto the street, following Sickie. The burnt frame of an abandoned car slid away from the sidewalk toward Sickie's van. He had to swerve hard to avoid the wreck as it tumbled in reverse cartwheels down the street. "Fuckermother," Sickie gasped. He stepped harder on the accelerator, but he seemed to be slipping backwards.

Cracker and the Ukrainian watched the tornado slice through buildings as it moved toward the piers. An explosion of white sparks flashed in the black cloud as it ripped into a transformer. Then the tornado slipped over the harbor for a moment and picked up some water before it writhed its way back onto the city. As it approached the warehouse, the twister hurled a van out of its funnel. The van fell to the earth and was torn to shreds as its cargo of grenades exploded.

"Now we go!" the Ukrainian shouted. He let go of the grate and scrambled for the fire escape leading down the building. A hard gust rushed over the rooftop and hurled him over the edge. His arms and legs flailed as he attempted to tread air. Cracker held the grate with both hands, hunkered against the storm, and hoped the tornado would change its course before it reached the warehouse.

The door to Something Fishy burst open and the guards from both families rushed in. "Tornado!" shouted Fuzzy Magee, pointing toward the open door. "Big-ass tornado! Coming this way!"

Macey shouted to the owner of the restaurant, "Do you have a walk-in cooler?"

The owner nodded and ran out of the room. Everyone else chased after him, fleeing the dining room and racing into the kitchen. Vladimir Borisova, who was near the back of the group, slipped on a spatter of oil on the tiled floor and fell flat on his stomach. One of the Borisova guards stepped on Vladimir's back as he raced for the shelter of the cooler.

When the cooler was packed with frantic bodies, Macey started to close the door until Increase shouted, "Where's Vladimir?" As Macey turned to look for the Russian, Increase rushed past her and ran back into the kitchen. Leon tried to follow, but Macey grabbed his arm and pulled him back into the makeshift shelter.

The floor began to shake, and the restaurant groaned like a wounded mammoth. Then the farthest wall of the dining room erupted in a spray of boards and splinters. Macey slammed the freezer door shut as pots and pans soared through the kitchen. The walk-in shook as it was hammered with debris. A steel rod punctured one side of the cooler, shot over the heads of the group, and pierced the opposite wall. "Fuuuuuck!" Fuzzy shouted as he dropped to a crouch and held his hands over his head. The others also fell to the floor or huddled behind boxes and crates.

Leon cowered behind several cases of wine, hoping the cardboard, glass, and Chardonnay would protect him from flying rebar and concrete. Peter Volkov appeared to be praying as he clasped his hands under his chin. Macey pressed her body flat against the floor, but she kept her eyes open as she scanned the cooler for signs of rupture.

When the rumbling and pounding had subsided, Macey was the first to stand. She cautiously opened the door and stepped outside. Leon followed. Outside the cooler, they saw only one wall along the kitchen remained standing. The dining room had disappeared. Gone was the great oak table where the two families had sang and laughed moments before. Gone were the nets and lobster traps that had been suspended from the ceiling, vanished like the ceiling itself.

KILL WHITEY

Gone were the paintings of fishermen and four-masted barks and the walls on which they hung. Gone were Increase Lynch and Vladimir Borisova.

Increase looked down at the docks of Butchers Harbor swirling madly a dozen yards beneath his feet. He was pelted with gravel and chunks of concrete, but he survived for the moment because he and the wreckage were traveling in the same direction and at roughly the same speed. Increase tried to push himself out of the path of a lamppost that nudged his back. When the air around him began to fill with water, he feared he would drown in the sky. Increase held his breath and closed his eyes. He collided with something solid and grabbed it for protection. The thing seemed to grab him in return, and Increase opened his eyes to see Vladimir Borisova staring back at him.

The two men grasped each other's wrists and screamed into one another's face. They spun as if their feet were opposite tips of a propeller. Vladimir seemed to be trying to say something, but Increase could not even hear his own howls over the pummeling wind.

Increase was torn from Vladimir and thrown from the twister. He plummeted for a moment until the earth slapped his body. The ground seemed to swallow him. In a panic, Increase realized he was underwater. He tried to swim to the surface, but his terror deepened as he realized he did not know which way was up. Increase tried to suppress his panic. Easy, old man, he thought to himself. Easy, old buddy. He allowed a few air bubbles to escape through his lips, and he watched them roll through the murky water. The bubbles rolled to the right. Right was up. Increase paddled under-water, moving his head toward the direction of the bubbles. He exhaled slightly again and followed the bubbles to the surface. Above water, Increase gasped and struggled to pull in air between the salt spray and rain.

Increase laughed wildly. "I'm alive!" he shouted. "I'm alive! Thank God! I'm alive!" He was about to shout more thanks and praise when a massive wave rolled over his head and kept him submerged him for several terrifying seconds. He popped to the surface again and cried, "Jesus Christ, I'm gonna drown!"

Walls of ocean surrounded Increase. He saw another mountain of water rolling toward him, and he kicked and paddled furiously to climb its slope. When he reached the summit of the wave, he saw the murky silhouette of Butchers Harbor. He swam desperately for the shore. He was not too far out, but the ocean was beastly. He could not tell if he was moving forward or backward. Undeterred, Increase decided that anyone who had survived a ride in a tornado could find the will to swim to safety under any conditions. He kicked off his shoes and began the strenuous swim to shore.

After several minutes of fighting the fierce waves, Increase thought he heard a call for help somewhere behind him. "Is that you, Vladimir?" he shouted as he treaded water. A wave lifted him high above the sea for a better view of his surroundings, and he thought he could see an arm flailing among the white crest of a far wave. "Hang in there, buddy! I'm coming to get you!" he shouted. He turned his course and swam boldly into the treacherous sea, taking himself farther from the shore of Butchers Harbor.

Increase never found Vladimir Borisova. Instead, Vladimir was recovered by the 5th District Fire Department. Actually, the fire department recovered only the portion of Vladimir that protruded from a dockside water tower. The remainder of Vladimir was scraped off the walls after the tank was drained.

Increase Lynch was discovered at the bottom of the harbor by hordes of crabs and lobsters. When Something Fishy on the Harbor was rebuilt three months later, Increase returned to the restaurant in the bellies of some of its entrees.

11
FUCKED

Leon was crumpled in the passenger's seat of the rented Town Car. He rested his head against the side window and watched thin snakes of rainwater writhing on the on the other side of the glass. "Man," he sighed. "When did the world lose its mind?"

"Long before we were born, I'm sure," Macey said. She drummed her fingers on the steering wheel.

"I just don't get it," he said. "All my life, I've wanted my father to respect me. Or just acknowledge me."

"Mm hmm," Macey said.

"My whole life, my father ignored me. Then, finally, he started paying some attention to me. He seemed—I don't know—he's seemed a little proud of me these past few days."

"He was proud," Macey said. She wished Leon would get out of the car, which had been idling in front of his house for nearly ten minutes.

"Yeah. I think he was a little proud of me," Leon said. "Finally. And then the sky just reaches out and snatches him away. The sky picks him up and throws him into the ocean. Just like that. I don't get it. I don't understand."

"What's to understand?" Macey asked. "The world's a horror show."

"Yeah. It is," Leon muttered.

Macey fidgeted in her seat. She was about ready to push Leon out of the car. She wished Fuzzy Magee or Frankie Baloney had driven the sad sack home. She wished she had called Wyatt and told him to pick his brother up at the remains of the restaurant. Leon should be with family at a time like this. Of course, that was the problem. Even Macey had to feel sorry for anyone whose remaining family was Wyatt Lynch. As she considered Leon's situation, she realized he had no one to turn to for support. She was probably the closest thing he had to a friend. Lucky her.

Macey felt strange. She could almost understand Leon's anguish. If Increase Lynch was dead, and he almost certainly was, she might actually miss the old man. She also felt sorry for Leon, this wimpy kid whining about his daddy. She had a bizarre urge to hold him and pat his back or stroke his little white dreadlocks. Talk about the world not making sense, Macey's sudden bout of feeble emotions did not make sense. Leon and Increase were just people. They were just things. She had seen plenty of folks come and go, and she had never cared before. Something was wrong with her this night. "So," she said, "you gonna be alright?"

Leon lifted his head from the window and glanced around him. "Oh," he said. "Right. I ought to go." He opened the door and stepped out of the car into the rain.

"Hey. Leon," Macey said.

Leon stooped down to look inside the car. Rain hammered against his back and streamed off the unknotted tie draped over his neck. "Yeah?"

"Everything will be fine," she said. "Okay?"

"Yeah. Sure." He closed the door, and Macey watched him lumber up the walk to his home. At the front steps, he fumbled with his keys, unlocked the door, and stepped inside. He glanced back at Macey with painful longing as he slowly shut the door.

Macey sat in the idling Town Car, watching the wipers battle the rain. She shook her head, shut off the engine, and stepped out of the car. Her first steps were slow, but as the rain soaked her, she ran to Leon's house. She raised her hand to ring the doorbell, and for the first time in her life, she hesitated. She stood with her finger hovering before the buzzer. Slowly, she reached forward and rang the bell.

Leon opened the door and the two faced each other in silence. Macey closed her eyes and turned her face to the sky, letting the rain wash her cheeks and lips. She lowered her head and smiled. "Can I come in?" she asked.

Leon stepped aside, allowed Macey over the threshold, and shut the door behind her. "I feel strange," Macey said. "I have feelings I've never felt before."

Leon saw the confusion in her eyes. Ashamed, he shifted his gaze to the floor. "Macey, I need to tell you something," he said. He raised his eyes again, just in time to see Macey's fist hurling toward his jaw. The uppercut knocked Leon's teeth together in a grinding clatter. He spun around in a half-circle and dropped facedown on the thin carpet.

Leon groaned and rolled onto his back. He tried to lift himself onto his elbows, but Macey pinned him to the floor by stepping on his throat. "What did you do to me?" she asked. "You drugged me, didn't you?"

"Sorry," Leon sputtered. "I'm sorry."

Macey applied more pressure to Leon's neck. "Don't apologize. Explain."

"I doped the meals at Something Fishy," Leon croaked. "I spiked the food with a harmony potion. I just wanted the meeting to go well. I wasn't targeting you, Macey. I drugged everyone.

"What's a harmony potion?"

"It makes people like each other," he gagged.

"How long will the feelings last?" Macey asked.

"They'll fade by tomorrow morning," Leon said, struggling for breath under Macey's foot.

"It's temporary?" Macey demanded.

Leon turned his head so his jaw took some of the weight of Macey's foot. "Depends. The drug loses all pharmaceutical influence in less than a day. Whether the harmony lasts is up to the user."

"Okay," Macey said, lifting her foot. Leon gasped for air and rubbed his throat. He started to sit up, but Macey pounced on him, shoving his shoulders back to the floor and pinning his hips with her knees. "As long as it's temporary," she said. She started to unbutton Leon's shirt.

"What are you doing?" Leon stammered.

"Take a guess," Macey said. She had trouble with a button, so she tore Leon's shirt open. She ran her hand up his flat stomach and narrow chest, then used her pinkie nail to scrape one of his colorless nipples.

Leon watched Macey lick her upper lip with the tip of her tongue. "Macey, this isn't right," he said. His voice and body quivered.

"Shut up."

"Macey, I want this too," Leon said, "but my father has just been carried out to sea by a tornado!"

Macey unbuckled Leon's belt and pulled it free from his pants.

"Macey, come on," Leon protested. "I don't think this is right."

"Your dad would want it this way," Macey said, unzipping Leon's pants. "Believe me, the old man was beginning to wonder if you liked women." She yanked Leon's pants and boxers down to his knees. "It looks to me like you do."

"Oh, man," Leon said, his voice shaky with anticipation and disbelief.

Macey, still holding Leon fast with her thighs, pulled off her black denim shirt. "Oh God," Leon gasped, watching the muscles that rippled on her shoulders. Macey leaned her chest against Leon and licked his eyelid as she slipped out of her jeans. "Oh, man," Leon whispered. He moved his shaking hands down the small valley of her back. Macey sat up and unhooked her bra. "Oh my god," Leon sighed. He slowly raised his hands and reverently touched her breasts. Macey pressed her hands over Leon's and guided his fingers across her torso. "Oh my god," he whispered again. Macey smiled sweetly as she slipped off her panties. "Oh Sweet Jesus!" he gasped. His body quivered as Macey straddled his hips. "H-h-h-o. H-h-h-o. Holy shit!"

Leon slept like a corpse. He did not stir or dream for nine hours. When he awoke, he was still exhausted. He opened his eyes and squinted in the sunlight that filled his room. He started to sit up, but his head and limbs felt thick and heavy. He dropped to the mattress again and closed his eyes. Slowly, memories of his night with Macey came to him. He pictured her pearly teeth biting her full lower lip. He recalled the slippery glide of soap on her skin, the flicker of candlelight in her dark eyes, and the patter of rain on the windows as she fell asleep in his arms.

The memories helped to draw him out of his slumber. Part of him was beginning to stir, at any rate. He imagined how it would feel to roll over and find Macey sleeping beside him. He would brush her hair and softly kiss her forehead. Then, he would slowly draw the sheets down her naked body as he kissed her flesh inch by inch.

He knew she was not beside him. She was not the type to stay until the morning. Still, it was nice to imagine she was there, and Leon did not turn for several minutes as he pretended she was beside him, sleeping so soundly that he could not hear her. When he finally rolled over, he saw he was alone in the bed. Although he had not expected to find her at his side, he felt a bit emptier seeing she was gone. Like Leon's father, she had disappeared.

As Leon thought of his dad and the tornado, his loneliness quickly turned into panic and shame. Increase had just died, and Leon had spent the night in a sexual frolic. It did not seem like an honorable way for a son to grieve. Leon wondered if his father had survived. As Leon considered the possibility, he became more convinced that his father was still alive. The tornado had thrown all sorts of debris into the harbor. Wooden beams, telephone poles, even boats were undoubtedly scattered for miles across the water. Increase could easily be clinging to some board even at this moment, desperate for someone to find him as the cold sea drew him farther from land. At that moment, his father might have been clinging to a sheet of plywood, struggling to keep his mouth above the waves, gasping for air and coughing up salt water as he scanned the turbulent horizon for the dark fins of sharks. And where was Leon at that same moment? He was lying in bed with a boner.

Leon wrapped himself in a sheet and leapt out of bed. He raced out of his bedroom and paced between his kitchen and den, moving with frantic energy but without purpose. When he stumbled over his pants crumpled on the floor, he dropped his sheet and began to dress himself in yesterday's clothes, which were strewn about the den. He did not waste time with underwear or socks. He just slipped on his slacks and dress shirt, stepped into his shoes without tying them, and raced out the door.

Leon drove through Butchers Harbor with uncharacteristic speed and recklessness until he arrived at the docks. He parked his car near the rubble of Something Fishy and scanned the harbor's horizon for some movement that could be his father. He saw nothing and wished he had brought a pair of binoculars with him. He ran back to his car and drove along the harbor until he reached a fish market. Behind the gray-shingled shops were several small fishing boats docked along two piers. Leon parked his car before a fire hydrant and ran out onto the docks. He leapt over wet garbage, broken branches, and splinters scattered across the planks. He approached a young fisherman who was crouched on the deck of his boat.

"Hey," Leon called. "Can I rent your boat?"

The fisherman looked up and brushed his long, gritty hair out of his eyes. "What do you want?"

"I need to rent your boat," Leon said. "My father was carried out to sea by yesterday's tornado. I need to get out there. I have to look for him."

The kid gave Leon a concerned look. "Dude, the Coast

Guard's already cruising the harbor looking for bodies. Or survivors too, I guess."

Leon nodded. "Yeah, fine, but I need to do something myself. I can't just stand here while my father drowns out there. He's my father."

"Yeah, man, I hear you. If it was my old man, I'd be freaking out too. But you can't take my boat, dude. For one thing, I'm inspecting it for damage from the storm."

"Can you help me find another boat?" Leon pleaded. "My father needs me. I can't waste any more time."

The fisherman wiped his hands on his jeans. "You got a boat license?"

Leon did not, but he nodded yes. The boat had a steering wheel. Leon figured it couldn't be much different than driving a car.

"You got the license on you?"

Leon groaned. "Come on! What are you doing to me? Listen, I'll hire someone to take me out. I just need to get out there. Now."

The fisherman nodded. "So how much money you got on you, anyhow?"

Leon reached for his back pocket and cursed as he realized he had left his wallet at home. The fisherman climbed off his boat and stepped onto the dock. "Listen, dude. You can't do anything out there that the Coast Guard isn't already doing. Let me walk you to a payphone, and I'll give you a number for the Coast Guard. Talk to them, find out how the search is going, and sit tight. That's all you can do."

For the next three days, Leon returned to the docks. From dawn to dusk, he paced the piers, scanning the horizon through a pair of high-powered binoculars. Every hour, he would walk to a payphone and pester the Coast Guard. At the end of the third day, Leon was told that the search was over. The Coast Guard had recovered any bodies it was going to find.

Leopard eyes drifted through Leon's greenhouse as a peacock butterfly fluttered through a cluster of slender Quang Ngai bamboo and landed on Leon's shoulder. Leon was crouched over his koi pond, dropping flakes of dried shrimp onto the water. The beautiful carp with scales painted like Mardi gras costumes darted after the food. A koi spotted with tiny gold hearts fanned its sapphire fins as it looked up at Leon and waited for some shrimp to be tossed in his direction. Leon reached slowly toward the water, trying to pet the fish on the head. The movement spooked all of the koi, and they retreated to the far end of the pond.

Leon studied the vacant spot from where the fish had fled, and he watched his faint reflection quiver over the emptiness. He scattered more food onto the water and rested on his heels. Leon felt relaxed in his greenhouse. He had started to calm down over the past two days. A week had passed since the tornado, and he no longer felt a blind panic to rescue his father. He knew his father was no longer alive. As Leon watched the fish ripple the water's skin, he tried to summon grief for his father, but the sorrow would not come. He felt only a sense of lost opportunity. It would have been nice to spend more time with his father, to get to know him finally. Increase had not been much of a dad, and hadn't been a very good man. It was shameful to think such things, but Leon could not deceive himself any longer. Still, family was family, and things could have been different.

Leon heard the telephone ringing in his house. He let it

continue to ring, but the caller would not hang up. Slowly, Leon walked through his greenhouse and entered his house. He picked up the phone and said, "Who is this?"

"*It's me,*" Macey said. Neither she nor Leon spoke for several seconds. "*Are you okay?*" she asked.

"I'm okay," he answered. "Should I have called you earlier? After the other night?"

Macey chuckled. "*No, that's fine. We both had things to sort out.*"

Leon sat on a stool by his kitchen counter. "I ... I'm glad you called, Macey."

"*Sure. No problem.*" She was silent for a moment. "*So listen. The reason why I'm calling ... Wyatt's calling a meeting, and he wants you to attend.*"

"Oh. I see," Leon said. "Well, Wyatt can fuck himself. I'm not going to any meeting."

"*That's not a good attitude to take right now. This is not the right time to piss your brother off.*"

"I don't have a brother," Leon said. "My family died with my father. I have no further interest in the family trade."

"*Good. Now you need to tell that your brother.*"

"I told you, Macey. I am not going to a meeting or any other place that will bring me in contact with Wyatt."

"*It's not a request, Leon. Wyatt wants you at your father's lighthouse in one hour. If you aren't there, I'll have to come and get you. Now watch your step from here on. If you aren't sensible, you'll put us all in a tough position. Don't make me do something I don't want to do.*"

Leon was silent. His listened to Macey's short, agitated breaths. "Fine," he said. "I'll be there."

Leon drove his Escort up the hill leading to his father's light-house. He pulled around to the back of the building and saw a crew of some twenty thugs drinking beers at the edge of the bluff. Leon parked his car and trudged toward the group. He looked for Macey, but she was not present. He helped himself to a beer in the cooler, then ambled toward the edge of a cluster of goons that included Cracker Jack, Fuzzy Magee, and Frankie Baloney.

Cracker acknowledged Leon with a short nod. Most of the other hoods looked out to sea or studied the beers in their hands. In contrast to the rest, Fuzzy Magee showed an intense in Leon. He stood with his arms clutched close to his chest and his hands tucked within the sleeves of his suede jacket as he stared and grinned at Leon. Speaking through chattering teeth, he said, "My mother had a saying about new brooms." Leon smiled and took a few steps away from Fuzzy.

A strong breeze was coming off the water. Wyatt zipped his dolphin-hide jacket up to his chin, and he forced a long, sorrowful sigh. "Here's to my dad," he said, raising his beer. The rest of the group raised their beers and drank. Wyatt walked to the edge of the bluff and poured the remainder of his beer over the side. "Here's to you, Dad." He watched the beer foam on the rocks and splatter into the ocean. He tossed the empty can into the waves and turned to face the group with his hands clasped solemnly before him.

"I think we have to face the sad fact that my father is not coming back," Wyatt said. "He's been missing for a week now. I suppose we could wait another week or two, just so we won't have an empty coffin at his funeral, but I don't think we should hold any delusional hopes that he's still alive." Wyatt reached into the cooler at his feet and pulled out another beer. "Dad loved the ocean. So I think he's happy right now, being at rest in the sea he loved." Wyatt cracked open his beer. "I think he would have liked it that way."

The others nodded and muttered in agreement. Fuzzy pressed his temples with the heels of his hands and said, "He's in a good place. The bed bugs don't bite in Davy Jones' locker."

Wyatt paused for a moment as he considered Fuzzy's remarks. He shrugged and continued with his speech. "Anyhow, we need to make plans for Dad's funeral. Then we have to make plans for *after* Dad's funeral. I'll get right to the point: a strong organization has only one leader, and the leader of this organization should be me. Any objections?"

The crew turned their attention toward Leon. He stared back at them, then laughed wearily. "I have no objection," he said. "I couldn't care less who runs your rackets. I'm out of it. I'm through. I never should've been involved with this insane business in the first place."

"Well, that's something I think we can all agree on," Wyatt said. "But getting back to my question. Does everyone agree I'm in charge?"

"Fuckin' A!" said Frankie Baloney, clapping his hands. "You the man, Wyatt! You the motherfuckin' man!" The rest of the crew showed their support with nods, shrugs, or muttered words such as "you're the boss" or "yeah."

Fuzzy rubbed his hands together. "Hey, is it cold out here, or is it just me? Because I'm fucking freezing. I'm so cold, it feels like ... " He held his hands before his chattering teeth and blew warm air over his fingers. "It's like the dark side of Pluto out here."

"Yeah, Fuzzy, it's chilly," Wyatt said. "Especially if you're wearing a skirt. In a few minutes, we'll get you a nice warm blankie and some hot fucking cocoa. But for now, I'd be grateful if you'd shut your goddamn hole for a minute so I can finish my discussion." Wyatt shook his head then took a chug of beer. "Now, a few things are going to change under my rule. I loved my father to death, but we all know he was a little off, and he was clearly a soft touch. I'm putting some balls back into the organization. The days of peace and love are over. We're back at war with the Borisovas. Now is the time to hit those Russki dildos. Right now, they're having a leadership crisis of their own. Also, they may assume that we won't act until my father is found and buried. If that's their assumption, they're wrong. We act now. Starting today, we wage a full-on offensive to reclaim Butchers Harbor. I don't want to hear any more talk about sharing this city, and I don't want to hear any more talk about a cease-fire. We'll have a cease-fire when there's no Borisovas left to shoot. I need an organization of warriors, not peaceniks and pussies." Wyatt glared at Leon for a moment. "We're also gonna hit our enemies in the unions, the courts, the press, and the police force. We've always been told that we're supposed to keep our hands off the civilians. Well, I say fuck that. We've got a long list of judges, hacks, and pigs that have fucked us over. Now it's their turn to get fucked. Any objections?"

Fuzzy clutched his elbows. "I have an objection," he said. "Why are we standing outside on this tundra? Huh? I'm not fucking around, you swine shits. I'm freezing!" He was shaking furiously now, and he seemed on the verge of weeping. "I need some goddamn heat. I need to stand before a flame before my muscles turn to slush. My brain is turning to a hunk of frozen meat in my skull. I feel the cells exploding under my skin. I feel the ice in my veins. The pipes are bursting all over. Don't you feel it? I can't be the only one."

Fuzzy looked wildly at the rest of the group. "God Almighty! Look at yourselves! You're pigs on the way to slaughter. Look in a mirror. You look like winter corpses in Warsaw." Fuzzy glared at Leon. "And look at you, you poor son of a bitch. Look at all of you. In a few minutes, ravens will perch on your foreheads trying to pull your frozen eyes from your skulls. Maggots will wait for the thaw so they can chew your flesh." He finally broke down in heavy sobs, then turned his back on the group to puke onto the rocks.

"Jesus Christ, Fuzzy!" Wyatt snapped. "What the hell are you on?"

Fuzzy shook violently and continued vomiting until gouts of blood splashed on the rocks. He turned to face the group with a weary smile. "Oh, yeah. Much better. I just needed to get that out of my system. Now, it's all clear, my friends. Now I get it." He pointed at his blood on the stones. "I see them. Can you? I can see the little pricks in my puke, and it all makes sense now. I'm fucked. We're all fucked. Don't even try to fight it now."

Fuzzy spit a gob of blood onto the grass. "Just look at me," he said. "I washed my hands until they bled. I put two sheets of asswipes on the shitter seat. What difference did it make? None. Nothing can stop the micro-phantoms. It's the micro-fucks that get you in the end. They'll eat their way into your veins, too. I'm warning you right now: if they got into me, they'll get into you. We're all finished." He chuckled sadly until puke-blood gushed over his blue lips. The thugs stumbled away from Fuzzy as his blood misted in the ocean wind.

"Goddamn it," Cracker muttered. He drew his Glock. "Fuzzy's got the pigpox."

Wyatt and the rest of the thugs drew their pieces and

aimed them at Fuzzy. "Alright, Fuzzy. Step back," Wyatt ordered. "Keep your distance, and keep your Willies to yourself. If you don't, we'll have to drop you!"

"Don't waste your breath with threats," Fuzzy said. He tried to wipe the blood from his mouth, but he only managed to smear the gore across his face. "Take a look at me, you imbecile. I'm bulletproof." A powerful convulsion seized him. His legs trembled, and his hands fluttered before him as if he were conducting a symphony. In a fit of violent shakes, he stepped closer to the group. Everyone with a weapon fired at Fuzzy, knocking him backward in reverse spasms. He dropped just short of the edge of the cliff.

Although Fuzzy had stopped moving, Wyatt continued to pump bullets into the corpse until his clip was empty. "Yeah, look at you Fuzzy," he said. "The bullets just bounce right off you."

"Aw, man," Leon groaned. He doubled over and held his stomach as a dry lump formed in his throat. He feared he might also vomit and meet the same fate as Fuzzy.

"Alright," Wyatt said. "Somebody get this dickhead out of my sight."

Cracker Jack Farrell pulled his sweatshirt over his mouth and stepped toward Fuzzy. He worked his boot under Fuzzy's shoulder and rolled him over the side of the bluff. Fuzzy bounced down the rocky slope until he splashed into the ocean. Cracker carefully untied his boot with two fingertips and threw the shoe into the ocean after Fuzzy.

"Alright, let's call it day," Wyatt said, keeping his distance from the others. "Why don't we all go home, take showers, burn our clothes, and rub our cars down with bleach and turpentine? For the next few days, we'll talk by phone. Okay? Meeting adjourned."

KILL WHITEY

Leon stepped into his house, closed the door behind him, and staggered to his refrigerator. He opened a can of beer and lowered himself to the floor. He sat on the worn tiles, with his back against a cabinet, and gulped the beer. He hoped the alcohol might quell the murky panic that overwhelmed him, but he wasn't relaxing.

Leon had put himself in a bad situation. He must have been insane when he had decided to return to Butchers Harbor. Irrational urges based on childhood memories distorted by time had drawn him back to this cesspool of killers and lunatics. He had wanted to end his years of drifting isolation by belonging to something. Unfortunately, things had not worked out as he had hoped. He had wanted to belong to a community. Instead, he had a dangerous and unstable association with a pack of thugs. He had longed for a romantic relationship. What he got was a one-night stand with an assassin. He'd wanted a family. All he had left was a psychotic brother who loathed him.

Leon had made a big mistake, but there was no time to mope about it now. Now it was time to move on, he thought. It was time to get the hell out of Butchers Harbor.

Leon decided he should take a long vacation. He felt that a trip to New Guinea was in order. He could sail down the Ramu, stopping along the shore to pick herbs. Then he could take a few weeks to hike along the Maoke Mountains, collecting mushrooms and drawing tree sap. Perhaps some friendly Papuans could turn him on to some other local medicines.

Leon crushed his empty beer can and lobbed it into the sink. He pulled himself up from the floor and wandered about his home, filling his medicine bag with a variety of powders, balms, and goofballs. He stepped back into his kitchen and moved a bookcase away from a wall. He crouched on the floor and lifted a loose tile, revealing a hole he had chiseled into a floor joist. He removed a small packet of aluminum foil from the hole and tucked the foil packet into his shirt pocket. If he needed nothing else, he would need this. Inside the foil packet were Leon's last doses of BMF. Billy Blake had been right; Leon had squirreled away a few doses for a rainy day. As Blake had said, it didn't rain much harder than this.

Leon felt a little more comfortable with the Rip in his pocket, but he was still frazzled. When he shut his eyes, he saw Fuzzy's corpse, the clothes and flesh ripped by bullets. Leon could still smell the gunpowder and the lethal blood that had pooled on the rocks beneath the carcass. For all Leon's anxiety, however, he was also exhausted. Since his heavy sleep after the tornado, he had only slept in fits. Now he was drained to the dregs. He needed something to calm his nerves, something that would give him a few hours of solid sleep.

In his kitchen cabinet, behind tins of Oolong, Cat's Claw, and Lapsang Souchong, Leon kept an herbal tea that filled his head with seraphic lullabies. Leon rummaged through the cabinet until he found the lullaby tea. "Man, do I need this tonight," he muttered as he placed a kettle on the stove. He set the herbs in a clay teapot, and when the kettle was steaming, he filled the teapot with boiling water. After the tea had steeped, he poured the brew into a steel camper's mug and stretched out on his couch, not even bothering to pull out the bed. He sipped his tea and waited to hear heavenly cradlesongs.

Leon did not hear any crooning cherubs. Instead, he

heard the low moan of a cat in heat. He tried to ignore the noise as he finished his tea, but the moans only grew louder and began to sound like a woman sobbing. Leon stayed on the couch, afraid that the crying woman outside would see him if he approached the window. She began screaming in a sustained, ear-splitting shriek.

Growing concerned, Leon stepped from the couch and tried to walk to the window, but the floor lurched beneath him, throwing him back onto the sofa. The room tilted to one side, dropped several yards, then shot upward again like a raft riding swollen waves. He felt something sprouting from his sides, and he was startled to see he had six arms. Each arm writhed with a different motion, like the complex dance of some Hindu demigod. He arched his back and began to crabwalk about the floor on all six hands and two feet, with his face and belly pointing upward. He raced frantically about the house, up walls and across the ceiling. He was racing just to stay in place, for the room was spinning on four shifting axes. All the while, cats moaned and women howled. "Damn," Leon muttered, as thousands of neon buffalo-headed gnats squirmed out of his pores. "I think I drank the wrong tea."

The air in the den became thick with Leon's belongings. Clothes, furniture, books, and appliances soared across the house, crashing into one another and slamming against the walls and ceiling. A coffee grinder, tumbling through the air with its chord whipping like a demon's tail, struck Leon in the ear. As he crumpled in pain, he was hit with a hardcover copy of *Art of the 20th Century*. Seven pounds of Western art slamming into the back of his head hurt like hell. He felt his bones burning and his heart beating as fast as a hummingbird's wings. Slowly, insight bore through the chaos and reached Leon's addled mind: Wyatt had sent some-one to tamper with his herbs.

A potted plant smashed a window, and shards of glass pierced Leon's flesh. He knew his heart would rupture soon, and blood would geyser from his lacerations. A briefcase whacked him in the ribs, and he snatched it for a shield. He opened the case and saw it was full of syringes and ampoules. He filled a syringe with what he hoped was a sedative and plunged the needle into one of his six squirming arms.

The room slowed its tumble, and Leon's belongings fell to the floor. The howls and moans slowly hushed to a low, reedy drone. Ferns began to grow about the house, sprouting from furniture and the carpet. Grape vines and ivy crept across the walls. Leon found himself sitting on the couch again. He had lost his extra arms, but his flesh was mossy green. His hair had grown into long fronds that rustled in the breeze drifting through the shattered windows. He felt his coccyx lengthen and worm its way out of his skin. It wagged like a puppy's tail then buried itself in the couch, where it branched and formed roots in the cushions. The couch curved toward Leon and cupped him like a great hand. He fell asleep to the smell of forest rain.

12
CATHARTIC

eon found himself sitting on a milk crate in a narrow alley. He was muttering to himself about the semiotics of dental hygiene in English period films. His own mouth felt grimy and stale. He ran his tongue over his teeth, and they felt slimy, as if he hadn't brushed for a few days. Apparently he had eaten, though, because he felt the jagged wedge of a popcorn kernel stuck between a canine and an incisor. As he tried to pry the kernel out of his teeth with his thumbnail, his head began to throb. He worked his fingers under his sunglasses and gingerly touched his forehead. He felt a large knot just above his left eyebrow.

He could not recall the hours or seconds before this moment, but now he saw his surroundings in perfect clarity. He looked about the dirt alley, at patches of weeds, cigarette butts, empty beer bottles, and wrinkled condoms scattered on the ground like shed snake skins. He glanced at small windows with shades drawn shut on the other side of brick walls covered with graffiti. Somewhere in a nearby apartment, a child practiced the flute. The wispy notes, beautifully labored, fluttered through the same air that carried the stench of alley trash.

Leon had a faint memory of his house in flames. He could

not remember if he had set the fire himself or if it was the work of Lynch goons. The home did not mean much to him, but he would miss the greenhouse. Those plants were the closest he'd had to family. Thinking of his drugs, Leon began to wander around the alley looking for his medicine bag. It was nowhere in sight. He must have dropped it sometime during his forgotten spell of wandering, or he had left it in his burning house.

Leon noticed he was wearing an unfamiliar, expensive overcoat. He searched the deep pockets of the coat and found a fast food paper bag filled with his stash of capsules, home-pressed tablets, and little baggies of various powders. He also found three pairs of cheap sunglasses, a deck of cards, a small pair of pruning shears, a wad of money, and a pencil sharpener shaped like a Civil War cannon. He threw the cards and pencil sharpener into a nearby Dumpster, but he kept the sunglasses, shears, money, and drugs. He patted his shirt pocket and felt the little packet of Slaughter. Good old BMF. He felt a little stronger and braver knowing it was still there.

Leon wondered how long he had been out of it. He wasn't wearing a watch, but that hardly mattered. He had a feeling that he had blanked-out for days rather than hours. He wandered out of the alley and through the streets until he found a familiar block. He bought a newspaper from a stand and read it as he walked. The date on the paper told Leon that three days had passed since he drank the bad tea. The Lynch family had been busy in that time.

The headline for the lead story read: "Two More Dead in Mob Slayings." The paper reported that Peter Volkov, chauffeur and confidant to the late Vladimir Borisova, had been garroted in the Fishkill subway and electrocuted after he was thrown onto the third rail. In a related story, Chip Darby, a labor boss who had been missing for two days, was found suffocated in a dockside grain silo.

A sidebar to the article summarized the other gangland murders of the previous three days. A career criminal named Butch Tyo, who freelanced for the Borisovas, had been bludgeoned to death in a porno theater on Stroker Alley. Parts of Nicky Samoshkin, consigliere to the Borisova family, were turning up in all parts of the city. His vivisectionists had been considerate to include a finger in each bag of body parts to simplify identification. Dwight Fishy Dulap, another mob lawyer associated with the Russian syndicate, had been drowned in an indoor swimming pool at DePrave High.

Two photographers for the *Butchers Harbor Register*, a newspaper that had been hostile in its coverage of the Lynch family, had died from toxic fumes in a darkroom after someone had switched their fixer with hydrocyanic acid. Joyce Nouveau, a reporter with the same paper, had died after prolonged convulsions and hallucinations caused by poisoned dentures. Lowell Porcer, the *Register*'s publisher, literally stopped the presses when his body was run through the massive rolling drums that were printing the evening edition.

Dennis Calloway, the lawyer who had prosecuted Wyatt Lynch, had been forced to eat four thousand dollars in crisp twenty-dollar bills withdrawn from his own savings account. The last bill had been soaked in arsenic. Rosanna Rivera, the judge who had tried Wyatt, had been detonated and dissolved after a chunk of potassium had been dropped in her Jacuzzi. Authorities were able to identify her by several teeth embedded in the stucco ceiling. Finally, Police Chief Bobby McLean had died of spontaneous internal hemorrhaging. Investigators suspected voodoo.

KEN HARVILL

Leon folded the newspaper and tucked it under one arm. He felt lightheaded, and a fuzzy darkness obscured his peripheral vision. He leaned against a telephone pole and shut his eyes until the dizziness passed. As he waited, he felt his shirt pocket again to touch the packet of Slaughter. When Leon opened his eyes, he saw a car slowly passing before him. He glared at the driver until the car disappeared around a corner. He felt he should move indoors where he could form a plan. He crossed the street and headed for a bar called Pig Iron.

The bar was nearly empty. The bartender, a large but weary man, approached Leon and greeted him with a nod. Two women in their early thirties sat at the back, loudly discussing art with an elderly junkie. Leon ordered a glass of orange juice and studied his surroundings. The place had a lot of metal. The floor was tiled with two-foot squares of steel. The barstools and chairs were made of wrought iron. Tables in the back of the bar were blocky and made of highly polished stainless steel; they had the cold, clinical appearance of morgue equipment. The countertops were chrome, and the walls looked like the interior of a sub-marine. "You have a theme going here," Leon said to the bartender. "That's nice."

Leon peeled a C-note from the roll in his coat pocket to pay for his drink. The bartender gave Leon an annoyed glare. "You got anything larger?"

"Sorry. It's all I have."

"Great. Let me run to the bank so I can get you change."

"Keep a twenty for your trouble," Leon muttered. "And give me a roll of quarters. You got a pay phone here?"

The bartender nodded toward a phone set in corner by the rest rooms. He handed Leon the roll of quarters and

277

the rest of his change minus a twenty-spot. He didn't thank Leon for the tip.

Leon carried his orange juice to the payphone. He set his glass on a metal shelf extending from the wall, and dropped two quarters into the phone. The phone rang several times before a woman answered. "*Yeah?*"

Leon hesitated before he spoke. "Macey. It's me."

"*Leon?*"

"Yeah."

"*Jesus, Leon. Where've you been?*"

"I don't know." He spoke softly. "Wyatt's trying to kill me, isn't he?"

"*Yeah.*"

"Can you give him a message? Tell him I want to leave the city. Tell him I'm not a threat."

"*I don't think he considers you a threat, Leon. I think he wants you dead for other reasons.*" They were both silent for half a minute. "*Why are you calling me?*" she asked.

"I need help," Leon said.

Macey did not answer immediately. "*If I help you, I'm putting my own life on the line. You know what Wyatt would do if he found out.*"

"I know. And I know you don't owe me anything. It's just…You're the only one left in this city who's a little friendly to me. I didn't know who else to call. I don't know what else to do."

"*Leon … I'm not really in the business of helping people.*"

Leon put his elbow on the top of the payphone and slumped with the side of his head in one hand. "I'm sorry I bothered you."

"*Wait. Don't hang up … I still have feelings for you, Leon. Is that from the Spanish fly you gave me?*"

Leon smiled. "No. I told you before; the harmony potion only lasts for less than a day. If you still have feelings for me, that's something from within you. And please believe me, Macey, I never intended to use the harmony potion to take advantage of you."

"*I had fun. Did you?*"

Leon blushed. "Yeah."

"*You're lucky you're a good lay, Leon. That's my only motive for keeping you alive.*"

He chuckled as he tried to think of a suave response. "Well ... I'll do what I can to earn my keep." He winced and shook his head at his dopey words. "So, you'll help me then?"

"*Yeah. I'll help your sorry, sexy ass. Where are you?*"

"I'm at a bar called Pig Iron."

"*I know where it is. I should be there in twenty minutes. Just sit tight. Get a beer or something. Stay away from windows, and don't talk to anyone if you can help it.*"

"Alright. Thank you, Macey. I can't thank you enough."

"*Oh, you'll thank me enough. You'll be thanking me plenty.*" She hung up the phone.

Leon grinned as he hung up the phone. Following Macey's instructions, he headed for the bar to order a beer. He swaggered a bit with his chin up and his shoulders held back. The bartender almost did not recognize Leon as the same gloomy schlub who had shuffled into the Pig Iron a few minutes earlier. Leon slapped a five on the bar to pay for a draft, and then he ambled toward the back of the bar, keeping away from the windows as advised. The two thirty-something women and the old man glared at Leon as he approached. Leon gave the ladies a little nod and a smile. Then he turned for a pinball machine in the corner. He draped his overcoat on the back of a chair and dropped two quarters into the machine.

As Leon played pinball, the threesome in the corner resumed their conversation. The old man rambled and droned about Andy Warhol, Christo, heroin, conspiracy theories, Hunter S. Thompson, and the beauty of various diseases. The women interjected occasionally with their own disjointed comments. To Leon, there seemed to be no connection between one person's comments and another's. In fact, any two sentences of one speaker seemed unrelated.

The pinball machine that Leon was playing had a sensitive tilt switch. The slightest jostle would shut the flippers down. After three low-scoring rounds, he stopped feeding quarters into the machine and simply loitered in the corner of the bar. The strange trio seemed suspicious of Leon. They soon finished their drinks and continued their discussion as they exited the bar through a side door. Leon became restless without the distraction of their conversation. He checked his watch and wondered how soon Macey would arrive.

Leon ordered a second beer and began pacing the length of the steel-tiled floor. Feeling a little claustrophobic, he stepped out the side door for fresh air. On one side of the door, grate-metal steps led from the sidewalk into the bar. On the other side was an alley that led to the far side of the block. Holding his beer, he walked three-quarters of the length of the alley. He stopped when he saw an Acura parked on the far side of the street. Cracker Jack Farrell sat in the driver's seat, and Frankie Baloney sat shotgun. Leon crouched behind a pile of wooden crates and watched Macey emerge from the backseat of the Acura.

Leon slumped a bit lower behind the pile of alley garbage. He felt dizzy, nauseous, outraged, and betrayed. He wanted to howl. He wanted to tear a board free from the pallet before him, charge down the alley, and attack Macey with the nail-studded club. He wanted to punch and kick the brick wall beside him. He wanted to smash his own head against the wall until he dropped to the ground bloody and unconscious. Instead, he sighed and muttered, "That figures."

Macey stretched her arms over her head as she scanned the street. She stooped down by the passenger window to speak to Frankie and Cracker. While her back was to the alley, Leon turned and scrambled into the bar.

Inside the Pig Iron, Leon walked back to the pinball machine. He set his beer on a nearby table, reached into his shirt pocket and frantically unfolded the aluminum foil packet. He removed two purple capsules from the packet, considered his situation, and removed two more. He stuffed the four capsules into his mouth and washed them down with his beer. He folded and returned the foil packet to his pocket just as Macey entered the front door. Leon gave her a cool nod as he dropped a dollar in quarters into the pinball machine.

Macey glanced around the bar as she walked to the corner. She stood silently for a moment, watching the pinball bounce off the bumpers. When she looked up at Leon's face, she saw the knot and scrape on his forehead. "What happened here?" she asked, brushing her fingers against the skin beside the wound.

"I don't know," Leon said. He pulled his head away from her as he tried to keep his pinball in play. The ball popped off the tip of a flipper and dropped into the drain.

Macey leaned into Leon and kissed him on the cheek. "Ready to go?"

"In a minute," Leon said. He needed ten to fifteen minutes

before the BMF took hold. Once the turbo kicked in, the icy nerves, high-octane strength, and bloodlust would last for the better part of a day. "I want to finish my game."

Macey smirked. "Sure. Why not?"

Leon pulled the plunger. The ball dropped straight down the playing field and through the flippers without scoring a single point. The machine taunted Leon with an electronic guffaw. "I still have another game in credits," Leon said.

"Play it, then," Macey said. "I'll get a beer."

When Macey turned her back to head to the bar, Leon fed four more quarters into the machine. His hands shook as he played. His goal was not to score high points. He simply wanted to keep the ball in play for long as possible. Macey returned with a pint glass of stout and sat on a stool beside the machine. She waited patiently as Leon played.

After five minutes, a user will feel the first effects of BMF: a boost in energy and confidence accompanied by subdued mental activity and a callous mood. Users often feel a tingling in their fingers, toes, neck, and genitals. Leon felt none of these harbingers of Slaughter's cool rage. Instead, he felt a little queasy. His stomach gurgled, and he started to fart. He struggled to keep the gas leak silent.

When Leon lost his third ball to the out-hole, Macey checked her watch. "Alright, Tommy. Let's hit the road."

"I still have more credits," Leon said.

"I thought you wanted my help so you could slip out of town. Come on, then. Let's go."

Leon sighed as he looked at Macey. "You weren't at my father's lighthouse for the meeting," he said. "You called to tell me I had to attend the meeting, but you weren't there yourself."

Macey tilted her head. "So?"

"So you're the one who switched my tea," he said. "You knew where I kept my tea. You had asked about my plants. You knew what to mix to kill me."

Macey sipped her beer. "I thought I did, anyway. I probably should have gone with something a bit more traditional: something like strychnine, arsenic, or lead poisoning. I thought it might be a bit more poetic if you died from your own plants. Somehow, I thought you'd prefer that."

"How could you do that to me?" Leon asked.

"I'm just the weapon," Macey said. "Your brother is the one who wanted you dead."

"Just the weapon?" Leon released a painful sigh. "Macey, this is insane. How could you try to kill someone after… after we did what we did? After we were together?"

Macey rolled her eyes. "Oh, grow up, Whitey. You had drugged me. Even if you hadn't, it still wouldn't mean anything. People need to fuck once in a while. What's the big deal?"

Leon slapped the side of the pinball machine, which drew an angry glare from the bartender. "I'm not just talking about the night we had sex! I opened up to you. I felt happy when I was around you. I know we were just working together, but we also talked. I worked with Cracker too, but I never said more than two words to him. It was different with you. You and I—we shared stories about ourselves. That's intimacy, Macey. How can you decide to kill a person after you've had that kind of contact?"

"An assignment is an assignment," Macey said. "Poisoning you was an assignment. Talking to you about your boring plants was an assignment. Did you really think I was interested in your greenhouse? It was all I could do to stay awake. Your father and your brother wanted me to learn about your plants to see if you had any products that they could sell. That's all that was. And after your father took a shine to you and brought you into the business, Wyatt wanted me to continue to stay close to you to keep an eye on you. He wanted to know what your ambitions were. That's why I endured all the small talk with you."

Leon smirked. "Of course. Why else would you be interested in me? How could I be so stupid?"

"It happens," Macey said. "You were thinking with your dick."

"No. I was thinking with my heart."

"Well, that's just as stupid." She reached into the waist pocket of her black leather jacket, removed a cell phone, and hit a speed dial. "Come on in," she said into the phone. "He's wise."

The heavy steel door swung open, and Cracker Jack Farrell and Frankie Baloney stepped inside and approached the bar. Cracker set a large duffel bag on the counter as the goombah Frankie admired his reflection in a mirror behind the bar. He brushed his goatee, adjusted his ponytail, and unbuttoned his jacket to have a look at the new Beretta Tomcat tucked under his alligator-skin belt.

Cracker unzipped the duffel bag and removed a sawed-off Mossberg shotgun. "We know where you work," he said to the bartender. "We're gonna find out where you live. Now fuck off." The bartender kept his hands raised as he stepped out from behind the counter and back-stepped out of the bar.

Leon hit the reset button on the pinball machine, and a new ball popped out and rolled down onto the plunger. "You'd better run along," he said to Macey. "In another minute,

you won't recognize me. I won't be able to recognize myself."
His stomach growled and gurgled. "Run now, or die with
Cracker and Frankie."

Macey smiled. "And how do you plan to do that, killer?"

"With superhuman strength and subhuman cruelty," Leon
said. He pulled the plunger and sent a new ball into play. As
the ball bounced off of bumper, Leon prayed for some sign
that the Slaughter was taking hold. He did not feel particularly strong, and he felt nothing resembling courage. He only
felt a strong urge to defecate. "Before you came into the bar,
I took BMF," he said. His stomach rumbled again, and he let
out a long, moist fart.

Macey crinkled her nose. "Smells more like BM," she said.
"I thought you told me you didn't have any Rip left. Don't
tell me you had some stashed away. Don't tell me it was
hidden in your kitchen. Under a loose tile. Beneath a bookcase. I never would have thought to look there while you
were sleeping."

Leon tried to ignore Macey as he continued to play pinball. Bells on the machine rang while Leon farted again and
his face flushed.

"I switched more than your tea, Whitey," Macey said.
"What was the name of that plant you pointed out to me
in your greenhouse? The laxative that you give to people
who've overdosed?"

"*Galenggang,*" Leon mumbled.

"Right. I found another use for it."

The sound of Cracker loading the shotgun distracted
Leon. He nudged the machine to the right when he should
have nudged left and lost the ball to a gobble hole. With a
shaky hand, he pulled the plunger again. As he sent the ball

into play, Leon felt a steady stream of piss warming his left leg. A small pond starting at his right foot began to spread across the steel floor.

Cracker Jack and Frankie Baloney strolled toward Leon. They stood on opposite sides of the pinball machine. Leon managed to catch the ball in the crook of a flipper and waited for someone to talk. No one spoke, but Leon's stomach groaned and whined. He clenched his buttocks as he tried to stifle a steady release of gas that squealed through his cheeks. After a five-second squeaker, Leon slumped into the pinball machine and allowed a tuba blast to sound from his ass.

Frankie Baloney chortled. "Somebody light a match."

"If you're done farting around," Macey said, "it's time to take you in."

Leon turned to face Macey and tried to look her in the eyes. "Macey," he said, his voice weak with desperation.

"Save it," she answered, returning his wretched look with cold indifference. "We're taking you in."

"For your own protection," Frankie added with a smirk.

Leon stared at a demented harlequin flashing on the pinball mural. He felt his wet jeans clinging to his crotch and his legs. "I appreciate your concern," he muttered. His voice was weak with humiliation and fear. "But I'd prefer to stay here and finish my game."

"No problem," Cracker said. He raised the Mossberg and smashed the butt through the glass top of the machine. The ball hopped out of the game and bounced loudly across the steel tiles. Cracker shook his head. "Looks like you tilted."

"Yeah," Frankie said. "Looks like your game is over." He pulled his .32 from his jacket and fired a round at the machine. The bullet ricocheted off the metal cabinet and struck Cracker Jack in the chest. As Cracker stumbled backward, Frankie winced and said, "Dude! I am *so* sorry!"

Taking advantage of the distraction, Leon stepped toward his overcoat draped on the back of chair. He reached into the coat pocket, removed the pruning shears, and plunged them into the side of Frankie's neck. Frankie's eyes slowly widened in disbelief, and he began to wail. Leon resisted a compassionate instinct to help the goombah remove the shears from his neck.

Leon turned his back on the thugs and took a step toward the front exit. Macey drew a garrote from her jacket pocket and slung it over Leon's head. "Get back here," she said, yanking the wire against Leon's neck. He tried to work his fingers between the wire and his flesh, but Macey had already pulled the garrote too tight. As she strangled Leon, his colon erupted in a powerful, wet explosion. "Jesus Christ, Whitey!" Macey shouted in disgust. "Did you shit yourself?" She dropped the wire noose and took two quick steps away from Leon until she slipped in the pool of his urine. As her feet slid out before her, she fell backward and cracked her head against the sharp corner of a steel table. She crumpled to the floor, and blood welled on the back of her head.

The wire had cut a thin, shallow slice into Leon's neck. Still standing, Leon held his throat and searched for deeper wounds when he heard the pump-action of Cracker Jack's shotgun. Leon raised his eyes to see Cracker leveling the Mossberg at his face. Cracker squinted with pain and anger as a patch of blood spread across his chest. Meanwhile, Frankie Baloney, shears still dangling from his neck, pointed his Tomcat at Leon and fired a round into his back. The bullet passed through Leon's shoulder and hit Cracker in the chest a second time.

"You fucking cocksucker!" Cracker shouted. He pushed Leon aside and blasted the shotgun pointblank at Frankie Baloney, shredding off the top half of his greasy head. As he died, the goombah's muscles, including his trigger finger, contracted in spasms, and he fired one last round into Cracker Jack Farrell, hitting him dead between the eyes.

Leon held the side of the pinball machine to keep his balance. Cracker Jack was slumped against the steel wall, staring dully at the fluorescent lights above. The small, neat hole on his forehead leaked a thin trail of blood that branched at his pug nose. Frankie Baloney was on his back with his arms and legs spread like a child making snow angels. He had no face above his nostrils.

Leon let go of the pinball machine and stumbled around the corpses as he searched for the goombah's gun. He found it next to a cigarette machine. He staggered back to Macey and held the Tomcat near her head as he felt her neck for a pulse. Her heat was beating. He held his ear over his lips, listened to her breath, and let her lungs warm his cheek.

Leon pushed himself away from Macey. He looked at the blood seeping from his shoulder and sopping his shirt. Then he returned his gaze to the woman that had tried to kill him. He pointed the Tomcat at Macey and stared down the sight as he took aim at her head. She looked small, delicate, and beautiful, but Leon knew better. He knew she was deadly, and her beauty only made her more dangerous. She had used him. She had betrayed him. Twice she had tried to murder him. He had plenty of emotional reasons to fire a bullet into her head, and he had practical reasons as well.

Leon set the safety on the pistol, and he wiped the gun down with his shirtsleeve. Still holding the grip with his shirt, he pressed the safety back to fire, and he set the gun on the steel floor. He crawled up to Macey, brushed her hair from her eyes, and sadly studied her face one last time.

Holding onto the nearby table, Leon pulled himself to a standing position. The effort strained the bullet hole in his shoulder. He groaned loudly as hot pain seared through his arm. He staggered for the exit, grunting and pressing his palm over his wound. He lost his balance halfway to the door and stumbled into a group of barstools arranged in a rough circle. As he fell to the floor, the stools crashed about him like bowling pins. He struggled to his elbows and knees and crawled for the exit. As he reached for the door handle, he could feel his flesh and muscles tear. He howled as he opened the door and collapsed onto the sidewalk.

Leon raised his head and saw pedestrians scurrying away from him. He had lost his sunglasses, and the light seared his eyes. He tried to call for help, but there was too little air in his lungs. He dropped his head to the concrete and stared blankly at spots of black gum ground into the sidewalk. He closed his eyes and felt himself sinking into the concrete.

"Hey, kid. Are you an organ donor?"

Leon opened his eyes and turned to his left. He saw an old man strapped to a hospital gurney beside him. The man was staring at Leon. "You an organ donor?" he asked again.

"Um. I think so," Leon said.

The man shook his head. He had a lumpy red nose and cauliflower ears. "Bad idea. Never tell anybody you're an organ donor. Not that it makes much difference. The hospitals have ways to get around that."

Leon tried to sit up, but he found that he too was strapped

to a gurney. He did his best to look around the room. A dingy curtain separated him from a hallway. In the space between the curtain and the floor, he saw feet and the wheels of other gurneys pass by his room. Beyond the curtains was a cacophony of telephones ringing, pagers and heart monitors beeping, nurses and doctors chattering, and patients wailing.

"Here's the lowdown," the old man said. "The organ donor program is a scam. These hospitals sell your organs to the Koreans."

"The Koreans?"

"Yeah. The Koreans use human gall bladders and livers as aphrodisiacs."

"I never heard that before," Leon said, still struggling to look around him.

"It's true. And the Indians—both kinds—they eat human eyeballs for powers of clairvoyance." He nodded for emphasis. "Meanwhile, the hospitals make a killing selling our organs. See, the hospitals rip off the insurance companies by giving us worthless medication and performing unnecessary operations. Then, after they've milked the insurance dry, they kill us off and sell our body parts to the Koreans and Indians."

"This is all news to me," Leon said.

"Yeah, well you can't trust anybody," the old man said. "Guys like you and me, we've got no chance. See, in my case, I've got a son that wants to inherit my business. The hospitals know they can do whatever they want to me 'cause my family won't ask any questions."

"That's terrible," Leon said.

"Yeah, well you're no better off, pal. Your brother has it in for you."

Leon lurched against his restraints. The movement tore at

the bullet hole in his shoulder, and he dropped back to the mattress in pain. "What did you say?" he gasped.

"I said your brother has it in for you."

"He was here?" Leon asked.

"Nope. Just heard some talk about him. Some gal was in here, though. A real looker. She was hovering around outside with a couple of cops, talking with a doctor-type about you and your brother. I didn't catch all the details, but it didn't sound good. The worst part is that the cops seem to be in on this deal."

"The cops? What did you hear?"

"Like I said, I didn't get all the details. But let me give you some advice. Don't let them put any drugs into you. It'll be tough, though. They already have you tapped." The old man nodded at the Heparin lock dangling from Leon's arm. Then he shook his head. "Ah, what's the use? You're screwed."

"What did you hear?" Leon demanded.

The old man cocked his head toward the sound of approaching footsteps. Then he dropped his swollen ear to his pillow and began to snore.

The curtain surrounding Leon and his roommate opened, and a tall, somber man in a white coat stepped inside. "Good evening..." He glanced at a clipboard in his hand. "Mr. Lynch. How are we feeling today?"

"I'm okay," Leon said.

The man walked halfway around the gurney. "You're looking better, anyway."

"Who are you?" Leon asked.

The man continued to study Leon without speaking. He shuffled through the papers in his clipboard and jotted down a few notes. Eventually, he answered Leon's question. "I'm Dr. Blint."

"Well, Dr. Blint, I'm feeling pretty good," Leon said. "How much longer do you think I need to stay here?"

A corner of the doctor's mouth twitched. It might have been a smile. He twisted Leon's arm under the restraint so he could take a pulse. His callused fingers were rough against Leon's skin. "You weren't in the best condition when you got here," the doctor said. "You had been shot, after all."

Leon tried to look at his shoulder. "Did you remove the bullet?" he asked.

"Didn't need to. The bullet passed right through you." The doctor let go of Leon's wrist and jotted a few more notes.

"Well, you guys did a great job of patching me up," Leon said. "So how soon will I be leaving?"

"You have an appointment somewhere?" the doctor asked.

"No, it's just that I don't have insurance. I can't be stuck with a big hospital bill."

"Well, you can't leave in your condition."

"Is that your advice, or is that the law?" Leon asked. "I mean, do I legally have to stay here? Can't I sign a waiver or something?"

"Everyone wants to know their rights." The doctor gave Leon a hard glare. "Why are you in such a hurry to leave, anyhow? You sound like a man on the run." He softly clucked his tongue against his front teeth. "I suppose that's why the police want to talk to you." The doctor walked around to the back of the gurney and pushed Leon out into the hallway.

"Where are you taking me?" Leon asked the doctor.

"Upstairs. A couple of detectives have been waiting to talk to you about a couple of murders."

"I didn't kill anybody," Leon said.

"I never said you did. But from what I hear, you were found bleeding outside of a bar with two dead people inside. Apparently, the police like to ask questions after that sort of incident." He rolled Leon down the corridor, past an obese man in a wheelchair. The fat man read an ancient copy of *Reader's Digest* as blood from a head wound dripped onto his gas station uniform. He looked up from his magazine and scowled as Leon rolled by.

"Wait. Hold up," Leon said. "I don't want to talk to the police."

"Who does?" the doctor asked. "But you said you're feeling better, so I guess there's no reason why you can't talk to the detectives."

The doctor stopped at an elevator at the end of the hallway.

"Did they find a woman inside the bar?" Leon asked.

The doctor shrugged. "I wouldn't know. Ask the cops." The elevator door slid open, and the doctor pushed the gurney inside. The elevator stunk of blood and ammonia.

"These detectives," Leon said, "did they show you any identification?"

The doctor ignored Leon and pressed a button for the twelfth floor.

"Did these detectives show you identification?" Leon demanded.

"You ask a lot of questions," the doctor said. He pulled a pack of unfiltered Lucky Strikes from his shirt pocket. He shook out a cigarette and lit it with a grimy disposable lighter.

The elevator stopped, and the door slid open with its little chime. The doctor rolled Leon out onto a desolate floor and pushed him down a dark corridor lit with a few flickering fluorescent bulbs. "Looks like you'll have lots of privacy here," he said. He pushed Leon's gurney into a large, empty patient's room. Standing before a tall window were a man and a woman in trench coats. They clasped their hands behind their backs as they looked down on the city lights. "Okay, *detectives*," the doctor said. "He's all yours." He gave Leon a quick nod, tucked his clipboard under his arm, and strolled out of the room.

The man and the woman remained standing at the window, their backs to Leon. The woman had long, black, slightly wavy hair. The man had a pale neck and dark, immobile hair that shined with heavy gel. "I don't know if I can be much help, detectives," Leon said. He clung to a desperate hope that he truly was speaking to detectives. "It all happened so fast. What do you want to know, anyhow?"

Wyatt and Macey turned from the window to face Leon.

"Yeah," Leon muttered. "That's what I figured."

Macey smiled at Leon. "Hello again."

Leon squirmed beneath his restraints. His winced as his thrashing ripped at his wound.

"You don't look so bad. Considering." Macey gingerly touched the back of her head. "Got a few stitches myself."

Wyatt walked across the room and leaned over his brother. He pushed two fingers against Leon's shoulder wound. Leon drew a sharp breath through his gritted teeth. "Does that hurt?" Wyatt asked. He furrowed his brow in mock concern. "How about this?" He tapped the bandage around Leon's neck where Macey had cut him with the garrote. Leon grimaced. Wyatt put his hands on the rail of the gurney and shook his head. "Whitey, Whitey, Whitey. You sure are a fuckup. Always have been. The problem is your bad luck's contagious.

Everything around you goes to shit. Ever notice that? Cracker Jack Farrell was one of the toughest motherfuckers our family ever employed. He never met a man he couldn't take, and he never encountered a situation he couldn't handle. Until he met you. Your incredibly bad luck killed the best soldier in my organization. I mean, goddamn! Most losers just have a black cloud hanging over their head; you've got tornadoes following your sorry ass. What am I supposed to do with something like you?"

"Just let me leave," Leon said. He tried to grasp his hands in a pleading gesture, but his wrists were strapped. "Listen Wyatt, I was on my way to the other side of the planet. I have no ties to Butchers Harbor, and I have no reason to come back here. Ever. You can have the shithole. And you can have the family business. I have no use for either. Just let me go, and I promise you'll never see me again."

Wyatt pursed his lips and tapped his chin with one finger. "Hmm. Nice offer. But no thanks. I've already made other arrangements for you." Wyatt peeled off his trench coat and draped it over the railing on Leon's gurney. "So how do you want to do this, Whitey? Suicide or overdose?"

Leon sighed. "What is that supposed to mean?"

"Oh, I think you know what I mean," Wyatt said. He cracked his knuckles. "Do you want me to throw you out that window over there, or do you want me to shoot you up with a lethal dose of heroin?"

"This is lunacy," Leon said. "You don't need to kill me. You just have to let me go. For your own sake, think about what you're doing. I'm your own brother." Even Leon knew this was a hopeless argument. He turned his attention to Macey instead. "Macey, I know you better than you know yourself.

You do have some decency in you. I've seen it in you. Let me live. I let you live back at the bar. I had a gun aimed at your head, but I didn't take the shot."

"Your mistake," Macey said. "I will give you a little advice, though. Go with the heroin."

"I agree," Wyatt said. "Heroin makes more sense. Just look at my scummy little brother. He's got overdose written all over him. Besides, he's already spiked." Wyatt flicked the Heparin lock protruding from Leon's arm. "And then there's the whole matter of unstrapping him to shove him out the window. As much as I love to see shit break, that would be a chore. So, overdose it is." Wyatt held out his hand to Macey. "Needle."

Macey reached into her trench coat pocket and fished out a plastic bag with a syringe. She opened the bag and handed the needle to Wyatt. "Fully loaded," she said.

"This is crazy!" Leon protested. "Don't you think the doctor's going to be suspicious? He leaves me in a room with you two, and I wind up dead from an overdose?"

Wyatt let out a low whistle. "Jesus, Leon, you are one retarded bastard. Your wethead mom must've been hitting the juice like a fiend when she was pregnant with you. Just because a man wears a white coat, it doesn't make him a real doctor." Wyatt pulled aside the lapel of his overcoat to display a badge. "I'm not really a detective either. It's sort of like make-believe." Wyatt tapped the tip of the syringe against Leon's forehead. "Here's what happened today, dickhead. You wandered out of your bed. You crawled away to this secluded room, and you booted up for the last time. You died just like the lowlife druggie loser you've always been. Like mommy, like son."

Macey patted Leon's shoulder. "It's not that bad," she said.

"Just try to relax. We all have to go some time, and this is a good way to go. Most people spend their last minutes in pain or terror. You'll be in Heaven even before you're on the other side."

Wyatt stuck the needle of the syringe into the Heparin lock in Leon's arm. He put his thumb on the plunger and turned to face Macey. "Now, you're sure this shit is lethal?" he asked. "I don't want Leon walking away from this thing with nothing more than a buzz."

"He won't walk away. He'll leave this room in a body bag," Macey said. "That drill is loaded with pure China white. I saw the test myself. Pure enough to put down a water buffalo. Factor in Whitey's blood loss, he doesn't stand a chance. But just to be sure, I cut the smack with a little strychnine. When you push that plunger, you'll put out your brother's lights for good. This fix is a permanent fix."

"Just what the doctor ordered," Wyatt said. He squeezed the plunger and felt a bit of resistance, as if the tip of the needle was clogged. He pushed harder and the plastic body of the syringe exploded, spraying smack across the sheets. Wyatt held up half of the broken syringe in amazement. "What kind of worthless piece of shit ... " Before he could finish his question, the closet door and the door to the hall swung open simultaneously. Police in body armor poured through the doors and filled the small room, jostling Leon's gurney as they surrounded Wyatt and Macey.

Wyatt and Macey stood dumbfounded as several of the officers shouted contradictory commands like "Get on the ground!" "Don't move!" and "Show me your hands now!" The room became truly chaotic when Wyatt made a grab for one of the automatic rifles. Within seconds, a half-dozen police had pounced on Wyatt and wrestled him to the floor, where Wyatt continued to flail his fists and feet. The cops bounced into one another, knocking elbows into jaws and skulls against skulls as they struggled to immobilize Wyatt and put his hands in cuffs.

While Wyatt shouted curses and threats, Macey stood patiently with her hands raised by her shoulders. Eventually, one of the officers helped her into a pair of handcuffs.

Detectives Kerns and Janes, the two young, pallid detectives who had arrived at Wyatt Jr.'s birthday party, stepped into the room. Kerns stood by the teaming heap of cops wrestling with Wyatt. At the bottom of the pig pile, concealed by their fellow policemen, a few of the arresting officers tried to settle Wyatt down with quick jabs to his face, neck, and stomach. Kerns unwrapped a stick of gum as he watched the fracas. "Alright, boys," he said. He folded the stick of gum in half against his tongue as he shoved it into his mouth. He chewed for a moment. "You think you've had enough time to slap a pair of cuffs on that shithead?"

A young officer sprung up from the agitated mess of men and reported, "Yes, sir. The perp has been restrained."

"Alright then. Stand him up."

The police yanked Wyatt to his feet, hauled him across the room, and shoved his face and chest against a wall. Bleeding from his lip and breathing heavily, Wyatt shouted, "What the fuck is going on here?"

"You're under arrest, that's what's going on," Kerns said.

"What'd I do?"

Kerns counted off the charges by tapping his right pointer against the fingers of his left hand. "Attempted murder, conspiracy to commit murder, possession of a controlled substance, practicing medicine without a license, and impersonating a police officer. That's for the both of you. Mr. Lynch, you get a few counts of assaulting an officer as well."

"Hold on a second," Wyatt said. "This whole thing was a setup."

Kerns smiled. "No. We just happened to be in the neighborhood."

"Fuck you," Wyatt said. "This is entrapment. This is bullshit. You might as well turn me loose right now. This setup doesn't mean shit." He turned to face Leon, who was struggling in his restraints to see the commotion about him. "And you!" Wyatt shouted. "You little asswipe! Did you set me up?"

Leon collapsed back into the mattress and tried to steady his breathing.

"Yeah, you did, you little rat. You fucking set me up! You set up your own brother. Rat prick piece of shit! You turned over your own flesh and blood to the pigs." Wyatt tried to take a step toward Leon, but an officer shoved him back against the wall. "When I get even with you, Whitey, you'll wish you had died today. Mark my words, fuckface!"

"Get him out of here," said Kerns. "Read him his rights on the way to the car."

Two officers grabbed Wyatt by the elbows and dragged him toward the door. Four additional police followed as escorts. Wyatt managed to hold an icy glare on Leon as the cops pulled him across the room. When he reached the door, Wyatt broke into a wild laugh. "This ain't over, little brother. Not by a fucking long shot. I am gonna settle this score." The cops shoved him into the hallway, where his cackles filled the corridor.

Detective Janes, looking frailer and sicklier than she had at

Wyatt's party, approached Leon and put a hand on his chest. She ran her fingers over the canvas strap that held him to the gurney. "Are you alright?" she asked.

Leon nodded weakly. His pulse hammered in his neck, and he felt as if he might pass out. "I'm okay," he gasped. "What's going on?"

Detective Janes smiled dreamily as she gazed into Leon's eyes. She reached toward him and brushed at the air around his head.

"What are you doing?" Leon asked.

"You have a halo," Janes said softly.

"What?" Leon asked.

Janes stopped fluttering her hand about Leon's head, and the odd smile faded from her lips.

"What did you say?" Leon asked.

Janes avoided Leon's eyes. "I said … Are you alright?"

"I don't know," Leon said. He jerked his chin toward the broken syringe dangling from the crook of his arm. "Can you take that thing out of me?"

Detective Janes looked at the broken hypodermic needle, and held one hand to her lips. "Oh no," she muttered. She took two steps away from Leon, cast her eyes to the floor, and slowly rubbed the back of her slender neck with two fingers.

"Please take the needle out of me," Leon said. "And please tell me what's going on." Janes didn't respond, and the rest of the officers seemed to have forgotten he was in the room.

Macey stood patiently with her hands cuffed behind her back as Detective Kerns approached with his arms crossed. They grinned at each other. "Well this went better than I thought," Kerns said. "Nice plan. Nice acting." He winked a bleary, raccoon eye. "Well done, Ms. Kick."

"Thank you, detective," Macey said. "Couldn't have done it without you. Now, perhaps you could help me out these bracelets?"

Kerns continued to grin as he cast his leer up and down the length of Macey's body. "I don't know, Ms. Kick. You look good in cuffs. I'd say you belong in cuffs. Maybe I should do Butchers Harbor a favor and put you behind bars as well."

Macey remained smiling. "Is that any way to thank me? I hand you Wyatt Lynch, and you suggest I'm a criminal. I thought you and I struck a bargain, detective. Lucky for me, I always take a few measures to make sure the deal sticks."

"What does that mean?" Kerns asked.

"Oh, we don't need to get into all the details, especially in such a public place." Macey lowered her voice. "I assume the cameras and microphones are still on? Let's just say we all have a few skeletons in our closest, Detective Kerns."

Kerns' face flushed as he chuckled. "There's no need for slander, Ms. Kick. I'm just having a little fun with you." He nodded to an officer standing nearby. "Cut her loose, will you?"

Macey remained smiling at Kerns as an officer unlocked her handcuffs. When her hands were free, she nodded to the detective and policeman, then made her way toward Leon's gurney. As Macey approached, Leon squirmed in his restraints. "Get away from me," he said.

Macey looked down at the syringe still dangling from Leon's arm. She turned to Detective Janes, who was loitering at the foot of Leon's gurney. "You want to take this hypo out of his arm?" Macey asked.

Janes stood for a moment, apparently confused. Then she removed an evidence bag from her jacket pocket, pulled the broken syringe from the Heparin lock, and placed it in the bag. She leaned close to Leon. A thin lock of her chestnut hair stuck to a film of sweat on her forehead. She whispered in Leon's ear. "Build your own religion."

"What? What did you say?" Leon asked.

Janes turned abruptly and retreated to the corner of the room. Leon tried to catch a glimpse of her as she wove her way through the clusters of restless policemen. Macey chuckled. "Is it my imagination, or was that detective flirting with you, Leon? I think I'm jealous."

Leon glared at Macey. "Get this woman away from me!" he shouted. "This woman tried to kill me."

Macey smiled reassuringly to the surrounding officers. "He's confused," she said. She turned back to Leon and began to unbuckle the strap over his chest. "This was a show. You were never in danger." She pulled the strap away from Leon's chest. He tried to sit up, but his wrists and feet were still bound. He began to thrash on the gurney. "Whoa, take it easy, Leon," Macey said. "Everything's cool now."

"What the hell is going on?" Leon demanded.

"We set your brother up," Macey said. "He was out of control. The police and other concerned parties were worried he might hurt someone. Including you." Macey unstrapped one of Leon's wrists. "I'm sorry we scared you. We had to keep you out of the loop. But as I said, we made sure you weren't in danger. That hypodermic had a plugged needle, and the body was designed to shatter under pressure. It's sort of like a dribble glass for junkies." Macey unstrapped Leon's other wrist. His skin was red where he had struggled against the canvas restraints. Macey gently massaged his wrist. "I'm sorry you had to go through this, Leon. It was necessary, but I'm sorry all the same. From here on, things get a whole lot better, okay?"

Leon pulled his wrist free from Macey. He propped himself on one elbow. "Just tell me what's going on here."

Macey nodded with an apologetic frown. "I know. I owe you a few explanations." She glanced at the police still milling about the room and cracking jokes. "Later. When we're alone," she said. "I'll explain everything."

The next morning, a chubby male nurse with curly orange hair, was completing Leon's discharge papers. "You may need a little help with some of your daily routines. Cooking, washing up, that sort of thing. Will a family member be visiting you for the next few days?"

"I hope not."

The nurse chuckled. "A friend, then? A neighbor perhaps?"

Leon didn't expect that Bea Carver could help him much. Besides, after the encounter with Billy Blake, Bea had been avoiding Leon. "I'm pretty much on my own."

The nurse gave Leon a condescending expression of pity. "Well, who will be picking you up today?"

"I'll call a cab," Leon said.

The nurse tapped his pen against the stack of forms in his clipboard. "I'm not sure I would recommend that. You've been shot in the shoulder, after all. You might need some help getting in and out of the car. Are you sure you can't think of *anyone* who might be willing to help you?"

Macey appeared at the door to Leon's room. "I'll take him home," she said.

The nurse looked at the attractive woman at the door, then glanced back at the sad, bandaged albino lying in the hospital bed. He raised his eyebrows. "Well. I guess you do have someone to take care of you, then."

Leon was quiet as he sat beside Macey in her Mustang. For all he knew, she was driving him to some lonely corner of the city, where she would put a round in the back of his head. His will to survive was feeble, but his desire to understand the events of the past few days was intense. He was willing to take a ride with an assassin if the conversation would give him some enlightenment. Even if he wound up with a bullet in his brain, at least that would give him some closure.

Macey did not drive Leon to the docks or the back parking lot of some abandoned factory. Instead, she took him to a nearby dive called the Crow Bar. "Come on," she said. "Let's get a drink." Inside the small club, three sleek, black ravens were kept in cages behind the bar, and the place reeked of their guano. Macey helped Leon to a bamboo booth by a window at the back of the dump. His arm was in a sling, and bandages still covered his neck. He was silent and sullen as he looked out the window, watching traffic roll by. Inside the cars, ordinary people were on their way to respectable jobs.

Macey ordered two beers from the bartender and carried them to the booth. She set one before Leon and smiled as she sat on the opposite side of the table. Leon sipped his beer, which tasted strange at the early hour. "So," he said. "You said you would explain things."

"What do you want to know?"

"Everything," Leon said. "Everything concerning us. What was real and what was a lie?"

Macey glanced at her watch. "Well, what I said at the Pig

Iron—before you nearly shit on me—what I said then was true. I was friendly with you because your family wanted to learn more about your stash, and then I stayed close to you because Wyatt wanted to keep tabs on you."

"You feigned interest in me."

Macey shrugged. "Yeah, I guess. I mean, you're a cute guy. You are interesting. I wouldn't say it was a chore spending time with you, but it was an assignment."

"So, you were working for Wyatt," Leon said. "But at some point, you decided to turn on him."

"Yeah, I worked for Wyatt. I also worked for your father. I was maintaining a couple of alliances. Ultimately, I worked for myself." She drank her beer, then used her thumb to wipe away a bit of foam on her upper lip. "When your father died, I knew the family business was done. I knew Wyatt would go on a killing spree. As I expected, he started killing judges, union bosses, hacks, and cops. You can't do that kind of shit and stay in business. Even if we won this insane war with the Borisovas, which was unlikely, there was no way we'd ever operate in Butchers Harbor again. The unions would never work with us, and the cops would be going ape shit until they shut us down. If I didn't do something, I would wind up in jail or a coffin. At best, I'd be looking for a new gang.

"A couple of days after the tornado, even before Wyatt started killing anyone, I went to Vladimir's kid, Josef Borisova. I could tell by looking at the kid that he wasn't cut out to run a crime family. I told him he was in over his head. If Wyatt didn't kill him, one of his own people would. Volkov or someone else would have clipped him in a power struggle. I offered to help him out. I suggested we combine the two gangs. One good thing about Wyatt's war, it was thinning out the ranks on both sides, so we were ripe for a merger. I told Josef I would help him maintain control of his father's operations, and I would be in charge of the Lynch crew."

Leon nodded. "And after a year or so, you'll take Josef out yourself, and you'll run everything."

Macey smirked. "Josef and I didn't get that far in our discussion. Anyhow, Josef had two conditions before he would agree to the merge. I had to take out Wyatt and you. Josef didn't want any alliances to the old Lynch family. He figured that without any Lynches, there wouldn't be a Lynch gang—just a bunch of thugs looking for a new boss."

Leon squirmed uncomfortably in the booth. "And you agreed to that?"

"Well, yeah. I didn't want Wyatt around either. Obviously, I didn't consider you a threat, but Josef did. So … " She raised her hands in a 'what are you gonna do' gesture. "Business is business. I figured I'd start with you. Wyatt wanted you out of the picture too. If I bumped you off, I'd be keeping both Wyatt and Josef happy. It would also keep me close to Wyatt until I had a chance to take him out."

"So that wasn't an act back at the Pig Iron?" Leon asked. "You really planned to kill me?"

Macey shrugged.

Leon started to slide out of the booth. Macey held his good arm. "Stay put," she said. "Don't be such a drama queen."

"Drama queen? Drama queen!" Leon shouted. "Jesus Christ, Macey! You tried to murder me. Twice! For all I know, you're planning to kill me today!"

The bartender, a Goth chick with white and black makeup and raven hair, looked up from her copy of People Magazine to stare at the two strangers in the corner booth.

Macey held a finger to her lips. "Inside voice. Okay?" She

turned and gave the bartender a reassuring nod. Then she turned back to face Leon and lean closer to him. "Why can't you understand that this is just business? This is the world you stumbled into, Leon." Her expression softened as she shook her head. "Besides, I've been thinking about things. I tried to kill you twice, but I also botched it twice. That isn't typical for me. Maybe some part of me wanted to fail. Maybe I wanted you to live. It's not beyond the realm of possibility that I do have something resembling feelings for you."

That was enough to keep Leon seated, but he continued to give Macey a hard glare. "How do I know you aren't playing me again? How do I know you aren't setting me up for a third attempt?"

"There won't be a third attempt," Macey said. "I spoke to Josef. You're off the hook. I convinced him you weren't a threat. I know you spared my life back at the Pig Iron. I'm returning the favor."

Leon nodded cautiously. "Okay. Thanks."

She shrugged. "Thank you."

They both sipped their beers to fill an awkward silence.

"What about Wyatt?" Leon asked.

"What about him?"

"You said Josef wanted me and Wyatt out of the picture. I can't imagine you convinced Josef that Wyatt wasn't a threat. So why isn't Wyatt dead? Why only have him arrested?"

"B.H.P.D. wanted credit for busting Wyatt. It gets the feds off their backs. If the FBI thinks Butchers Harbor's finest are cracking down on organized crime, they'll turn their attention to some other corrupt city. Putting Wyatt in jail works out better for the Borisovas and the police. Plus, I thought I'd have an easier time working with the old Lynch crew if I wasn't responsible for clipping their old boss."

One of the ravens started squawking and flapped its wings. The bartender slapped its cage with a wet bar rag.

"So what happens to Wyatt now?" Leon asked.

"I've made sure he won't be a threat to me or Josef," Macey said. "Unless you plan on getting arrested, he won't be threat to you either. So you can breathe easy."

"Actually, that wasn't my concern," Leon said. "I want to know if you have plans for him while he's in police custody."

"Once he's behind bars, he's out of our reach." Leon gave Macey an incredulous glare. She laughed. "Okay, maybe he's not entirely beyond our reach. So what do you want, Leon? You want your brother to fall on a shiv?"

Leon shook his head. "No. Let him live. I want him to think about me walking free while he rots in jail. Besides, he's my brother. I don't want you to have him killed."

"Well, it's really not up to me at this point," Macey said. "Josef is content to leave him locked up. The Borisovas have enough pull in the courts to ensure that Wyatt gets life, so we have no plans to rub him out. You don't have to worry about your beloved brother."

"Okay then," Leon said. His shoulder throbbed, so he drank some more of his beer to numb the pain.

"Any other questions?" Macey asked.

Leon looked into his beer. "Well ... I know we've had a strange relationship, Macey. Maybe I'm just the loneliest person on the planet, but ... I'm not even sure how to say this. Can we still be friends?"

"What do you mean?"

"Can I just—I don't know—just talk to you once in a while? I enjoyed our talks in the past, even if I was just an assignment for you. I enjoyed a lot of what we did together." He smiled coyly.

308

Macey did not return his smile. "We really shouldn't have any future contact. That wouldn't go over well with Josef. In fact, Josef wants you out of town. It's one of his conditions for letting you live."

"Oh." His smile drooped into a frown.

"That's good news, isn't it?" Macey asked. "You have no reason to stay in Butchers Harbor. Your father's passed on. Your home burned down. You knew that, didn't you?"

"I had a vague recollection."

"So why would you want to stay in this shit heap of a town?"

Leon looked up from his hands and looked Macey directly in the eyes. "No reason at all," he said.

"Good." She returned Leon's stare until he looked away. "You'll be leaving town in style, at least." She reached into her pants pocket and held up a set of car keys. "Josef and I are giving you a going-away present."

Leon looked at the car keys and scoffed. "I get a car? Well, that make it all worthwhile."

"It's a nice car," Macey said. She pointed out the window to a slick black convertible parked in the lot outside the bar. "Looks nice, huh? Don't be surprised by its compact size either. It has a lot of trunk space. In fact, I've packed four good-sized suitcases in the trunk."

"Oh?"

"Yeah. They're in the trunk right now." She grinned. "The luggage is packed too, but don't expect to find any clothes or toiletries."

"So what's packed in the suitcases?" Leon asked. "Explosives?"

She laughed and shook her head. "Nothing but good things, White Boy. I took care of you. In the good sense."

"Fine." Leon took the car keys and slid out of the booth. His shoulder burned as he stood. He spoke through clenched teeth. "It's been a pleasure, Macey. Have a nice life."

"Where are you going?" Macey asked. She remained seated as she finished her beer.

"What do you care?" Leon asked. He turned his back on her as he shuffled out of the bar.

Wyatt sat in the back seat of an unmarked police car, his hands cuffed behind his back. He tried to make himself comfortable by leaning against the door and stretching his legs out across the torn and cracked upholstery.

Detective Kerns eyed Wyatt in the rearview mirror. "Get your dirty shoes off the seat," he snapped.

Wyatt ignored him. He was watching Detective Janes. She was a frail, sickly thing, but Wyatt liked her. He liked her thin neck, her pert little nose, and her sharp chin. He wanted to run his tongue along her porcelain-gray skin. The detective gazed out the window, either lost in thought or thoroughly fascinated by the filthy streets of Butchers Harbor. Her hands trembled slightly as she rubbed her temples with her knuckles.

"What's the matter, sweetie pie?" Wyatt asked. "You got a little headache? You want Wyatt to give you a neck rub?" He let out a lusty chuckle.

Wyatt's laugh made Janes giggle. "Neck rub," she repeated. "That's a good one."

"Oh, you like that?" Wyatt cooed. "Well, just uncuff my hands, sexy, and I'll put my magic fingers to work all over you. Head to toe and everywhere in between."

KEN HARVILL

Kerns chewed his gum with frantic, angry energy as he glared at Wyatt in the rearview mirror. "Watch the gutter talk, fuckface." He looked jealously at his partner. Gradually, he began to smile. He returned his gaze to the rearview mirror. "You know what? Go ahead and run your mouth all you want. Pretty soon, you'll be using your mouth for something else. Skinny little has-been hood like you. The boys in the big house are gonna love you."

Wyatt snorted defiantly, but the detective thought he sensed something resembling fear. If Wyatt wasn't afraid, he should have been. Kerns and Janes were transporting him from a holding cell in the Butchers Harbor Police Department to a prison outside of the city. While he was at the prison, Kerns was to meet with a correctional officer to hand him a payment from Macey and Josef. That night, the c.o. would ensure that several inmates gave Wyatt a long and hearty welcome to his new home. When the new prisoner had suffered enough humiliation to warrant his suicide, the c.o. would hang Wyatt in his cell.

Wyatt chuckled as he watched Janes rub her temples. "Oh, honey, it looks like you're really hurting. What's the matter, sweetie? You going through withdrawal? Huh? Are you and Detective Demerol running low on idiot pills? Is that why you two are so moody? Poor little pill popper. If you turn me loose, I'll make sure you get all the medicine you need. I'll take much better care of you than your limp-dick partner."

Kerns laughed. "Okay, tough guy. Keep it up. Just remember me tonight when you got a line of brothers in front of you and behind you waiting for their turn to plug you from both ends. We'll see who gets the last laugh."

Janes did not appear to hear her partner or Wyatt. She

311

turned to watch a dog pissing on a hydrant. "Shimmer," she said.

Kerns veered the car off the city street and onto an on-ramp for the highway. The morning rush hour was over, and the highway was nearly empty. Kerns unrolled his window and spit his gum outside.

"Hey! You mind rolling that window up?" Wyatt demanded. "You're letting all the heat out."

Kerns snickered. "Yeah, Mr. Tough Guy. Can't even handle a little breeze. I'm sure you'll do just fine in the joint tonight, tough guy." He shoved a fresh stick of gum into his mouth.

"I think he's right," Janes said. "I'm chilly too." She held her forearms and shivered. "Chilly."

Kerns gave Janes an annoyed glare. He shook his head as he rolled the window shut.

"So tell me something," Wyatt said. "How long has my brother been a rat for you fucking pigs?"

"Sorry, we can't discuss our investigation with shithead, soon-to-be prison bitches," Kerns answered. He blew a small bubble and sucked the gum back into his face.

"That's fine. You protect your rat," Wyatt said. "I'll conduct a little investigation of my own. In the meantime, you might want to give my brother a warning. Tell him to watch his back."

"You're brother is not a rat," Janes said. "He's pure. I've seen your brother's aura." She cupped her hands before her mouth and blew warm air on her fingers. "The whole world has an aura these days. The Earth is shimmering."

Kerns laughed. "Earth is what?"

"There's a shimmer on everything," Janes said. "See? Look at the edge of those trees. See how the leaves shimmer?" She laughed. "Shimmery."

Kerns glanced sidelong at his partner. "Are you high? Did you take something without me?"

"Shimmer," Janes said slowly. "Shimmer-glimmer." She laughed again. Her soft giggle began to sound a little wild.

"Jesus, Janes," Kerns scolded. "Pull yourself together."

Janes held her shaking hands over her face and tried to stifle her laughter. "Oh, man," she sighed. She wiped a tear from her eye and tried to catch her breath. "I feel good. I feel funny. I feel cold." She reached forward and turned the heat up to its highest setting. "There's chilly shimmers all over the car now. See them? Cold luminosity in front and liquid light just underneath."

Wyatt's cocky smile slipped into a gape. "Oh shit," he said. "Shit! Let me out of this car!"

"Shut up," Kerns said, turning to face Wyatt. The car drifted across a lane.

Wyatt kicked the seat in front of him. "Let me out!" he shouted. "Your partner has the Willies!"

Kerns laughed. "She's got what?"

"The pigpox, you fucking retard! Pork flu! Let me out!"

"Don't be an idiot," Kerns said. "She's just stoned."

"She's just insane!" Wyatt shouted. "The Willies have fried her brain! She's chock-full of the goddamn virus! Now let me the fuck out before we all die in here!" He twisted and thrashed in the back of the car, working the handcuffs under his feet until his hands were before him. He began to pound the window with both fists.

"Hey! Cut that shit out!" Kerns yelled.

Detective Janes convulsed in her seat and vomited blood over the dashboard and windshield. Detective Kerns gasped at the sight of his partner and inhaled the wad of gum he had been chewing. As the gum lodged in his windpipe, he let go of the steering wheel to clutch his throat with both hands. In his panic, he also stepped hard on the accelerator. The car lurched forward, swerved across three lanes, and hopped over a guardrail. The front bumper tore into the earth, sending a spray of dirt before it. The car upended, landed hard on its roof, and tumbled down a grassy embankment until it finally slid to a groaning stop at the bottom of a gully.

Wyatt writhed on the car ceiling and stared at the seats and floor above him. He was covered with pebbled glass. He was also splattered with blood, which he hoped was his own and not from the cute detective with the deadly virus. He groaned and whimpered as he squirmed through the shattered window that had been narrowed by the half-flattened roof. Outside, in the muddy gully, he tested his legs and was surprised that he was able to walk. He felt his face with his cuffed hands. Blood ran from his forehead and nose and streamed across his shirt. As he staggered away from the wreck, he glanced through the broken windshield at the two detectives. They had survived the crash as well, but Kerns was still choking on his gum, and Janes was still convulsing and puking bile.

Wyatt staggered up the embankment and peered over the twisted guardrail. If anyone had witnessed the accident, they hadn't stop to help. Wyatt was glad. He scampered across the highway and disappeared into the surrounding woods.

Leon drove his new convertible out of the Crow Bar parking lot. The autumn air was chilly, but he drove with the top down. He was too numb to feel the cold. He hadn't looked in the trunk yet, but he imagined that the suitcases were packed with money, jewels, or precious metals. He didn't care what was inside as long as it helped him get far away from Butchers Harbor.

He drove by the piers and looked out on the harbor where the fish had gone mad on his drugs. He looked out to the sea where the winds had carried his father. He left the harbor and drove into the city, back to see his old home one last time. As he drove into his neighborhood, he found a pile of charred timber and scattered ashes where his home had been. The greenhouse was nothing more than a half-collapsed frame with shattered glass glinting in the noon sun. Leon parked his car on the street and glanced at his neighbor's house. Bea Carver was not sitting on her doorstep, and the shades behind her windows were all drawn tight.

Leon walked across his yard. Cinders crunched under his feet as he wandered through the ruins of his greenhouse. He was looking for any remnant of the sensory-enhancing tea that Bea enjoyed so much. Unfortunately, none of these plants had survived the blaze. Leon felt ashamed that he had never given Bea a larger supply of these herbs. He had always supplied her in weekly doses just so he would have an excuse to visit her. He had been selfish, and now the old woman would have to live in a world of fading vision and growing silence. She would have only memories of tastes and aromas.

Leon was heartbroken by the devastation around him. The Tomaki tree, which he had spent years trying to cultivate for potent fruit, had withered in the heat of the fire. The delicate Ferns of Tranquility had turned brown, and the leaves had crumbled to a powder scattered by the fall wind. Precious cacti and mushrooms he had collected from a secluded corner of a Hopi reservation were nothing more than charred stumps. The koi pond was just a muddy pit filled with rotting, broiled fish.

A few plants had survived the blaze. He found some purple cornflower seedlings, some ginseng root, a flamingo bush with a handful of half-decent berries, and a basket of peyote buttons. However, nothing that remained was remarkable or worth collecting. He had lost all of the most exotic plants. He had lost his favorite green friends. They never said much, but they were good company all the same. Now he was utterly alone. He doubted if he would ever matter to anyone.

Wyatt slumped in the corner of a freight car and felt the wheels rumble over the rails. He didn't care where he was headed, just as long as it was out of Butchers Harbor. His shoulders and elbows ached terribly, not only from the beating he had received in the tumbling police car but also from nearly 48 hours of restricted arm movement. His hands were still cuffed before him, and he longed to spread his arms or to simply lower them at his side. Once he got off the train, wherever that might be, he needed to find a hacksaw or a file. His nose was broken, which caused a throbbing pain in his face whenever he moved his head. A gash above his eye had become infected, and the top eyelid had swollen shut. His face, the front of his shirt, and even his pants were covered with crusty blood.

If anyone had opened the door to the freight car and seen Wyatt slumped in the corner, he would probably have thought Wyatt was dead or well on his way to the grave. Despite his appearance, Wyatt never felt better. This was a defining moment for him. Before this night, his life had been a dull haze of indirection. He'd always had trouble setting and following goals. Now, all of that had changed. Now, he had a clear purpose and a reason to survive. "I'm going to live," Wyatt muttered. "I'm going to live so I can kill my brother."

Wyatt took a deep breath. It hurt his bruised ribs, but it was a satisfying pain. He breathed to live. He breathed to see another day. He breathed to fan the flames of his life-defining rage. He felt in the darkness for the bag of stale potato chips that he had found beside the tracks. He reached into the bag and grabbed a handful of chips. The salt burned his bleeding lips, but he forced himself to continue eating. He ate with a purpose. He ate to fuel the engine of anger that drove him toward revenge. "It's all for you, Whitey," he muttered. "From now on, everything I do is for you." From this moment forward, every step Wyatt took would be a step toward his brother. The route would not be direct, for he had to elude his hunters. Nevertheless, his journey had a clear destination.

Destiny is liberation.

Wyatt curled on the floor and fell asleep to the rocking of the train and the lullaby of its rumbles and creaks. His sleep turned purposeful as he dreamt of new ways to torment and destroy his brother. Whitey was all that mattered. Wyatt now lived for a single, unwavering purpose: to kill Whitey.

ACKNOWLEDGEMENTS

I owe a depth of gratitude to Tom Fassbender and Jim Pascoe for taking a chance on a newcomer, for the guidance that improved my novel, and for the freedom to tell my tale my way. Thank you also for founding UglyTown and for the care and joy you take in cultivating small batches of beautifully ugly novels

To my friends who read early versions of my manuscript, including Steve St. Thomas, John Tessier, Eric Eisnor, and Kelly Carter, I appreciate your kind words, critiques, and encouragement. I owe special thanks to Tom Gianakopoulos for particularly close readings and solid comments. Rick Koster, without your mentoring and motivation, I would have never turned my short story into a novel.

Thanks Mom for having faith in my pipe dreams. Maybe my next novel will have a nicer title and fewer dirty words. But don't hold your breath.

Greg Christian, thank you for eighteen years of true friendship and for your example of strength and courage. I still lean on you in tough times, and I never fail to laugh when I recall your antics and twisted wit. The world isn't the same without you, buddy, but it's better for the time you spent here.

And thank you, Dad. I didn't know you for long, but my memories of your love and lessons are always in my heart.